BEVERLY KNAUER

THE
LINE
BETWEEN

A NOVEL

Wise Words Press

For information, address the publisher at:
wisewordspress.com

Excerpt from *The World As I See It* reprinted by permission of
Albert Einstein Archives, the Hebrew University of Jerusalem.

This is a work of fiction. All the characters, organizations, and events
portrayed in this novel are either products of the author's imagination or
are used fictitiously.

Printed in the United States of America
wisewordspress.com

Wise Words Press
1611-A S. Melrose Drive #265
Vista, CA 92081

First Printing, 2016

Ebook ISBN: 978-0-9977303-0-2
Paperback ISBN: 978-0-9977303-1-9
Hardcover ISBN: 978-0-9977303-2-6

*To Jonathan Rosenthal, who taught me the
soul is immortal and love eternal.*

*To Samantha Rosenthal, who taught me to
face fear and push through it.*

*To Janet Rosenthal, my best friend, my "Lizzie." It would
take another book to list all the things she's taught me.*

"I couldn't be here in spirit, so I came in person."
—Red Buttons

PART I

CHAPTER 1
AUGUST 21, 1987

THE FRAMED PHOTO of her husband, Neil, fell from the wall as Sophie Beaumont plodded down the steps, in her pajamas, still wiping the sleep from her eyes. Bits of shattered glass covered the wooden floor near the bottom step. She stopped in her tracks, wondering if it was an earthquake; after all, their house sat on the Rose Canyon fault. No, nothing was shaking. Seeing no reason for the strange occurrence, she continued down the steps, carefully avoiding the pieces of glass, surprised the noise hadn't seemed to wake her sleeping husband. She decided to clean the mess up later, after her coffee, when she felt more awake.

The night before, she'd filled the coffeepot with water and ground beans and set the timer to begin brewing at 6:30 a.m. She didn't actually need an alarm, as she woke to the herbaceous scent of coffee permeating the house. She shuffled into the kitchen and fixed herself a cup with exactly one teaspoon of sugar and two tablespoons of cream.

That was her typical morning ritual before work—she'd sit at the kitchen table, drink two cups of coffee, and read her horoscope.

Sophie grabbed the newspaper off the front porch, shook the rain off the plastic wrapping, snapped open the paper, and turned to page four of the entertainment section to the horoscopes.

Libra: A partnership demands attention. Proceed with caution as an imagined scenario may come to pass. Something may disrupt your domestic tranquility—be prepared for the unexpected. This is a good day to stay home. Count on friends for support.

That sounded a bit foreboding. Maybe it wasn't a bad idea to skip work. She hadn't slept well the previous night, feeling on edge and restless. Not wanting to hassle with getting stuck in rainy-day traffic, she picked up the phone to call in sick—then hesitated, deciding she should go in. As she set the receiver down, she knocked her elbow into her full cup of coffee, smashing it on the floor. Two strikes in a fifteen-minute period. She hoped bad luck didn't really come in sets of three.

Sophie figured the signs were there that it wasn't going to be a good day—some days are just like that. Hopefully, nothing catastrophic would happen. Her edgy feeling intensified.

It took Sophie an extra hour to get home after work due to the weather. It was good to be home. Other than gridlock on the freeway, she was happy she'd had an uneventful day at work. She noticed a note taped to the refrigerator from Neil stating he'd be home no later than 5:30 for dinner. But it was already 7:00—and he still wasn't home. Feeling concerned, she wondered if he was stuck in traffic. Sophie glanced at the clock every five minutes while listening for the sound of his car pulling into the driveway.

At 7:30, she wrung her hands and paced the kitchen floor. *Where is he?* She hoped he hadn't been in an accident. The local news had described a multitude of traffic collisions due to the heavy rainstorm.

They say it never rains in Southern California, yet it had poured off and on for twelve days straight in San Diego. The night air even tasted wet. But once the howling winds of the latest deluge had died down about fifteen minutes ago, it grew calm. No sounds of cars driving by outside, no barking dogs, no noise from the neighboring children. The quiet seemed unusual to Sophie, almost haunting.

An unsettling shiver traveled down her spine, making her feel something was not right. Something was amiss. She shook the feeling off. Maybe Neil was picking up something for dinner. Knowing he might want to house the car in the garage for the night, safe from the rain, Sophie decided she'd go out back and turn on the light for him.

She stood in the backyard looking toward the detached one-car garage behind the house. The lawn was drenched. Pink rose petals, blown about from forceful gusts during the earlier downpour, floated in mud puddles.

She thought she heard a faint sound from inside the garage—perhaps a raccoon seeking refuge. She felt uneasy and nauseous. Something beyond curiosity, beyond fear, spurred her to take slow, halting steps across her yard, barely avoiding a pile of feces from a feral dog. Her canvas shoes were already soaked with water, causing squishing sounds as she walked. She didn't know why she clenched her fists tightly or why her lips were trembling. Her inner voice was screaming at her to turn around. She ignored it.

The black color of grief tinted the night sky. The only illumination came from the yellowish glow of a neighbor's porch lamp. Her left eye twitched as a sinking feeling in her gut diffused throughout her body. *What's wrong with me?*

A waxing gibbous moon, nearly full, showed between streaks of gray clouds, partially spotlighting the pale white garage. The garage door, like a barn door with two sides that swing open from the middle, faced a dirt alley that wasn't visible from the backyard. The smaller side door, completely off the hinges, leaned against the battered clapboards.

She stepped into the doorway. An unfamiliar creaking sound made her hair stand on end. Reaching into the darkness, she flicked the switch. As light flooded the garage, her worst nightmare flashed before her.

It was too late to unsee the grotesque scene: Neil—suspended from a rope that was tied to the beam of the garage. It was a gruesome sight, a gruesome way to go.

At first, Sophie refused to accept what she saw. Her eyes read one thing, but her brain wouldn't compute. It was too repugnant. As though it required censoring, the image started out pixelated and blurry. Abruptly, it transformed into a well-defined picture with focused, distinct edges. The image, once fully developed, engraved itself permanently in her brain like an inscription on a tombstone.

The beam continued to creak from holding the weight of his 175 pounds. Sophie's mind went numb. Through suffocating gasps, she felt like she was breathing through a straw. Her abdomen tightened and her stomach heaved. Deep, guttural noises, which she didn't quite recognize as her own, came from the back of her throat, followed by piercing screams, as though her skin were being peeled with a dull knife. Her heart seemed to stop until a rush of adrenaline flooded her body, releasing her from a temporary paralysis.

What do I do? She wasn't thinking clearly. The six-foot ladder Neil must have knocked over when he dropped was lying on the cement floor. Sophie set it upright near his body, climbed it, then frantically dug her fingers into the knot at his neck that cut deep into his flesh. It was too tight. As his limp body swung toward her, she lost her balance, toppled the ladder, and crashed onto the cold floor, hitting her head.

She stood and regained her footing, then grabbed a saw that hung precariously on a cup hook on the wall above the woodworking table. She righted the ladder and climbed it again. She attempted to cut Neil down, but the never-sharpened teeth on the saw only frayed the rope and lacerated the web between her thumb and index finger. Blood spurted and pooled in the palm of her hand. The saw wouldn't work. Unable to get Neil down, Sophie stared at him face-to-face—close enough to gag at the sight of the deep discolorations and red grooves where the noose dug into his neck.

No. No. Oh my God ... How can I save him?

His tongue, swollen and dry, protruded at an angle from his slack lips, his face pale in color. The stench of urine permeated the air from his damp pants.

Why? The word repeated in her mind. There was no adequate answer. Sweat poured from her hairline. Her heart raced out of control. She jumped from the ladder to race to a phone to call for help. As she landed, she twisted her ankle and cried out in pain. That's when the horror of the situation sunk in.

She couldn't save him.

She screamed for help, then black spots performed a macabre dance before her eyes and, mercifully, she passed out.

CHAPTER 2
NEIL

B Y NOON, I'D decided to commit suicide today. It was an emotional struggle to get to that point, but once I'd made the decision, I felt detached about the process. I knew Sophie would be at work all day, so I had sufficient time. I just needed to get it over with and stop constantly thinking about it. I'd spent way too much time contemplating ways to kill myself over the years. It's not like I hadn't thought of it at least a hundred times before. I distinctly recall making the final decision to end my pathetic life after I realized I'd been in an endless loop of repeating the same destructive mistakes. I wanted out. It was a disturbing yet defining moment.

I needed to die.

So many decisions to make—so many things to consider. Pills, gunshot, or hanging. Rope or telephone extension cord. Slip knot or bowline. Three-quarter diameter or one-inch rope. To write a note or not. Hanging was my chosen method, but I even had to decide where to place the knot. I remembered reading somewhere that, for a successful hanging, the placement of the knot was very important. Although some people put the knot behind the neck, others have said it should go high, closer to the top of the head. I decided to place it underneath my jaw near my ear—the goal being quick constriction with a rapid loss of consciousness.

The timing of the deed was my final decision. I needed to be sure no one would be around to interrupt the process, leaving me brain-damaged instead of dead. Being a fearful person by nature, I wondered if I could go through with it. Ashamed of my cowardice many times during my life, I'd taken ridiculous risks to prove otherwise. I couldn't back down. I didn't want to be a wimp. So I practiced making the noose a few times, and that made me feel more confident.

After securing the rope over the beam, I downed a pint of vodka. My final drink. No profound, insightful thoughts drifted through my mind. All I thought was: *Am I really going to do this?*

I climbed the ladder and positioned the knot. I kicked the ladder and swiftly dropped. Swirling colors of light sprang before my eyes like fireworks, and hissing noises buzzed in my ears—then, an explosive headache. Excruciating pain shot through every nerve fiber in my body. My muscles twitched and jerked. That very moment defined the word *surreal.*

What a surprise when I released from my body as easily as a banana from its peel. An unseen power, a strong suction, pulled me out and up. The pain stopped, and an odd feeling registered—like I had become newly fallen snow: fresh, clean, pure, and light.

I'm confused. How am I able to be aware of anything right now—unusually aware, in fact? My heart function and respiration have ceased, my reflexes are absent, my eyes are set, and my corneas are opaque. I'm dead. At least I think I am.

But how can I be dead and still have thoughts? I'm afraid.

I had the sensation of rising upward until I came to the top of the garage. Now I'm floating near the ceiling, looking down at a body that appears to be mine hanging from the beam, still jerking and twitching. Apparently, my inner self has separated from my physical self, and only my consciousness is still functioning—a shocking sensation.

What I do know is that I've transitioned from my life on Earth. But to what? I always wondered about the afterlife, and here it is. I'm face-to-face with death. As a Catholic, an unconfessed Catholic, I think I might be going to hell. I haven't been to confession for years.

My last attempt at confession was at age fifteen. My parents had hosted a New Year's Eve cocktail party. Hats, horns, and confetti were plentiful, and so were fancy bottles of wine, scotch, bourbon, gin, and vodka. Even then, I found the bottles tempting and enticing—they looked beautiful as the crystalline and amber liquids shimmered inside. I wanted to try some. People always laughed and had fun when they were drinking.

When no one was paying attention, without a second thought, I grabbed a bottle from the bar and hid it under my shirt as I ran for my bedroom. There were so many bottles, who'd miss one? I was out of breath when I reached my room. Looking to see what treasure I had secured, I saw it was a bottle of vodka. *Score!*

Like prospectors discovering gold, my brother and I had our own party while the adults were downstairs ringing in the new year. We drank enough to feel great without getting sick—a balance impossible to find later on. I relished my feeling of confidence, my insecurities dropping away sip by sip. Vodka, meet Neil. Neil, meet vodka, your new best friend. As a young, self-conscious boy, I'd found my panacea, my elixir to make me feel sociable and accepted. For quite a few years, I thought of liquor as my magic potion. Drinking it had been like casting a spell, instantly making me believe I exuded an aura of charm and charisma.

I knew it was wrong to steal the bottle, but I didn't get busted. When I went to confession, I couldn't make myself tell the priest. I didn't want to acknowledge the sin. I didn't want to repent and ask for God's forgiveness because I knew I'd do it again—and again. After that, I stopped going to confession.

Quite a few creatures molt. Is that what happened to me? Did I molt? Looking down at my former physical body makes me feel like a tarantula after throwing off its skin. As I float, my essence feels light and unrestricted. The hanging body looks like me, yet it doesn't. I recognize my receding hairline, my wide-set eyes, my overly long nose, and my off-kilter jaw—even my gold wedding band with the lapis lazuli stone on my ring finger. My feet, in mud-covered shoes, are still twitching. It's strange to view myself from the outside, to see my body as others saw me.

I feel no attachment to my body. It served my needs while I played the role of Neil. But now, releasing the essence of me feels like coming home after a hard day, pulling off my stiff work boots, then kicking back and relaxing. Only it's my body I've shed instead of work boots. The realization that I'm much more than my physical entity is a bit daunting.

This floating-above-everything perspective gives me a much broader viewpoint, like looking at a landscape from an airplane window. To observe the world from a bird's-eye view gives rise to a sense of omnipotence. Death provides a new, clearer perspective of life. Too bad this insight has come too late.

Being free of the flesh feels invigorating. All of me, the essence of who I was—my consciousness, my thoughts, my memories—remains with me, not in that lifeless vessel. I wonder what will happen next. Will the dark people come for me and take me straight to hell? I saw them in a movie once, and frankly, it kind of haunted me over the years.

Sophie talked of disincarnate beings from another dimension—good guys—who, before we were born, agreed to assist us to meet our missions and goals throughout our human lives and who would meet us when we died. She called them "spirit guides." If they exist, where are mine now? I'd like them to appear and guide me out of this garage.

I seem to be untethered to time, but I know Sophie will be home soon and wonder where I am.

The horror of what I've done to her starts to sink in.

The light switch in the garage flicks on and Sophie enters. I'm not happy to see her. If I still had a beating heart, it would be shattering as I watch her. I hear her thoughts, see her horror and fear. My decision to end my life came from a need to relieve my own agony. I didn't think about what it would do to Sophie.

I watch as she climbs the ladder and falls as she's trying to free me. I want her to stop trying to save me, but she's attempting it again with a saw in hand. Desperation breeds perseverance. I worry she might die herself because of how she's gasping for air. An animalistic, wailing sound rips from her throat. Keening. Blood, *her* blood, is dripping from her hand. Oh God, I feel the full intensity of her pain, and now I fear she'll never forgive me. I was a shit when I was alive and a shit to choose suicide as my way out.

What have I done? If only we could press a button to show us a foretelling of the repercussions from an action. I want to go in reverse and undo the deed. That's me, only thinking of myself. But we don't get do-overs when it comes to death.

While I float above, observing my dead body, a welcoming, brilliant light envelops my essence. I want to follow it, to go with it. The light is intense and compelling, but I'm going to ignore it. I don't deserve light. I deserve darkness and fire. I know I'll be harshly judged for what I've done to my family and to Sophie. I might deserve hell, but I'm sure not going to go there without being forced. I feel as if I'm standing at a precipice, not knowing what lies below and afraid to look. I think I'm going to stay right here in this garage.

I don't want to go to hell.

CHAPTER 3
AUGUST 22, 1987

I T STARTED LIKE any quiet morning in La Jolla, California, with Lizzie Cohen following her usual Saturday routine. Curled up on the family room couch in sweatpants and an old Jimi Hendrix T-shirt—an ensemble she called her "anti-aphrodisiac outfit"—Lizzie relaxed while she scratched in the answers to the *Union Tribune* crossword puzzle, in ink. A dollop of cream swam on the top of the coffee she sipped from her favorite SKI ASPEN mug. She was feeling clever after quickly penning in the first five words when the phone in her husband's office rang. It took her until the fourth ring to nonchalantly pick it up.

"Hello?"

An eerie cry came from the other end of the phone, followed by a sound reminiscent of a dying, wounded animal. She knew immediately it was her best friend, Sophie.

"Sophie? What the hell is wrong?" She set her mug down.

Sophie choked on her words, finally shouting, "He's dead! He's dead!" More heaving, racking sobs.

Lizzie's heart sank faster than a plunging roller coaster as she was sucked into a swirling, plummeting vortex of doom—she knew at once who "he" was. It was no surprise. In fact, she wondered why it hadn't happened sooner.

Lizzie clenched the phone. "Calm down, I can't understand you. What happened? Where are you?"

"I'm in the kitchen at home."

Lizzie pressed the phone closer to her ear. "Why do you sound so breathless?"

"I'm pacing the floor. I spent the worst night of my life at the hospital. I accidentally cut my thumb while trying to cut him down, and I banged my head pretty badly."

Lizzie gasped at her words. *This can't be happening.* "Cut him down?"

Sophie mumbled something incomprehensible, then, "Neil didn't come home when he said he would, so I worried and—"

Lizzie stood perfectly still, unable to move while she waited out another round of gut-wrenching sobs.

"There was a voice in my head telling me, 'Sophie, don't go back there.' But I walked back there anyway and—" She released another wail. "He was hanging in the garage! He hung himself with a rope. I wanted to tear my eyes out after seeing that horror. I tried to cut him down, but I couldn't. It was too late. I was screaming bloody murder, and Phil, my neighbor, came over from next door and took me away from the scene. My hand was a mess. I don't remember much of what happened other than someone took me to the hospital to stitch me up and take a scan of my head. I can't believe this. I can't cope with this. I can't breathe. I don't know what to do!"

It was hard for Lizzie to take it all in. Maybe she was in shock. She knew Sophie's world, as it had existed previously, had just turned into a monstrosity of a nightmare, but all she could hear was a loud roaring noise in her head—like jets taking off on a runway in her brain. She was listening to Sophie's words, but she couldn't comprehend them. She felt like she was swimming in a cloud that tangled up her auditory input.

Sophie continued lamenting. "It can't be. This can't be happening. I hate him for this. I hate what he did to me."

Lizzie snapped out of the fog she was in. *Could all this be real?* She knew she needed to get to Sophie. She put her tennis shoes on while she talked.

"Wait there," Lizzie said. "I'll come get you. You're staying with us."

Running around the house, gathering her keys, her purse, she called her husband—almost falling to her knees as she told him what had happened. David offered to pick Sophie up, but Lizzie wanted to go. She knew Sophie had never needed her more.

On autopilot, Lizzie jumped into her car and drove off, careening around corners and flying on the freeway in her Volvo. She couldn't get there fast enough.

As she drove, Lizzie relived memories of Neil. She'd been all too aware of the rocky status of Sophie's three years of marriage. She'd often say to Sophie, "Alcohol abuse wreaks havoc on the body of the abuser, but it destroys the souls of those who love them." She'd always hoped it wouldn't destroy Sophie's soul. Not so silently, Lizzie had watched the impact Neil's addiction had had on her friend over the years. *Why did it have to come to this?* She should have recognized how unstable he was. After all, she was a doctor!

When Sophie had first introduced Neil to Lizzie and David, he'd been clean and sober for years, and Sophie wasn't aware alcohol had ever been an issue for him. Lizzie recalled the emotional day when Sophie had told her that she'd found out he'd been keeping a secret from her. A big one. The addiction monster had found its way back into his life, bit him hard, and wouldn't let go of its hold—like a beast grabbing on to the tail of his coat, pulling him back deep into a cave, then eating him alive. His addiction was ugly and insidious, toying with him like a seductress. It lured him, bottle after empty bottle, drawing him into a place of total darkness. His blackouts made him forget what happened while he was under the seductress's spell, but Sophie carried the memories for him, and Lizzie helplessly watched as those memories eventually wore away at Sophie's sparkle and joy.

Glancing down at the speedometer, Lizzie noticed she was going well above the speed limit. Wanting to avoid a ticket, she slowed down, but her mind still raced, her thoughts flip-flopping between trying to figure out how to help her best friend and the intense sadness she felt for Neil. She turned the radio down so she could think.

Lizzie had tried to talk Sophie into leaving Neil when he'd started to heavily drink again. She'd tried to convince her that Neil regaining, and then retaining, his sobriety was about as unlikely as uncracking an egg. But Sophie was a fixer by nature and research was her specialty. She was determined to help mend him—to put Humpty Dumpty together again—so she read every book on the subject of addiction and coaxed Neil to try the recommended solutions. Nothing worked. He lost jobs, crashed cars, slept in places he couldn't remember, spent countless hours in multiple emergency rooms, and blacked out frequently.

With her brain on overload, Lizzie missed the exit to Sophie's house by several miles. Realizing her error, she filled the car with expletives and turned around, but her thoughts continued to bombard her.

Lizzie remembered not feeling at all hopeful the last time Neil went to rehab. Heck, it was his seventh stint! She didn't have any faith that it would be successful. After completing sixty days, he vowed to stay clean and sober forever. His promise lasted a week. His indescribable demons compelled him to stop at the grocery store one morning, where he bought a pint of vodka. One bottle was all it took to set him back on the never-ending loop of self-destruction, dragging Sophie and all her self-help books and research along with him.

Lizzie knew Neil was in big trouble when Sophie told her about an overwhelming feeling Neil had shared. He was desperate to get off the merry-go-round of ongoing relapse, he'd told her. It felt as if he'd tried everything and failed. So he just resigned, literally and figuratively reaching the end of his rope. Neil confessed he couldn't stop the pain and anguish and could take no more. All he wanted was peace, no more suffering, and, in his mind, there was only one way to achieve that. Lizzie figured that was probably when he began planning his death. She knew his one true love was the bottom of an empty bottle. He lived in a space between lost and found. And then he died.

Traffic slowed to a crawl as Lizzie approached the exit to Sophie's house. Her urgency made the stagnant traffic seem doubly frustrating. She combed her fingers through her hair in an attempt to soothe herself while tears rolled down her cheeks. She didn't want to focus on Neil's negatives. She just wanted to focus on what she could do to help Sophie.

*

Finally, she arrived, driving too close to the curb, scraping her tires as she parked in front of Sophie's house. She saw her standing out front talking to a policewoman, vigorously gesturing with her arms and shaking her head vehemently.

Lizzie barely got the car door closed before Sophie ran to her and buried her tear-streaked face in her neck, arms wrapped tightly around her. "Lizzie, I—" No other words came out.

"Honey, I'm so sorry. I'm here now and will help you get through this."

As Lizzie hugged Sophie's rigid body, she tried to inspect her for visible signs of physical distress. "Will the police let you leave now? If so, get in the car and let's get out of here."

Sophie pulled out of Lizzie's embrace far enough to answer, "Yeah, the policewoman said I could leave. I've already given a statement, but I have to go to the police station later for further questions."

Lizzie was shocked to see that it had taken only one night to age Sophie ten years. She was only thirty-five but now looked forty-five. Her stonewashed blue jeans, lime-green jelly shoes, and off-the-shoulder T-shirt were stained with grief, fear, dried blood, and fresh tears. She reeked of rubbing alcohol and despair. She held her hands up trying to shield her mascara-streaked face from the sun as rivulets of sweat from her forehead streamed over the bridge of her dripping nose.

There was a long moment of silence.

"Lizzie, was it my fault in some way? I tried everything I could to get him help."

Her voice was raspy from screaming, but Lizzie heard something underneath the words—a dark cloud of dread mixed with a touch of guilt.

She stroked Sophie's shoulder-length hair, pulling it back off her face as she spoke. "You know this wasn't about you. It was about a pain he could no longer endure. He was a broken person. You tried to fix him, and you learned you couldn't. He was gone long before this day."

Opening the door to her car, she signaled Sophie to get in. Standing on the sidewalk, Sophie didn't move.

"I can't shake the visual out of my head. How could anyone do that to another human being? How could he do that to me when he knew I'd find him hanging there? In our garage! How will I ever get the image out of my mind? I can't cope with this."

"When did it happen?" Lizzie said.

"Last night."

"Really? What? Why didn't you call me?"

"I couldn't. They took me to the hospital for this." Sophie held up her hand bandaged in white gauze. Dried blood dotted the tape. "And they were observing me for a concussion."

People had started to gather around them but kept their distance. Lizzie ignored them. They whispered and pointed toward the backyard while staring. Sophie didn't seem to notice.

"Sophie, get in the car and we can talk there. You'll need special counseling for this. This is beyond anything I'm trained to handle. Specialists know how to guide you through situations like this. Group counseling or private. Whatever it takes. Right now, I'll prescribe something for you to calm you down—something so you de-escalate a bit. You're coming to stay with us, Sophie. You need to be around people. David and I will look out for you."

She nudged Sophie in the direction of the car.

"Okay, but I need to go to the bathroom before we go. Can you throw some clothes in the duffel bag in my closet?"

"I will. Go wash your face and run a brush through your hair, and I'll pack some stuff for you."

Lizzie closed the car door and headed up to the house with Sophie.

As if the universe needed to cry along with her, the clouds opened up and dumped a bucket of rain again, and the winds picked up with force. When they entered the front door, tree branches smacked against the side of the house like a woman slapping her cheating lover.

Lizzie quickly packed the bag with essentials for Sophie and waited in the bathroom doorway watching Sophie throw toiletries into a smaller bag. Neither spoke. She watched Sophie jerk open the medicine cabinet, grabbing her toothpaste, toothbrush, deodorant. Sitting on the shelf was a bottle of prescription medication, and Lizzie observed as Sophie nervously counted out the pills, placed them back into the container, and shoved it into her pocket. Lizzie looked directly at her and raised her eyebrows.

Sophie responded to her look. "My stomach medication," she said. "I'm ready to go now."

Lizzie put her arm around her friend as they walked down the steps to the car and tossed Sophie's bags into the trunk. Lizzie sat in the driver's seat, with the motor running, chasing raindrops from the windshield with the squeaky wipers on fast speed, waiting for her hands to stop their intense shaking.

Trying to maintain her composure, Lizzie drove to her house in utter silence. There were simply no words. What more could be said? Neil's hanging was the punctuation mark to a final statement.

CHAPTER 4
THE ASTRAL PLANE

S OMEWHERE IN THE cosmic realm where existence is timeless, several souls, appearing as light-bodies—each soul radiating a color indicating a level of consciousness depending on their frequency—watch over the human beings they assist. These entities are spirit guides, nonphysical beings of vibrating energy assigned to human souls before they're born to help guide them as they strive to attain their mission and purpose on Earth.

Nephesh, a senior guide emitting a teal-colored transparent light, works at a complex computer-like monitoring device designed to help guide a person's life path. He controls the device by moving his light-hand in a pattern on an invisible wall as though he's playing a piano without touching the keys. As he works, his light-arms carve the air like a maestro conducting an orchestra. Another senior guide, Malach, also emitting a teal-colored transparent light, assists. Ruach, radiating a transparent yellow—an intern spirit guide—observes in the monitoring area. They communicate telepathically.

Malach: Who are you monitoring, Nephesh?

Nephesh: Sophie Beaumont and Lizzie Cohen. Sophie is going through a life crisis right now, so I'm making myself available if she wants help.

Malach: Let me know if you need my assistance. Are you almost finished with your book?

Nephesh: Not yet. This has been one big undertaking. I think my book will help people on Earth understand how to navigate their lives using wisdom instead of so much suffering. Life would be easier for all of us spirit guides as well. I think it will help people like Sophie.

Ruach: As I understand it, both positive and negative experiences are a part of life on Earth.

Nephesh: That's true, but I think there are ways to gain life experience without so much drama and pain. Understanding some basic concepts might help people evolve faster.

Malach: Why do you think they need to evolve faster? Time isn't something we deal with here, but it helps people in the physical world structure their lives and stay directed. I function fine in a world without it. I do like the idea of the book, but it's not like it hasn't been done before. Many people on Earth have published books like the type you're talking about. What makes yours different? And how would you get the book to people from here? You can't take anything with you when you're born. What's your distribution plan?

Nephesh: People live in a world influenced by time even if we don't. I know other books have been channeled from some of us here, but I hope to present my information with the wisdom from this dimension—a knowing and an understanding not available from the earthly perspective. I haven't resolved the distribution plan, but I hope to present my information in a different way.

Ruach: I do know, from past incarnations on Earth, that it takes participation in actual experiences to grow and expand consciousness.

Nephesh: Yes. I think people *are* raising their consciousness. Many refer to that as "awakening." My goal? To help people evolve faster to bring the planet to a higher level of consciousness. You know, less war, terrorism, and hatred. More love and compassion. Malach, don't you agree, for the sake of the world, that it would be better to accelerate the positive changes?

Malach: Not necessarily. Souls evolve at their own speed. And I already see many positive changes going on.

Nephesh: Anyway, it's almost my birthday. The council of spirit guides and I have been reviewing my upcoming soul agreements and life plan. I've chosen my parents, made my agreements with fellow souls, formalized my life goals, and I'm finalizing some details. I'm going to Earth to be born. Happy birthday to me.

Malach: Wish I were going with you this time, but I'm not ready to leave this dimension yet. I have some missions to accomplish right here.

Nephesh: Good, because I need an experienced guide like you here to assist me. I missed you at the last meeting, and you'll need to catch up on everything since you'll be my main guide. No screwups. Right now, I need to get this book completed before I go.

Malach: Sorry I missed the meeting, Neph. I'll catch up and be ready for your transition to Earth.

Pneuma, an intern guide emitting a transparent pink light, enters the monitoring area.

Pneuma: Wow, this monitoring device completely amazes me. I don't know how I'll even begin to learn some of this stuff. Since I'll be one of your assistant guides, Nephesh, how about letting me in on the information in your book before you go?

Nephesh: Absolutely. I *want* you to read it. Like I've said before, I don't want any screwups happening. I have soul agreements with people who have already been on Earth for years, and there are some things I definitely want to accomplish. On the other hand, I might not be able to finish the book before my birth date arrives. I think I might have to memorize everything I've already compiled and write it into a book when I'm on Earth—that could be one of my life missions.

Pneuma: Why don't you stay here and guide them? Wouldn't that be more powerful?

Nephesh: Ah, grasshopper, we leave this utopia for our own spiritual development, yes, but also to promote the growth of those we love.

I can guide from here, or I can physically incarnate and assist people directly there. Some of them don't believe in us and will hear my message better if I come in physical form. For what I want to do, I'll be more effective on Earth, but I'll have to deal with the veil. The veil will be a huge deterrent to me with this mission, and of course I'm going to have to deal with expanding my own consciousness while I'm there, which is part of the gig.

Pneuma: I get it.

Nephesh: One of the members of our soul group on Earth, Sophie, is struggling and off her chosen path. That's okay, of course—it's her choice. But I think I need to bring her some hope so she can decide if this is really the direction she wants to go. There's free will, but she's distraught, acting out of fear, and she's cried out for help more than once. So help is on the way, and that help would be in the form of yours truly.

Malach: Pneuma, spirits take on a physical form because it's the only way to gain certain kinds of experiences that will heal or expand them. How do we grow in consciousness? By taking on challenging experiences in physical form.

Nephesh: Hey, Malach, our beloved pup, Betty Rose, will be joining me. I want her with me this time around.

Malach: That's great, but I'll miss her. She'd miss you too much if you didn't take her along. Maybe she'll keep you out of trouble.

Nephesh: It's not so much about keeping me out of trouble—she's going to serve a significant role for me.

Malach: Okay, I'll study up on the updates you've made to your life plan. I need to be on top of everything.

Nephesh: Yes, you do. I'm counting on you.

CHAPTER 5

SEPTEMBER 1, 1987

S OPHIE SAT IN the Cohens' guest room and ripped off each page of the daily calendar, stacking them in a haphazard pile on the wooden desk. She counted eleven days since Neil's suicide. She must have been functioning mechanically, in a daze, the whole time because she didn't remember the days passing. One word kept playing like a stuck record in her brain: *Why, why, why?* She couldn't come up with an acceptable answer, especially because Neil hadn't left a letter to explain himself. Not that something like suicide could be explained in a note. Maybe it was better he'd left nothing—she couldn't have dealt with it if he held her responsible in any way.

Suicide. Sophie couldn't even say the word out loud, so she referred to what he'd done as "it." She thought about other words no one ever wants to hear in relation to life: *kidnapped, cancer, abuse, murder, prison.*

Getting through the funeral had been almost unbearable. Following Neil's burial, Sophie's emotions raged out of control. She hated feeling out of control. At times, she was so angry, she wanted to smash things—angry that Neil had abandoned her, angry that he hadn't loved her enough to work things out.

The trauma of the past couple of weeks brought back other long-buried memories. An image of her father came to mind and, with it, the days of her childhood.

Sophie's father had been diagnosed with juvenile diabetes at the age of fourteen, and the medical community didn't understand the best ways to manage it back then. Over time, his illness had progressed, requiring him to stay home, so he took care of her and her brother while their mom worked. Sophie loved spending time with her dad. In spite of being ill, he still enjoyed singing with his smooth baritone voice and playing sweet melodies on his violin.

In the center of their living room sat a well-worn armchair, where her dad would squeeze between her and her brother and read them their favorite storybooks. He took on the voice of the characters, making the stories come alive. She loved *Dumbo* and *Howdy Doody's Circus*. Sometimes the three of them baked. As a diabetic, he needed to avoid eating sweets; but he ate them anyway, and once a week they'd bake his favorite chocolate chip cookies.

Eventually, he had difficulties reading the books because he couldn't see well, and his feet were always swollen, requiring him to keep them elevated on a footstool. Pain became a way of life, but he never said so, always acting cheerful. Even though he was sick, Sophie loved the bonding time she spent with her dad and her brother. Most nights, he'd play them to sleep with the melodious sounds of his violin.

One night, no more songs came from his instrument. Instead, Sophie woke to the haunting sound of sirens. Climbing out of bed, she peered around the corner of her bedroom door. Two men rushed up the stairs of their second-story duplex with a stretcher and carried her father away. Her mother collapsed, sobbing on the chenille bedspread in their bedroom. Someone arrived in a car to take her mother to the hospital, while Sophie's grandmother came upstairs to stay with her and her brother. She remembered her grandmother answering the phone and crying. When she gathered herself together, she called Sophie and Dean to her and told them their precious daddy had gone to live with the angels. He never came home again.

For years, Sophie had nightmares about the night the sirens blared. She vividly recalled the funeral. Everyone was dressed in black— women in black dresses with hats and veils and men in black suits. The nauseating scent of too many carnations permeated the room. For the rest of her life, she hated that smell. She saw her dad lying in a fancy box with his eyes closed, thinking it was odd that he was sleeping there while everyone around her was crying. Standing on the step stool in front of the coffin, she reached up and pulled an eyelid back. "Daddy, wake up," she said. But he never did. She didn't understand why he'd gone to live with the angels instead of living with her. Why had he left them to be with the angels?

Sophie doodled on the scratch pad sitting on the desk. Lately, it seemed as though all she did was live in the past. She thought about how she missed her dad.

She figured it was because of her dad dying when she was so young that she had trouble establishing deep relationships with men in later years, so she'd eventually seen a therapist about it. "Abandonment issues," he'd said. The therapist told her the fear of being abandoned was what created her severe anxiety and worry that people around her were going to leave her or die. He said the problem could lead her to unconsciously attract and be attracted to people who would abandon her in the future. He called it "repetition compulsion," where you repeat your childhood traumas and play them out over and over. All the psychobabble didn't matter because all she knew was that it was happening again. Neil had abandoned her. But this time, she doubted Neil went to live with the angels like her dad had. He must have gone somewhere bad and dreary. A small part of her hoped so.

Sophie's daydreaming was interrupted by a barefooted Lizzie standing at the bedroom door.

"Soph, can I come in and talk?"

"Sure. Pull me into the present. I've been reminiscing too much about the past."

It was only 8:00 p.m., yet Sophie was already in her pajamas—her blue and green plaid top misbuttoned and stained with a combination of grease, chicken soup, and something burgundy in color, most likely wine. She'd been avoiding mirrors because she didn't want to see the dark circles under her eyes, swollen from crying, the pallid complexion of an invalid.

Sophie watched as Lizzie plopped down in the peach chair in the corner, nervously twisting the hair at her temple. She felt annoyed as Lizzie visually inspected her and furrowed her brow.

"Honey, you just aren't looking good at all. Your beautiful green eyes are so sullen. Your reaction to something so horrifying is totally natural, but you've now reached the point of not functioning. You even look like you've shrunk."

"That bad?"

"I'm just concerned. You hang out in your pajamas all day, eating only chicken noodle soup and tea, and I'm not even sure I've heard the shower running recently."

Sophie nodded. "Forcing myself to go back to work and face people just isn't possible right now."

"I do understand that. But you can't just sit in this room day after day staring out the window. Tomorrow you need to get up and get dressed—we'll go for a walk on the beach and smell the ocean. You need some exercise and fresh air as well as some nutritious food. You look like you've dropped too much weight."

"I can't. The pain is overwhelming, and no one understands the hell this is. I don't know if *he* went to hell, but he certainly sent me there. How could he hate me so much? How could anyone do this to another person? The condolences and prayers from everyone can't change the destruction—it's like a bomb exploded in my head."

"I know, I know."

Sophie shook her head. "Actually, you don't know. It's an emotional roller coaster, and I don't know how I'll feel from one moment to the next. I dive down feeling depressed, and then I ride up in a fit of anger that something like this could happen to me. Then I have days where I'm numb and feel nothing—protection days—followed by days of crying uncontrollably. My perception of life has changed completely."

Lizzie stood and reached for Sophie's hand. "You're right, I can't say I understand because I've never gone through it, but I imagine it's beyond horrible. But you were also living in hell while he was alive, going through his cycle of addiction. You need to try to move a bit forward now—at least take a shower," she said with a hint of a smile and a playful pinch of her nostrils.

"Soph, Neil's behavior controlled your life when he was alive, and it continues to control you after his death. You've used up your sick time at work. Do you want to ask for a leave of absence? What do you want me to tell them? They want to know your plans."

Sophie turned her head to the side to avoid Lizzie's direct gaze. "I don't have the energy it takes to even get up and get dressed, much less function at work. I can't do occupational therapy with little kids in this state of mind. Please tell them I need more time—a period of bereavement. If I need a doctor's note, write me one, okay? Having a physician for a best friend should reap some benefits."

"I'll do that for you."

"I don't see any way out of this pain. All I want to do is stay in bed. I know it seems like I'm sleeping my life away, but it's my only escape. Every night, I have nightmares where I see flashbacks of him hanging. I can't concentrate on anything, and I don't want people around me because they all say the wrong things. I have no interest in anything."

"It takes time, I know," Lizzie said, "but you also need some professional help to deal with the trauma. You can't do this alone. I found a grief group you can attend. I think it'll help to discuss this with other people who've gone through the same thing. David thinks it's better than doing individual counseling because in a group setting, you'll feel like others understand your situation."

"I don't see how anyone can understand this. I never will." Sophie pushed out her lower lip. "I don't want to remember anything good about him. Like, I remember this really awful day at work when there was this big personnel issue going on, and I was so tired and ready to call it quits. When I got home, he greeted me at the door with a cold martini, followed by a gourmet dinner and a foot rub. I was so touched by his sensitivity." Sophie paused, then her voice changed. "But now I just want to despise him."

"It's natural to have all these mixed feelings. We'll call to enroll you in that group tomorrow. No excuses. You're going. Neil committed a desperate act, but there's no reason to ruin your life because he destroyed his. And you need to eat. You want a bowl of soup? I'll go heat it up and bring it in here."

Sophie climbed into the bed, snuggled down deep, and pulled the covers up to her chin. "No, I don't want anything, but thanks. You're a good friend. I'll deal with all this tomorrow, okay? Tonight I just need a good night's sleep."

"Okay, hope you have sweet dreams instead of those nightmares. See you in the morning."

Lizzie leaned over and kissed her friend on the forehead, then closed the bedroom door on her way out.

As soon as Lizzie was gone, Sophie threw back the covers and made a beeline for her purse, scrounging through her wallet full of old receipts, credit cards, and stamps in search of a particular photo. It was a picture of her and Neil at a charity dance a few years ago—her favorite picture of the two of them. Neither of them were photogenic, but in this particular shot, the photographer had captured a happy time of a couple in the initial stages of love. Now she wanted to destroy the photo in the same way he'd destroyed her illusion of happiness.

Digging through the top drawer of the desk, Sophie found a pair of scissors and started snipping at the border, creating fringe all around. That didn't improve her mood, so she took a pen to his face, eventually obscuring his features, then his entire body.

Still her anger overflowed, like a clogged-up toilet. With a red pen now, she vigorously scribbled all over his face. There—the photo was utterly ruined, just like the relationship he destroyed.

Sophie was convinced talking with a group of people wasn't going to stop the unbearable pain. She couldn't stand thinking about it anymore.

There was no future for her.

There was only one way out.

She grabbed her crumpled-up jeans on the dresser and dug out the bottle she'd shoved in the pocket a couple of weeks ago.

I shouldn't have lied to Lizzie, but I didn't want her to take my pills. They were leftover narcotics from a previous shoulder surgery. She unscrewed the cap and stared at the pain pills, hoping there were enough to do the trick. *What if they only give me brain damage?* She spilled one pill into her palm, tentatively fingered it, then placed it on her tongue and swallowed. It wouldn't be so bad.

She climbed back into bed and reached for the bottle of water on the nightstand, considering if she really wanted to die. She longed for freedom from the pain. *There's only one way to escape. This is what it must have felt like for Neil. I'll probably join him in hell.*

CHAPTER 6
THE ASTRAL PLANE

NEPHESH WORKS IN the monitoring area, where the other guides join him, peering over his light-shoulders watching him work. Shifting the display with a slight wave of his light-hand, he zooms in on a scene. He's a disciplined observer searching with intent. This time, he pinpoints a home in La Jolla, California. He zooms in closer and sees a woman in her thirties sitting on a bed, head in hands, crying like her heart has been broken, her body limp with hopelessness and sorrow. She holds a bottle of painkillers, ready to take the pills.

Crap, Sophie, he thinks, transmitting his thoughts to her. *No. I know you don't want to do this. You aren't hearing me! You have missions you want to accomplish. Hang on until I get there in person. You don't want to do this. I'm going to try to help you because I know this isn't what you want to do.*

With a wave of his light-hand, he gives Lizzie the inspiration to say good night to Sophie one more time. *This better do it. Sophie, I'm not going to Earth for a while. I'll give you a sign that I'm coming.*

He pans to Lizzie and watches as she receives the thought—the inspiration—and acts on it. She immediately heads to the guest room to check on Sophie one more time.

Nephesh carefully observes the interaction between Sophie and Lizzie on his monitor and listens to Sophie's thoughts.

Sophie startles to the sound of knocking on her bedroom door.

"Sophie, are you awake?"

"Just a second," she says. She shoves the container of pills under her pillow and pulls the covers under her chin. "Come in."

"Oh, good, you're still up. Come have a glass of wine with me. Let's watch a movie on TV. David's already asleep, and I really could use some company. Please. I could use a friend myself right now."

Sophie fakes a yawn. "Can we do it another time? I'm tired and actually feel like I could fall asleep now."

"You sure? Okay. I love you, my friend. We'll get through this. Hang in there and remember, we'll face this together. *You aren't alone.*"

Lizzie places her hand tenderly on Sophie's cheek, then leaves the room.

Tears of relief roll down Sophie's cheeks. It seems as though Lizzie's words are like magic. Soothing. Lizzie's caring and kindness appear to have a profound and immediate impact on Sophie's state of mind. It's as though that small heartfelt gesture of camaraderie subdues the intensity of the moment. Sophie is touched by her friend's love—it's healing. She remembers she is loved and not alone. She smiles for the first time in months.

Sophie realizes she isn't acting in her right mind. What had she been thinking? Killing herself? How could she do to Lizzie what Neil had done to her? How could her head be so clouded by emotion? She takes the bottle of pills out one more time and gently shakes it. She figures there probably aren't enough of them, anyway, and she'll likely just vomit them up. She flings the bottle across the room, slides her head into her hands, and sobs.

I need help. I'm ready for help.

But Sophie isn't sure what kind of help she wants to seek. She doesn't want to see another psychologist—she just doesn't think that kind of counseling is what she needs right now. As a child, though, her mother had taught her to trust her intuition and listen to the voices of her spirit advisors—guides from another dimension who watched out for her well-being and helped direct her on the right path.

She needs her guides now.

She crawls out of bed, kneeling at the side. "Dear spirit guides," she says. "I need you. I'm feeling lost. Please help me. I can't make it without you."

She hears Nephesh's buttery soft, yet confident, voice in her head. *Hang on. You can and will hang on. I'm coming and will be with you shortly. Do you understand?*

Goose bumps spring up on Sophie's arms. She whispers back, *Yes, I understand … I knew you'd come. I knew it.*

On the astral plane, Nephesh notes Sophie's response. He makes an entry into the system: *Message received.*

CHAPTER 7
OCTOBER 17, 1987

THE LATE-AFTERNOON SUNLIGHT poured through the oversized picture window behind the sink in the kitchen, and the light bounced off the burgundy walls, forming soft pink shadows on the gray countertops. Lizzie, having returned home from a run, stood in front of the open refrigerator guzzling bottled water. The enticing smell of cinnamon and butter diffused through the room— Sophie must have baked.

After throwing her bottle in the trash, Lizzie grabbed a red marking pen from the kitchen junk drawer and scribbled a phone number on the kitchen calendar. As she did so, she noticed that Sophie had been living with her and David for two months.

"Sophie," Lizzie yelled toward the back of the house. "You know the real estate agent I told you about? I called him, and he's starting the process of selling your house, like we talked about."

Lizzie opened the refrigerator again, this time rummaging through it until she found a block of Jarlsberg cheese. With deliberation, she opened the cellophane wrapper and carved thin pieces with a sharp knife.

Sophie sauntered into the kitchen, in her pajamas again—this pair adorned with pink poodles—and plopped onto a bar stool at the island. She picked up one of the lemons from the crystal bowl sitting on the counter and tossed it back and forth from hand to hand.

"Thanks, Lizzie. I can't wait to get out from under that evil place."

"Sophie, the place isn't evil, but what happened there was tragic." She nodded with her chin. "Could you get some apples from the refrigerator bin and wash and slice them? We need a snack. You know, of course, it's always more difficult to sell a house when there's been a murder or suicide in it. The neighbors aren't helping by telling prospective buyers it's haunted."

Sophie pivoted on the stool. "Of course it is." She shrugged. "I almost do believe he's haunting it. Anything to make things more difficult. I want the house sold. I never want to have to look at it again." She retrieved the plumpest apples she could find in the refrigerator. "This is my favorite brand, and they aren't in season long enough." She washed a few of them and cut them into wedges. "Want some wine?"

"Yep, I found a new one to try. An Oregon wine from the Willamette Valley. A pinot noir. Can you get two glasses down?"

"Sure." Sophie retrieved two wineglasses from the cupboard and set them on the counter. "I discovered this great taste sensation—sprinkling some lemon juice on these apple slices. It tastes delicious."

"Are you two drinking again?" David strolled into the kitchen holding two paper bags filled with groceries. He leaned over and gave Lizzie a kiss. "Hi, sweetie. You look particularly beautiful today. Did you just get your hair done?"

"Thanks. I refreshed my highlights, so it has more blonde streaks."

"Makes your eyes look more crystal blue, if that's even possible."

Lizzie eyed her husband for a moment, his angular face. *He really is a handsome man.*

David was a six-foot-two former basketball player with wavy black hair with a shocking stripe of gray running through it. He wore outdated silver eyeglasses, but they highlighted his doe-brown eyes, expressive and shining with compassion. He was what Lizzie called a "good soul," a mensch. She was a fool for David Cohen the minute she set eyes on him—she knew she was fortunate to have him in her life.

David stood behind Sophie and gently massaged her shoulders with his strong hands. "And you, my friend—you're in for a treat. I'm grilling rib eyes tonight with chimichurri sauce. Don't fill up too much."

Sophie rolled her head clockwise, making little moaning sounds. "This is just a little appetizer. Mmm, that feels good. Thanks."

Sophie layered the sliced apples and cheese alternately on a plate, squirted a burst of lemon juice on the apples, and gave David a hug and a peck on the cheek. "Okay, you big lug. What's your drink of choice?"

He unpacked the groceries as he talked. "Wine is good. So how are you feeling, Sophie?"

Lizzie noticed as David leaned in toward Sophie and furrowed his brow. "I've been thinking about you. And I'm worried you aren't eating. You're looking too thin."

"Ha! Words I never thought I'd hear in my life. This is a weight loss diet I definitely don't recommend."

As Sophie reached up for a third wineglass, she said, "I guess I'm doing better. The thing is, I don't know where I'm going to live. Without Neil's income, I'm not sure I can afford much in this city, and I'm not up for a roommate right now." She stood still for a minute and rubbed her temples as she spoke. "I'm not sure how long I can live on the 401k account. I won't be able to collect his life insurance because he only bought it a year ago and it has the two-year suicide clause. Hopefully, the house will sell for a good price."

Lizzie's eyes lit with excitement. "Come on, let's sit in the living room. David and I talked about it, and we have a scathingly brilliant idea. David, you tell her, it was your idea."

They sat on the U-shaped gray and white couch and placed the food and glasses on the coffee table. David drew out the suspense as he chomped on an apple slice.

"Okay, this is it," he said. "Two things. First, I found a great therapist for you. I know you didn't follow up on the idea when Liz presented it before, but I'm putting my foot down now. It's time, if for no other reason than to get you out of your pajamas. You need to get into some group therapy to help you through this."

He picked up the wine bottle, cranked the lever wine opener, removed the cork, and allowed the wine to sit and breathe.

Sophie vehemently shook her head. "I don't want to take drugs."

"I didn't say anything about taking drugs." David turned and glanced over at Lizzie. "Liz, did I mention the word 'drugs'? I'm suggesting group grief therapy. Talking to other people who have been in your shoes and relate to what you're going through."

Sophie popped a slice of apple in her mouth, talking with her mouth full. "I do want to sleep through the night again without horrid nightmares."

"That's what I'm saying. I know it's been difficult for you."

"I have you two to talk to. I don't want to talk to a bunch of strangers. And I haven't found therapists very effective for me in the past." She stacked her apple slices in a tower.

"We don't know what it feels like for you," Lizzie said. "Other people who have been through it do. So I think a group environment is best for you. We're not the professionals to help you through this, Sophie."

"You sure as heck are. You're doctors!"

Lizzie swallowed a piece of cheese before speaking. "You know if I could give you a pill to mend your heart, I'd do it, but I don't know how to fix emotional heart pain. And David's a great surgeon, but even he can't cut the pain out of you."

Sophie sucked in a deep breath and released it slowly. "You know, I hate to admit this, but I have to tell you something. I need to say it out loud."

"Okay, go ahead," David coaxed, leaning forward.

Sophie ran her fingers through her hair and blew air, sputtering her lips. "I stopped loving him. There. I said it out loud." She paused for a few seconds. "I stayed with him out of obligation. I don't know when the love actually died or if it was ever even there. Maybe it disappeared somewhere between him falling down that airport escalator and smashing his car head-on into that ditch. Somewhere between the autumns changing to winters, the love slipped away quietly without alerting me it was going to happen. There was a blurry line between love and hate, and then the love faded away. I didn't even realize that until recently. I don't like to think, or don't want to believe, love can die or go away. For anyone. I hate that thought. I believed love was a constant in life. I thought it would always be there."

Lizzie nodded her head as Sophie spoke. Sophie's revelation wasn't news to her.

David filled each glass with wine and passed them out. "Think about this. Maybe it never was love. Maybe you liked being needed, and his need filled some empty space inside you."

Sophie cocked her head and thought for a minute. "See? You would be a good therapist for me."

Lizzie laughed. "Nice try. But you need professional counseling— either one-on-one or in a group. Your choice, my friend. Now, let's toast to new beginnings."

David and Lizzie held out their glasses, and Sophie toasted with reluctance.

Sophie sipped her wine. "Mmm, this is good. You know, there's this part of me that does believe things work out as they're supposed to. Life always has twists and turns."

Lizzie set her glass down on the coffee table. "Life is always a surprise, isn't it? It never seems to go as we expect it to or think it should. We have to expect the bad with the good. Opposing forces give us perspective. So today is a good day. We're enjoying a wonderful afternoon together drinking this pinot noir with my favorite cheese and my favorite people. But here's the best part. David, do continue."

David took the pass and ran with it. "Okay, Soph. I think we have the solution to your living situation. A brilliant solution, if I do say so myself. Drumroll please. You can live in the guesthouse behind us. We aren't using it—no mother-in-law who wants to live in it—and you love the place. It's cozy, homey, and perfect for one. You won't have to pay any rent, so you can save up for another place of your own. We'd love to have you closer to us. And you can house-sit for us when we're working out of town, if you don't mind."

Lizzie sat on the edge of her seat. "We can fix it up any way you like. It'll be fun. What do you think? We could use a joint project." She knew she'd love having Sophie in her backyard.

"Wow, I don't even have to think about this," Sophie answered quickly. "That sounds great. Why not? It's such an adorable little cottage, like something that belongs in a fairy-tale forest. Just my style—cozy and cute.

"I'm excited that you're excited," Lizzie said. "It will be your refuge, your shelter. And the best part is, no one has killed themselves there—at least as far as we know."

Sophie started crying. "I'm sorry. I'm not sure if these are tears of relief or if I'm just feeling so loved and cared for by you two." She fanned her face with her hands. "I think it's a perfect idea. I could be happy anywhere there's room for my bed, my easel, and my loom, but this is more than I could have hoped for. I can't live there rent-free, though. When the house sells, I can give you some cash. I'm not sure how I'll ever thank you guys."

David wore a big grin on his face. "No need for thanks, Sophie. And no need for rent, either—honestly, we don't need the rent money. Since you can't collect on Neil's life insurance, you could use a rent-free place to live. It's just sitting there anyway, so why not use it?"

"It's a deal. I'd love to. And one day, I'll think of a way to thank you."

Lizzie drank the remaining drops of wine from her glass. "My dear friend, thank us by healing and becoming your old self again," she said. "Maybe not your old self—maybe a new and better self. We'll get through this, Sophie—just hang on. Something good is coming your way. I can feel it."

"Okay. And for you guys, I'll call that therapist tomorrow."

Lizzie winked at Sophie. "Thanks. On another note, now it's *my* turn to tell you something." She bounced on the edge of the couch, ready to burst. She leaned forward to watch Sophie's expression.

"What?" Sophie asked. "I can only handle good news."

"It is. At least I hope so. David and I have been working on getting pregnant! It's getting to the point where we'd better do it now or never. Some women can't even get pregnant after thirty-five. Do you think we're doing the right thing?" But Lizzie didn't stop long enough to let Sophie answer. "I've never been completely convinced that bringing more kids into this world is a wise decision. I mean, working for the People Saving People Project has been wonderful for us, but with all the traveling to sometimes pretty unsafe places, raising a family seemed out of the question. But now we think there are ways we can work it out. I love doing humanitarian work, but I don't plan to continue it much longer."

David nodded in agreement as he put his arm around his wife.

Sophie teared up again. "I know it's the right decision. Deep in my soul, I know it. We need to toast again because soon you won't be drinking. Cheers, my friends. Cheers to the new life you'll be bringing to this earth. I guess I'll have to find a new wine buddy."

David raised the nearly empty wine bottle in the air. "I'll be your wine buddy, Sophie."

They toasted again.

"I feel high at the thought of you guys having a baby. I'm not sure why I'm so excited, but it feels like a wave of relief flowing through my veins, like I was a dying person about to give up the struggle, but now the heavenly sensation of surrender has taken over."

Lizzie was thrilled at Sophie's reaction to their news. For the first time in months, Lizzie felt optimistic, a feeling she'd almost forgotten. The thrill of anticipation filled the air. She had the feeling that something good was on its way.

Finally.

CHAPTER 8
THE ASTRAL PLANE

Pneuma: Nephesh, last time we met, you talked about the veil. I know what it is, but why could it be a problem for you?

Ruach: Let me attempt to explain that one.

Nephesh: Go for it.

Ruach: When you're incarnated on Earth, the veil is an amnesia that makes you forget our nonphysical world. While we're here, we enjoy the omnipotence of this dimension. We know who and what we really are before we have to adjust to physical life in a three-dimensional world living in a body.

Malach: Good explanation, Ruach. And everything in the universe— including you, of course—is pure energy vibrating at different frequencies. When we're born on Earth, most souls forget about life here. When we die, our consciousness is free to expand again and to remember once more.

Nephesh: Yes, as spirits, we know the purpose of the lives we're going to lead before we incarnate. When we're born and pass through the line between the physical and nonphysical worlds, we forget. Sometimes we don't remember for the whole lifetime.

Malach: Challenges we face in life help remind us of our purpose for becoming physical beings. Think of the veil as a barrier of sorts—the line between—that separates various planes of existence. It's necessary for most people to function on Earth. But Nephesh needs to remember our nonphysical world this time to accomplish his goals. He doesn't want to forget his limitless potential. Right, Neph?

Nephesh: That's correct. We're a bundle of highly vibrating energy, right? When we go to the physical world, we have to decelerate. Imagine a race car going a hundred eighty miles per hour and decelerating down to thirty miles per hour as it dives into the body. We slow down to low frequencies of vibration, and then we pass through the veil and forget who we really are—spirits! For most people, remembering everything they know about the spiritual realm would be too crazy and confusing while they live their lives.

Pneuma: Makes sense, I guess.

Nephesh: Think of it like a magician and his art. There's a saying, "Magic is the art of changing consciousness at will." A magician creates an illusion—he is able to manipulate how we see things, right? When we watch a magic show, we know what we're seeing isn't real at all, but momentarily, we think it is—we believe it is. The magician uses his veil to cover the magic trick while he hides the truth from us. Taking off the veil reveals his secrets. When we move from the spiritual world to the physical world, you could say the veil essentially covers us—we forget we're really spiritual beings underneath our human disguise.

Pneuma: Seems a daunting task.

Ruach: What's that?

Pneuma: To plan a physical life. I wouldn't even know where to begin.

Ruach: It requires a lot of planning and experience, for sure.

Nephesh: We incarnate to have experiences to expand our consciousness. At this time on Earth, suffering seems to be the most effective way to make a person quickly understand that a situation is painful or negative. The more compelling the pain, the faster the attempt to resolve it. Pain can motivate a person to take action very quickly, but there are other ways to expand consciousness, like raising your vibration through joy, gratitude, and compassion. But most people are still relying on painful experiences to grow. I'd like to see that change.

Pneuma: Hopefully, it will.

Nephesh: I want—no, I need—to remember everything from this dimension when I'm born. Everyone on board with that?

Malach: Yes, and I have just the plan to avoid the amnesia.

Nephesh: Here's my concern, Malach. We won't know for certain if your plan is working until several years into my life on Earth. Children often hang on to memories of this dimension when they're very young, but they start to forget as they get older. The age when the memories seem to appear, when kids start to talk, is usually between two and four, but the memories fade between ages five and eight. I don't want to forget this spiritual dimension while I'm on Earth. Let me repeat: Forgetting is not an option. This has to work.

Pneuma: Isn't falling under the veil a requirement?

Nephesh: Not at all. Some people have avoided falling under the illusion. I can do it too. It'll be easier and faster for me to accomplish what I want to do without it, and I want a direct link to all of you for guidance. I do know, even for those who fall under the illusion, there's always a way to communicate with those of us up here.

Pneuma: Well, good luck. I hope it works.

Nephesh: Pneuma, when you're on Earth and you get a knowing feeling deep in your gut, when you experience a lightbulb moment or have a sudden flash of inspiration—that's the spirit in the incarnated individual remembering relevant knowledge from here. As Wordsworth said, "Our birth is but a sleep and a forgetting."

Malach: You and your quotes. They make me nuts.

Nephesh: One of my many talents. The real reason I want to go to Earth is that I want to eat pizza, drink beer, and snowboard. I can create a huge list of benefits to living in the physical world.

Malach: No doubt. That'll be worth the trip alone. No worries, though, Neph—we'll put my calculated plan into action when the time is right. You won't forget.

Pneuma: Pizza? Beer?

Nephesh: Once you've spent as much time guiding and monitoring people on Earth as we have, you'll start to pick up their style of language and you'll see that some of their experiences look fun. Observing Earth has made me want pizza, and many other things, once I get there. You'll also learn that when we appear to people or communicate with them on Earth, we do so in a way that is within the context of their lives and belief systems—something they can easily relate to.

Pneuma: Makes sense. So, Malach, tell us your plan for ensuring that Nephesh won't forget.

Malach: Okay, everyone, gather around—you need to hear this.

Nephesh: There better be a plan B. Just in case.

Malach: No need.

Nephesh: No really, there's a plan B, right, Malach? Right?

CHAPTER 9
THE ASTRAL PLANE

AS HE WORKS at his monitor, scanning the orbiting planets, stars, and other celestial bodies, Nephesh turns his attention to Earth, focusing in on California. He quickly locates what he's looking for: a man and woman spending a romantic evening out under the stars, sailing on the San Diego Bay. The night is serene, and the mild westerly breeze fills the sails, pulling the boat gently over the sea. The moonlight sparkles like diamonds on the water, and the air smells as sweet as harvesttime in Tuscany, so fragrant it's intoxicating. The captain keeps the boat on course while the man and woman dine on fresh sea bass and caviar. The crescent moon slips beneath the horizon while the woman exhales a breath she didn't know she was holding. They had hoped for a glorious evening such as this—a magical moment in which to create their first child.

Nephesh zooms in closer to see the woman and man toasting each other with their drinks. He listens to her thoughts: *No more alcohol after this. If we conceive tonight, the baby will arrive in the summer. The timing is right. I'm not afraid anymore. I'm ready.*

The couple gaze into each other's eyes, a silent understanding and hopefulness passing between them. The moonlight, the cocktails, the food, the rocking motion of the boat all churn into a lustful sea of desire. They head belowdecks, where the man and woman make love like it was the first time, then they fall into the deep slumber only heated passion provides.

The world of the conscious slips away, and the woman enters an alternate dimension where dreams are reality. Her heart rate increases and her arms and legs twitch and jerk. Her breathing becomes more irregular and shallow, while her eyes, beneath closed lids, move rapidly. As she dreams, the face of a towheaded boy about three years old appears, first within a foggy mist, then transitioning into crystal clarity. He's playing with a hobbyhorse, riding it in a circle in a grassy yard. He's dressed in a child's American Indian costume, including furry knee-high moccasins.

The woman in the dream asks, "Who are you?" A sensation of something powerful, loving, and familiar washes over her.

She clearly sees his face and hears him speak to her: "It's me," he says. "I'm to be your son and you my mother. I'm coming."

Message sent.

CHAPTER 10
NOVEMBER 9, 1987

SOON AFTER LIZZIE and David offered their guesthouse to Sophie, she moved in. The time she spent decorating and personalizing it proved a good diversion for her.

She glanced at the clock on her night table as she made her bed. Predictably, Lizzie was late, as she usually ran about fifteen minutes behind. But just then, Sophie heard the front door open, and Lizzie proceeded to speed through the bedroom door, her fingers frantically clutching a wrinkled paper bag. She immediately plopped down on the bed, upsetting the neat pile of toss pillows Sophie had just finished arranging. Sophie could feel the floor vibrating slightly under her from the beat of Lizzie's tapping foot.

"Okay," Lizzie said, "I got it. I'm too nervous to open the package and read the directions. I have all the signs, though. My boobs are swollen and getting bigger every day. I missed my period, and I'm sick every morning. But if this is real, it happened fast. Like right away!" She tossed the bag to Sophie. "Hurry up and open it, and tell me how to do the test."

Sophie ran a hand through her hair before reaching into the bag. After twenty-four years of friendship, she knew how anxious Lizzie could get when things were important to her. In fact, there wasn't much they didn't know about each other.

"You don't even have to take the test," Sophie told her. "I already know you're pregnant. And you're right—that sure did happen fast. Like it was meant to be." Sophie opened the box and started unfolding the white sheet of directions. "I've been having dreams about him, actually. He's coming. He's on his way."

Lizzie scooted to the edge of the bed, grabbed one of the pillows, and hugged it to her chest. "So it's a boy? You feel sure?"

"As sure as anyone can be. And I'm telling you, he's already on his way."

Lizzie jumped up and started pacing the floor. "You know, I had a dream a while ago too, and it seemed so vivid, so real. The most adorable towheaded boy was telling me I'd be his mother. He was the cutest thing ever."

Sophie stopped in her tracks. "And you didn't think to mention this before? Really? Oh my God! I've had pre-birth dreams and now you had a pre-birth dream. He's letting us know he's coming."

Lizzie rolled her eyes. "A 'pre-birth dream'? Where do you get these things, Sophie?"

Sophie looked directly at Lizzie, crossed her arms, and let out an exaggerated sigh, deciding to ignore what she thought was a stupid question. Then she busied herself with the sheet in front of her. "Let me read these directions."

As Sophie summarized the important points for Lizzie—hold the stick, tip pointing downward, directly in the urine stream for a full five seconds, check that the tip turns pink to indicate that urine is being absorbed—Lizzie's pacing intensified, until she was almost jumping around the room.

"Honestly, Lizzie, if you don't calm down, I'm going to give you a tranquilizer. Go, go, go. Get on with it. While you're in the bathroom, I'll start looking through this baby book of names for the perfect one."

"Don't forget it has to start with a J," Lizzie called through the open bathroom door, "for David's grandfather, Jack. I like Joshua and Jake and Jonathan."

"Let me look up what they mean," Sophie called back. Running her index finger up and down several pages, she reported, "Okay, Jacob means 'held by the heel.' … Jonathan is a common masculine given name meaning 'gift of God' in Hebrew. That's it. Why look any further? It's absolutely perfect to describe him—a gift from God."

She giggled a little as Lizzie came back in the bedroom and laid the testing stick on the flat surface of Sophie's dresser to develop. "I suppose it isn't up to me. I guess David will want to have a say."

"Set the timer for three minutes, Soph. I'll do the test again when David gets home so he can enjoy the anticipation too. Don't mention I did it with you first, okay? I couldn't wait."

Then she and Sophie sat on the bed, just staring at the dresser and listening to each second ticking out loud on the timer.

A look of sheer panic was on Lizzie's face. "I'm scared and I don't know why."

"Don't be scared," Sophie said, though she herself couldn't stop chewing on her cuticles. "Nothing to be afraid of. Nothing at all. Of course, that's easy for me to say. I think I'd be afraid of the childbirth pain. You'll take drugs for the delivery, right?"

Lizzie plopped on her back, staring at the ceiling. "I don't know yet. You're jumping the gun here, anyway."

"No, I know that it's all going to be okay, because he's a soul we've both known before. I just have this overwhelming feeling for some reason. I get goose bumps on my arms whenever I think about it. My mom used to say that goose bumps mean my spirit guides are giving me a message through my intuition, because intuition is the voice of the nonphysical world."

"Really, Soph, you're so out there sometimes."

"I wish we were sisters so I could be his aunt," Sophie said as she traced her finger along the bedspread pattern. "I want to play an important role in his life."

"Godmother!" Lizzie offered. "You can be his godmother."

"Great! That's what my role will be. I'll be in charge of his spiritual awareness and development."

The timer finally went off, and when it did, Sophie and Lizzie both held their breath, trying to make time stand still.

Slowly, Lizzie rose from the bed, picked the stick up from the dresser, then started jumping up and down. "You're right, you're right. He's coming! Baby Jonathan is on his way!"

As Sophie's smile expanded to match Lizzie's, she looked deeply at her friend, already reading a noticeable shift in her. She was carrying a precious life inside of her now, a life that was going to change everything. But just how much?

A sensation of warmth flooded Sophie's chest, filling it with a peace she had never experienced before. *Yes, he's coming. What the heck took so long?*

CHAPTER 11
THE ASTRAL PLANE

Ruach: By the way, Neph, I reviewed the rough draft of your book. Are you interested in some constructive criticism?"

Nephesh: Sure, go ahead.

Ruach: The content is interesting, but it's textbook-like. Do you realize what age you'll be living in by the time you're able to publish this message on Earth? People will have short attention spans, preferring to get their information in one hundred forty characters.

Nephesh: Good point. I'm not sure I can fix it quickly enough, though, since I'll be born shortly.

Malach: Never mind your book for a minute. The important thing is getting your memory plan in place. I've been working on how to keep Nephesh from forgetting this dimension when he incarnates for quite a while, and I think I've got it. It's called Project Detaching the Veil.

Pneuma: We're all ears.

Malach: I'll use a special process with the monitoring system. We all know that we're all bodies of light, and the higher the dimension we're in, the faster and brighter the vibration of the light. As we transition to the physical dimension, the vibration becomes slower and denser. When we're only our light-body, we have complete awareness. When we're incarnated, we lose that awareness. It's all about the rate of vibration.

Pneuma: Okay, so far, so good. But can you just boil down in simple terms how you're planning to allow Nephesh to retain his awareness?

Malach: I'm going to program Neph's light-body to continue to vibrate at an accelerated rate when he enters the physical body at birth. If I sustain the vibration for a specific duration at just the right moment, Neph will *stay* open and there will be no forgetting.

Nephesh: I don't like your use of the word "if." I'm not so sure this is going to work.

Malach: Don't throw water on my fire. It'll work.

Nephesh: Can we pre-test this somehow?

Malach: It'll be different once you're in the third dimension. We can't pre-test it, but it's a surefire plan. You'll remember, and all of us guides will continue to have direct telepathic communication with you.

Nephesh: "The best laid plans of mice and men often go astray."

Malach: Seeing as I'm neither mouse nor man, your quote doesn't apply here. Where's your faith in me, Neph? After you made such a big deal about it, I did develop a plan B, but I'm not going to need it. I've mastered how to control vibrational rates.

Nephesh: Those better not be famous last words.

CHAPTER 12

THE ASTRAL PLANE

Nephesh: Ruach, why don't you see if you can come up with an inspiration for Sophie Beaumont to seek professional assistance from Matthew Hobbs in his earthly incarnation. I think it would do her some good. She's struggling and he'll be able help her. Present the opportunity and see if she'll take it. Besides, you need some practice providing inspirations before I go to Earth.

Ruach: Matthew Hobbs—he's the spirit guide known as Tejomaya, correct?

Nephesh: Yes. He's an empathetic, wise soul. Currently, he has incarnated and is living close to Sophie in California. He's the perfect soul to help guide her right now. So make that connection happen, please.

Ruach: Piece of cake, my friend. Piece of cake.

Nephesh: Never mind the cake. Pretty soon, I'll be eating pizza.

CHAPTER 13

DECEMBER 13, 1987

ALTHOUGH SOPHIE HADN'T found much personal happiness in the preceding month, she was thrilled her house sold quickly. Living in the guesthouse suited her perfectly. It was quaint, yet roomy enough, and she didn't have to worry about landscaping, maintenance, or rent. That was a blessing in so many ways.

The living room was large enough to hold her couch, an ottoman, two armchairs, a coffee table, and an end table, with just enough room left to squeeze in her easel and vertical loom. The bedroom barely fit her king-sized bed, a bedside table, and a dresser. A larger kitchen would have been nice, but it would do, although it was a bit cluttered with all her cooking paraphernalia and twenty-some flowerpots of herbs. The bathroom met her needs with both a full tub, for bubble baths, and a shower stall. With some fresh paint, new drapes, and some throw pillows and rugs to add some color, the guesthouse was ideal. Not only was it free, but it was close to her friends and support system.

On this particular Sunday morning, all Sophie wanted to do was drink a pot of coffee and read the paper. She shuffled across the kitchen's tile floor in her bare feet, looking disheveled in her orange pajamas with purple octopuses and with her unkempt hair hanging in her face. She wasn't much into appearances lately. She tripped over the too-long cuff of her pajama bottoms, barely catching herself. "What the hell," she mumbled as she reached for the bag of coffee, followed by "Double hell" when the scoop in the bag came up empty. *Is a lousy cup of coffee too much to ask? I can tell what kind of day this is going to be.*

After pulling on a pair of sweats, Sophie sprinted to the corner store to grab a fresh bag of ground coffee beans. She felt too lazy to dig out the grinder and pulverize them herself. The long line at the store was filled with people impatiently waiting to buy their weekend apple fritters and sprinkled doughnuts. To pass the time, she glanced at the bulletin board to see the home sales postings. *These houses are so out of my price range. Good thing Lizzie and David offered me the guesthouse.* Something caught her eye—a bright yellow business card with black printing:

DO YOU FEEL LOST AND CONFUSED ABOUT

WHAT DIRECTION TO TAKE?

Spiritual advisor will help you learn to understand how the universe works in your life and how to live a life of harmony.

Trauma and grief counseling, spiritual counseling, and past-life regression.

LIVE YOUR BEST LIFE

CALL:

MATTHEW HOBBS

As if it were fate, Sophie pulled the card from the bulletin board and put it in her pocket. Despite her many assurances to Lizzie and David, she hadn't yet followed through on going to grief therapy, but this piqued her curiosity.

Back at the guesthouse, Sophie brewed a pot of coffee. It smelled like a heavenly combination of Jamaican Blue Mountain and Kona. She found her favorite mug, dirty, in the dishwasher. She cleaned it, poured in her cream and sugar, and topped it off with fresh, hot coffee. In a few moments, she'd feel human again.

The business card crunched in her pocket as she sat on the living room couch. Pulling out the card, she read it again, noting the local phone number given at the bottom. *I think I'll call.* She picked up the phone and dialed. No answer. She remembered it was Sunday and left a message on the machine, looking forward to the return call.

I have a good feeling about this, she thought.

CHAPTER 14
THE ASTRAL PLANE

Nephesh: How did you do with your assignment, Ruach?

Ruach: Success. Message received. Sophie took the business card and called. Action taken.

Nephesh: Good work. Maybe I can trust you to do a good job guiding me.

Ruach: Of course. Would I ever let you down?

CHAPTER 15
DECEMBER 21, 1987

O N HER WAY out the door to her first appointment, Sophie picked up the yellow business card from the kitchen counter and turned it over to read the back side again:

HELPING PEOPLE OPEN DOORS ON THEIR PERSONAL

JOURNEY OF TRANSFORMATION

It was odd how much better she felt about going to a spiritual counselor than a therapist. She had nothing against therapy—she knew its value—but after years of watching Neil go through session after session, she wanted to try something different. She wasn't exactly sure what a spiritual advisor did—was he perhaps a medium? could he perhaps channel messages from beyond?—she only knew this alternate route appealed to her.

A little while later, turning onto Matthew Hobbs's street and scanning the addresses, Sophie noticed that his Cape Cod–style house looked out of place with the other beachy residences in the neighborhood. She liked the idea of his home-based office, though—it somehow seemed less intimidating to her. She started scouting for a parking space amid all the cars on the curb, when suddenly a woman vacated the spot directly in front of his house. *Well, that was lucky!*

After Sophie walked up the pathway to the front entrance and rang the bell, a young woman with coal-black hair swept into a ponytail answered the door. "You're here to see Dr. Hobbs?"

"Doctor? No, uh, I'm—" A bit flustered, Sophie glanced at the slip of paper in her hand to double-check the address.

The woman laughed. "Don't panic. He's a Ph.D., not a physician—you're not going to get a shot or anything. My name's Nancy. Come in and have a seat."

She waved in the direction of the waiting room. A pair of expensive-looking red shoes with four-inch heels accentuated her well-developed calves.

Sophie stared at her shoes. "Holy cow, you're impressive. I never could walk in those."

"It takes practice, like anything." The girl's voice sounded like Minnie Mouse. She giggled and batted her false-eyelashed eyes. "Have a seat in here. Dr. Hobbs is on a phone call and will be with you in a moment. Can I get you a cup of tea?"

"How about a gin and tonic?" Sophie said.

Minnie Mouse giggled again.

She thinks I'm kidding.

"Darjeeling or Lapsang Souchong—your choice."

"I'll pass, but thanks."

The waiting room was neither masculine nor feminine. The walls were covered with burgundy-and-cream-striped wallpaper. Along the north wall was a seating area with two wingback chairs, upholstered in a soft, biscuit-colored fabric. The design was geometric in a room layered with asymmetry. There was an enormous entryway table and a salon-style gallery wall covered with a display of mandalas in various sizes, shapes, and colors. In front of the couch, on the west side of the room, was a round ottoman neatly stacked with a variety of books and magazines.

She picked up a book—*A Life Without Limitations*—with a photo of Dr. Hobbs on the back. *Intriguing title,* she thought.

Within five minutes, Dr. Hobbs opened the door of his office and approached Sophie.

She quickly sized him up: a very attractive man in his late thirties, early forties, with a very kind face. He smiled with his eyes—eyes of the most unique aqua color, like the Caribbean Sea. A determined, steady gaze conveyed an air of authority, yet his demeanor was charismatic and soothing. His well-trimmed beard sharply outlined his square jaw. Sophie's eyes moved up the length of his body, solid and slim. His salt-and-pepper hair was slicked back like Al Pacino's in the movie *Godfather II*. Small, thin lines formed under his eyes when he smiled. A comforting, pleasant scent of Prince Albert pipe tobacco wafted from him, making her think of her grandfather. There was something extraordinarily familiar about him. She liked him instantly.

He extended his hand. "I'm Matthew Hobbs." His voice was smoky and confident.

"Hi, I'm Sophie. Thanks for seeing me on relatively short notice." She shook his hand. She was a bit nervous and tended to ramble when she was anxious. "It's actually an interesting coincidence how I found you—," she started to say.

"There are no coincidences." He smiled so broadly, the lines around his mouth looked like cracks.

She was a bit taken aback at his response and just stood there smiling in return.

"Please join me in my office. Were you offered refreshment?"

"I was. Thank you."

"Sit over there in either chair by the window, please." He nodded toward two chairs sitting in front of a fireplace.

She walked briefly around the room before selecting her chair. "How cozy—with a fireplace and all, I mean."

"I'm glad you think so."

Dr. Hobbs picked up a sheath of papers from the table between the two chairs and shuffled through them looking for something in particular. "I do know why you're here and have read all the information you filled out on the forms you mailed me. I reviewed them in great detail. Now tell me in your own words."

He sat down in the chair opposite her, set the papers back down on the table, and leaned back as if he were preparing for a long explanation.

"Well, in a nutshell, my husband committed suicide. He hung himself in our garage, I found him, and I've pretty much been a basket case since."

When he didn't say anything, she continued, determined to get through the explanation without a single tear: "I float between moments of despair and guilt—mostly guilt, I think. No, maybe mostly anger. I quit my job and I can barely function. I have a hard time getting out of bed and taking care of myself. I'm at a loss as to how to fix this." She starting weeping. "Damn, I keep promising myself there'll be no more tears. How can I have even one more tear to shed? I know the grieving process can take years, but I don't want to continue on like this. It's so ... so destructive."

Dr. Hobbs uncrossed his legs and sat a bit more upright in his chair. Catching a whiff of his signature scent, Sophie could imagine him smoking his pipe—or maybe it was his aftershave. His light gray sweater, dark gray slacks, and gray socks and shoes—it was all a little too monotone for her taste. There was a long, uncomfortable silence.

He tilted his head to the side and spoke. "Have you ever been on a road trip, Sophie? You know, when you're traveling in your car and you're on your way somewhere to do something or see someone? Where you've had some kind of destination in mind?"

"Yes, I have. My best friend and I took a road trip across the country from Wisconsin to California years ago."

What an odd way to begin, she thought.

"Tell me about it."

She watched him, looking for an observable tic. All of Neil's therapists seemed to have some kind of nervous tic.

"We'd just graduated college and decided to move to California together, me to complete my occupational therapy training and Lizzie for her pediatrics internship and residency."

"So your destination was to drive to California, set up residence, and complete your professional trainings. Correct?"

"Yes."

"Tell me more."

"About the trip? There wasn't anything really spiritual about it."

"Yes."

"Mostly, we camped along the way. At night, we'd set up a tent and cook simple meals over cans of Sterno. Sometimes we'd stay in a cheap motel so we could have a shower and a nice mattress. We drove a Dodge Dart—my first car. We did stop and sightsee along the way … I'm not sure what else to tell you."

"Did everything go smoothly on your journey across country?"

Sophie didn't even have to think before answering. "Good heavens, no. We had some bad weather, our tent wouldn't go up one night, we got lost … one morning we got chased by a wild animal, and we had a broken fan belt."

"And yet, here you are."

She furrowed her eyebrows. "What does this have to do with anything? Yes, here I am. Should this make sense to me?"

"Look at it like this. Say you were on a road trip and had driven three hundred miles, and all of a sudden, a tire blows and you steer straight into a ditch, but you're not hurt. What would you do? Would you sit there forever and not continue on? Would you feel singled out and upset, thinking that of all the people in the world, you were the one to blow a tire that day, you were the one to hit a kink in your journey? Would you do nothing? Or would you find a way to patch the tire or replace it and continue on your way? You can stay there in the ditch as long as you need to. That's allowed. It's your prerogative. But at this point, it doesn't serve any purpose. You can choose to get a new tire and continue the journey, to complete the things you intended to do in the first place, or you can sit in the ditch."

Dr. Hobbs jotted something on his pad of paper.

He continued. "So my question is: What did you choose to do when your fan belt broke? I see you're here today, so at some point, you made the decision to deal with what was stopping you from progressing on your journey. It was a choice you made. You decided, 'I need to fix this so I can continue on my trip.' "

"I guess I see the point you're making."

"It's so much easier to see clearly when you take the emotion out of a situation. Right now, of course, you're filled with negative feelings about the situation that happened in your life, and it clouds your vision. You're not able to see ahead of you. I'm looking at it differently, as I don't have any emotion attached to it."

He stood and took a picture down from the wall. "Take a look at this picture." He propped it in front of her. "You maybe have seen it before. Stare at it and tell me what you see."

Sophie leaned forward and stared hard at the picture. "I see a white vase on a black background."

"Now shift how you look at it. Change the focus of your eyes. Look at it for about fifteen seconds. Then tell me what you see."

Sophie did as he said. She leaned forward again and returned her gaze to the picture, narrowing her eyes. "Weird. Now I'm seeing black profiles, in silhouette, of two individuals facing each other, on a white background."

"Precisely. What made you see something different, do you think?"

"I looked at it differently."

"Yes, you did. When a situation is clouding your vision, and you're standing still in one place and unable to move forward, you need to reframe it. Look at the situation from a different perspective.

"You've been stuck in the mire and choking your mind with useless chatter. You've been struggling with all the what-ifs. 'What if I'd come home earlier? What if I'd taken him to one more doctor? What if I'd been more sympathetic?'

"None of that matters, Sophie. Your guilt is like the broken fan belt. It's temporarily stopped your journey. You can choose to make the car run again and proceed to your destination, or you can choose not to. It's up to you. You're at a crossroads, and you—only you—get to decide which path you'll choose. It's like the illusion of the vase and the profiles of the people. You look one way, and you see one thing; you look at it another way, and you see it differently. Change your focus."

"I see your point." Sophie felt tension drain from her body. *This is actually helping me.* She eyed a teapot and cups on a side table. "I've changed my mind. I would like a cup of tea, Dr. Hobbs."

"Of course." He stood and poured her a cup of tea and placed it on the table next to her chair.

"Thank you."

"You have a choice, Sophie. You always have a choice. Decide how you want to look at this situation. We can work together as co-creators helping you see it differently, if that's what you want. Bottom line is, you're overcome with pain and feeling awful. And the feeling of ongoing pain is a sign that you have disconnected from the source of all that is."

"Could you define what the 'source of all that is' means to you?" Sophie tilted her head and raised her brow.

"Yes. People use different language to describe the essence behind existence—God, the Source, Buddha, Creator, the Divine, the universe, Allah, Great Spirit, Elohim, the Supreme Being, and many others. It's a matter of semantics. I often find when trying to get on the same page with someone that talking in his or her language is key. Don't let the language used make you miss the messages.

"I'm speaking about an energy out there greater than us, energy each of us is part of—the thing we speak of with reverence and wonder. The universe is still a mystery no matter how we describe it. What name do you prefer? What do you call it? Let's go by what's most meaningful and powerful to you."

"I guess I like 'Source' as well—the Source."

"Okay, that's how we'll refer to it."

Dr. Hobbs rested his index finger against his cheek with his thumb pressed under his chin. "So what's your decision, Sophie, what do you choose?"

Light dribbled in from the corner window, cutting long, rectangular shadows on the striped walls.

Sophie spoke with an uncharacteristic confidence. "I choose to move on."

"Good. Then we can begin the inner work. We need to work on getting you back in sync with the Source again. You're experiencing the momentum of negative thoughts gone too far. The laws of the universe dictate this concept—as you think your thoughts, you're creating the world where you'll live, your reality. So we need to restore some balance to take you out of the negativity and create things to make you feel good and bring you to a new energy level. That, in turn, will create more positive feelings and dig you out of this ditch. You've probably beaten this issue to death by now, and no amount of talking about it has made you feel better, has it?"

"No, it makes me feel worse. Everyone's opinion on how I should act and what I should do only confuses me."

"I'll teach you a marvelous secret. When you're thinking and feeling negatively, all the bad energy perpetuates more of the same. What's needed is to break the cycle. So first, I don't want you talking about the bad stuff anymore to anyone. I'm not saying you shouldn't grieve. Grieving, feeling the pain of your situation, is very important. I'm referring to when you get stuck or unbalanced and not able to move forward.

"We need to intercept then. Step in and change the vibration of your energy with meditation. I'd like you to meditate to get to a place where you're not thinking at all—where you've eliminated your mind chatter. This will provide you with the mental rest you need and provide clarity. Meditation happens to be one of the tools I use to communicate with my spirit guides, and so can you. Are you familiar with spirit guides?"

"I am. My mom, when she was alive, communicated with her guides. She talked about it sometimes." Sophie took a quick breath in and gave Dr. Hobbs a hesitant smile. "I'm ready. Let's do this."

"Great. But remember, Sophie, the inner work you'll be doing is a journey. Some people expect or hope for instantaneous and dramatic results. I'm not saying you can't make rapid progress, but integration of what you learn can take some time. Please recognize that."

He handed her a cassette tape. "I want you to listen to this tape, and I'd like you to meditate with it daily. You'll work toward sitting in stillness until you are able to empty your mind. If a thought enters, let it pass through. Our goal is to change your energy vibration. Are you game?"

"I am."

"For now, no negative thinking is the way to go. We can move on to positive energy later."

Sophie couldn't resist—she felt like she just had to ask at this point, somewhat playfully, "So … no séance today, no talking to the dead or something like that?"

He smiled his comforting smile and answered simply, "No. No channeling today. Let's just start with the plan I outlined."

The two talked for several more minutes. When Sophie rose from her chair to leave, she felt the bitter remnants of her guilt drain from her body, replaced by a sense of peaceful buoyancy. Where her chest had been blocked, it was now open with hope for the future, her future, one in which she no longer had to feel trapped.

As she headed down the walk to her car, she felt giddy, almost tipsy with relief and release. She was breathing easier than she had in months; she could feel herself beginning to let go. She couldn't believe how different she felt leaving Dr. Hobbs's office than she had going in. Opening her car door, she felt a tear roll down her cheek. It was the last tear she would shed over "it"—the last time she would think of it as something Neil had done to her.

CHAPTER 16
NEIL

I WANTED TO FLOAT into the beckoning light. It looked so welcoming and warm. But I couldn't. I just couldn't. Hanging around, most of the time in a dingy garage or at my father's house, is no way to spend eternity. But I'm confused. Where am I? Is this hell? If so, it's missing the heat, the fire, and the goat-like little man with his pitchfork. It doesn't look like hell, but it feels like it. It's heavy—like wearing a winter coat of guilt—and it's weighing me down.

The effect of my suicide on Sophie, my dad, and the rest of my family is really bothering me. Selfish and narcissistic—that was my nature throughout my life. Everything was always about me. All I thought about at the moment was releasing my own pain, not how I'd inflict it on others. Everyone remains so angry with me, and I feel so guilty. Worse, I feel ashamed, inadequate, and worthless.

I had this feeling that always plagued me throughout my life: that I didn't belong on this planet in the first place. Always present was a sense of discomfort in my own skin, and I never felt I was like other people. Shrinks prescribed antidepressants for me. They said depression was why I self-medicated, but the prescription meds didn't give me the same feeling booze gave me. I liked the numbing sensation that allowed me to avoid the fearful, painful moments of life. The problem was that everything else was anesthetized as well, like joy and happiness. What's the point of being on Earth to experience life when you don't let yourself feel any of the emotions?

Maybe the bright light is heaven. I know it's calling me to step into it. I figure I'll be judged harshly, and I'm scared of my punishment. Unfortunately, I've always been like that. As kids, when my siblings and I were caught lying or taking something not belonging to us, we'd be sent to Dad's room for the strap. Hitting a child isn't allowed now, but that's the way the four of us were raised. Dad instilled fear in all of us.

Sometimes I shadow Sophie like I'm attached to her by an invisible cord. If she knew I was following her, she'd be so pissed. Other times I hang out with my dad. I need to let go, but I can't yet. This heaviness is overwhelming, and I feel myself holding back from moving on so I can work through the sadness, the guilt, the remorse. I can't absolve myself because I'm too weak. Forgiveness takes strength. I wish I could get the forgiveness of those I hurt so badly. But when I look in on Sophie, she seems so depressed, and I know she's angry with me. I deserve it. I'd be ticked off too.

I have no clue how to move forward. So I hang around, not able to talk to anyone, touch anyone. I guess I'm in hell. It's a different kind of experience than I expected. I think hell is a place you create.

That's it: I created my own hell.

CHAPTER 17
THE ASTRAL PLANE

Pneuma: Why hasn't Neil Beaumont gone to the light yet? Why does he mostly hang around in an old, dilapidated garage? It doesn't make any sense.

Malach: Sometimes it can take a long time before people who commit suicide can free themselves. It all depends on the person. Some go into a self-created holding area. Their consciousness is dense, and they feel heavy with their guilt.

Pneuma: Can they get out of it if they want to?

Malach: Of course. They're always in control. Those of us here do encourage them to come home, but they make the choice of when to do so.

Pneuma: Kind of their own self-imposed hell?

Malach: In a way.

Pneuma: Did any of the guides try to help Neil before he killed himself?

Malach: Quite often. Many of the accidents he was in were incidents we set in motion to help awaken him prior to his suicide. Sometimes an accident can prompt the individual to recognize he's on a spiraling, destructive path, and then he can turn things around. We also initiated situations to provide him with hope. We can try to influence, but we can't make decisions. Neil made his own choice.

Pneuma: I see. Sometimes they don't get the messages.

Malach: People ignore messages quite often. Neil could use the assistance of Sophie and his family, his father especially. Sometimes people in Neil's situation can move on if they get the support from their loved ones on Earth. Sophie isn't feeling good about him now. If she can't forgive him, the weight of his guilt can make it more difficult for him to let go. He also needs to forgive himself and accept the consequences of what he did.

Pneuma: From what I'm observing, Sophie won't be sending loving thoughts to him anytime soon.

CHAPTER 18

JANUARY 11, 1988

H IS SCENT WAS a comfort to her. Simply a whiff of his cologne was like sixty minutes of deep meditation—relaxing and peaceful. Dr. Hobbs looked particularly handsome today. Sophie hadn't previously noticed his upturned lips and angelic smile. There was something so familiar about him, like she had known him for eons. She relaxed in the overstuffed chair in his office as he stood to the side of her, placing a firm, comforting hand on her shoulder.

"I haven't seen you for a few weeks. I hope your holidays were enjoyable. How have you been, Sophie? Tell me what's been going on."

He took the chair across from her, as before, and crossed his legs.

"Mine were good. I hope yours were too. Happy new year, by the way. I'm doing better, but I'm still having bad dreams. I guess I still don't get *why* this happened with Neil."

"You can ask that question forever, but you'll never get an answer. Most persistent negative emotions and feelings we have are because we resist the experience. The key is to not fight any of your experiences—go with the flow. Everything in life changes, so you need to embrace what comes. If you feel it's negative, go ahead and allow the feelings to flow through you. Then find the gift it holds for you. Don't bother struggling against the universe, Sophie. There's no point. Have you ever ridden in a hot air balloon? It starts out with sandbags tied to the sides of the basket.

Once it's inflated, the operator starts releasing the bags to allow it to ascend. You'll never soar without letting go."

Sophie pursed her lips and shook her head. "Why do I have to go through this? I'll never be the same."

"Is that so awful? To never be the same? Is your goal to remain stagnant?"

Her voice shook slightly. "No, but in some ways, I'm not seeing how I'm growing."

"And yet you are." He turned the corners of his lips into his mesmerizing smile. "These kinds of trials in life bring rapid, life-altering change. That's the power of loss. We all deal with loss—every one of us. It's a powerful catalyst for change."

"I want to go back to the way things were before it happened."

"Do you? Think about that. There's no point in trying to recoup what was because it no longer is."

"It scooped out a chunk of me and left a gaping hole." She drew in two deep breaths and blew the air out slowly.

"I agree. Loss makes room for something new. Create and fill the gaping hole with something fresh, something different. Often, people mistakenly think the ultimate goal of being on Earth is achieving happiness. But really, we're here for experiences—not just happy ones, but all kinds of experiences. Don't deny them. They come at us each moment. The trick is to feel fulfilled *now* regardless of what you have or where you are. Let the moments flow through you. The pain comes when you resist. Let the experiences work for you and expand your consciousness."

Sophie drummed her fingers on the armrest. "And how do I do that?"

"I like a phrase you may have heard before: 'Melt into now.' The key to becoming present in the moment is an awareness of what's around you. Try it now. Try being aware of what you're sensing at this moment. Smell the scents in the room. Taste the air. Hear the silence. Become aware of the space around you. Feel your breath. Feel your pulse. Feel life flowing through your body. Relish what you're experiencing without judging it. That's melting into the now."

They sat quietly for a moment while Sophie looked around the room and took it all in through her senses.

Her playful side was beginning to reemerge. "Okay, so I smelled the air, and it smells like sugar cookies, but it tastes like it needs more sugar," she said with a smile. "No, seriously, that's a powerful tool."

Dr. Hobbs laughed. "Help yourself to the cookies on the table over there. I assure you there's enough sugar. Now, when you find yourself thinking about the past or the future, keep practicing melting into the now."

"I'll use that. Thanks. I do want to move forward."

Sophie pushed herself out of her chair and went to the table set with glasses and a pitcher of water. She poured a glass. "Do you want one, Dr. Hobbs?" She didn't wait for his response, just handed him the glass and then poured herself another, grabbing a sugar cookie from a tray on the end table on her way back to her chair.

"This is what I recommend. Reach inside yourself, find forgiveness, and send it to Neil. It's the most powerful tool there is. Forgiveness is an act of grace."

"Easier said than done. How do I know when I've gone through the storm?"

"You'll feel peace. Like a tornado tearing through a town destroying things. When it's done, it's quiet."

"Sounds too simple to me. Forgive Neil and I'll find peace."

"I'm saying the actual act of forgiveness is simple, and it's a step toward healing. However, the process of getting to that point can be difficult to master. The spirits of those who have committed suicide are given multiple opportunities to release what holds them back so they can move forward into the spirit life again. It's their choice. Sometimes, however, they're unable to see and understand that what they have to do is let go and move forward, like I'm asking you to do now. I think you're ready to move beyond your guilt, to forgive Neil, and to proceed to true healing. You just need to do it instead of making it as hard as driving up a hill in fourth gear."

There was that disarming smile again. It seemed so familiar to Sophie. She couldn't place why or how.

"I'll think about that. I agree. That gives me something to work on. Although I wish you could wave a magic wand and just fix me."

"But, dear Sophie, that would defeat the purpose of your existence on Earth. We learn through physical experience. And you don't need to be fixed." His expression was gentle and comforting. "If you read the word 'run' on a page, it's far different from actually feeling the sensation of running, isn't it? That's the way things are. I'll talk you through it, guide you through the experience. You'll find a lot of books telling you how to do things, but if you don't put what you read into practice, it's just a random collection of words. No matter how many people might be around to guide you, there are times in life where the only way you'll learn is through actual experience. So give it a go. I'll be right here beside you."

"What you just said—it's all so familiar to me. Like I heard it a long time ago. Have we ever met before? It seems like maybe we have."

In response, Dr. Hobbs just smiled a knowing smile, looked up as though he were peering over invisible glasses, then glanced down at his watch. As he slowly stood to escort her to the door, he placed his hand gently on her shoulder and spoke with genuine sincerity. "Work on forgiveness, Sophie. In the simple gesture of forgiving, you'll find peace."

CHAPTER 19
JUNE 6, 1988

LIZZIE, SWEATY AND hot, heaved and gasped as she pushed her bike up the incline instead of riding it. The hill wasn't very steep, but thirty-one weeks into her pregnancy, it felt like Mt. Everest. More fatigued than normal, she couldn't catch a deep breath. The only book she'd been studying recently was *What to Expect When You're Expecting,* and she'd read that morning that baby Jonathan probably weighed close to three pounds and was about sixteen inches long by now. At that stage of his development, he could recognize her voice, so she talked to him all the time.

She glanced behind her, watching Sophie walk her bike too, pushing it up the hill. She also looked hot and tired. The weather report had said the temperature was going to hit ninety-two degrees this afternoon, and Lizzie was feeling every bit of it, beads of sweat dribbling into her eyes, causing her mascara to run and making her eyes sting. *I need a break,* she thought.

Lizzie turned to Sophie and waved toward the nearest cross street. "Let's get some ice cream. I think I need more calcium."

"Ha-ha. I love that excuse."

Lizzie leaned her bike against a tree and slumped down to the grass-covered ground. Her sweaty blonde hair clung to her neck, temples, and brow. *I'm too old for this.*

"Park your bike, Soph. I need a rest. I'm beyond tired. You may have to get the car and pick me up." She stretched out on her back with her hand on her forehead while she rubbed her protruding belly with her other hand.

"Really? Of course I will. You poor, exhausted thing. I'll go and get the ice cream first. Be right back. You want your usual? One scoop of chocolate chip and one scoop of mint chip, in a dish, no cone. Right?"

"That sounds great. Or just get a pint of each and we'll take it home with us."

Lizzie felt like she'd barely had time to recover before Sophie returned on her bike, two pints of ice cream packed in a bag of dry ice in her basket. "Got it," she said, grinning. "You ready to ride home, or do you need me to get the car?"

"No, the rest helped. My feet are really swollen, but I can make it back."

"Well, if you're sure … head back to my place—I mean, your guesthouse. I want to show you one of the cakes I made."

"Okay, and feel free to call it your place, Soph. That's how we think of it, and we love having you there."

Once Lizzie made it home, she gratefully pedaled up her driveway to the back of the house and leaned her bike against the garage. "Just leave your bike here with mine, Sophie, they'll be fine. Let's get out of this heat before I collapse."

The minute Sophie unlocked the door, Lizzie waddled to the living room couch and heavily plopped down.

"You stay there and rest, Lizzie. I'll dish us up some of the delicious stuff."

"Have any cold water?"

"I do—a dozen bottles on the top shelf of the fridge." Sophie tossed a bottle to Lizzie. "Don't get dehydrated."

Lizzie glanced around the room. "You're getting tidier. The place looks great. We're like the odd couple, aren't we? You're messy, and I'm the tidy, organized one."

"I do need to be neater. Especially in the kitchen. I love to bake, but I sure hate to clean up."

Lizzie could see directly into the kitchen, and she watched as Sophie got out two bowls, unpacked the cartons from the bag, and set them on the counter while she searched for a scoop. She didn't know why she felt so exhausted. Maybe it was just the heat.

"The ice cream partially melted in spite of the dry ice," Sophie said.

"Doesn't matter. Hand it over," Lizzie demanded, immediately digging into the dish Sophie handed her. *God, this hits the spot.* "Beware, I might eat both cartons."

Sophie settled in next to Lizzie. "Okay, so remember how I've been telling you for months that Dr. Hobbs seems oddly familiar to me? It's uncanny how much I feel as though I know him from somewhere. Well, I was going through some old boxes the other day and came across a story I wrote about you and me when we were kids, in the days when I was driving the old stick-shift Volkswagen. Remember? For English class. It's kind of weird because Dr. Hobbs says some of the exact same things I wrote in that story."

"Like what?"

In response, Sophie launched into an extensive memory. "You remember that day we met that stranger who helped us? When I hadn't yet mastered how to drive the stick up steep hills? Gosh, that car made for some hysterical stories over the years."

Lizzie remembered the day perfectly, back in Wisconsin, when she was still Lizzie Rosenbaum and Sophie was Sophie Russell. They were both sixteen years old, and Sophie had recently passed her driver's test on the first try in her parents' car. After she got a used VW Bug, her brother, Dean, spent hours teaching her to work the clutch and shift gears in the Kmart parking lot, but getting up hills was still a difficult task.

About two weeks before Christmas, the girls had gone shopping in the town of Wauwatosa. Driving there on the flat surface streets had been a breeze. But after a full day of shopping, so much snow had accumulated that the girls saw signs for a detour as they loaded the backseat with all their bags and boxes.

Lizzie noticed Sophie's lips tremble slightly as she scanned the road they'd have to take to get out of town. *Uh-oh.* There was a king-sized hill they'd have to crest if they wanted to get home anytime soon.

With no other choice before them, Sophie let the engine warm up, idling loudly, as she gathered her courage. The first part of the incline was fine, and she easily made it to the four-way stop. But the second part of the hill was really steep until it plateaued off into a residential area.

Lizzie remembered hearing Dean tell Sophie over and over that it takes practice to master the hills—the important thing was to stay calm, to not panic, until she'd gained confidence. He told her to start in first gear with her left foot on the clutch and her right foot on the brake. She had to find the sweet spot between letting the clutch out, releasing the brake, and quickly moving her right foot to the accelerator to give it more gas than usual. The problem was that the clutch in the Bug was old and needed replacement, so she had to let most of it out before finding the spot.

The girls sat at the stop sign in silence for several minutes. Despite the chilly air and the falling snow, Lizzie noticed drops of sweat on Sophie's forehead. She wished she could offer to take over, but she'd never even driven a stick shift. Still, she knew enough to realize that continuing on in such an old car, from a completely stopped position and at a slight incline, was going to require a bit of skill.

"Just try to relax, Sophie. Try to take it easy, like Dean said." Trying to look nonchalant as she nervously sucked on a candy cane, Lizzie encouraged her. "You can do it."

"I'm not so sure. I'm really not so sure we're going to make it up this hill."

Lizzie tried not to say anything more as Sophie ever so slowly lifted her left foot off the clutch, lifted her right foot off the brake, and pressed down on the accelerator pedal. The VW rolled backward. The car jolted as Sophie slammed on the brakes. Lizzie gripped her armrest as Sophie attempted the motion again—and the car rolled backward once again.

"As soon as I lift my foot off the brake, we start rolling. I'm freaking out here."

Lizzie turned and peered out the rear window. "At least there's no one behind you. Try again, maybe moving faster from the brake to the accelerator."

But every time Sophie lifted her foot off the brake, the car rolled a little bit farther down the hill. Lizzie didn't know what to say as Sophie burst into tears, her hands shaking on the steering wheel. Gaining control of herself, she tried once more. But eventually, the car rolled all the way down to flat ground again, basically where they'd started from.

"We'll have to leave the car here and walk to a pay phone for a ride. My mom is going to kill me."

"Whoa, Soph, let's not do that. Try again."

"I don't think I can. I give up. I wish someone would help me."

Just then, as though magic had answered Sophie's wish, a guy appeared out of nowhere and knocked on the driver's side window. He was young—maybe twenty-one or twenty-two—attractive, with kind, aqua-blue eyes. As Sophie rolled down her window, the scent of her grandfather's pipe tobacco wafted into her nostrils.

"Having some trouble, ladies?" he asked with the perfect combination of gentleness and concern.

Sophie, near tears, spoke between deep sighs. "I can't make it up this hill without rolling back down. I just can't do it. We're stuck."

"New to manual driving?" He didn't wait for a response. "I can help you."

Turning to Lizzie, he said, "Hop in back and I'll sit in the passenger seat. We'll get this car up the hill."

"Please," Sophie begged. "Can't *you* drive us up?" She bit her lip. "I don't want to try it again. I've failed enough."

"I could, but you'll learn by actually doing it yourself. I'll talk you through it—guide you through the experience. You can read a lot of instructions telling you how to do things, but if you don't put what you read into practice and actually apply the lessons, it's all just a collection of words. So give it a go. I'll be right here with you."

"I'm afraid to do it again."

His smile was compassionate and soothing. "What are you afraid of?" he asked.

"That I won't make it up. That I'll look like an idiot. That I might roll back into someone behind me. I might get in an accident. I might kill us. I might wreck the car. What if I never get up the hill?"

"That's a long list of fears. You have to push through the fear to get to the other side. And that holds for all hurdles in life—you have to learn to tackle the fear. What's your name?"

"Sophie."

"I'll help you, Sophie." His gaze was like that of a parent watching a young child at play. "Don't let your fears get to you. Focus on this moment and let go of the what-ifs."

Sophie got her feet back into position, this time knowing the stranger was there to help. She released the brake, gave the car gas ... and still rolled backward some more. She let out a deep grunt and laid her forehead against the steering wheel. "I give up. I can't do it."

"You're letting your emotions interfere," the young man said. "But the bigger problem is, you just tried to get up the hill in fourth gear. That's not going to work. There's certain principles to driving a car, and if you don't apply them, it'll be difficult. I think you'll find that starting in first gear will work."

Sophie felt her face flush red. "I was so flustered, I didn't even notice."

"It's okay—it's a good lesson. Don't make things harder for yourself than you need to. Sometimes when things seem futile, you need to literally shift gears. Now, try again. Focus on what you're doing, let go of the fear, and let's get up this hill."

Sophie held her breath, proceeding through all the motions one at a time, concentrating only on them, and this time, the car started climbing up the hill. *Finally!* At the stop sign, encouraged by the forward momentum of the ascent and by the calm demeanor of the man next to her, she just kept going up and up until they reached the top. Releasing a huge sigh of relief, she told the stranger, "I can't thank you enough."

As he got out of the car, he said, "My pleasure, girls. Have a merry Christmas."

Before Lizzie could reclaim her original seat, Sophie told her, "Grab that box of chocolates in the backseat and give them to the guy for helping us out."

"Great idea," Lizzie said. But once she had the box in her hand and turned around to present them, he was nowhere to be seen. "He's already gone," she told Sophie, who was fiddling with the dials on the radio.

"What? How could he disappear so quickly? That's so weird. But it was so nice of him to help us. Let's go home now—this time starting in first gear."

"Lesson learned, huh?"

"I'll never make that mistake again," Sophie said.

Now, on the couch, Lizzie was struck by how vivid that particular memory had remained for both of them. "But what's so weird about the story you wrote about that day and Dr. Hobbs?"

"The guy's face, his eyes, his smell. And Dr. Hobbs used some of the same words with me—the same messages."

"You don't think it could *possibly* be the same guy, do you, Soph? That's insane! That was—what?—twenty years ago and thousands of miles away! What are the chances that this guy just shows back up in your life, here, now?"

Sophie shrugged. "I don't know, Lizzie—slim to none—but I'm open to the possibility. Sometimes meeting people again is simply meant to be, and it can happen in strange ways. I'm telling you: His voice sounds the same, and from what I remember of the guy, he looks like him, too."

"You gotta ask him, then."

"I did. And he just avoided the question and smiled."

"If I didn't know better, I'd think you have a crush on this doctor."

"I could, if I were in a different place in my head. He's so empathetic and kind."

"Is he married?"

"His wife died a few years ago, and he hasn't remarried. No kids."

"That's sad. But even if you don't date him, you should start getting out more, start dating *someone.* The loneliness is bound to replace the grief one of these days."

Sophie let out a deep sigh. "I will when it's time. I'm working on me now."

"Don't work on you for too long." Lizzie gave Sophie a kiss on the cheek. "Just want you to feel happy in here," she said, pointing to her heart.

CHAPTER 20
THE ASTRAL PLANE

Nephesh: Malach, I'm ready be born. Are we all set? I've been going in and out of the baby's body for months now. I want to get the show on the road.

Malach: I'm ready. I'll be there for you, no worries. I won't let you forget your connection to us, and I'll be here with Ruach and Pneuma to guide you. We'll be in close contact. Now go accomplish everything you want to do.

Nephesh: I'm counting on you. Remember, I'm not only going there to help guide people, but I want to get my message to people. I'll finish the book when I'm there.

Malach: I know, I know. I'm here for you. Don't worry about it, okay? It will all work out.

CHAPTER 21
AUGUST 5, 1988

S OPHIE CROSSED THE yard from her cottage to the main house, stepping over piles of lumber and around scaffolding. The Cohens lived in a permanent state of remodeling, and this time, they were revamping the master bedroom and en suite bath. They relished change as much as she dreaded it.

She knocked on the back door while holding one of her mini cakes decorated with blue icing. In the relatively short period of time since she'd resigned from her health care job, Sophie was doing surprisingly well with her cake business. Baking had always been therapeutic for her and brought her fond memories of the days when she and her brother had made cookies with their dad. She'd thought it would be less pressure for her than her former job, where she'd dealt with people's health issues all day. But her new venture carried its own kind of stress. She was a pleaser and hated to disappoint or let anyone down. So making a mistake on someone's special-occasion cake, which was usually the centerpiece of a wedding, a birthday party, or a bar mitzvah, was something she never wanted to happen. And delivering the cakes caused her the most anxiety. Inherently heavy, the cakes were hard to transport, and the inevitable bumps on the road would sometimes shake and bounce off many a delicate decoration. She hired a helper, Jerry, who lifted the cakes and transported them, but ultimately, she was the one responsible for meeting the expectations of the client.

Sophie turned the knob on Lizzie's door only to find it uncharacteristically locked. She knocked again, vigorously this time, in case Lizzie was napping or on the other side of the house.

"Hold on," she heard Lizzie yell. Then, as the door slowly opened, "It's taking me forever to get out of a chair these days. And we've been locking the door with all the construction workers around lately."

Sophie breezed in, planted a kiss on Lizzie's cheek, and headed directly for the kitchen, Lizzie plodding behind her. She set the cake on the counter and asked, "What do you think? It's for Jonathan's pending day of birth—his first birthday cake." She grabbed two clean cups from the dishwasher, filling one with coffee for her and one with juice for Lizzie. "I'm going to make Jonathan a birthday cake for every birthday of his life that I'm alive."

"That's a pretty big commitment, Soph. This one's really beautiful—I love all the detail. Can we have it now and not wait until his actual birthday?"

"Of course. Now is always the perfect time."

Sophie gazed at her friend, an overwhelming sensation of warmth flooding her veins. "I love you, Lizzie. I want you to know that. There's no one like you. Everything's going to be okay, and I can't wait to meet baby Jonathan. I know you're worried, but you'll be the world's best mom."

"Thanks. I love you too. Your faith in me means so much. I know I can only do the best I can, but I hope David and I raise a happy, content, loving human being. And I hope you won't be too disappointed if the baby turns out to be a girl."

"Oh, he won't be. He's definitely Jonathan."

Sophie watched from behind as Lizzie lumbered into the living room, hands on her lower back and belly protruding.

"You're waddling like a penguin," Sophie said.

"You think? God, I'm so uncomfortable. Finally, the upward pressure on my diaphragm let up, but now all my joints ache, especially my hips and pelvis. And just so you're warned, I'm feeling cranky too. Really cranky."

"I'd be amazed if you weren't."

"I think I've been having contractions since this morning."

"You have? This is feeling very real now!"

Sophie set the tray with the drinks, two forks, and two slices of the cake on the coffee table. She hoped the worry she was feeling for Lizzie on the inside didn't show on the outside. "What did the doctor say about the swelling in your ankles? I'm a bit concerned. I know that's normal to a degree, but your bloating looks pretty extreme. I wish you could drink coffee because it can act as a diuretic and push some of the fluid out of you."

"David's going to take me to see the doctor as soon as he gets here." Lizzie's bare legs under her shorts squeaked on the leather couch as she leaned toward the tray. She sunk her fork into the cake and took a bite. "Wow, this is delicious. You have a winner here. I could never go into business making cakes—I don't even like it much. Give me a sour cherry pie any day. I wonder what the story is behind why we eat cake for celebrations."

"Funny you should ask! They were offerings to the gods and spirits. It goes way back to ancient times and their ceremonies. My favorite story is how the Chinese made round cakes at harvesttime to honor their moon goddess. In the old days, all the ingredients were rare and expensive, so the cakes were made to honor—"

A wail from Lizzie interrupted Sophie's narrative.

"Holy crap. It feels like someone put a hose between my legs. My water broke. This is really happening!" Lizzie awkwardly pushed herself up from the couch as Sophie started frantically collecting the cups and plates and running them back to the kitchen. "Call Dr. Browning for me, okay?" Lizzie called after her. "His number's by the phone. No rush, there's plenty of time … but I think it would be a good idea if we just headed straight over to the hospital. Leave a message for David, tell him to meet us there. Get the car, Sophie, he's coming. Jonathan's coming!"

CHAPTER 22
AUGUST 6, 1988

S OPHIE HAD A feeling it was going to be a difficult birth. Even before labor began yesterday around noon, she'd dreaded hearing updates about the struggle—Lizzie's struggle to remain in the world and Jonathan's struggle to enter it.

Sophie was relieved when David had arrived at the hospital, but after he'd met up with her to relay what she hoped would be some good news about Lizzie and Jonathan to help soothe her anxiety, the look on his face said otherwise. Normally cool and calm, he appeared frazzled and concerned. She'd listened as he'd formulated a plan out loud. The situation wasn't optimal—Lizzie's blood pressure was too high and the baby was showing signs of distress—so he'd called in a small army of his physician friends to take the helm of Lizzie's case as he stepped to the side with a sheet-white pallor and eyes filled with fear.

Now, in the early-morning hours in the hospital waiting room, Sophie paced the floor and bit her nails, praying for a fortunate turn of events. She knew it wasn't the nineteenth century anymore—when as many as 40 percent of women died during childbirth due to severe bleeding, a statistic she recalled from a maternal and child care class she'd once taken—but still, she knew Lizzie's team was expecting complications.

Perspiration trickled between her breasts. Worrying about what could go wrong wasn't helping anybody, so Sophie shifted her focus to sending out positive thoughts to the universe. *David is doing everything in his power to give her the best medical care possible*—that provided some comfort. The original plan was for her to be in the room during the birth process, but she had been asked to wait outside so the doctors could perform their work.

Try as she might to stay calm and optimistic, her mind buzzed. *I can't stay still. I can't shut my brain down. Dear spirit guides, great Source of all, I beg you, I plead with you, I beseech you to make everything okay. Save baby Jonathan and Lizzie. If you honor my plea, I'll spend the rest of my life doing charitable acts for others. I swear. Please! I'll make donations to the homeless and work at the soup kitchen to feed the hungry and …*

Spiritually exhausted from her mental bargaining and physically exhausted by the endless wait, Sophie eventually slumped into a waiting room chair and fell into a fitful sleep.

The sun, blazing through the window, woke Sophie from her disturbed dreaming. As she rubbed her eyes, taking in the activity in the room, David approached her. He looked completely drained, yet his walk was deliberate and rushed. She couldn't read his stony face to see what news he was bringing her.

He grabbed Sophie and gave her an uncharacteristically deep hug, sobbing as he rested his head atop hers. *Oh God, no,* thought Sophie. She began heaving.

"No, no, Sophie—these are tears of joy. He's here, he's here! He arrived at four twelve this morning. He's doing okay, and Liz's vital signs have stabilized—she's out of the woods now. I'm laughing and crying at the same time because I'm so relieved. In fact, I'm euphoric! Liz went through a rough spell, but—" He drew in a deep breath and shook his head. "Honestly, it was touch and go there for a time. The blood transfusion turned things around, and she's getting some much-needed sleep. Thank God they're both okay."

With hunched shoulders, looking as though he was going to collapse, David leaned on Sophie for support. Her arm around his waist, she guided him to a chair as a wave of relief rushed over her, relaxing her tense muscles. She slowly expelled a breath she didn't know she was holding.

"So what happened? I don't know any details."

"The baby got stuck in the birth canal with the cord wrapped around his neck. He was faceup and in distress. The doc resorted to forceps to flip him and pull him out. When she did that, the forceps tore Lizzie's uterine wall, causing the bleeding. ... But it's all over now, let's not dwell on that—they'll both be okay."

"I'm so grateful," Sophie said, wiping her wet cheeks. *Note to self: Make those donations and sign up for volunteer work, stat!*

"Hey, Soph, you look like crap. Did you sleep at all? Have you eaten? Lizzie will likely sleep for a while, but I'm going to go back in and sit with her. You can't see her right now, anyway, so why don't you go take a peek at the baby in the nursery, then get a cup of coffee in the cafeteria." He shook his head. "Thank God, thank God, Liz and the baby are okay. I don't know what I'd do without her."

He dried his own tears, then admitted, "I've never known fear like that before. I feel like a bathtub with an open drain, all the life sucked out of me, but at the same time, I'm so damn relieved and happy."

Sophie reached out and touched his cheek. "I'm so glad they're okay, David. And I do need a shot of caffeine. Can I get you some? Can I get you anything?"

"Not now. Maybe later. Just go take a break and see the baby." David grinned. "He's such a handsome little devil—looks like his proud daddy. I'm telling you, this is the crowning glory of my life, Soph, to be a father. I can't wait to do so many things together—fishing, playing ball, taekwondo, sailing, camping ..."

"I know. You'll be a wonderful father. You already are."

*

Sophie skipped the cafeteria and went directly to the nursery to see Jonathan. She wondered if they would recognize each other right away. *Of course we will!*

Peering through the window, her heart beat in an unusual way—a thundering sensation like a herd of bison galloping over the prairie. Not the kind of heart pounding that meant excitement or fear. It was something she'd never experienced before—an anticipation she couldn't name.

She found his name on the sign, and then there he was in the flesh, just like he'd told her in her reverie. Baby Jonathan. The sight was intoxicating. *You're finally here,* she told him silently. *You've come like you promised.* She was trembling from head to toe.

"Would you like to hold him?" asked a ponytailed nurse wearing teddy-bear-patterned scrubs and a stethoscope around her neck.

"I can? Of course I want to." She was breathless.

"Dr. Cohen already gave permission. You can go wash up and put on a gown in there." She pointed toward a door leading to another room.

Sophie couldn't believe this was happening—being able to hold him so soon after his birth.

The nurse placed the swaddled baby in Sophie's open arms. Apart from a few bruises on his face, he was the picture-perfect baby. His miniature hands looked so delicate and pristine. *Oh, the things these little hands will touch, the things these hands will do!* She offered a pinkie to his curled fist, and he immediately clamped down on it. She knew it was a reflex, but she nevertheless heard a message in his firm grip: *I'm here for you. Ride this wave with me.* She bent toward his face and smiled. His barely visible eyebrows lifted as if in recognition.

Sophie wasn't prepared for what happened next. As her gaze settled upon something familiar in his eyes, her body erupted in a mosaic of emotions. Her knees went weak. The crown of her head seemed to open to form a cavity directly linked to all that was above—to the universe, the Source—while a vortex of spinning, vibrating energy surged in an upward spiral, through her spine and back to the top of her head. She was literally vibrating. Her eyes opened wide—to see life in a way she'd never seen it before.

The energy was white and electric and expanded into the space within her chest. Her rib cage seemed to part as the vibrating light filled the vacuum, and the energy spread, unable to be contained within her heart. A sensation of lightness enveloped her, and her body seemed to levitate upward. Light, glorious white light, filled her, caressed her, lifted her, making her as buoyant as a balloon in air. Simultaneously, she was drinking, eating, sleeping, running, floating, expanding. Her ego disappeared, replaced by an awareness of total connectedness. A sense of purpose wrapped around her like warm rays of nurturing sunlight. She wasn't alone—she felt this to her very core. She was plugged in and linked to this little soul and to the universe. She morphed into all that ever was and ever will be. There was nothing else but that moment, that second. She was in a place of everything. Ecstasy and union. Surrender.

This is the purest form of joy, she thought. *Satcitananda—pure, unadulterated bliss.*

This is love.

Pressing the precious soul close to her breast, Sophie's eyes streamed with tears. She had heard about this before but had never experienced it—moments in the physical world when one is fully open to love, allowing feelings of incredible intensity to spring forth. It felt like an overwhelming emotion—the kind that can bring on a rush of tears when listening to a musical composition of carefully chosen notes arranged in a soul-moving way to percolate through one's entire being … the kind of peaceful ecstasy one finds while sitting in a majestic wooded forest under a darkened sky filled with dazzling stars, transcending normal consciousness to an altered state.

This is joy.

Sophie finally found words. "There you are," she whispered in Jonathan's ear. "I've waited for you for a very long time. I hoped you'd come."

He eagerly suckled the tip of her pinkie finger, and she held him close until their heartbeats fell in sync.

Sophie now knew what it was like to feel whole, to be complete. The answer was there in her arms. A strong sensation of familiarity swirled through her body—a feeling of coming home. In that moment, she knew beyond all doubt that she was experiencing a slice of heaven: the reunion with a soul she had deeply loved before on Earth, here in the flesh again. Not knowing when she'd ever feel this bliss again, she absorbed every second of elation with her entire being.

"How much do I love you?" she asked the miracle in her arms. "Since you can't talk, I'll answer for you. More than you'll ever know."

CHAPTER 23
THE ASTRAL PLANE

I N SPITE OF being positive he had the situation completely under control, plan A for Jonathan Cohen's birth didn't go as Malach intended. At the beginning of the birth process, he played his part like an Oscar-winning movie director. But as often happens on the earthly plane, he couldn't control the situations that developed. He couldn't stop Jonathan's fetal distress or keep Lizzie from hemorrhaging, and as a result of those circumstances, he wasn't able to control the vibrational rate he was sure he could sustain at the moment of birth. He never served in the role of a physician on Earth, but he'd done his research. He knew that lack of oxygen to the baby—what the doctors called "anoxia"—is one of the leading causes of death among infants and that it could occur at any time during the birth process, so he thought he was on guard for that.

As the birth process progressed, a chaotic collection of medical problems moved liked a sequence of collapsing dominos, and the vibration Malach tried to hold steady at a high rate suddenly plummeted and couldn't be sustained for the duration he intended. It was as though he were driving around a racetrack with a restrictor plate limiting his power. Malach was now unsure if he recovered the vibrational level fast enough to avoid the loss of memory Nephesh was adamant about preventing. He didn't know to what extent the brief period of decreased vibration would impact him. If Malach sustained the vibration at a high

enough level at the precise moment of entry into the physical world—
the moment he promised Nephesh—he'd still remember his connection
with the spirit world.

*Unbelievable. This can't be happening. I planned this so well. Only time
will tell ... I don't want to have to resort to plan B.*

I just don't.

CHAPTER 24

NEIL

I'VE CERTAINLY HAD time to reflect on what went wrong in my life and how I got to the point of suicide. In fact, all I have now is time—time to reflect on the various things I could have done differently. From my vantage point, I've been watching people and observing how they handle various life situations. I'm mesmerized by the differences I see in attitudes and coping mechanisms. I think part of my problem was my endless pursuit of that elusive thing called "happiness." I expected it and was disappointed when I didn't have what others had—or at least appeared to have.

I didn't realize it (or maybe I didn't think about it because I was so focused on myself), but no one's life is free of pain. All people experience loss, and all people experience some kind of suffering. Unfortunately, I was afraid of that pain—not because I couldn't handle some of it, but because part of me thought it would never go away. I couldn't run from the unpleasantries of life, so I numbed myself to avoid feeling them. I numbed all my emotions by choosing to live my life in a liquor bottle instead of living in the world. A hopeless heart is a desperate heart.

Since we're all individuals, what we can tolerate varies from one person to the next—we all have differing coping mechanisms. In my case, I played the role of a victim who was always looking for someone to blame for my problems, and blaming others is a barrier to healing. How did I not see that?

I appreciate having a broader viewpoint now, greater knowledge of how the world works. It's altered my perception of life. In hindsight, I wish I had been open to the experiences life brought me because that's exactly what I signed up for by being born. Obviously, embracing any kind of pain isn't such an easy thing for human beings to do because it can involve working through some pretty nasty stuff. Most of us are looking for happiness, wanting only good times because they're easier. But I understand now that true soul growth comes from developing strength when the crappy things in life happen. It's all about how we handle both the positive *and* the negative experiences we encounter. So my big aha revelation? Pain isn't pointless.

Sometimes we have to look for alternate ways to cope. Our approach is the key—it's about the attitude we take. I went through my adult life with a pretty dismal attitude. Even though I couldn't see the bigger picture of my life, I should have recognized there was one. We all have a life plan. I didn't have faith that things would turn out okay for me or that my suffering was temporary.

I thought killing myself would end the pain once and for all. Big mistake! My consciousness is still here with me, and I'm still feeling the pain.

Another revelation: My suicide didn't resolve my problems, it only created more.

PART II

CHAPTER 25

JANUARY 15, 1992

TIME MOVED FORWARD as fast as a meteor streaking across Earth's atmosphere, with Sophie acutely aware of how time seemed to accelerate with each passing year. Already, Jonathan was almost three and a half, and the greatest joy in her life had been participating in his.

Sophie stood at the Cohens' front door, ringing the bell with her signature ring—five sustained rings followed by two short bursts—which was her signal to Jonathan that she was there. She waited for his response and wasn't disappointed. Squealing from upstairs, he tore down the steps as fast as his sturdy legs would carry him, then pushed his tiny hand through the mail slot in the door, eager to touch her.

Sophie smiled broadly at the sight of that hand. *I can't believe how happy this one little act makes me feel.*

"Toffee," he screamed. Initially unable to say "Sophie," he'd been calling her Toffee since he could speak, and the nickname had stuck. His squeals of joy filled her soul with an indescribable pleasure.

Lizzie answered the door. "Hi, come in. I find it adorable how much you guys look forward to seeing each other."

Jonathan grabbed Sophie by the hand, led her to the family room, and started playing on the rug. With the eye of a trained pediatric occupational therapist, Sophie noted some unusually advanced behaviors for his age. When he was two and a half, he already had a large vocabulary and spoke in full sentences, always asking lots of who, what, and why questions. He was keenly observant and curious about his surroundings and people. He showed early development of his motor skills, a high level of understanding, and an advanced attention span. He was a gifted child, like his dad. Even as a baby, he was socially engaging and clearly liked people, greeting them with his big, toothless grin. Sophie loved to watch him play.

Sophie accepted the cup of coffee Lizzie handed her. "It makes me feel so good that we can leave him with you. David and I can comfortably go about our work knowing the two of you are having such a great time together. It's hard to leave my little boy, but it's much easier because of you. David agrees. He said just that the other night."

"I hope you know the happiness he brings me. I know it's terribly hard on both of you to leave him."

"We're both torn about continuing our work, but you know us—it's in our blood."

"I do know that. You two were made for each other."

Sophie recalled the phone call she'd received from Lizzie eight years ago, after she'd first met David. She'd been so excited, she could hardly get her words out. They'd met at a fund-raiser for the People Saving People Project. Lizzie was determined to attend because she was intrigued about the agency after having researched several international medical aid organizations once she'd first felt the calling.

Immediately following the event, Lizzie called Sophie to tell her she'd met her future husband—they were an instant match. Lizzie and David both saw the world with the same let's-save-lives eyes. They were each a good fit for the PSPP—Lizzie a pediatrician and David a general surgeon—and David had some interesting stories to share with her about the few assignments he'd already been on for the agency.

Although they were both still committed to their humanitarian work after Jonathan was born, Sophie knew there'd been a definitive shift in their priorities. How could there not be?

Sophie and Lizzie relaxed in the family room, watching Jonathan transform a large, empty box into a fort. Sophie laughed as he peeked at them through a hole in the cardboard.

"I could be happy just spending my days with him, yet I always feel like I should be doing something on a grander scale than child care or baking cakes. Something important that helps others, like you and David."

"Don't compare. We all have our purpose in life. And anyway, you helped people for many years when you were treating kids. And now you help David, me, and Jonathan, not to mention all your clients. Your baking talents bring a lot of joy to the world. Just think of all the celebrations you make special."

"I guess so. But I have to say, I hate it when you and David go away at the same time—I worry about the two of you all the time."

Lizzie didn't respond, just started picking lint off her sweater.

"I'm sorry. Did I upset you by saying that? You're rarely at a loss for words."

"Yeah, I worry about the risks as well. But as my mom says, something can happen right here at home crossing the street."

"I know, I know—but your risk is way higher when you go to some remote location, to unstable parts of the world."

"You're right. Of course there's some inherent danger in what we do. All the more reason we're so grateful that you take care of this little guy for us. And I think I've finally decided: I'll finish out this one last assignment, and then I'm packing it in to devote my time to being a mom."

Sophie let out a huge sigh. "I'm beyond relieved to hear that, although I'll miss taking care of him as much as I've been able to. It's given us such a unique opportunity to bond, to connect. My love for him, the contentment he brings me in such simple ways, it fills me completely. When you take him with you on some of your trips, I miss him more than I can say."

"Well, start looking for more things to fill you up, because he's growing and will be starting school soon. And you know what happens a few years into school—it's all about friends and playdates and after-school practices."

Sophie frowned. "I'm acutely aware that that time will be here before we know it. That's why I appreciate every moment I have with him now."

Lizzie took a sip of her coffee. "Hey, I have a favor to ask. We decided at the last minute to attend a medical seminar in Paris in preparation for our next assignment. It starts next week. Will you be able to watch Jonathan for two weeks? I mean, I know you'll watch him—you always do when we're working. But this is extra. Can you do days *and* nights at such late notice? Will that interfere with any plans you have?"

"Are you kidding? Of course I can. No plans that I can't rearrange. I have a lunch date with my former co-worker, Anne, next week, but there's no reason Jonathan can't come along. And I have a few cake orders to fill, but he always loves helping me, and Jerry can take care of the deliveries."

"Great. David already booked his flight for tomorrow, and now that I know you're on board, I can meet up with him there sooner. ... I have something else to discuss with you too."

"Sure, shoot."

"It actually relates to what we were talking about earlier. David and I have been discussing it, and we'd like to name you as Jonathan's legal guardian. You're already his godmother, we know, but that's not a legal title. And if anything ever happened to David and me ... We considered our parents, of course, but they're getting up there in age, and honestly, Soph, there's no one who loves him more than you. Or knows him better. Since we'll both be out of the country for an extended period this time, I'd like to tie up this loose end before I go."

Sophie put an arm around Lizzie and gave her a reassuring tug. "Nothing is going to happen to you guys. You'd better not abandon us!"

Jonathan crawled up on Sophie's lap just then and clasped his arms around her neck. "Play the reindeer game," he said.

"Okay, junior reindeer, give me a minute to finish up with your mom."

Lizzie continued. "We certainly don't plan on anything happening, but we need to be prepared. Just in case. We'd be irresponsible parents if we didn't make provisions."

"Of course I'd raise him, Lizzie, protect him, love him. I'm beyond touched that you asked me. I'm deeply honored."

"Great. Okay. We need to take care of this before I leave. We already asked our attorney to draw up the papers since I had no doubt you'd say yes, and we can meet him later today to make everything official—David already signed. And just so you know, Jonathan would be taken care of financially by us—we've already made those arrangements too."

"Wow, that sort of gives me the creeps. I don't like even talking about this kind of stuff."

"You'd want him taken care of, wouldn't you? It's part of raising a child. And guarantees in life don't exist, so preparation is a good thing. A necessary thing. Okay, enough on that."

"You always were the practical one of the two of us," Sophie agreed.

Lizzie grasped her hand then. "How about you, my friend? How are you doing? You seem at peace these days—content and grounded. How are things going with Dr. Hobbs?"

Sophie plumped the toss pillow on the couch. "Good, good. It's been years now. I always feel more at peace after a session with him, and even though we've made great progress, it feels like there's always more I can work on."

"That's great. Just keep progressing. So do you think you'll ever go back to OT … or stick with the cakes?"

"The cakes for now. Baking has always been so cathartic for me, it gives me a creative outlet, and like you said, it gives people pleasure. But there's some stress involved. For example, it's hard to make some of the bigger cakes—like the wedding cakes—in my little kitchen."

"It's settled, then. While we're gone, just live in the house. The kitchen is huge, there's the extra freezer and fridge in the garage, and all of Jonathan's things are here. It'll be so much easier all around than packing him up every night for your place."

"Thanks, I'll do that."

"I'm going to go get dressed for the attorney's office and make my travel arrangements. Can you drive me to the airport?"

"Of course. Now we've got some reindeer to herd while you get ready."

On Friday, Sophie pulled into the Cohens' driveway to pick up Jonathan and Lizzie. All the papers were squared away, the fridge was fully stocked, and Lizzie had printed up detailed instructions for Sophie—Jonathan's vitamin schedule, his pediatrician's emergency number, which clothes he insisted on wearing lately. After Lizzie buckled Jonathan into his car seat, she climbed in back with him.

"Hey, little guy, you know Mommy and Daddy have to go bye-bye again, but we'll be home soon. You be a good boy for Sophie. We love you so, so much."

Jonathan scrunched up his face. "Nooooo … Mommy, don't go away. I don't want you to go." No amount of kisses planted all over his face stopped him from crying and pouting all the way to the airport.

Lizzie dabbed at the tears in the corners of her eyes. "This is awful," she told Sophie through the rearview mirror. "I hate leaving him like this. But like I said, one more assignment and then I'm retiring." Lizzie sighed deeply. "I'm so torn about leaving. I hope we at least have good weather this trip."

"In Paris," Sophie said, "any weather sounds good to me."

"Remember our trip after college?" Lizzie perked up a little at the memory. "In spite of all the rain, it was a great adventure, wasn't it? All the Parisian shops, the clubs, the handsome French men. *Ooh la la.* We should go on another trip again."

"I'd like that. I really would."

They arrived at the bustling San Diego airport with twenty minutes to spare. Sophie pulled to the curb in the departures area, then jumped out to get Lizzie's bags from the trunk.

"Okay, guys, hugs and love for all," Lizzie said through her tears, again covering Jonathan with kisses.

Sophie pulled Lizzie close to her. "We'll miss you very much."

As she headed for the terminal, Lizzie turned to give one more wave, one more good-bye. "See you in two weeks."

"Bye, Mommy," Jonathan shouted through the open window, sticking out his lower lip. "I love you." He waved back at her.

"Love you more," she called out.

Chapter 26
January 23, 1992

SOPHIE WOKE AT the crack of dawn. The orange-yellow rays of the early-morning sun peeked through the window amid layers of patchy, gray coastal fog. Sophie loved baking in Lizzie's big kitchen, and she rose easily with a happy anticipation. Wearing her baby harp seal pajamas, she padded into the kitchen and started preparing for the day. A little while later, Jonathan shuffled in to join her, still a bit groggy and with a serious case of bed head.

"Good morning, sweetie. Want some breakfast?"

He nodded and climbed onto his regular stool at the counter—his favorite sitting spot in the kitchen. Sophie poured him a bowl of Froot Loops and then watched as he cradled it like it was his life support—much like she felt about her coffee.

First on the agenda, they had a birthday cake order to complete. Baking with Jonathan was always fun because he found delight in all the new tastes he experienced. Sophie loved seeing life through his eyes, with each discovery still so exciting.

The kitchen was already a mess of bowls, scrapers, and flour—lots of flour on every surface. After drinking the last bit of sugary milk from his bowl, Jonathan was ready to dump the ingredients Sophie handed him into the mixing bowl.

"What does this say?" Jonathan pointed to a pink cardboard box.

"It says 'The Icing on the Cake,' the name of my business. Okay, now let's get the chocolate cake ready for the oven."

"I like frosting."

That was rather obvious. He was covered in white buttercream from his toes to the towheaded locks on his head. His upper lip was slathered in frosting as he licked the beaters.

Sophie melted when she looked at him. *Could anyone love him more? He's so inquisitive. So thoughtful.*

"Yes, I see that. It's good, isn't it? How did you manage to get it on every square inch of your body?"

He shrugged. "It's fun to cook. Can we make the same cake for Mommy's birthday? She'll like this flavor."

"She will. Sure, it'll be fun to surprise her with a birthday cake when she gets back. After we're done baking, let's go shopping for a birthday present for Mommy."

"I want to get her an Elmo."

"An Elmo, huh? Elmo's nice, but Elmo's something *you* love. When you give gifts, you should give something the other person loves."

"Mommy loves Elmo."

"You know what? I guess that's true. We *could* buy her an Elmo … but what does Mommy like? What does she enjoy doing?"

Jonathan tilted his head to the side, his blonde bangs falling slightly askew. From his expression, Sophie could clearly see that he was putting a lot of thought into the question. She was impressed by that.

"She grows flowers."

"Yes, she does. Maybe we could think of something she needs for gardening."

He looked perplexed, and Sophie watched him deep in thought for several minutes.

"I could get her dirt."

Sophie laughed. "Good thinking. But there's already a lot of dirt in those big bags she has out there. What else might she need for planting her flowers?"

"Her gloves have holes."

"True. We could get her new gardening gloves."

Seemingly satisfied with this decision, Jonathan returned his attention to the nearly empty frosting bowl in his lap, holding it tightly against his body as he wiped the icing from the sides with his fingers, licking each one methodically.

"Last time I was big, you were my mommy. I made you a present. It was pretty with beads." He kicked his feet rhythmically against the cabinet below him, grinning with his white-frosting lips.

Sophie was only half listening as she greased the cake pans and tossed in a bit of flour. She tilted the pans to the side to cover the bottoms, then tapped them over the sink to remove the excess. "You made me a present with beads?"

"Yep, last time, when you were my mommy."

"Sometimes I am like a mommy to you, aren't I? I love you that much!"

"No, you *were* my mommy. Last time I was big."

Concentrating on her task, Sophie didn't look up from pouring the batter into the pans. "When you were big, huh? You're a big boy now."

"No!" He kicked the cabinet harder, sounding frustrated as he repeated, "No, last time I was big. You were my mommy."

Now Sophie raised her gaze to his face. "Last time you were big?" she echoed.

"Yes. When you were my mommy. We shot arrows. I fished. My hair was long here." He pointed to the left side of his head. "It was short here." He pointed to the right side of his head. "So it didn't get stuck in my bow."

Sophie froze. Holding her breath, she looked deep into his eyes. Was she hearing what she thought she was hearing?

Gathering her composure, she tried to sound casual as she said, "Tell me more."

"Not now, Toffee. I want to lick the batter next."

CHAPTER 27
THE ASTRAL PLANE

Ruach: Malach, there's been an indication that Nephesh hasn't forgotten the spiritual realm. He seems to be remembering one of his prior lives. Let me play this back for you to see what you think.

Malach: That's definitely a sign he's remembering a previous life with Sophie. This is good news for us. Maybe I didn't screw up after all.

Ruach: Maybe not.

CHAPTER 28
JANUARY 31, 1992

LAST NIGHT AT bedtime, Sophie had told Jonathan that his parents would be home the next afternoon. Now she wished she'd waited to tell him, because it was all he could talk about and think about all day. He wouldn't let the front door out of his sight, not wanting to miss the moment they arrived. Wearing his favorite pair of jeans with rolled-up cuffs, his red sweatshirt that said THE KID, and a pair of blue sneakers, he knelt on a dining room chair staring out the picture window in the living room.

"When will they be here?" he yelled into the kitchen for about the thousandth time. Unable to stand the anticipation for another second, he ran to the door and opened it. When no one was there, he resumed his post on the chair.

Sophie came to the doorway between the kitchen and the dining room. "You asked me that five minutes ago, sweetie," she said. "I'm not exactly sure what time they'll get here, only that they're due this afternoon. But sometimes planes are delayed and sometimes there's a lot of traffic on the roads coming home. Want to help me in the kitchen? I'm making elderberry syrup for flu season."

"No," Jonathan said, never taking his eyes from the window. "I want to wait for Mommy and Daddy."

*

Finally, a car door slammed. Jonathan ran to the front door and threw it open. "Mommy, Daddy!"

Sophie waited to greet them until Jonathan had had his fill of first-round hugs. She watched as Lizzie and David dragged their suitcases and bags of souvenirs into the foyer, looking happy and refreshed from their trip. They dropped their packages on the floor so they could start in on their second round of affection. Jonathan basked in the warmth of their loving arms—his face revealing to Sophie how safe he felt there, how cherished.

David picked him up, clasped him to his chest, as Jonathan wrapped his legs around his father's waist. "Boy, did I ever miss you!" David said, slathering kisses on Jonathan's neck and head.

"My turn," Lizzie said as she took Jonathan's face in her hands and pressed her lips against his. "Did you have a good time, sweetie?"

He nodded as he continued to nuzzle David.

Lizzie gave Sophie a hug. "It was a great conference," she told her. "Best of all, we had plenty of time to enjoy Paris, dining at all the best spots. And, of course, we lugged back tons of souvenirs. Want to see yours?"

"Absolutely. And I want to hear all the details."

At the mention of gifts, Jonathan clambered to the ground and started searching through the bags.

"Wait, buddy," David said. "Let's sit in the living room and open your presents. But let Mommy and I take a bathroom break before we start, okay?"

Jonathan rolled his toy car on the back of the living room couch until they returned. "Mommy, what did you bring me?"

David tousled Jonathan's hair on his way to the couch. "Come gather round and we'll show you." Jonathan crawled up on his dad's lap as Lizzie brought all the bags in the room.

She handed Sophie a slim box from her suitcase. "Oh, wow, a silk screen scarf. It's gorgeous. I love it." She tied it around her neck, modeling it.

"We thought the colors would look great with your auburn hair," David said. "And this is for you, Jonathan."

Jonathan squatted down on the floor with his bag and pulled out a long white cylinder. Inside was a poster. "It's Albert Einstein!" he exclaimed as he unrolled it. "Can we put it on my wall?"

"How amusing that such a little boy has a fascination with Albert Einstein," Sophie commented.

"Just like his daddy," said Lizzie. Then she handed Sophie another elegant box. "Jonathan, you and Daddy can put the poster up later. Let's finish up here first. You'll like this one, Sophie."

Sophie lifted the lime-green cover of the box, and the decadent smell of artisan chocolate immediately hit her nose. "Oh yeah … now we're talking! This is great. From Cacao et Chocolat. I'll even share these."

"You won't want to after one bite," said David. "We ate the first box we got you, went back for a replacement, then got another box for us as well. Finished it off in one night. I think we each gained five pounds on this trip."

"Um … David, that was going to be our little secret," Lizzie teased.

Lizzie handed Sophie a rectangular package wrapped in tissue. "And one more for you."

"This is like Christmas," Sophie said, tearing the tissue paper. "Oh my, this is great—a watercolor of the Seine. Thank you so much. I know exactly where I'll hang this."

"Yeah," Lizzie explained, "there was this little old man who sat on the street with his easel, painting the scenery. He even wore a beret."

"What about me?" Jonathan piped up. "Any more for me?"

David handed him another bag. "Yep, here you go."

Inside were two T-shirts and a Paris baseball. "I want to play catch!"

"We sure will, buddy," David assured him as he started gathering all the wrapping paper up from the floor. "But first we have one more special gift from France that I know you'll like. You can save it in your coin bank. Mommy and I know you love coins, so we brought you a piece of French money. This is a lucky 50-francs piece from 1978."

Sophie had always been fascinated by Jonathan's interests. She'd worked with lots of children over her career, but none of them were intrigued with coins like Jonathan. Sometimes he liked to take them out of his bank and line them up and look at them.

Jonathan took the coin from David and turned it over, studying it as if it were a piece to a puzzle. "It's my favorite, Daddy."

Sophie laughed. "You guys should go away more often so we can get more of these great gifts."

"No!" Jonathan yelled. "Don't go away more. Mommy, Daddy, I missed you." He crawled into Lizzie's lap and put his hand on her cheek, then said, "I've got presents for you too. It's your birthday, Mommy. We made you a cake."

"You did? That's exciting. Tell me what else you did when we were gone."

"We made cakes. Toffee took me on her bike. We ate lunch with Anne. We sat outside. She has a dog named Barney. I want a dog."

"Sounds like you had fun," said David.

David gave Sophie a big hug. "Thanks so much for taking such great care of him while we were gone. We missed him more than we can say, but we knew he was in the very best of hands."

"It was nothing but a joy for me. You know how much I adore that kid."

David stood and held out his hand to Jonathan. "Come on, buddy, it's time for some ball." David snatched him up and placed him on his shoulders, holding him securely at the knees. "Hang on." He danced around the living room. "Let's go practice throwing your new baseball in the backyard." Sophie's eyes teared up at the sudden, sweet memory of riding on her own dad's shoulders when she was a little girl.

Once the guys were gone, Lizzie stretched out on the couch, propping her feet on the dark gray ottoman. "Come sit by me, Sophie. Let's talk. We had a great time, and I actually learned a few things. It's good to be home, though." She tilted her head, pressed her lips together, and gazed at Sophie. "You good? You look a little different somehow."

"I'm feeling a bit different—kind of energized by my latest obsession. I've been reading about reincarnation day and night. I'm literally inhaling the books. Get this, there's a guy named Stevenson who did all this work on children and reincarnation."

"Warning: You're talking to a person with a scientific brain here, you know."

"So is his. He's a psychiatrist who worked for the University of Virginia's School of Medicine for fifty years, and he was the chair of the psych department as well as a professor there. He investigated over twenty-five hundred cases of kids around the world who claimed to remember past lives."

"I have a hard time grasping the concept. I have enough dealing with this life, much less thinking about others I might have had."

"Sure, there are moments when I find it hard to believe too, but it's also hard to argue away someone you actually know who talks about experiencing it."

"Would this someone be Dr. Hobbs?"

"No. It was your son, actually—something he said. We were in the kitchen baking a cake, and he talked about the last time he was big when I was his mommy. Since then, he's kept saying things like that, things I find stunning. Once I started thinking about it, I realized he's said things like that in the past, but I didn't ever see a greater meaning. But now, after reading these books—it's a textbook sign of reincarnation when a child talks about the last time he was 'big.'" Sophie was doing her best to restrain her excitement, not wanting to sound too "out there" for Lizzie.

"That doesn't really mean anything—it's not any kind of proof. Jonathan has always had a vivid imagination and an advanced intellect. That doesn't mean I don't find the concept intriguing and maybe even feasible. So if we reincarnate, we can change gender, race, religion, the places we live, right?"

"Apparently, yes. I agree that there's not any conclusive evidence or anything, but I *was* dumbfounded when I read that what Jonathan said is one of the signature phrases suggestive of reincarnation. I'm just relaying an experience we had, and it was pretty amazing. It's all pretty fascinating and interesting."

"Definitely, yes," Lizzie agreed.

"Stevenson said children usually begin to talk about their past-life memories between the ages of two and four. The memories usually aren't there for long and start to dissipate when the child is between four and seven years old. But exceptions to the rule exist, like when a child continues to remember a previous life but stops talking about it for various reasons."

Jonathan came back into the room then, interrupting their conversation. "Mommy, I want cake."

Lizzie sat up straight to hug him. "Okay, it's cake time!"

David brought the platter to the dining room, and Sophie carried in a tray of coffee for the adults and milk for Jonathan. They all sat at the table waiting for Lizzie to cut the cake.

She swiped a taste of the frosting with her finger. "The cake is gorgeous. Jonathan, you did a great job."

He beamed. "It's chocolate. And Toffee helped make it. Open your presents, Mommy. I got you Elmo."

She laughed as she tugged off the paper, exposing Elmo in a box. "Well, don't tell me. Let me unwrap my gifts and be surprised." She removed Elmo from the box. "Oh, finally, all my life I've wanted my own Elmo. Thank you, sweetie." She leaned over and planted a kiss on the top of his head.

"See, Toffee? I told you." Then he grabbed another package and handed it to Lizzie. "Here."

After opening her second gift, Lizzie said, "A perfect choice. Garden gloves. Let's see if they fit." She tried them on and, sure enough, they fit perfectly.

Jonathan was glowing.

"We'll have to do some planting tomorrow. Thank you so much, baby boy. I love you."

Once everyone had enjoyed their cake, David and Jonathan went out back again to play and Lizzie and Sophie resumed their talk.

Lizzie scrunched up her nose and grimaced. "Gosh, I hate to even tell Jonathan we're leaving again on assignment, but at least I can tell him this will be my last one. And we have a little time with him before we have to pack up again. Usually only surgeons are allowed to sign on for less than the full six months at this site, but since I come in a package deal with David, they agreed to let me return early with him. I'll show Jonathan where Peru is on the map before we go. He likes to look at maps, and the communication will be easier there than from some of places we've worked."

"Everything will be okay on this end. I'll take wonderful care of him."

"I know that. You're the best. Want to help me throw a dinner party before we go? I owe so many people so many thanks, and I think a lovely dinner party would cover a lot of bases all at once. I could use your help in a big way."

They stood and hugged, coffee mugs in hand. "Of course, my friend. I'd do anything to help you."

CHAPTER 29

MAY 10, 1992

S OPHIE WAS DEFINITELY in the mood for something fun to do with Jonathan; whenever Lizzie and David were away, she liked to entertain and educate him with unusual diversions. Perusing the newspaper, she found what she was looking for: a pow-wow at the American Indian Culture Days event in Balboa Park. It looked like it would be a wonderful day filled with lively traditional dances, storytelling, music, beading and crafts, and native foods. Jonathan would love it, and she herself had always had an affection for Native American culture. When she was a little girl, she'd prayed each night for a pair of moccasins. She had no explanation for her affinity for all things Native American other than her mother's belief that Sophie had been an American Indian in a previous life.

It was a perfect day for a festival—cool springtime was in the air, with a sunny, cloudless sky. They arrived early, but lines of cars were already circling for parking spots, like vultures ready to pounce on their prey. Sophie released a deep sigh. "Jonathan, wave a magic wand and make an open parking space appear."

"Okay," he said. He waved an invisible wand in the air and said, "Abadaba."

"Close, it's 'abracadabra'!"

Sophie raised her eyebrows in disbelief when a car backed out of a spot right in front of them. She reached into the backseat to rumple his hair. "You're a magical little boy, aren't you? Let's go and have some fun!"

The festival was one of the most well-attended events in the park each year, and the grounds were swimming with visitors. Jonathan was a delightful companion for Sophie. A curious child with a naturally inquisitive mind, he was constantly asking stimulating questions. He observed everything around him and came up with thoughtful ways to express how he saw the world. She loved introducing him to new things, seeing his mind absorb information like a sponge. Sometimes she'd catch herself just staring at him—the pursing of his lips, the drawing together of his eyebrows, and the slight tilt of his head when he was heavy in thought.

They stopped to watch a group of young boys warming up to perform a dance. One boy sported a headdress of white and black feathers and a feather fan. Others wore brightly colored regalia decorated with detailed beadwork, free-flowing ribbons, and animal furs.

The smell of baked goods and sweet sugar filled the air. Lured by the steady beat of the animal-hide drums, Sophie and Jonathan strolled into a large open area where a group of dancers had gathered, stopping at a vendor's booth along the perimeter.

"Wait till you taste this," Sophie said, placing an order for two servings of fry bread. "You're gonna love it." After she paid the vendor a few dollars, she handed Jonathan his plate. "Careful, it's hot."

Jonathan bit into the bread, a soft plume of white powdered sugar spraying his face. "Mmm, it's good!"

Enthralled by the mesmerizing drumbeat and the chanting, Jonathan stared wide-eyed as the men began their traditional dance. Diligently, he watched the dancers bend and hop rhythmically, taking in the whole performance. At one point, spectators were invited to enter the dance ring. Without saying a word to Sophie, Jonathan handed her his plate and scampered into the ring to join in.

With her mouth agape, Sophie stood on the side watching. *What the heck? Where did he learn to do that?* Jonathan wasn't as fluid and practiced as the tribal dancers, no, but he didn't look like a novice, either. She was stunned. When the music stopped, a broadly smiling Jonathan returned to Sophie, slightly out of breath.

"Honey, where did you learn to dance like that?"

"I did it last time I was big. The drumbeat tells us how to move our feet. We danced around the fire. We had animal skins on our heads. I told you before, Toffee."

"Well, I want to hear more," Sophie said. "I want to know everything."

He shrugged. "It was when you were my mommy, like I said. You were a good mommy. We hunted deer. We ate corn."

"Maybe that's why you like it so much now."

"We made flour. And good stuff to eat. We fished. We made boats out of logs."

"That's very interesting."

"I had a knife. We made it out of stone. We told lots of stories too."

Sophie didn't want to push him—she wanted him to just talk freely—but she hoped he'd go on and on.

Instead, he started eating the rest of his fry bread as they sauntered among all the showcases. Demonstrations for making bead jewelry and leather crafts were on the left, and medicinal herb tinctures, lotions, drums, and moccasins were for sale on the right. Booths stocked with pottery, sculptures, dream catchers, and music recordings were arranged in a circle in the center.

Jonathan glanced down at his sneakers. "I want some Indian shoes."

Sophie stopped in her tracks, remembering her nightly childhood prayers, which had eventually been appeased by a gift from her grandmother. She cherished those shoes for years.

"There's a stand over there. Let's go see if we can each find a pair we like."

On the way, their eyes feasted on more colorful images, more demonstrations on shaping flints, on making bows, on starting fires.

Jonathan spontaneously started talking again. "We loved drums," he said. "We named them. I liked to dance to the drum."

Sophie quietly listened, but she was bubbling with excitement inside.

At the moccasin booth, Sophie watched as Jonathan scoured through the inventory like a miser inspecting his gold pieces.

"We didn't sew ours like this. They look different." He tried on a pair. "But I like these. Can we buy them?"

"Yes. Yes, we can." It felt incredibly fulfilling to Sophie—to be providing him with an item she'd so desired in her own youth.

As the vendor handed her the merchandise and Sophie started to stuff the moccasins into her satchel, Jonathan said, "No, I want to wear mine. Toffee, put on yours too." So she did, putting their shoes in her satchel instead.

They wandered through the fairgrounds some more until a dream catcher stand caught Jonathan's eye. He turned to Sophie and pointed to one of them. "This is like the one you made me last year. We didn't have those when I was big."

The vendor, with two long braids and a leathery, wrinkled face, gave Jonathan a solemn smile. "What's your name, young man?"

"Jonathan."

"Do you know what this is?" he asked. He held up an unusual-looking dream catcher.

"It catches bad dreams," Jonathan said. He pointed to Sophie. "She made me one."

"Mine are different from the others you'll see here. I use a tear-shaped frame of willow branches and tie sinew strands in a web around the frame. Do you know what sinew is?"

"I know what that stuff is," he said, pointing to the web of the dream catcher. "We cut it from a deer leg. It's strong. We put it on our bows."

The old man stopped, cocked his head, and dropped his jaw slightly. He glanced at Sophie with a puzzled look that transformed into a knowing nod. "That's absolutely correct. It's the tendons of the animal. You're a special boy, you know."

Jonathan grinned. "I know."

Digging through his wares, the old man pulled out a round object to show to Jonathan. "This is a mandala," he began. "It's—"

Jonathan interrupted him with a rush of knowing enthusiasm. "I know what it is. It helps us know what's in here." He pointed to his heart.

Again, the man looked surprised. "That's correct. You are very smart. Our people understand what lies beneath this." He gestured to his body. "And they know there are deep messages that live in our hearts. The mandala is used to uncover the messages."

Jonathan nodded as though he understood.

"I have a special present for you," the man said. "I know you'll appreciate it." He handed Jonathan a beautiful handmade dream catcher. "Here is my gift to you. And for your mother, I have a mandala bracelet."

"Thank you," Jonathan said.

"I'm also giving you a coloring book, young man. The book is full of mandalas for you to color or paint. Coloring these will help you see what messages are in your heart."

He held out his hand to Sophie. "Come, please give me your wrist, my dear. I think you'll benefit from this." He fastened an energy bracelet around her wrist made of two strands of stones connected in the center with a silver mandala charm. "This is bloodstone," he said. "It's used for circulation of energy in the body and will help to remove your energy blocks."

Why am I feeling so emotional over this? she thought.

Jonathan's eyes were filled with emotion too, Sophie noticed—a joy that twinkled in them as though he had been away for a long time and had finally come home.

Impulsively, Jonathan reached out and hugged the old man. "Thank you," he said.

"Yes, thank you," Sophie echoed. "Please let me compensate you somehow for these lovely items," she said, reaching for her wallet.

The old man put his hand up. "I said they're gifts, and I want no other payment than to see what's now in his eyes. That's all I need. Please accept the gifts in the manner in which they were given. It's been my joy and pleasure to meet young Jonathan today."

Sophie thanked him for his generosity, wondering if it was appropriate for her to give him a hug as well. As she debated this, he showed her a labyrinth mandala. "It says life is a journey. And it has no ending because we're eternal. We always *are*," he said.

The intricate mandala was unlike any Sophie had seen before. It was composed of a square center point and four gates. She knew the mandala held great spiritual and ritual significance—Matthew had them hanging all over his waiting room. It would be the perfect gift for him.

"I'd like to buy this one for a friend." This time, the old man accepted Sophie's payment and repeated how pleased he'd been to meet them before they bid one another good-bye.

As they slowly made their way toward the exit, Sophie gently urged, "Tell me more about when you were big."

"I don't want to talk about it anymore," Jonathan answered. "It will make you sad."

"Why would I be sad?"

"Because you were a good mommy. You loved me a lot. I loved you. You were sad when I died. Now you're scared to be a mommy because I died. I came back here to tell you something. I'm always with you. You don't have to be sad now."

Sophie was beyond speechless. His words resonated so profoundly in her core, she was momentarily breathless. He had touched a truth deep inside her—one previously covered up by the noise of life. She fingered her new bracelet, and maybe it was just her imagination, but she felt as if her heart were fully opening in her chest. She felt like she'd received his message to her loud and clear.

Jonathan quickly shifted back to the present moment, startling her with the rapid transition. He looked up at her with an innocent grin. "Let's make corn tonight, okay?"

"Sure," she said, laughing. Then she bent down and hugged him tightly. "How much do I love you?"

"More than I'll ever know."

He stated this beloved phrase between them as a known fact.

CHAPTER 30
AUGUST 6, 1992

PERIODICALLY, PANGS OF loneliness, felt as something like the aches of the flu coming on, began to hit Sophie. She was used to missing the company of Lizzie and David when they were gone, but when they took Jonathan along with them—as they had a few days ago—the loneliness could become overwhelming.

To celebrate his fourth birthday, David and Lizzie had taken Jonathan to Pennsylvania for a week to visit David's parents. Sophie already missed him, having come to depend on his companionship, finding it more fulfilling than dealing with some of the judgmental adults in her life. His innocence was so refreshing to her, his eagerness to learn, and she particularly relished her conversations with him. Story time was their favorite part of the day, and although Sophie had always felt maternal toward him, that bond had only strengthened since he'd started sharing memories from another time, another life, with her.

But now, Sophie figured, the loneliness was likely a good sign—a sign she was ready to become a participant in the world again. Hopefully, it was an indication that she was ready to fully put the tragedy of Neil behind her. She didn't need Dr. Hobbs or Lizzie to point out the improvements in her—she noticed them herself. She was no longer isolating herself from people and had slowly but steadily been accepting invitations from friends and acquaintances over the last few years to lunch and dinner, the movies, baseball games, and various activities. One night after a few glasses of wine, she'd even let Lizzie talk her into scanning the personal ads, maybe even attend a singles event in town, but she hadn't been quite ready to take *that* step yet. Romantic love didn't feel safe yet, whereas her love for Jonathan was nothing but pure, enriching, and enchanting. Still, she knew all the one-on-one intense time she had with him wouldn't continue forever, so she made a conscious decision to start rebuilding a life of her own.

While the Cohens were gone, then, she'd invited a couple of friends over for a summer cookout this Saturday night. In the meantime, she had several cake orders to fill, she was looking forward to working on a tapestry she was making, and her reading table was filled with more books on reincarnation. She enjoyed her time alone in her cottage, but she was aware of missing Jonathan every minute of the long week.

Missing out on Jonathan's birthday was a whole different matter, though. She hadn't missed one of his birthdays yet, and she didn't intend to go back on her promise to make him a cake every year. So while she baked a cake for a client, she baked a birthday cake for Jonathan too. She'd freeze it for when he got home, when he could have a second celebration with her.

Sophie put the finishing touches on the three-tiered sweet-sixteen cake in front of her. She swirled pink rosette frosting around the border of the top tier and dropped white candy pearls in the center of each. Putting the cake on a cardboard circle—extending beyond the cake by at least an inch on all sides—would help prevent it from sliding in the delivery box. Jerry was on his way to pick it up.

She was feeling a bit rushed because she had an appointment with Dr. Hobbs this evening. He'd already agreed to work after-hours today to accommodate her schedule, so she didn't want to be late. As she started placing the pearls on the lower tier, she thought about his generosity, how it was in his nature to go out of his way for others. He was always so patient with her and understood when she had to work her appointments around her child care obligations to Jonathan, but he'd also been very accommodating about her finances, proposing a payment schedule for their bi-monthly sessions that she could afford.

She still had a nest egg from the sale of her house, and her business was doing fine, but money wasn't exactly flowing out of a fountain. The real game changer for Sophie had been when Lizzie and David had come to her with a proposition: Would she stay on in the guesthouse indefinitely, rent free, in exchange for being Jonathan's primary caretaker when they traveled for work? Although she didn't receive a salary, they compensated her in many other ways—prepaying all the household bills, stocking a bank account with plenty of cash for groceries and expenses, having her over for dinner often and gifting her in unexpected ways, like with play tickets or a spa appointment—and this arrangement had made it possible for Sophie to live a comfortable life in such an expensive area and to add some extras to the mix to boot, like therapy with Dr. Hobbs.

She'd been seeing him a good long while now, and they no longer spent much of their time dealing with the aftereffects of Neil's suicide. She felt far down the path of healing from the tragedy and was enjoying exploring more of the spiritual path with him. He added insight into many areas of her life, and so she planned to stay on the ongoing journey of spiritual development with him as long as she could.

The doorbell rang. "Hey, Soph. All ready?" Jerry was about twenty-five, with a baby face that radiated warmth and kindness. His large, expressive eyes revealed a mischievousness beneath the surface, along with his lopsided, toothy grin. To Sophie, his muscular arms were his best feature—perfect for hauling the heaviest of cakes.

"Yep. Come see what do you think."

He followed her back to the kitchen to admire her work, but then raised his eyebrows in alarm. "Wow, looks like there was a hurricane in here."

"Yeah, yeah—no comments needed. I'll clean it when I get back."

"The cake is perfect. Great job, as always. The birthday girl will love it. You have the address for me?"

"Yes. Oh, and those special cake stackers you found? Well, I used them this time. It took me a few minutes to figure them out, but it'll make the delivery easier, I think." Sophie rummaged through some papers on the counter. "Here you go. It's not far from here." She handed him the order, which would require the client's signature upon acceptance.

"Are you coming, or am I going solo this time?" he asked as he carefully slid the cake box onto the wooden support he'd created.

"Solo for this one. I have an appointment, and I don't want to be late. So don't mess up the cake, and take my emergency kit with you just in case." She gave him a friendly pat on the back.

He leaned close to her ear. "Just call me the cake whisperer." Then he dipped his finger into a bowl of frosting for a taste. "I'm still such a kid. I love the icing. And don't worry: I won't forget to take pictures of the cake once it's there."

"Don't forget to blast the air-conditioning in the van, either, while you drive like a little old lady. Thank you, Jerry."

"See you later, Soph."

Sophie washed the frosting off her hands and face—she always managed to get some on her nose—and ran a brush through her hair. Swiping on some lipstick at the hall mirror, she grabbed a package off the console underneath it and headed out the door. She'd made sure to put the package there so she wouldn't forget to bring it.

Even though Sophie knew Nancy would have gone home for the day, she was still startled to see Dr. Hobbs answering the door himself. He'd never done that before.

"Hi there. I really appreciate you seeing me this late. The cake I was working on all day couldn't be delivered until the parents were home from work, so I had to arrange things this way with my delivery guy. But I think I found a way to thank you," Sophie said, holding out the package wrapped in brown paper with a raffia bow. "Actually, I got this for you months ago at the American Indian festival, but I've been waiting to give it to you until your birthday."

"How thoughtful of you, Sophie. Not just the present, but remembering that it's my birthday tomorrow."

"I always do," Sophie said, following him to his office, "because it's the day after Jonathan's."

"Come in and sit while I open this." She watched him gingerly untie the bow, then saw his eyes light up when he pulled away the tissue. "A mandala!" He looked genuinely pleased as he turned it this way and that. "It's quite unique. I'll hang it on the wall tomorrow. It's beautiful. Thank you so much."

"The first time I came here, I was impressed with your marvelous gallery of them, so when this wonderful old man at the pow-wow showed me this labyrinth mandala, I thought of you immediately."

"I do have an extensive collection from many places. This one is now my favorite. Since you're familiar with the mandala, perhaps you know it's the word for 'circle' in Sanskrit, the root word *manda* meaning 'essence' and *la* meaning 'container.' The fascinating thing about a mandala is how it can stimulate the two sides of the brain. It helps us find our inner peace. Focusing on it helps clear the mind, freeing it from clutter. It was so thoughtful of you to think of me, Sophie. I'll cherish this. Now tell me what's been going on since I last saw you."

They relaxed in their usual chairs.

"I'm actually doing quite well. Thankfully, my energy has been high lately. And although I've been feeling a bit lonely, I'm looking for the gift in that—thinking it's a good thing because it's prompting me to interact more with people. I think what I'm struggling the most with right now is letting go; as you've helped me worked toward letting go of Neil, it seems these residual feelings of abandonment from other periods in my life have cropped up: my dad's passing, my mother's death from breast cancer, my brother moving out of the country. It seems like I have to work on the letting-go part of all that too."

"Quite astute of you. I've been thinking about that as well, in fact. Thinking of ways I can get you through that barrier." He took quite a long pause, swallowing deeply from his teacup. "You know about regressions, not just past-life, but present-life as well. We've talked about them before, and you know I facilitate them. I'm thinking maybe the time is right for you now.

"Would you be interested in trying a regression—starting with your father's death, since that was your first experience with abandonment, and working through the emotions surrounding that? When one experience is healed, sometimes other similar wounds spontaneously heal as well. Regressions can help relieve painful emotions by clearing out blocked energy. You may be holding back from love and engaging more fully in relationships with people because you fear they'll abandon you. If so, let's try to release that."

Sophie's curiosity was greater than any trepidation she was feeling. Completely trusting Dr. Hobbs, it was easy for her to answer, "Yes, okay. What do we do?"

"First, I'll help you move into a deep, relaxed state. Then I'll assist you in traveling back through your past as we try to trace the root of the problems impacting your present life. Sometimes to go forward, we need to go backward. If you can release the emotions you've been holding on to since your dad's death, it can be very cathartic. We'll aim to discover those emotions while you're in a trance-like state—not unconscious, more like deep meditation."

"Oh, like a hypnotic state, right? I studied hypnosis during my freshman year of college and even tried self-hypnosis a few times."

"Good, then you have an understanding of what it will feel like. Some people have intense recall and others don't. The deep state of relaxation helps you access your subconscious memories. But know that you're always in control of what's going on. You'll be able to communicate with me if the emotional pain gets too great."

"Okay, I understand. But it's late. I imagine you want to get home. Do you want to do this during our next session instead?"

Dr. Hobbs glanced at his watch. "I've got time now. I'm game if you are."

"I am."

"Okay, then. Make yourself comfortable on the sofa over there. Loosen any tight or constricting clothing. Close your eyes and concentrate on your breathing."

When Sophie had done what he'd said, Dr. Hobbs began. "Breathe in to the count of four, hold it to the count of seven, and breathe out to the count of eight. Ready? Breathe in—one, two, three, four. Now hold—one, two, three, four, five, six, seven. Now blow out—one, two, three, four, five, six, seven, eight. ... Keep breathing just like that as I talk.

"Imagine a pure white light above your head, a spiritual light protecting you. Let it come in through the top of your head ... through your brain ... let it flow down your spine, protecting you and filling your entire body. With every breath you take, you feel more and more relaxed. You're so relaxed.

"Now imagine you're in an elevator on the tenth floor. The elevator is slowly going down to the ground floor. Slowly, slowly. With every floor you pass, you'll go deeper and deeper into a state of relaxation. Deeper and deeper. Down, down. Every muscle in your body is relaxed and ready to go deeper and deeper into a state of complete relaxation.

"You're going down in the elevator—ten, nine, eight, seven, six, five. You're deeply relaxed, going deeper and deeper—four, three, two, one. You're in a deep sleep in a place of peace and calm."

Sophie was aware of feeling relaxed, of experiencing a transitioning sensation in her body. Her eyelids felt heavy and her facial muscles slackened, causing her jaw to open slightly.

"You'll remember everything that happens in this session when you awaken. You'll always hear my voice as a friendly one. ... Imagine a movie screen in your mind. On the screen, project a big clock with an hour and minute hand. Watch the clock go backward in time. The clock starts at the number twelve and moves backward as you drift back in time to your childhood. When the clock reaches one, you'll go to a pleasant childhood memory and remember it in detail. Twelve ... eleven ... ten ... nine ... eight ... seven ... six ... five ... four ... three ... two ... one.

"Look around you and tell me where you are."

"I'm back in my house in Wauwatosa, Wisconsin."

"What year is it?"

"Nineteen sixty-three. It's my birthday. I'm eleven."

"How do you know it's your birthday?"

"The dining room is decorated. My mom decorates for birthdays. Pretty red and white crepe paper streamers are coiled around the banister and hanging from the ceiling with lots of balloons. My favorite cake is sitting on the table—a confetti angel food cake with pink icing. The milkman delivered a quart of chocolate milk for me. Something they do—free chocolate milk on your birthday. Wrapped packages with red polka dots on white paper and red ribbon are sitting on the table."

"How are you feeling?"

"I feel really happy."

"Why are you feeling so happy?"

"I feel special."

"Okay, you're now going to go back in time again. Watch the hands on the clock go backward from twelve to one. When you're at one, go to a day of significance around your father's death. Twelve … eleven … ten … nine … eight … seven … six … five … four … three … two … one.

"You're there. If you feel any anxiety, detach from your body and float above it and watch."

"I see the date on the screen: March 1958."

"Where are you?"

"It looks like a funeral home."

"Tell me what's happening."

"My brother and I are both here. My mom is sitting on a chair, crying into a handkerchief. She's wearing a black dress and a hat with a veil. She has black gloves on. The room is filled with bouquets of flowers. There are too many white carnations, and the scent makes me feel sick. Lots of people are crying. Grandma is crying too, and it feels really sad. A lady is patting me on the head. She's also dressed in black with a black hat. She's saying, 'Your daddy is gone now. He's gone to live with the angels. Poor little girl with no daddy. Poor little sad girl.'

"I see my daddy in his casket, and I'm confused. I don't understand what happened and why everyone is crying. His eyes are closed, and he doesn't wake up. Oh … I'm leaving this place. I'm floating."

"Let yourself go with it."

"I'm in a new place now."

"Describe where you are."

"I see nature all around me—trees, a river, and clothes lying on a rock. I see naked women washing themselves in the water. They're laughing and talking."

"Look down at your feet. Are you wearing shoes?"

"I can't see myself."

"Step out of the body and look down. What do you see?"

"I see a girl with dark, braided hair. She's me. I'm washing myself in the stream. I'm about eighteen. I have a swollen belly. I'm pregnant, and I'm feeling sad."

"Why are you feeling sad?"

"Oh, I'm back in the body now. I'm sad because I'm lonely. My husband died in a skirmish, my mother and father are dead, and I'm ready to give birth. I have others in the tribe to help me, but I wanted my husband and mother and father with me. They all left me alone."

"Move forward in time. What do you see?"

"I'm eating a meal with a utensil made of seashells and wood."

"Move forward again. What do you see?"

"I'm pounding corn, and other women around me are doing beadwork."

"Go to the most important event of that life. One … two … three—you're there." Dr. Hobbs snapped his fingers. "What's happening to you? What are you aware of?"

"I just delivered my baby boy. I'm hearing an indigenous language spoken, but I'm actually comprehending it in English. His name sounds like Naantam. In English, 'wolf'—Mystic Wolf."

"Do you recognize that boy in this life?"

"Yes, it's Jonathan. I'm his mother."

"Move forward in time again. What do you see?"

"He's a wonder. I'm always happy when he's around me, and life is full. He likes to hunt deer with the men and go out in the canoe to fish. We're very close and I adore him. He's my life, my joy, my everything."

"Move forward and backward through time as you wish. Tell me what you see and feel."

"I'm so happy and content. I'm beading with a group of women. Mystic Wolf is a young man now, and he's preparing to go out on a hunt with the men."

"Move ahead."

"He's going to marry a beautiful woman. I'm happy he's such a strong and wonderful man."

"Move ahead to a significant event in that life—an event that connects to this life."

"I have an important role because I'm a medicine woman, and I spend large parts of my day creating medicines and potions to heal those who are sick and in pain. I make my medicines with herbs and plants. I'm gathering mullein to make a sweetened syrup from the boiled root to give to the children with coughs.

"There's a stabbing pain in my heart. It's a shocking, urgent pain, and I know at once it's Mystic Wolf. His spirit is before me. I sense him, and I know his spirit has left his body. I find his body, facedown in a pool of water, and I rush to him. I turn him over, and his body is empty of life. He's no longer with me."

Sophie started writhing on the couch, tears flowing from her closed eyes.

"I can't bear it. I'm wailing and screaming like a wounded animal. I can't breathe."

Gasping for air, Sophie tore at her blouse, as though she were trying to free her heart so it could beat again.

"Oh no, oh no!" she screamed. "He's been shot. My boy is dead. I'll never let go of his lifeless body, I'll never release him. Kill me now! Take me too! Please take me too! My son, my son, my son. *Ko.wama.nes.* I love you, I love you, Mystic Wolf. Without you, I cease to exist. I can't bear any more."

Dr. Hobbs spoke loudly, so Sophie would hear him above her sobs. "Sophie, listen to me. Rise up and watch the scene from outside your body. Detach and float above the scene. One, two, three—now." He snapped his fingers again.

Sophie calmed down rapidly. Her arms went to her sides again, her respiration improved, she stopped crying.

When she was breathing steadily, he asked, "What's happening now?"

"I'm holding him to my heart. Others hear me screaming and come to lead us away. I can't go on. I'm so lonely and depressed. I'll never have more children—the pain of the loss is just too great. I've lost everyone who means anything to me. My mother and my father, my husband, and now my son. My beloved son. I don't want to live without him, so I give up on life. I will myself to die." Sophie shook her head slowly from side to side. "I don't want to see any more of this."

"Leave there now and come back to consciousness here. You've lived through the pain and can now leave it in the past. When I count back from five, you'll be wide awake and will no longer feel the pain and grief. You will remember everything you just experienced, but you will not feel the pain and grief."

He leaned over and tapped her forehead between her eyebrows. "Five, four, three—eyes are open. … Two, one—you're awake and feeling refreshed and pain-free." Dr. Hobbs snapped his fingers one last time.

Sophie immediately sat up and gestured wildly as words rushed from her mouth. "Oh my God, Dr. Hobbs. I can't even express what just happened." Flushed, she started pacing the floor to release some of her energy. "That was one of the most powerful experiences I've ever had in my life! I knew it was me the whole time. I felt it. I lived it. That was me. I knew it was Jonathan too! … Oh my God, it explains so many things to me on so many levels. Wow, that was unbelievable! I felt *every* emotion."

Dr. Hobbs poured some water from a nearby pitcher into a glass. "Here." He handed the glass to her. "Drink this. I was thinking we'd go back to your father's death to see what we could uncover there, but then you unexpectedly transitioned to a past life. Apparently, that was the experience requiring the soul healing. Do you remember everything?"

"I do. If I hadn't just lived through this myself, I never would have believed it. It was me experiencing a past life. It explains so much to me, pulls together all the isolated puzzle pieces in my life. My affinity for American Indian culture. My otherworldly connection to Jonathan. My feelings of abandonment. My fear of having children. A husband who died in that life, a husband who died in this life. Everything Jonathan said to me makes sense now—I mean, I understood what he was telling me, but now I understand it from *my* side. I think I released a powerful energy blockage or something. I have this incredibly free feeling. This regression tied together so many loose ends for me. I'm blown away."

"I'm also thinking it's possible that you and your father made a soul agreement prior to your birth to work out some of your issues," Dr. Hobbs offered. "He may have agreed to come to Earth for a short period of time to trigger your abandonment issues in this life to help you on the path to your soul healing."

"That would change my whole perspective on his death—that he died to help my soul heal instead of leaving me for no reason."

"Is that the takeaway you're feeling right now?"

"Well, I'm sure much more will come to me as I go back over all this in my mind, but at the moment what I'm feeling is that we're all interconnected, and although the role we play in any one life ends, the soul is eternal. Jonathan's soul came back to be with me in this life, and since that's true, probably other people in my life now were with me in other times and places. Like Lizzie or David … maybe Neil … maybe even you. Jonathan and I are together again. I can't believe what that has shown me—that the spirit in us always lives. The regression put so much into perspective for me. I can't wait to share this experience with Lizzie. She's actually been reading about this topic, and I'm sure this will fascinate her."

"You were ready to learn that now. You weren't before. Our existence is a vast web of energy connecting everything. How do you feel, Sophie?"

"I'm giddy, cleansed, full of joy! And also a little hungry!"

"I have a great idea. It's seven-thirty. Why don't we go grab a bite? I'm hungry too, and we can continue talking about this over dinner."

"Together?"

He smiled. "Yes, together. My treat. There's this great Italian restaurant around the corner—we can walk there from here. They make their own noodles and simmer their Bolognese sauce for hours. All we'll need is two forks and a bottle of Chianti. Their pasta is almost as good as my own."

"You cook?" she asked, surprised but delighted by this peek into his private life.

"I do. Italian is my specialty."

*

The restaurant was quaint and cozy, and the tantalizing smell of oregano and sausage permeated the air. They sat in the back patio area under cascading grapevines and white twinkle lights. Dr. Hobbs ordered a salad, pappardelle pasta, and red wine.

Sophie scooped up a spoonful of sauce, blew on it, and took a taste. "This is delicious. It's like there's a little old grandmother back in the kitchen ladling it out. What a day this has been! My head's still going a mile a minute. Thank you for giving me that incredible experience. I feel like life is a school, that our souls evolve as we learn through various lifetimes. I've read so much about reincarnation this year because of Jonathan, but now that I've actually had a firsthand experience myself, it all feels so magnified. When you talked me through the regression, it felt like being in a waking dream state, only the feelings in the dream were so vivid, so real. It's weird, Mystic Wolf didn't look or sound like Jonathan at all, but I knew him instantly."

"Everyone has a certain energy vibration, and we can identify them by that vibration," Dr. Hobbs said. "Kind of like a fingerprint. I think it was helpful that you'd worked with self-hypnosis in the past—it usually takes a bit more work to get a person into past-life recall. Your experience was so spontaneous. Remembering past lives requires a thinning of the veil to tap into the past. We're all on a journey, and when we incarnate again and again, the soul can become splintered from some of the traumas experienced. The result can be that part of your energy gets stuck in the past. When that happens, it impacts your current life. Going back and living through the experience can spontaneously release the trapped energy so it no longer interferes."

Sophie liked hearing him talk. "I read it's common to travel through different lives with the same group of souls—'soul companions' or 'soul families.' I think that's incredible, don't you? Loving the same souls through all of eternity, healing together, learning our lessons, expanding our consciousness, balancing our energies—all together. Even though the soul stays the same, our relationships play out differently from life to life."

Dr. Hobbs smiled and slowly sipped his Chianti. "I do think it's incredible."

"And it's so comforting, too," Sophie added, biting into a crusty piece of garlic bread and waiting to speak again until after she swallowed. "Because that means we're always being reunited. Plus, it plays into my sense of fairness. I worked with kids with some pretty serious disabilities. I always thought how unfair it would be if they only got one crack at life and it was such a difficult one. Or think of the babies who live only a few days and die. It makes sense to me that this could be just one life among many for them where they're learning specific things or teaching others."

The good wine, the good food, the good conversation—it all blended together into one of those intoxicating moments in life for Sophie. Feeling cleansed to her core, she wanted nothing more than to harness that dynamic moment and preserve it forever.

Dr. Hobbs leaned back in his chair and grinned. "And with that, dear Sophie, I think you no longer need to see me in a professional capacity. You've made a major breakthrough."

Sophie put her fork down and stared at him. "If I had known this was going to lead here, I wouldn't have done it. I don't think I can go without my regular dose of guidance from you."

"We don't have to stop seeing each other," he suggested. "We can transition the relationship to a friendship." He extended his hand to her. "Call me Matthew."

She extended her hand back and they shook. "Hi, Matthew. Pleased to meet you. But now I'm wondering if we perhaps met in a past life."

In answer, Matthew only smiled and said, "Let's take a walk out on the pier."

He paid the bill, and they strolled across the street to where the waves were pummeling the pilings—the beaches were the real jewels in La Jolla. The night sky was black with a dimpled moon hanging like a lopsided smile. They stood on the pier watching the surf crash against the rocks, the spray from the breaking waves dampening their clothing.

Matthew placed his hand on Sophie's shoulder. "I have a suggestion for you. You want to hear it?"

"Of course I do."

"The final step in letting go of Neil is to forgive him. You're holding on to him with your negative energies. When you're ready, you need to forgive him. I have a sense his spirit needs that. Although it will help him, the forgiveness is for you. It releases the pain and anguish in you. Forgiveness is a choice you make."

"I think you're right, as usual, and I'm ready. I have an idea of what I'm going to do."

"What's that?"

"I'll tell you when I've done it, okay?"

"Okay."

Matthew walked Sophie back to her car. "I rather like our new relationship status. What do you think?"

"I know we spent a great deal of time tonight in the past, but looking into the future, I see a special friendship ahead of us." Sophie slowly got her car keys out of her purse, seeming hesitant. "Matthew, I have one more gift for you. I haven't been sure if I should give it to you or not, but now seems like the right time."

Sophie unlocked her car, reached into the backseat, and handed him a bag. Her eyes stayed locked on his face, wanting to see if he'd understand her unspoken message.

He pulled a box of chocolates from the bag.

"It's a December day around dusk, back in the Midwest … twenty-some years ago … an old blue VW Bug on a snowy hill."

Matthew nodded his head slightly in acknowledgement. He reached down and squeezed Sophie's hand. "Night, Sophie," he said. "Drive safely."

As she slid into the driver's seat, Sophie turned to look at him. "Hey, Matthew …"

"Yes?"

"Have a happy birthday."

"Thanks. I just did," he said.

CHAPTER 31
NEIL

I WISH I DIDN'T keep coming back to my hometown to see my dad, but sometimes I need to get away from the garage. It's weird enough to come back to the town you grew up in when you're an adult, but it's even weirder when you're dead. I almost think he can feel my presence whenever I'm near him because he'll do things like suddenly pick up my high school graduation picture and stare at it while tears well up in his eyes.

I'm sorry, Dad. I'm sorry I caused you so much pain. I wanted to escape my own pain, but the suffering is still there. And to make matters worse, I inflicted it on you. I wish I could have your forgiveness for what I did to you—I can feel you thinking about me. Please know this: I regret causing so much chaos in your life.

When I was alive, it seemed as though I lived in a state of constant blackouts, never remembering the messes I created all around me. Sometimes I didn't even believe Sophie when she told me the things I did, like the time I flew to North Carolina for a job interview. I don't even know what happened then, because I have only snapshots of individual moments from that trip, nothing linking them together. Apparently, on my way to the interview, I got rip-roaring drunk and fell down the escalator and tore up my face. If it wasn't for the physical evidence like a row of black stitches going down the entire length of my face and no recall of how the hell they got there, as well as a huge hospital bill, I'm not sure I ever would have believed that particular story.

Sophie was my memory. She was the one who carried around the details of things that happened, and she resented me for living in an unconscious state, never remembering what went on. I didn't experience the emotions that went along with my awful behaviors, so I couldn't quite understand her rage, pain, fear, and the overwhelming sense of aloneness she experienced because of me. She also wanted to forget, yet she couldn't. I wonder if she ever will.

It may seem like I'm floundering in this vast nothingness, but I don't think I am because I've learned so much. As I observe the world from this perspective, I see there are things happening in everyone's life much more significant than a bunch of random acts having no meaning to them. There's this magnificent interconnectedness to everything and everyone. It kind of blows me away.

When you're going along day after day, just living your life, your viewpoint is so different—it's like when you're driving a car, and you see only the road ahead through the windshield. From where I'm sitting now, though, I see so much more. I can actually see where the road is going, where it might split or even stop. I can see the obstacles ahead. That's how it is when we live a human life—it's like looking through the limited view of a windshield, and we're seeing only part of the whole picture. And even though we can't see the full scope of our lives, there's always guidance present if people learn to listen to their intuition, the voice of their soul.

Oh, Dad, now you're lighting a candle and setting it next to my picture while saying a prayer for me. I'd do things differently if I could change them, I really would. You were a good father to me. You didn't let me down. You did everything you could for me, and you're not to blame for what happened. I'm sorry, please forgive me.

Wait … I think you might be hearing my thoughts. Yes, you are! You're saying you love me and you forgive me. Dad, those are the most powerful words ever. Thank you. I love you. Thank you for your forgiveness.

Thank you.

Chapter 32
The Astral Plane

Ruach: Great news, Malach. Neil Beaumont is starting to get what it's all about. His father just did a pretty great thing. Forgiveness is powerful.

Malach: Good. I predict we'll be seeing him come home soon.

CHAPTER 33
SEPTEMBER 12, 1992

S OPHIE WOKE UP thirty minutes before her alarm went off, feeling excited about her plan. With David and Lizzie volunteering at the Apple Days Festival in Julian this weekend, she'd asked Jonathan if he'd like to accompany her on a day trip instead of manning the booth with them. He'd happily agreed.

After securing him in his car seat, they took off, heading fifty miles east of San Diego to the Cuyamaca Mountains area. Sophie wrapped her navy-blue cardigan closer to her body as the cool breeze made its way through the open car window. As she drove, she noticed more volume than usual on the road, a stream of cars no doubt also on their way to Julian, since one of the highlights of the small town was this two-day festival of music, dancing, contests, and fresh, homemade apple pie.

The sky was a crystalline blue, and the clouds were puffy and round—a perfect day for a leisurely drive into the country. After enjoying an hour and a half of travel games and songs, Sophie pulled into the parking lot of the Plainsbrook Cemetery, impressed by the peaceful, dignified setting. She unbuckled Jonathan from his seat, and he climbed from the back in his jeans, sweatshirt, and baseball cap worn backward. Sophie, too, was dressed for the outdoors in her typical blue jeans and a retro pair of loafers she'd found at a consignment shop.

Hand in hand, they walked between two enormous wrought-iron gates, entering an area where the grass was lush and green. The view from here, set high up on the hillside and overlooking a heart-shaped lake, was pretty enough to inspire a poem. A gentle wind rustled through the row of trees lining the walking path.

From their vantage point, they could see row upon row of graves. As they strolled through the land of the dead and buried, they noticed numerous bouquets of bright flowers left to honor loved ones. A group of people was sitting near one gravestone having a picnic, maybe to celebrate a significant date. Others seemed to be there for the peace and the beauty of the place, to walk their dogs, or to jog somewhere tranquil. They slowly roamed around the large plot of land with many winding pathways and stairs.

"Where are we going, Toffee?" Jonathan asked. His pants were too short already, a sure sign that he was growing way too fast. Curls of blonde hair peeked out from his Padres cap.

He needs a haircut. He's so beautiful, people often mistake him for a girl, Sophie thought as she smiled down at him.

"People are having picnics, are we going to?"

"No, I have a different surprise for you after we finish. You'll like it."

"What is it?"

She threw her head back and let out a hearty laugh. "Not telling." She loved to tease him.

"Where are we?"

"This is a cemetery, Bunkies." Lizzie had come up with his nickname— Sophie had no idea why. "This is a place where people who have died are buried."

"Are we going to see dead people?"

"You won't see them. Their bodies are buried in the ground."

Jonathan squatted down on the grass and picked some lingering dandelions. They continued walking along a quaint cobblestone pathway among elegant sculptures and relaxing water fountains until they came to a wishing well. It was an ordinary well, standing slightly off the path, made of stacked stones, with a cedar slanted roof and a wooden bucket.

Sophie handed Jonathan a penny. "Toss your penny into the wishing well and make a wish."

"Like it's my birthday?"

"Yes, like that."

He leaned over the well, tossed the penny inside, and waited to hear its gentle splash in the water.

"What did you wish for?"

"I wished that Mommy and Daddy wouldn't go away so much."

"And we already know that wish will come true because Mommy retired from that job, remember?"

He nodded happily as he pointed to the coin purse in her hand. "Now you make a wish, Toffee."

She got out another penny and tossed it in the well.

"What did you wish?" He cocked his head, looking at her intently for her answer.

She brushed a stray curl out of his left eye. "I told you about Neil—the man I used to be married to? Well, I wished that he would forgive himself, as I have. I feel him around me all the time, and he needs to move on to wherever he should go."

"Why are the bodies buried in the ground?"

"Once we die, we don't need the bodies. It's hard to explain these things in a simple way, but I'll try. There's an energy inside our bodies that gives us life, and it moves on to a different place after we die."

"Grandma's dog died. He didn't move or bark anymore. She buried him in the ground. I didn't like that. We can't see the dead people, so why are we here?"

They started walking on the path again. "I need to talk to Neil's spirit, and he's buried here. I want to help him."

"You get sad when you talk about him."

"I know. But I'm not going to be sad about him any longer after today." She spotted a wooden picnic table up ahead. "Want to sit down for a while? I brought a snack. Are you hungry?"

"I'm hungry."

They sat side by side at the table, thoughtfully munching apple slices.

Jonathan pointed to the small collection of wildflowers peeking out from Sophie's tote. "Why did you bring flowers for Neil if he can't see them?"

"This cemetery, the headstones, flowers, and funerals—they're all for the people who are left behind when someone dies. It helps them feel less sad. I didn't have to come here to talk to Neil. I could have talked to him anywhere. But this place feels nice. It's so peaceful here, and I can think easier when it's quiet. Just Neil's body is in the ground because the spirit that was inside him moved out of it."

"Will we see his spirit?"

"No, we won't. It's invisible to us. But this is still a good place for me to do what I need to do."

"Where do spirits go?"

"I believe that when people die, they usually go to another place. But I think Neil's spirit stayed here on Earth. He died in a way that was very sad for me and his family. Sometimes I can feel he's still here. I'm trying to help him so he goes where he's meant to go."

"It's good to help people. Can I help him too?"

"You are, just by being here and thinking good things about him. We all come to this Earth to have experiences, and through those experiences, we learn, like being in school. I don't expect you to understand this, but one of the lessons I'm supposed to learn is to forgive. Neil chose to be with me in this lifetime to help teach me this lesson. I was very angry with him. But now I've forgiven him, and I need to let him know that it's time for his spirit to move on."

"Toffee, don't let your heart be too mad."

Sophie bent down and kissed his cheek. She was astounded at his ability to understand complicated concepts. *Such a wise old soul,* she thought.

"You're one smart, sweet boy. You're exactly right. When you think someone's done something wrong to you, you might feel angry. When you forgive, you let your heart fill up with love instead of anger. I want to free Neil's consciousness. Setting it free is like letting a balloon loose as it floats away into the sky."

"What's that?"

"Consciousness? Honey, it's so hard to explain some of these big words. ... Um, okay, it's like this. While we were walking, were you thinking about your heart beating?"

"No."

"But now that I'm talking about it, you're thinking about it and feeling it, aren't you?"

"I feel it when I put my hand here." He placed his hand over his heart.

"Consciousness is like that—like being awake. When you're asleep, you're not aware of what's going on in the world."

Sophie could tell by his face that he was confused. He was silent for a few moments, then, "So only his body is in the ground, huh?"

"Yes, only his body. His spirit needs to go to another place. It's a place we can't see. I came here to help free Neil's spirit to go there."

Sophie pulled a map of the cemetery from her bag and pointed to a spot. "Look, Bunkies, we're here on the map"—she pointed to another spot—"and Neil's grave is over here. We need to take a right turn over there. It's a good thing we have this map, because I wouldn't remember how to find his grave otherwise. You ready?"

Jonathan tossed their empty plastic bags in the trash can, then took Sophie's hand to resume walking. After a few minutes, they found the grave. Neil's father had purchased a fairly large headstone of solid granite, upright style with a serp top. Jonathan stood and watched inquisitively as Sophie kneeled in front of the stone.

The corners of her lips turned up. There was no sadness. There was no anger. Jonathan stood next to her, placing his hand on her shoulder, as if he knew it would keep her calm and grounded.

Sophie spoke out loud. "Neil, it's me, and this little guy is Jonathan."

"Hi, Neil," Jonathan said. "Can you hear me?"

"He can hear you. He hears your thoughts." She paused for a moment. "We're here visiting you today because I have an important message for you, and I'm finally ready to send it.

"I think your spirit is still here on Earth. But it's time for you to let go now and forgive yourself. I forgive you, now you should too. Things happen for a reason to help us grow and learn. I was angry with you when you took your life, but I realize you didn't love yourself enough while you were alive. It's time to love yourself. Forgive yourself.

"I'm fine. Go now and be free. It's time to move on, Neil. I forgive you. I'm sending you love. Forgive yourself."

When she finished speaking, Jonathan tapped her on the shoulder as she remained kneeling. "Toffee, did your heart fill up with love?"

"It did, Bunkies, it did."

She stood, picked him up, and hugged him. "How much do I love you?"

"More than I'll ever know." He flashed her his cherubic smile.

"Since we finished that important task, we're going to do something really cool now. I'm going to show you how to do a grave rubbing using Neil's stone." She reached into her tote again. "Look, I brought rice paper and crayons. You put the paper over the engraved words and rub it with the crayon. I did this on my grandma's gravestone. Don't mark on the stone, just the paper. What color crayon do you want to use?"

"Blue. My favorite."

Sophie taped the paper on the granite stone and showed him how to color across the engravings. "Watch me, then you do it. Hold the crayon to the side, like this. That's his name I colored. Now you try it."

She handed him the blue crayon, and he vigorously rubbed it across the paper over Neil's epitaph, careful not to get any on the actual stone itself.

"This is fun. But what are these numbers for? One, nine, five, zero and then one, nine, eight, seven?"

"I see you and Mommy have been practicing your numbers. The first group of numbers is the year Neil was born, the second group is the year he died."

He pointed to the dash between the dates. "What's that line?"

Sophie took a deep breath before answering. "That line stands for the whole life you live here on Earth. That's the most important part of all. Everyone lives and everyone dies. But the thing that is different for everyone is their story. That little line between the numbers is Neil's story. That's how we live on, through our stories."

"That line is so important, I think I'll color it." He gently returned his hand to the paper, right over the dash, and rubbed the crayon over it. "I'm going to take Neil's story with me," he said. "I love stories."

Sophie stared at the innocence on his face, utterly overcome with her love for him. "Me too," she said.

"Will your spirit go away someday?"

"Yes, it will, but I hope not for a long time."

"When your body is in the ground, I'll come to talk to you. I'll bring you a Christmas tree. I'll read you stories."

"I can see you doing that. That's very sweet, honey."

"Remember last Christmas when I was with you? It was scary watching that ghost on TV."

Sophie had rolled up the gravestone rubbing when they were done with it, and Jonathan was now coloring big circles on a new piece of rice paper. Sophie started coloring with him.

"Oh, you mean *Mr. Magoo's Christmas Carol*? That was my favorite holiday show when I was a kid. I know you were scared of the ghost of Marley when he let out such a scary moan." She let out a long groan like Marley, and Jonathan giggled. "Marley's spirit was trapped on Earth by all the chains he created when he was alive."

"Does Neil have chains?"

"We don't actually have real chains like you're thinking, but our unloving thoughts can feel heavy like chains."

"I'm still hungry, Toffee."

Sophie glanced at her watch. "Remember that surprise I told you about? Well, we're going to go meet Mommy and Daddy at the Apple Days Festival for chicken pot pie for lunch and apple pie for dessert!"

"Yay! What a great day! First, we helped Neil go free. And now we get pie!"

"All days should be this great," Sophie agreed.

As they walked back to the car, sunlight danced through the trees, falling on Jonathan's hair so it appeared golden, like a miniature Greek god's. When she finished getting him settled in and turned to close the door, a brown striped butterfly landed on her shoulder, circled her head, and fluttered up into the light. Knowing that the butterfly is a symbol of transformation, she inhaled deeply and closed her eyes.

"Go home, Neil. Go home now."

CHAPTER 34
NEIL

IT'S HAPPENED. SOPHIE reached out in love. She has forgiven me, and I'm overwhelmed by that. There's a tremendous healing power in forgiveness. It's like melting an icy heart and planting a seed of love in it, then watching the seed grow and flourish.

I'm finally more at peace, and that's a fantastic feeling. Forgiveness is powerful, but so is gratitude. If I had focused on the things I was grateful for instead of what wasn't present in my life, I think I'd still be living my life on Earth, as Neil, in my body.

Living. Breathing. Experiencing.

Going back in a time machine to my younger years would be so interesting because there are many things I'd do differently. Even the smallest action is powerful, like the simple act of smiling at someone at the right time. It could change their day.

It's time to forgive myself and move on. Sophie learned to forgive me, so I can too. The power of her forgiveness and her message of love fill me.

Thank you, Sophie.

CHAPTER 35
THE ASTRAL PLANE

Malach: Good for you, Sophie. You did it. You forgave Neil, and now Neil is free. And good for you, too, Neil. Now come home where you're loved. Float into the light.

Pneuma: You were right. He's on his way.

CHAPTER 36
NEIL

MESSAGE RECEIVED.

The light is beckoning me to come, but this time, I'm not scared. It feels liberating, fluid, and balanced—free of negativity and obstacles. The warmth of the compassionate light surrounds me, and a magnet-like force is sucking me into a giant vortex of energy, followed by a sensation like I'm floating, drifting like a feather falling through the air.

What's so cool is that I remember everything—all the things I had forgotten when I went to Earth. With incredible awe, I find I'm instantly flooded with a vast amount of knowledge.

One more thing I now understand: There isn't a place up in the sky that's "heaven," and there isn't a place down below that's "hell," hot with fire and a pitchfork-wielding devil. The universe is filled with many dimensions, and the location of each is no different from the Earth plane.

Imagine this: We think we live on this planet alone, but we live in a range of frequencies. There's a whole slew of different vibrations out there. When we live our physical lives, we're tuned in to a specific frequency similar to a certain station on the radio. That's our world, our environment. Like we're tuned in to 91.2 FM WKT Earth. Our five senses are limiting, and we don't pick up on all the frequencies out there, but they're all around in the same space as our bodies. We can't see them or feel them until we tune in to them at the proper frequency. So the ironic thing is, I was never going to a place called "hell." Death is simply a change to a new frequency, a new dimension.

I'm feeling this overwhelming connection with love. I am the love. I'm vibrating faster now, moving into a state where I don't feel judgment. I don't feel fear. I now understand that death doesn't sever love. I'm not afraid of what others think—I'm at peace, no competition, no coveting. It keeps washing over me in waves.

My vibrational frequency is increasing, the warmth and brilliance of the light has enveloped me, and I feel the unconditional love of being with a strong, magnanimous presence. The spirit guides Sophie told me about are here. I'm a bird released from its cage, light and weightless. I'm tuning in to a new frequency now.

At last, I'm home.

CHAPTER 37
SEPTEMBER 25/26, 1992

A S OFTEN HAPPENS with Southern California weather, the cool streak of fall-like, crisp air was fleeting, and the summer heat returned with a vengeance. Sophie's little cottage felt hot, so she cranked up the air conditioner in the kitchen window a few degrees.

A sensation of change filled the air. The artistic side of Sophie's brain wanted to have a party, so she decided to paint, realizing she hadn't put brush to canvas for quite some time. She pulled out her easel, placed a blank canvas on it, and squirted a few blobs of oil paint onto her palette. She stood in front of the large, white canvas, envisioning a composition. She felt free to paint herself a new life. She boldly dunked her fan brush in the crimson red paint on the palette and made crisscrossing strokes on the canvas. Life was about to change—she could sense it.

She mixed her own colors and outlined her own design. In front of her canvas, she used her brushstrokes to blur the boundaries between tragedy and a place of inner peace. Her poem was in the strokes, strong and resolute.

She got lost in the task for about an hour, at which point she looked up to take a break. A red circle around tomorrow's date on the calendar hanging on the refrigerator reminded her that she had a wedding cake to finish.

Marion, the bride-to-be, was the kind of person who had a knack for putting people at ease, and Sophie found herself instantly liking her and wanting to create an exceptional cake for her. Every now and then, one of her clients would invite her to stay for a party or wedding reception after she set up the cake, but she never did. This time, when she received an engraved invitation in the mail to attend the wedding, she thought, *It's time I start being more social.*

Setting her easel aside and hastily tidying up her paint supplies to prep the kitchen for the next steps in the baking process, she let her mind wander over her emotional journey over the past several years. It had taken time, but as Dr. Hobbs said, she'd weathered the storm, happy and relieved to have come out on the other side. The healing process had allowed her to feel excitement and joy again—emotions that she had learned to repress.

"The Freeing of Neil," as she called the whole journey, opened a space in her heart—one that had been blocked before. She now had room to develop other relationships. As she thought about new people she might meet at the wedding, Sophie realized she wasn't just glad she'd decided to go, she was actually looking forward to it. When was the last time she'd gotten dressed up? The last time she'd been out after dark with adults? The feeling that something good was going to happen was palpable.

Sophie picked up her to-do list and reviewed it carefully—the precise timeline she'd constructed to keep the project on track. The sugar pieces for the cake decorations took the longest, so she'd started in on them first. Each piece had to be formed and dried overnight, which had taken the better part of last week. This particular cake would have an unusually large number of sugar flowers, so there were trays and trays of them sitting in the Cohens' fridge in their garage. Being able to use the large freezer in there as well had been a godsend for her business, as she was able to bake and store her cakes ahead of time. For Marion's cake, four layers were carefully wrapped and stowed—carrot, marble, dark chocolate, and banana—and Sophie set off for the garage to go retrieve them now, so they could defrost while she was out.

Next on her list was clothes shopping. Sophie had no choice—she had nothing nice enough to wear to an evening wedding that currently fit her. She'd never been a fan of shopping as most women were—she didn't know why—preferring comfort over style. But she'd promised herself weeks ago that she would go to the effort to buy a new dress, which would keep her committed to attending the reception in case she started waffling on the idea. The issue was: Where to look? Lizzie would have been delighted to drag her around Fashion Valley Mall, trying on dress after dress, but Sophie wanted to keep the process short and simple—she had to get back to finish up the wedding cake.

Sophie drove herself to the immense mall, looking in several windows before entering a shop where an angular saleslady quickly emerged from behind the counter to assist her. She wore reading glasses dangling from a chain, the skin on her neck hanging in soft folds like a shar-pei, her face pinched and pale. Nothing she picked out for Sophie from the racks of cocktail dresses felt right to her in any way, so she moved on to another store … and yet another … before giving up and heading home—not at all confident of her shopping skills and wishing she'd brought Lizzie along after all.

But on the way home, Sophie remembered a vintage store on the corner of Elm and Date. Pulling up in front of the shop, there was her dress in the window. She hoped it was her size because it looked perfect. It was a 1950s-style, flirty, sleeveless dress, soft petal pink in color with small, frosted mint-green polka dots. The dress had a sweeping skirt and a flattering V-neck, which was sexy without being too revealing. The formfitting bodice was shaped to give off a sensual, feminine look. The cotton material would be perfect for a late-summer night, and Sophie knew she'd find just the right accessories to match if she raided Lizzie's closet. She gave a small prayer of gratitude that they wore the same shoe size.

Sophie sighed with relief in the dressing room when the dress fit her. *It was meant to be,* she thought. After paying the salesclerk, she happily headed home with her treasure to start in on bowls and bowls of specialty frosting.

The next afternoon, the cake was ready for delivery, and Sophie was ready too—jewelry, handbag, and pointy pumps compliments of Lizzie. When she greeted Jerry at the door, he let out a low whistle. "Hot babe!" he exclaimed. "I don't think I've ever seen you in heels and a dress. Looking good, girl. Something tells me you aren't riding with me in the van this time."

"Not this time, no. I've been invited to the wedding, so I'll follow behind you in my own car." Sophie took one last glance in the hall mirror, twirling the unfamiliar curls of her auburn hair with her index finger. "Thanks for the boost of confidence, though. I needed it."

Once the cake was safely loaded in the refrigerated van, they were ready to head to the venue, jointly hoping for a smooth ride. "See you there, Soph," Jerry called out the window with a wave.

The wedding was being held at a large estate in Rancho Santa Fe, a wealthy part of the county. The backyard was beautifully arranged with more than a hundred white folding chairs fanning out in an arc, encircling a decorated canopy. The alcove in the garden area, surrounded by greenery on three sides, had been dedicated just for the cake. White roses filled two golden Grecian urns flanking the entrance to the space, and miniature white lights cascaded down the corners of the alcove forming a dreamy effect. To truly showcase the cake, a large circular table was centered in the middle of the area, draped with a shimmering silver-white cloth falling gently to the floor.

Jerry successfully maneuvered the cake into place as directed by the wedding coordinator, which left only the finishing touches for Sophie. Jerry watched her as she discreetly retrieved her pastry bag of icing, tending to some minor repairs needed due to a bit of a bumpy transit. Guests started arriving early for the ceremony, peeking in on her work as she finally positioned the cake topper into place.

"You outdid yourself with this one, Soph. I think it's the most beautiful one yet. Let me just snap a few photos for your cake book, and then I'll be on my way." Servers were circling the grounds with platters of hors d'oeuvres and drinks, and when Jerry was done cataloging the cake for posterity, he plucked two glasses of pink champagne from a silver tray. "Let's toast with some bubbly—which matches your dress, by the way—to celebrate your latest achievement."

Sophie accepted the glass and took a sip. "Mmm, so refreshing and good. Thanks, Jerry—not just for this, but for everything you do to help me. I don't think I'd even be able to operate this business without you."

"My pleasure. Have fun tonight." He winked at her. "You deserve it. I'm going to head out now."

Sophie blew him a kiss and then turned to conduct her final inspection of her work. The bride had wanted colorful, and that's what she'd gotten: yellow and white daisies, red roses, purple violets, blue forget-me-nots, and green bells of Ireland.

Suddenly, a familiar, smoky voice came from a man behind her. "Are you stealing a taste of the frosting?" She spun around to find a specimen straight out of an Armani ad, dressed to the nines and smelling of a marvelous cologne.

"Matthew!" Even as a blanket of comfort enfolded her at the sight of his handsome face, she couldn't help but look him over head to toe, in a smart beige linen suit—ideal for the occasion, she thought—with a light blue shirt and a pastel yellow and blue striped tie. He looked casual but suave, confident, and romantic. It had been a long, long time since she'd flirted, but she found herself instinctively slipping into a role she thought she'd forgotten how to play. "No, I'm not tasting the frosting, but why don't you!" And with that, she squeezed a dollop from the icing bag onto her forefinger and playfully planted it on his upper lip. A bold move. Suggestive.

They gazed at each other intently, forming an instant intimate connection in this sea of strangers. She couldn't deny their chemistry any longer. She'd first felt it when they'd had dinner together last month, but since then, she hadn't let herself think any more about it lest he didn't feel the same.

But her worries were put at ease when, maintaining steady eye contact with her, he drew his tongue slowly over his lip and smiled. "Delicious, like you. You even look a bit like cake frosting in that pretty polka-dot dress."

"And you look quite mouthwatering yourself, if you don't mind me saying. Looks like we both took the vintage route, huh? What are you doing here? Friend of the family?"

"Yes," he answered. "Spiritual counselor to the bride."

No wonder she'd liked Marion right off the bat—evidently, they had quite a bit in common.

Sophie felt herself slowly losing her composure as sensations like lightning bolts rippled through her. She thought she'd lost her capacity to feel inflamed like this, but so unexpectedly seeing Matthew in a social setting after years of only office appointments was kindling a spark she found very pleasant. Out in the sunshine, in his dapper suit and a smile to match, he exuded a charisma that was distractingly disarming.

As he lightly touched her shoulder, she felt like she was floating in his buoyancy. "But seriously, Sophie, you look stunning," he murmured softly.

"That means a lot to me. Thank you."

"Where are you seated?"

"I have no idea."

"Well, you finish up and let me go see if I can arrange it to sit at the same table for the reception." When he walked away, the electrical charge followed in his wake.

The night was unlike any Sophie remembered. She'd never been to a wedding before that was so much fun; normally, they'd been more of an obligation. Everything was the same as at all the other weddings—the bridal party, the strewn flower petals, the vows, the kiss, the first toast—but everything was vastly different because he was there.

With stark clarity, Sophie realized that everything was better when Matthew was present.

She was like the bashful schoolgirl who'd landed a date to the prom—not just any date, but her dream date, the prom king. The lobster tasted like it came directly out of the ocean, the lights above them seemed to cast them in a fairytale land, and the music sounded like it was telling a sweet love story. The entire evening was sensual and enticing, and Sophie found herself most aroused by Matthew's ability to make her laugh—a trait of his she'd never experienced before when their relationship was purely professional.

When dinner was over, a dance floor magically appeared on the lawn, and the DJ started playing a collection of classic rock songs to cajole guests out of their seats.

"Care to dance?" Matthew asked, pushing his chair back and extending his hand to Sophie.

"Ah, you dance too? A man of many talents. It would be my pleasure."

As they moved to a slow, romantic tune, Sophie felt her inhibitions slipping away. She relaxed fully in his arms, feeling like she could live inside of him.

At that moment, she felt a change in his rhythm and she opened her eyes in alarm, afraid she'd done something to break the mood. "What's wrong?" she asked him, looking at an expression on his face that she couldn't read.

He shook his head kindly. "Nothing. Not a single thing. I didn't realize until now—until after you stopped being my client—just how much I wanted this."

"This?"

"To be with you. Until very recently, I never allowed myself to even imagine a magical night like this with you."

"Oh, Matthew, I feel the same way. I think I have for a while, actually—I was just holding back my feelings." He pulled her close to his chest as they swayed in sync.

When it was time to cut the cake, they returned to their table, gazing at each other like it was the first time they truly saw each other. Everyone raved over Sophie's creation, but nothing tasted as good to her as that moment in time.

A little while later, his finger stroking the back of her hand, he asked her, "How about I come over to your place for a nightcap?"

She didn't even hesitate to answer.

They drove back to her place in separate cars, arriving at the same time. Sophie opened the front door to her cottage, and within seconds,

Matthew was nuzzling her neck with his lips as she breathed in his intoxicating scent.

A man hadn't touched her like this for so long that the pressure of Matthew's hand on her back was like lighting a match in a forest. The flame spread throughout her body rapidly, and rather than futilely trying to resist it, she willingly let it flow through her, inviting the giddiness of release. As he kissed her lips tenderly yet firmly, they seemed to blend as one into a mixture of intimacy and instinct. In that moment, all of the heartrending loneliness in Sophie's life simply melted away.

In its place, her senses were heightened. She was in a trance where physical boundaries dissolved, time disappeared, and nothing else mattered other than his body pressed against hers.

She felt the muscles in his forearms ripple. She saw his lips turn rose-colored as they flushed with blood. She saw a future with this man. Everything fell silent. Everything was in the present moment. Breathing in sync with him felt so natural, and his energy shot directly into her core, filling her with new life and fresh vitality. Nothing could get her off this thrilling train heading to their destined outcome.

He fit her like a lock and key. With the weight of his body on hers, it happened—a feeling she hadn't experienced before. Their bodies melted together like two sticks of butter, intensely heated until they were reduced to a pool of liquid, inseparable and whole. An overwhelming feeling of unity and connection filled her. She was limitlessness.

She realized what had been right in front of her all along, for years. How had she gone through life without ever really seeing? How had she lived without the sunlight that flooded her breast now, permeating every particle of her being and radiating warmth to every part of her, body and soul?

Oh God, she thought. *I love him.*

CHAPTER 38
APRIL 3, 1993

SOPHIE SANG EVERY morning as she prepared for her day. For years following Neil's death, she hadn't really taken an interest in her appearance, but ever since her relationship with Matthew had blossomed, it had become routine again to primp and preen, to style her hair, and to apply makeup, particularly her newest favorite—a vivid pink lipstick shade called Glam. She even looked forward to using Lizzie's treadmill and had taken to running on it daily, losing the ten pounds that had kept finding her. After her success at the vintage store last fall, shopping had become fun too, and she'd recently bought herself a sexy jade-green negligee to wear to bed instead of her vast collection of patterned flannel pajamas. Glancing at herself in the mirror, she realized she no longer resembled glued-together pieces of a broken glass pitcher. She looked, and felt, whole and intact.

Sophie sat at her dressing table, deep in thought, as she brushed her hair. She missed being with Matthew when he wasn't around. The personal things he kept at her place seemed to take on a life of their own. She liked to pick them up and touch them—his razor, his cologne, his toothbrush.

His towel—of white Egyptian cotton, with gold embroidered letters—hung on a hook on the back of her bathroom door. After using it, he'd hang it there; and sometimes after her own bath, she'd take it down, smell it, and wrap it around her body. Her desire to feel close to him was, at times, unbearable. She'd imagine him whispering in her ear and lightly nibbling on her earlobe. Sophie wondered if maybe she'd had to learn some major life lessons before she was able to appreciate and feel worthy of someone like him.

She basked in the glow of his perception of her, for he saw things in her others didn't. He saw Florence Nightingale when she created her herbal tinctures and medicines, Renoir when she painted, Julia Child when she cooked, and Céline Dion when she sang. He mirrored to her a woman she had never seen before—he, seeing through her defenses and insecurities, loved her in spite of them.

The connection they shared reached beyond the physical plane. To Sophie, the love she'd found was grand—beyond the limits of time and space. Moments of joy and euphoria danced in her body at random, making her feel she didn't have a care in the world. It felt like bliss to her to finally be free of her fears of abandonment, which would have tarnished their union.

Sophie relished this feeling of freedom as she drove to La Jolla Cove to meet Lizzie for brunch. She easily found street parking, then walked to the seaside restaurant set high up on a hillside as a gentle ocean breeze kissed her cheeks. Lizzie was already sitting outside on the Brockton Villa patio wearing oversized sunglasses and a wide-brimmed hat, watching the birds swoop and glide. The pounding of the ocean surf, in harmony with the sound of the seagulls, provided the ideal background for their first girls' day out in a long time. They each ordered a Ramos gin fizz and egg entrées before settling in to catch up on their personal news.

"I feel like we never get a chance to talk alone at home—one of the guys is always around. And I want to hear everything! The relationship is clearly going well?" Lizzie didn't let Sophie answer before adding, "By the way, you're both invited to dinner on Saturday night so I can try out a new recipe." Ever since retiring from the People Saving People Project, Lizzie had been immersing herself in several interests, watercolor painting among them, not only to distract herself when David was at work, but to help keep her stimulated and busy while she decided what she wanted to do next with her own career. The joint pediatric practice she'd been part of for years was anxious to have her back full-time, but she was weighing her options—even thinking about starting a practice of her own so she could keep her hours flexible for Jonathan.

"That would be great, thank you. I can't tell you how happy I am that you guys seem to like him so much. I'm still at the point where I feel compelled to talk about him, to keep digesting and analyzing all these emotions inside of me."

"Go for it. Now that you two are past the point of pure infatuation, I'd be interested to hear you describe him to me through your eyes, not as Dr. Hobbs, the professional counselor you've been telling me about all these years, but as Matthew, the man."

"There's so much about him I adore. First of all, he's so kind and loving, and he radiates a peacefulness that draws people to him. He's charismatic, with a sentimental side, yet there's a strength about him I admire. He lives his convictions, and he's fun, laid-back, and interesting. He exudes a gentle power. When he talks about something that really matters to him, he's fully engaged, vigorously gesturing with his arms and hands. I'm sure you've noticed some of this yourself by now, though, right?"

"I have, yes. I like you two together. He seems to bring serenity and stability to your world, and I think you draw him out a bit, loosen him up. But what I find most interesting is that you interacted with this guy for years, communicating about pretty deep things month after month in his office, and then—boom! All of a sudden, you experienced him in an entirely new way."

"Well, I wasn't ready to be open to my attraction to him before the night of the wedding, and I think all that talking we did during our sessions really laid a solid foundation for a mature friendship. But once the physical thing happened? Oh man, that sealed the deal for me. I remember thinking that that's what it must feel like for a person coming out of a coma. I felt completely awakened to a new reality."

"It's that good, huh? For me, I realized I was in love with David when I was overcome with a monumental sense of connectedness."

"I know what you mean. After Neil died, I think I was bound and determined to compartmentalize all my feelings. I took my beliefs about romantic love and put them in one box, my need to be desired in another, my vulnerability in yet another, and I sealed them all up with duct tape and put them on a shelf. They were too dangerous to look at. But with all the work I've done—all the healing, the processing, the growing Matthew led me through—I finally opened doors that were shut before, collected all my boxes and unwrapped them and integrated them again, and now I feel … well, unblocked. I trust myself now and feel I'm able to recognize true love. The realization that my love for Neil wasn't authentic love was an eye-opener. Neil and I came together out of a mutual neediness, and neediness is not love."

"That's quite an insight, Soph, and not easy to admit."

"It wasn't that I didn't have love in my life, because I've always felt tremendous love from you guys. But this fullness I feel inside from my love for Matthew has just taken things to a whole new dimension. I'm really glad that I took the time to work through my past pain and issues. I know you were worried about me there for a while, but now, looking back, it all created a new space for me to inhabit."

"I'm so, so happy for you. I've always wanted this for you. You were so crushed by Neil's tragedy—not just losing him the way you did, but losing belief in yourself in the process. You've done a lot of hard work, and I can see it—the sense of peace about you now."

"As Matthew says, each person you encounter has a gift for you. Some people come into your life and quickly give you their gift and leave, some stay a while longer, some stay for a lifetime. I'm grateful for what I learned from Neil, and now I'm hoping that Matthew is the love that will last forever."

Matthew had already taught Sophie so much. In guiding her to grow, to see herself and her life in a new way, it had become safe for her to be more visible in the world. Under her previous cloak of invisibility, she'd been living a less-than-colorful existence. But Matthew had restored the color to her life, iridescent, brilliant, magnificent colors—that was his gift to her. Now her spectrum was full of hues, those from her other loved ones, too—a beautiful array of neutrals, pastels, and neons, all commingling in harmony.

"Thank heaven we grow and change, right?" Lizzie said as she dug through her omelet looking for more cheese. "The truth is, we aren't constants. We grow, change, experience new things, and as a result, our way of thinking is altered."

Sophie nodded in agreement, swallowed a mouthful of eggs Benedict, and readied herself to share another piece of news with Lizzie. "Okay, I have one more announcement, and then I want to hear what's going on with you—how you're really adjusting to all this stay-at-home mom stuff. Actually, your future plans are related to what I want to tell you, so here goes: If things keeping going as well as they have been, Matthew and I are talking about living together—about me moving into his place, not right now, just planning ahead … maybe sometime this year, maybe once Jonathan starts school in the fall and you don't need me around so much? I know that will depend on what you decide to do about work and all … but what do you think?"

Lizzie slowly put down her fork. "You'll have been dating for a year by then—I think that's great timing, actually. But let me sit with this for a minute. It'll feel so strange not having you within arm's reach anymore. And it will be a big adjustment for Jonathan."

"I know. For me too. But Matthew lives pretty close by, and we both always knew I couldn't live in your backyard for the rest of my life. Anyway, it's a long way off … I just wanted to give you lots of notice so we could make plans for Jonathan—and I don't want to tell him anything about this until it's definite. Regardless of when it happens, Lizzie, I want you to know that living in the guesthouse has been one of the greatest things to ever happen to me—right when I needed it most. I'll never be able to adequately thank you and David for all that you've done for me."

"Sophie, how far do we go back? No thanks needed. We were happy to do it, and we've reaped many benefits from the arrangement as well. Whatever you decide, we'll make it work. You'll always be part of our family, no matter what your address is." She took a long sip of her drink. "So do you think you guys will get married?"

"I don't know," Sophie trilled. "We'll see how living together goes. He's open to whatever I want—a spiritual partnership is more important to him than a legal one—and I'm not so sure I want to go down that path again. It doesn't feel necessary."

"I wonder if you'll change your mind."

"Hard to say right now. My first marriage didn't work out so well, as you know. Then again, when I look at you and David, what you have together, I'm inspired to just take the leap and do it."

"I'm very fortunate—I know that. And I wish the same for you, my friend. You deserve to be loved."

"That's another realization I've come to, Lizzie. It's not that I think people *deserve* love—I think we *are* love. We just need to recognize that."

CHAPTER 39
THE ASTRAL PLANE

Malach: Pneuma, I'm going to have you work on transmitting some inspirations.

Pneuma: I'm up for that. Can you explain a bit more about inspirations, please?

Malach: Sure. I'd describe them as inner messages that come to a person in the form of physical sensations or feelings. Some people believe that receiving inspirations is a special gift only a select few have, but we know this is something naturally inherent to *all* people as long as they are open to it. As spirit guides, we're messengers between the Source and another soul. It's a means we have to communicate and put information in their path.

Pneuma: I know what you're talking about. Some people sense the energy of others around them, including those of us in this dimension.

Malach: Sometimes people don't hear the ongoing communication because they expect something grandiose or clearly supernatural, when in reality, it can come to them in a countless number of ways.

Pneuma: I've noticed that when Sophie picks up our messages, she often gets goose bumps.

Malach: Yes, and they're transmitted in various ways. Sometimes she'll ask a question and find the answer in a book she picks up, or she'll receive a message from us while in a conversation with a stranger. Some people receive messages through movies or TV shows or number sequences they see. And, of course, through synchronicities.

Pneuma: Synchronicity?

Malach: It's when a person's energy or vibration matches what they're seeking. It's the universe's way of communicating. On Earth, people think certain occurrences are coincidences, but there are no such things as coincidences. What's happening is events that *seem* improbable to align themselves actually *do* align themselves at exactly the right moment. The events hold great meaning, but a person has to be consciously aware to receive it.

Pneuma: So people need to quiet their minds and listen and watch for the messages coming to them.

Malach: Exactly. As technology changes, it makes our job so much easier—to bring messages to people and to make connections between people where they might have been highly unlikely before. Wait until you see how the Internet is going to facilitate our connections with people in the future.

Pneuma: Okay, I get it.

Malach: The holiday season is coming up for them on Earth, so please give an inspiration to Lizzie to host Thanksgiving at her house, inviting Matthew's brother.

Pneuma: Sure, but why am I doing that?

Malach: I'm going to hold off telling you for now, if you don't mind.

Pneuma: Okay, but now I'm really curious.

CHAPTER 40

NOVEMBER 1993

I T WAS A crisp autumn afternoon, and Lizzie was on her way to the elementary school to pick up Jonathan. She wasn't superstitious, but—just in case—she knocked on wood because life was going particularly well for everyone. Jonathan had started kindergarten and loved it. David and Lizzie had met with his teacher in October, and she'd talked at length about how impressed she was with his creativity, imagination, and his storytelling skills. It had been a relief to hear he was doing well, had lots of friends, and looked forward to going to school each day.

For his first Halloween party at school, Jonathan had been determined to dress up as his favorite character of the moment, Aladdin. David had found him the perfect costume with tattered harem pants, distressed vest, maroon fez, and a stuffed monkey to sit on his shoulder. He wore his costume around the house all month, carrying his magical lamp, and Lizzie saw him secretly rub it as though he hoped a real genie might actually appear.

Once she arrived at the school, Lizzie waited in a line of cars with the other parents. She waved when she saw him. As he slid into the backseat, he seemed a bit miffed.

"What's wrong?" she asked, as she turned around to talk to him.

He sat with pouty lips, eyes turned down, and arms across his chest. "Mom, you need to talk to my teacher."

"Why? Your dad and I just did and everything's good."

"I'm feeling mad."

"I'm sorry to hear that. Tell me why."

She inched the car out of the congested area, weaving around the collection of idling vehicles.

"We're going to have a pretend Thanksgiving feast at school, and we're dressing up as American Indians and Pilgrims. My teacher told me I have to dress up as a Pilgrim. I told her I didn't want to be an ugly, old Pilgrim. Last time I was big, I was an American Indian, and I already have the clothes and everything."

"That's true, you do."

"She told me no. She already made plans for everyone."

"I'm surprised she said no when you had such a compelling reason, but I say go ahead and have the experience of being a Pilgrim because I have a scathingly brilliant idea."

"What is it?" he asked.

Someone was honking at Lizzie, signaling to let him cut in front of her. She waved him in, wishing they would come up with a better system for parents to pick up their kids.

"Sophie and I were talking about it, and we're planning to host Thanksgiving at our house this year. We can invite Grandma and Grandpa Cohen and my mom and dad, Sophie and Matthew, and anyone else who wants to come. So here's my idea. We can have people dress as Pilgrims or American Indians there too, and you can be the leader of the Indian tribe. You can make headpieces for people to wear at the table. Wouldn't that be a hoot? Can't you just see Grandma Cohen in a Pilgrim hat?"

When she glanced at him in the rearview mirror, she saw Jonathan break out in a smile.

"I like that idea. I'll wear my Indian outfit. Toffee has to wear hers, too."

Thanksgiving was Lizzie's favorite celebration of the year. It seemed the least commercial of all the holidays, and she liked the idea of giving gratitude—she had so many blessings.

The dinner invitations went out weeks in advance, and when the RSVPs came in, almost everyone confirmed they were coming, except for a few who already had other obligations. Grandpa and Grandma Cohen planned to stay a few days, but Lizzie's mom and dad weren't feeling up to the flight. However, Matthew's brother planned to attend, as well as two couples who were friends of the Cohens.

Lizzie knew the idea of costumes would appeal to Jonathan, and she helped him make feathered headbands for the event. The Pilgrim hats were too hard to construct, so they'd bought them at a party store along with other Thanksgiving decorations.

Lizzie and Sophie busied themselves planning the menu. Grandma Cohen's traditional chestnut stuffing made the cut, along with David's smoked turkey, jellied cranberry sauce (the canned kind, for Grandpa Cohen), Lizzie's pumpkin pies, Jonathan's favorite lime-pear gelatin salad, and Sophie's pumpkin curry soup.

"Let's make the rolls and piecrust from scratch because Grandpa Cohen goes crazy over those," Lizzie suggested.

Sophie scrunched up her nose and lips. "Yikes, ambitious. Okay, well then, why not go whole hog and add an apple and a pecan pie to the menu as well?"

After that, it was as though Martha Stewart had moved in. Lizzie returned to the party store for a beautiful, gold-embossed tablecloth and fancy cloth napkins. She, Sophie, and Jonathan sat around the table for hours hot-gluing plastic vegetables into individual cornucopias and making turkey-shaped place cards out of pinecones.

A few days before the holiday, Lizzie was so exhausted by all the shopping and preparing that she wasn't sure why she'd decided to take on such a big task. But by Thanksgiving Day, all the effort seemed worth it when she looked around her house. Logs were burning in the fireplace, candles were lit, the table was set perfectly with coordinating plates and napkins, and the mingling aromas of cinnamon, sage, and cloves filled the air.

Lizzie and Sophie were busy in the kitchen putting last-minute touches on the dishes and planning cook times so that everything would come out hot together. "Where's Jonathan?" Sophie asked. "I'm surprised he isn't helping."

"He's occupying himself with all the costumes for the dinner. I'm glad we were able to find a solution to what bothered him so much at school by letting him be an American Indian today. I'm not so sure how all our guests will feel about wearing headpieces at dinner, but it's made him happy. And I'm so glad you remembered to dress in your own Indian outfit—he was counting on it."

"I'm surprised they even had a Thanksgiving celebration at school," Sophie said.

"Why? It isn't a religious holiday."

"Just something I heard. Apparently, much of what we learned in history class wasn't accurate. Like, there's controversy over how the first Thanksgiving really went down—that it wasn't actually a lovefest between the settlers and the natives and that they didn't even eat the foods we eat today."

"Well, next year, we won't focus on anything but giving gratitude. To me, this holiday is about gathering with people I love to enjoy our connection and to focus on what we're thankful for. I want to teach Jonathan to be grateful for what he has."

"I second that motion, Lizzie."

As the guests started arriving, Jonathan ran around like a puppy anticipating a treat. His grandparents brought him gifts, of course, and Jonathan gave them a complete tour of the house, pointing out everything that was new since their last visit.

Lizzie confirmed that everyone was on task. Her oven and stovetops were simmering away on schedule; Matthew and David were manning the turkey in the smoker in between breaks from the football game on TV; the guests were chatting in the living room; and Sophie was mixing cocktails—Mayflower martinis.

No one else was available to answer the doorbell when it rang except Lizzie. She wiped her hands on her leaf-patterned apron—a gift from her mother that she wore once a year—brushed her hair out of her eyes, and headed to the entryway.

"Hi, I'm Mark, Matthew's brother. And I assume you're Lizzie?" He extended his hand.

"Hi, yes, so nice to meet you." Lizzie immediately noticed his resemblance to Matthew, the same aqua-colored eyes accentuated by a deep, penetrating gaze, about the same height and weight. Is that why he looked familiar? He was tan with a short, scruffy beard outlining his strong, square jaw. His hair was dark, wavy, and styled. "Glad you could come today. Matthew is so excited you were able to join us. Come in."

He handed her a bottle of wine as he entered. "I drove directly from the airport, but I had to stop for a small token of thanks. I really appreciate the invitation."

"Oh, nice. A pinot noir, my favorite. The guys are out back with their smoker and their beer. Let me show you the way."

"I haven't seen Matty for too long, so this is great," he said.

Lizzie walked Mark to the backyard to witness the reunion between the brothers.

Mark gave his brother a big hug. "Matty, so good to see you. You're looking fantastic."

"Ah, my baby brother. And you're looking exceptionally well too. Mark, this is David, host with the most. David, this is my brother, Mark."

David set his beer down, and they shook hands. "Really great to meet you. Any friend of Matthew's is a friend of mine. Matthew talks about you often and with great pride and affection." David gestured toward the mini fridge on the deck. "What can I get you to drink?"

"I'll have one of those." Mark pointed to David's beer. "It smells great all the way down the block. What wood are you using for smoking?"

David handed him a cold beer. "I'm trying a fruitwood because they say that flavor works best with turkey. According to *Bon Appétit*, something like cherry or apple wood chips work well with poultry. I'm using cherry. Babe, do you want a beer?"

"No, but thanks. I've got to finish up dinner first."

On her way back to the kitchen, Lizzie alerted Sophie that Mark had arrived and was out back, then she attended to the sweet potatoes before taking a break to mingle with her guests in the living room, with their martinis and hors d'oeuvres. Jonathan descended upon the group wearing his costume: a soft deerskin breechcloth and leggings, with a mantle fastened on one shoulder and wrapped around his body. He'd decorated his face with ceremonial paint and wore a breastplate made of toy bones.

"That's some cool outfit," Grandpa Cohen told Jonathan as he eyed him up and down. "You even have moccasins."

"Toffee got them for me at a festival," Jonathan replied.

Lizzie realized she couldn't stall any longer—it was time to put on her Pilgrim costume. As she went upstairs to change, she thought, *I'm never doing this again. Why did I suggest this ridiculous idea?* It was even worse when she came back down, and Jonathan laughed so hard at the sight of her that he couldn't catch his breath. "I feel silly. This is the most boring costume ever. I want to be an Indian."

Jonathan stopped laughing long enough to say, "Too late, Mommy."

Grandma Cohen said, "I think your dress should be black, Lizzie."

"Well, Irene, Jonathan said he learned in school that it wasn't easy to dye cloth in a long-lasting color like black and that the Pilgrims wore black only for their most reverent occasions. So their everyday outfits were often yellow and blue, like this."

Grandma Cohen shook her head and pressed her lips together. "The things they're teaching in school these days. It hardly pays to learn new things because everything keeps changing over the years anyway."

Lizzie thought Sophie got the better outfit by far—a soft-looking, deerskin dress, a black wig with braids, and her moccasins.

Getting into the spirit of things, Matthew and Mark happily donned their hand-painted headbands with feathers, and David and his parents pulled their Pilgrim hats snugly on their heads. The other guests, Vivian and Charles Wu from the hospital and the Silvermans from next door, didn't look too keen on participating, and when Lizzie gave them an out—"You don't have to wear them if you don't want"—they all too readily took it. She thought they were spoilsports.

Lizzie began the final countdown to dinner, and Jonathan and Sophie followed her into the kitchen. She liked listening to the interaction between them.

Jonathan perched on his regular stool and watched Sophie reach for a whisk. "What are you making, Toffee?"

"The gravy. I'm using my frozen turkey stock." She emptied a frozen block into a pan."

"Can I help?"

"Of course."

Jonathan reached into the spice cabinet above him and started pulling out random bottles and jars: cinnamon, ginger, sugar, mustard, cayenne pepper. He sprinkled copious amounts of each in a bowl, moistened the mixture with some water, then joyfully stirred it all together with the whisk. "This will be my secret sauce," he said. "Every year from now on, I'll make the secret sauce. Taste it, Toffee!"

A new holiday tradition, Lizzie thought. She laughed when Sophie dipped a pinkie into the bowl ... and then tried not to gag when the taste hit her tongue.

"I'll just set this here until it's time to add it to the gravy," Sophie said. "I hasn't melted yet. So why don't you go see if your dad needs any help carving the turkey?"

"Okay," he said. "Hey, Mommy, can I put the whipped cream on the pies?"

To Jonathan, she replied, "Yep, at dessert time." Then, to Sophie, once Jonathan had run out back, she snickered, "Nice cover-up."

Once Lizzie had covered the buffet table with piles of steaming food and David had brought in the magnificently browned bird, all carved and ready for serving, dinner commenced to much fanfare. Grandpa Cohen did the honors of saying grace before the meal, then everyone began with Sophie's soup. All the while, the smells were heavenly, the food was delicious, the wine flowed, and the conversation steered clear of politics, religion, and finances.

"Lizzie, this gravy is absolutely delicious," Vivian Wu complimented.

"It isn't gravy," Jonathan said. "It's secret sauce, and I made it. I'm going to make it every year now."

Grandma Cohen shook her head and muttered, "Imagine a five-year-old making gravy."

Lizzie quickly changed the subject by asking everyone to share what was new in their lives. She started by announcing that she'd started a part-time job at Scripps Memorial Hospital, attending to kids on the pediatric wing. David had fulfilled the surgical hours requirement he needed to keep his hospital privileges for the year and was awaiting word on his next PSPP project. Sophie happily reported on her plans to open a cake and cupcake shop in La Jolla, and Matthew had an upcoming speaking engagement on a cruise to Hawaii.

Grandma and Grandpa Cohen were tired of the cold Pennsylvania winters but didn't want to move. The Silvermans were excited about a new deck they were building in the spring, while the Wus were gearing up for a vacation to Australia. Mark, a photojournalist, was in the process of moving from his small, overly expensive apartment in New York City on his way overseas for an assignment for a couple of months. Evidently, the afternoon had gone so well for the Hobbs brothers that Mark was now considering making San Diego his temporary home base.

When it was Jonathan's turn to speak, he said that he loved going to school and wanted to tell them the story he'd learned about the first Thanksgiving. After that, everyone took turns going around the table talking about what they were thankful for during the past year—Lizzie's favorite part of the holiday.

About midway through his story, Jonathan slowed down. "Are you full, honey?" Lizzie asked him. "You have a lot of food left on your plate."

He was biting into a piece of cornbread the Silvermans had brought. "This is good," he said, "but it isn't like the kind we ate when I was big. Toffee and I used to grind our own cornmeal on the rocks when we were *real* Indians, like this." He knelt on his chair and vigorously rotated his fist in the air.

"You made cornbread in school, Jonathan?" Grandma Cohen asked.

"No, Grandma, we made it when I was an Indian with Toffee."

Grandma Cohen laughed heartily. "Oh my, you have such an imagination. But you shouldn't make things up," she told him. "Do you know the story about the boy who cried wolf? People won't believe you if you tell tales. It's always better to tell the truth."

Jonathan's lip trembled slightly, and he crossed his arms over his chest. With narrowed eyes, he said, "But, Grandma, that *is* the truth. It's real. Toffee was my mom then, weren't you, Toffee?"

Sophie smiled at him and nodded. "Indeed I was," she said rather quietly.

But not quietly enough. "Sophie, you shouldn't encourage the boy to tell fibs," Grandma Cohen said.

"Let it go, Irene," Grandpa said. "This isn't the place."

Lizzie was annoyed with her mother-in-law for clearly upsetting Jonathan, who was silently looking down at the table now with slumped shoulders, averting everyone's eyes and fighting back tears. She got up and kissed him on the head on her way into the kitchen with a stack of plates.

"Don't worry about it, honey. Some people believe in these things and some don't. Some people remember things from long, long ago and some don't. But just because they don't believe or don't remember, it doesn't mean it isn't true. You know what's true for you, and that's all that matters."

After pie, it was like kindergarten naptime had descended on the house. Jonathan had retreated to his room, Grandpa Cohen was comatose in a recliner, and everyone else was in various states of recline in the living room, some sipping coffee and watching TV, others playing cards.

Mark took it upon himself to clear the table, bringing armloads of platters, bowls, and cups to Lizzie as she loaded the dishwasher. "You don't have to do that, Mark."

He flashed his 200-watt smile. "Oh, I like to help clean up. Besides, I wanted to get a chance to talk to you a bit. I feel comfortable with you, like there's something so familiar about you."

She laughed. "Funny, I was thinking the same about you."

"That does happen sometimes. Anyway, the dinner was excellent. Best meal I've had in a long time. I appreciate all the time and effort you put into it."

"Glad you enjoyed it. ... So you're a photographer," Lizzie probed.

"I am."

"Has that always been an interest of yours?"

"Yes, I'd say telling visual stories has been a longtime interest of mine. With photography, you must have interesting stories to tell and you need the passion to communicate the stories you feel are pertinent."

"Where do you work?"

"I'm freelance—about to go on assignment for *National Geographic*. You and your husband know all about overseas assignments, don't you?" They exchanged a knowing smile. "Great kid you've got there." He nodded his head toward the stairs. "He looks photogenic. Mind if I take some candid shots of him?"

"That would be great. But maybe another time. He's still feeling a bit distraught about his grandmother scolding him in front of everybody."

"Sure, another time, then. You know, if you think it would make him feel better, maybe I could to talk to him about memories I have that are similar to the ones he was talking about at dinner." Mark stopped scraping bits of food from plates into the trash to look directly at Lizzie, as though to gauge her reaction to what he'd just said. "I don't know what your own beliefs are, but I carry memories from my own past lives. I'd be happy to talk to him about it."

Lizzie didn't say anything for a moment, then took a step back and gazed into Mark's face. When she again saw the kindness there, her shoulders relaxed and she was flushed with warmth. "Really? Yeah, I think that might comfort him—make him feel more understood. Thanks, Mark."

A little while later, when the Cohens' friends had left and Grandma and Grandpa Cohen had retired to the guest room for the night, Mark knocked on Jonathan's door.

"Come in."

Mark found him sitting on his bed—no TV on or toys out, evidently just sitting and thinking. He didn't look like the happy little boy he'd met just hours ago.

"Bit of a tough night, huh?"

Jonathan bit his lower lip and turned his head. "Yep."

Maybe because Mark didn't push him to say anything more, or maybe because he already felt at ease with him, as Lizzie had, Jonathan starting telling him how he was feeling.

"I'm kind of sad. I was thinking about running away. I don't know why people don't believe me when I tell them about the last time I was big. I mean Toffee does, and Mommy and Daddy always listen to me, but other people laugh at me and tease me. Grandma even told me not to fib. I wasn't fibbing. My stomach felt sick when she said that. I don't think I should talk about it anymore."

"Well, I believe you, kiddo. In fact, I went through this same thing when I was your age."

Jonathan perked up immediately, as though rays of sunshine had just broken through dark clouds. His jaw dropped. "You did? What happened? What did you do? Who did you used to be?"

"It wasn't just me, actually. Matthew and I aren't just brothers in this life, we were brothers in a past life as well—we were soldiers together during the Civil War. As little kids, we didn't know how we knew this, we just both always knew … I don't even remember when the memories started. But we'd play outside together and re-create scenes from our past life, and when we told adults about it, they just assumed we were making up stories. Even when we made it clear that we weren't imagining anything, nobody believed us. It bothered us, sure, but since we had each other and we both knew we were telling the truth, that made it a lot easier on us. It must be really hard, though, when you're the only kid you know who feels this way."

"Yeah. I just want to be like everyone else."

"It does sometimes seem like that would be easier, doesn't it? Sometimes. But actually, I discovered that I could use it as an advantage in my life—being different, I mean. You know how your mom and dad stand up for what they believe in no matter what? How they go off to help other people in the world even though most parents stay home with their kids?"

That seemed to resonate with Jonathan, and he sat up straight and gazed at Mark's face as he continued talking. "That makes your parents special. And you're special too, Jonathan. You carry with you your soul's knowledge and compassion from long ago, and that doesn't make you different, it makes you special. Very, very special."

Jonathan leaned over and hugged Mark. "Thanks, Mark."

"You're welcome, buddy. We can talk about this anytime you want. We're coming back over tomorrow to throw the football around, so I'll see you then, okay?"

Jonathan did feel better after talking to Mark. His words were like a warm blanket of understanding that comforted his soul. But he still didn't think he should talk about his past life with other people anymore, not unless they talked to him about it first.

Then it was Sophie's turn to check on Jonathan. Before she and Matthew left, she told him she was going to head upstairs for a few minutes. "I just want to tell him good night."

Sophie slipped into Jonathan's room and headed straight for his bed to kiss him good night when her eye went to the wastebasket by his desk. She stepped back in surprise. His loincloth, his breastplate, his dream catcher, even his moccasins—they were all in the trash. She reached down and picked up the moccasins pressing them to her heart.

As she sat on his bed, she asked him, "Why are these in the trash, Jonathan?" although she already knew the answer.

His face was still smeared with ceremonial paint, the remnants of his earlier tears.

"Because people make fun of me when I talk about being an Indian. They don't believe me, so I don't think I want to be an Indian anymore."

She stroked his blonde locks. "Sweetheart, I can tell you it doesn't matter what other people think and say, but I know it does. I know it hurts to not be believed. But we know what's true, right? Maybe you can keep all these things, and maybe we can just keep this between us from now on, not share our memories with others. What do you think?"

"I don't know. I don't even know if any of it was real. Maybe it's all from my dreams. Even if it was real, I don't think I want to remember anymore."

Sophie felt like the wishbone in the turkey—broken in half and left with only the short side, without her wish. She wanted to preserve the life they'd had together forever, for it to always be special to him. With each tear that rolled down her cheek, her heart broke a little bit more.

She tucked Jonathan in and kissed him on the forehead. "I don't want you to forget," she whispered.

He didn't answer.

Sophie emptied the wastebasket in her arms on the way out. Maybe he'd want all these things again someday.

She turned off the light switch near his door, then turned back to look at him as he snuggled under the covers. The moonlight shone brightly through the tilted blinds, casting soft yellow stripes on his face. His breathing was rapid and shallow.

I'll miss you, Mystic Wolf.

Downstairs, she pulled Matthew aside. He saw her wet cheeks, heard her deep sigh, but he waited for her to speak. "It's happening, Matthew. Jonathan is starting to let go; he's choosing not to remember our past life together. I feel so terribly sad, like I'm losing a piece of myself."

"Try not to be so sad—not for your sake, but for his. It seems he needs to do this, to take this step, to incorporate himself fully into this life. It's a process and won't happen overnight. But there will always be a part of him that remembers. The soul always remembers."

Matthew put his arm around her. "I'm sorry this is so painful for you, Sophie. Come on. Come stay with me tonight. Mark's staying in the downstairs guest room so we have the whole upstairs to ourselves."

"Come on, Mark," he yelled. "We're ready to leave. You can follow behind us to the house."

Sophie got a bag from the kitchen and put all of Jonathan's American Indian gear into it. *I love you, Mystic Wolf,* she thought. *I'll always love you.*

Matthew reached for her hand with one hand and tilted her chin to the side with the other as he gave her one of his gentle, knowing smiles. "Tomorrow the sun will rise again and life will go on. It's going to be okay," he assured her. "It will all be okay."

CHAPTER 41

DECEMBER 9, 1993

O N THE DAYS Lizzie worked at the hospital, Sophie picked Jonathan up from school. She loved splitting after-school duties with Lizzie, not only because it gave both of them the flexibility they needed in their work schedules, but because she'd be moving into Matthew's place at the start of the new year—once the renovations he was having done to better accommodate her were complete—and the schedule she'd worked out with Lizzie would allow her to stay a part of Jonathan's daily life. He'd been pretty emotional when she, Lizzie, and David had sat him down to break the news to him, but once he learned that his beloved Toffee would be picking him up after school half the week, he'd bounced back beautifully and had given Sophie a big hug. They'd all laughed with relief when Jonathan asked if he could use the guesthouse for a fort once she'd moved out.

At precisely 2:01, Jonathan was waiting at the curb, wearing khaki pants, a blue sweater, and athletic shoes, his backpack over his shoulder, his lunch box in one hand, and a container of juice in the other.

Sophie rolled down the passenger window and called out to him. "Wow, you look like the weight of the world is on your shoulders. Get in and take a load off. How was your day?"

Jonathan piled his stuff in the backseat and climbed in next to it. He'd only recently outgrown his toddler car seat and was very proud to now be able to buckle himself into his booster chair in the back.

"It was good. We're going to share about our holiday traditions, and I'm going to bring in my menorah to show, but they won't let me light the candles."

"Oh, I like that idea of people sharing their holiday traditions— almost as much as I like sharing our holidays together. Do you want to help me get my house ready for Christmas today? You know, put ornaments on the tree? Make cookies? Watch a Christmas show? I could use some help."

"Yeah. Sounds great."

Sophie smiled warmly at him in her rearview mirror. It was the last Christmas she'd spend in the house in his backyard, and she wanted to make it as special as she could.

Once they got home, Sophie and Jonathan stood in her small living room, sizing it up. "I'm not sure where to set up the tree this year. There's not much space left now that my loom is out here."

Jonathan ran his hands across the vertical threads on her loom, as though he were playing a harp. "How does a loom work?"

"You weave on it with special yarns."

"What are you making?"

"It's a tapestry representing stories from my life. I use the colored threads to create scenes, sort of like painting pictures, but with the yarns instead of with paints."

"How do you know how to do that?"

"I learned how to weave back when I was in training for my old job, when I studied occupational therapy. I don't think they teach it anymore as part of the curriculum, but I'm glad I learned how to do it. I find it very relaxing."

Jonathan rummaged through her box of bobbins. "It looks fun. Will you show me how you do it?"

Sophie pulled the loom closer to the two of them and pointed to the vertical threads. "These up-and-down threads are called the 'warp.' I put my thread on these bobbins—they're called the 'weft'—and I weave them between the warp threads where I want the color."

Jonathan laughed. "Those words are so funny."

" 'Warp' and 'weft'? I guess they're kind of funny. And the design I use that goes behind it is called a 'cartoon.' "

"That's funny too. Show me, show me!"

Sophie picked up a bobbin of thread and weaved it in and out of the warp threads. "The weft threads are like filling. They go under and over the warp threads wherever I want a certain color, like this, and then I push the threads down with a beater, which is kind of like a comb."

"What do you do with it when you're done?"

"I'll hang it on the wall. Like a piece of art. See, these weft threads don't go all the way across the whole piece—they change when I want a certain color."

Jonathan drew his finger over a long yellow thread. "But this one goes a long, long way through it."

"That's the thread representing your mom. Yellow means constancy— always being there. That's my friendship with her."

He traced his finger along another thread. "This one is pretty and shiny."

Sophie laughed. "I knew you'd like it. It's a shimmery golden silk thread. You know when I put that in?"

"No."

"When you were born."

"Will it be a long thread too?"

"Absolutely. My story is made from all of these threads representing the experiences in my life."

"When will you be done with it?"

"Probably not for a long time because I have more stories to add."

"I love the stories we make together."

A familiar wave of overwhelming love for him washed over her, and she had to restrain herself from scooping him up and crushing him in her arms. "Me too, honey." She turned away from him long enough to brush a tear from her eye. "I know: Let's move my loom back into my bedroom for the holidays. Then we can put the tree next to the sofa, in front of the window. What do you think?"

Jonathan already had one side of the loom in his hands and was ready to help her hoist it before her sentence was out.

Sophie lugged her huge, weather-beaten box of decorations from the Cohens' garage. They set up her Santa collection on the windowsill, put the lights on the artificial tree, and carefully unwrapped each individual ornament.

Jonathan searched through the box. "Where's my first ornament?"

Sophie knew he liked to hang that one first.

"Here it is!" He held up his find. "My red wooden airplane."

"When you were little, you'd point at it on the tree and say, 'Er-plane, er-plane.' It seems so long ago already."

"It's my favorite."

As they decorated the tree, they listened to Christmas music and sipped on hot cocoa. When they were finished, Jonathan stood back admiring his work. "Can I turn the lights on?"

"Sure." Sophie pointed to the closest outlet, and Jonathan plugged in the cord.

"Wow, that's so pretty."

"It is. Thanks for helping me. It's more fun doing this with you, so I'm glad your mom and dad let you help me with my Christmas traditions."

"Me too."

"I made some gingerbread dough—it's been chilling. Ready to cut out some cookies?"

"Yeah. Let's decorate some too. Have you always loved to bake?"

They went into the kitchen, where Sophie pulled the bowl of dough from the refrigerator, plopped it on a floured pastry cloth, and got her rolling pin from a drawer. "I have—ever since I can remember. My dad used to bake with my brother and me when we were little, and it gave me good memories. I hope it makes good memories for you too. I'll start rolling and then you can finish, okay?"

She added more flour to the pastry cloth and set to work on the cold, brown ball, starting in the center and pushing outward on all sides until it was a large circle about a quarter of an inch thick. "Your turn," she said to Jonathan, handing him the roller as she reached for the big tin of metal and plastic cookie cutters on the counter. "Look through those and pick whatever shapes you want. I have Christmas ones *and* Hanukkah ones. I was thinking you could use the menorah and the dreidel, and I'll use the tree and the wreath."

They spent the next few hours cutting out shapes, baking and cooling the cookies, then icing and decorating them all. As the sun set, her little cottage was filled with the sounds, smells, and colors of the holiday season.

"I picked up a new video for us—*The Muppet Christmas Carol*. Want to watch?"

"Is it with Kermit?"

"Of course. We can have milk and gingerbread cookies while we watch. I heard it's good. Next week, we'll go shopping for things on my Christmas list."

Snuggling on the couch with Jonathan, Sophie was conscious of experiencing pure joy in the moment. She said a silent prayer of gratitude for having made it through all the suffering of Neil's suicide and having come out the other side a stronger and wiser person.

"This is so much fun," Jonathan said. "Are we going to watch the Mr. Magoo tape next, with the ghost in chains? I wish we could free the scary ghost like we helped free Neil. It wouldn't be so scary and sad then."

Sophie was momentarily flabbergasted that Jonathan had brought up Neil just as she'd been thinking about him and their visit to his gravesite over a year ago. *You'd think by now that I wouldn't be surprised by this kid's extraordinary gifts.* Recovering quickly, she said, "That's so true."

Then she tightened her embrace around his shoulders, kissed his head, and sent another prayer of thanks upward, for the perspective she'd been given to appreciate such simple, precious moments as this.

CHAPTER 42
FEBRUARY 1994

THE EVENING TEMPERATURE was cool, yet pleasant enough to sit outside. The hunger-provoking scent of burning charcoal, smoke, and caramelized meat percolated through the Cohens' backyard—a last supper of sorts, a farewell dinner for David as he was about to embark on his upcoming PSPP assignment. Matthew and Sophie were helping prepare the feast Lizzie had planned, knowing David wouldn't be eating wholesome, nourishing foods for some time.

Lizzie handed Matthew a stack of plates to set on the large outdoor oak table. When she'd discovered the table in an antique shop in Ohio, she knew she had to have it, and they'd dragged it across the country in a trailer, with hopes of using it for many future family celebrations.

An outdoor barbecue in the dead of winter was definitely one of the advantages of living in California. David manned the grill, carefully turning the seafood kabobs to achieve the perfect grill marks and the right degree of char while avoiding overcooking the succulent flesh. Lizzie gazed at her husband as he cooked. She knew how empty the house was going to feel once he was gone. Just his presence gave her a sense of peace. She loved her home and their life.

Returning to the kitchen, she and Sophie made the side dishes. Sophie wielded her chef's knife, julienning carrots for the salad.

"Sophie," Lizzie said, "would you make your Meyer lemon dressing while I finish the salad? It's so good." She pulled out a glass carafe and handed it to Sophie.

"Sure, where's the avocado oil?"

"There's a new bottle in the pantry behind a bag of pasta."

As Lizzie washed the greens, she said, "I also made your heirloom tomato and mozzarella salad. It's marinating in the fridge. Jonathan inhales that stuff like a hungry dog wolfing down a steak."

As if on cue, Jonathan meandered into the kitchen, his chest puffed with pride. "Mom, wait till you see what Toffee and I made for dessert." His golden-green eyes twinkled with the secret bubbling inside him.

"What is it, sweetie?"

Sophie jerked around and pointed a wooden spoon at Jonathan. "Don't you tell!"

He laughed. "I won't."

The wine was open and breathing. Once dinner was ready and everyone had gathered around the table in the gazebo area, Lizzie turned on the overhead heater and lit six metal lanterns for ambient lighting. In the setting sun, Lizzie thought the scene looked like a painting by Thomas Kinkade of cozy, domestic contentment.

Matthew placed a platter of vegetables on the table. "What a team we make. This all looks and smells delicious!"

Jonathan sat in the chair next to David. "Daddy, I want to sit next to you."

"Sure thing, slugger. I made a special kabob for you. Give me your plate."

Jonathan held his plate up in the air with two hands, and David used his tongs to transfer a steaming kabob to it. "Let it cool a bit before touching it. It's really hot."

Then David retrieved the rest of the kabobs from the grill, sat down with everyone, and poured the wine for a toast. "There's nothing more comforting than preparing a home-cooked meal to share with friends and family. Cheers to all my loved ones."

"Hear, hear," they all chimed in, clinking their glasses.

"I like how Jonathan always eats grown-up food with us instead of a peanut butter and jelly sandwich," said Matthew.

Lizzie passed the salad around the table. "Yeah, he has pretty cultivated tastes for a kid. We never did go the boxed macaroni-and-cheese route with him. Once when he was about four years old, I found him in the kitchen with an open jar, munching away on pickled herring. It was so funny."

Everyone laughed and continued to enjoy the good food and company until Lizzie's eyes welled up with tears. She couldn't hold back any longer. "So tell Sophie and Matt where you're going tomorrow," Lizzie said to David.

Matthew helped himself to another kabob. "Yeah, what's all the mystery been about? Where's your next assignment?"

"Do we really have to discuss this now?" David asked Lizzie quietly. "Maybe it can wait until after dinner, over a brandy."

Lizzie frowned. "You're leaving tomorrow. I don't think you can stall any longer."

"Uh-oh," Sophie said. "Now you're making me nervous, guys. I've been asking Lizzie for weeks, but she keeps avoiding the question. So where are you off to?" Sophie wiped her mouth with her red-and-white-checkered napkin.

"Well, let me give a bit of backstory first," David replied. "You know that I think the PSPP does great work and that I feel gratified that Liz and I have been able to work for such a respected organization for so many years. We like their nonpartisan ways of giving aid to the needy. They sincerely want to help make the world a better place, and that fits in with my concept of how life should be, you know?"

He paused to place half an ear of grilled corn on Jonathan's plate. "And because they put humanitarian efforts above all else, that frequently means providing aid in areas of conflict, often under dire circumstances. Liz and I have both made significant contributions we're proud of."

David paused again, this time reaching for the wine bottle to fill Sophie's empty glass. "Now that Lizzie has retired from the organization, I want to spend more time at home with my family too, and I am planning to do that. I've been talking to my chief at the hospital about a full-time appointment in the very near future. But having said that, there are some things happening right now in the world that I can't overlook and turn away from. I have to help."

"So lay it on us, David," coaxed Matthew. "Where to?"

Just then, Jonathan slid off his chair and stood. "Daddy, I'm done eating. Can I go play on the slide now?"

"That was awfully fast," David responded. "Did you like your dinner? Are you full?"

"It was yummy. But I want to save some room for dessert."

"Okay, let me flip the light on over there. We'll call you when it's time for your special dessert."

As Jonathan ran to his swing set, Sophie prompted David again. "So where, David?"

"I'm going to Rwanda."

Silence immediately followed, heavy and thick. No one spoke, no one even moved.

Sophie shook her head slowly. "I don't even know what to say other than to ask you not to go. It's a powder keg waiting to explode over there."

"Sophie, how can I not go? How can I not help? Pretend not to see what we all know? I can't turn my head away."

"So what's your role going to be? What are they pulling you in for?" asked Matthew.

David pushed a tomato around on his plate as he spoke. "Various humanitarian aid teams are working in the camps in the Ruhengeri district close to the Ugandan border, giving aid to displaced people."

"David's friend Max said there's little aid for these people," Lizzie added solemnly.

David continued, "Just this past October, over a half million people were trying to escape the massacres going on in Burundi, and some of the humanitarian aid agencies sent teams to the camps in southeast Rwanda."

Lizzie pushed her plate away, too upset now to eat more.

"And with famine and an outbreak of shigellosis, thousands are dying. There's been a terrible problem with poor quality of distribution of humanitarian food and many political killings. They anticipate that a high volume of violence is going to create an overwhelming demand for surgeons."

Sophie poured more wine for everyone. "How can doctors and other medical people stop what's going on there?"

David shifted uncomfortably in his chair, uneasy talking about the details. "We won't stop it, but it's not about that—it's about healing the wounded. They have needs of colossal proportion there, and I can't deny the calling. I've tried numbing the thoughts floating around in my head, but they persist. They nag at me like the pain in my knee from my basketball injury, hounding me so I have to pay attention. Bottom line for me? I need to be true to the inner me, the authentic me. It's hard to explain."

Matthew nodded empathetically. "No, I get it."

"I owe it to my father, a Holocaust survivor," David went on, "and his parents and siblings, who were murdered, not to turn my back. The lesson I hoped that we, as a society, learned during the Holocaust was 'never again.' … Well, it seems that was just political rhetoric to many people."

"I understand, David, I do," Lizzie said. "It's all a nightmare. Having you go is unbearable to me, but asking you not to go is unimaginable."

Jonathan returned to the table and everyone stopped talking. "Hey, are you guys done eating yet? Let's play a game."

"Let us finish our wine, buddy," David told him, "then we'll serve your dessert."

Jonathan climbed in David's lap. "Daddy, I don't want you to go away again."

David tousled his hair and gave him a hug. "I know you don't, but this will be my last time. When I get back, I'm going to work right here in the city, like Mommy."

"I'm glad, Daddy. I love you."

"I love you too."

And I love both of you more than I can ever say, Lizzie thought. Afraid she'd burst into tears, Lizzie abruptly stood up and announced that it was time for dessert.

As everyone made one trip into the kitchen to clear the dishes, Lizzie smiled as she spotted Jonathan and Sophie's secret signals. They snuck away to the pantry to get their dessert while the others returned to the table to finish their wine.

A few minutes later, Jonathan, beaming with pride, reappeared in the backyard carrying a huge cake in the shape of an airplane. As Sophie helped him set the platter down in front of his father, David saw what was written on it: *Bon Voyage, Daddy! We Love You and Will Miss You.*

"Wow," David exclaimed, looking truly surprised. "This is fantastic. It looks exactly like the plane I'll be taking. I hope it tastes better than a plane would, though."

"Daddy, you're silly. It's your favorite. Carrot cake. I helped make it."

"Thank you so much," said David. "What a special night this has been. Now let's dig into this cake!"

After Sophie and Matthew said their good-byes—with effusive good wishes and extra-long hugs for David—Lizzie and David put Jonathan to bed.

Then they sat next to each other in the quiet of the family room. David was all packed and ready to leave in the morning. Lizzie reached over to take his hand, wondering how she'd be able to handle this particular farewell.

She faked a smile as she looked into his eyes. "I wish you weren't going. I'm worried something will happen to you."

"I know, baby. But this assignment is much shorter than most. I'll be in and out." He placed his hand on her knee, rubbed it lightly. "I'm looking forward to coming back—to settle in at home and live like a regular family. You, me, and the little guy."

"Think you'll be bored without the adrenaline rush? I mean, when you get back?"

"No. Have you been bored since you quit?"

Lizzie paused for a moment to think. "Nope. Well, rarely. For me, returning home after an assignment was almost more of an adjustment than going. I always struggled more after coming back to my creature comforts when I knew I was leaving behind people living with poverty, famine, disease, brutality. It's something I never got used to, but it gave me the gift of gratitude and an appreciation for what we have. I think my experiences left me profoundly changed."

"I know exactly what you mean."

"It's going to be agony not having much contact with you this time, not knowing what's going on except through word of mouth. At least when I'm there with you, I know what's happening. Did you call your mom and dad?"

"Yeah, that's always so tough. My mom always cries buckets."

They sat in silence for a moment.

"You'll be okay. I'll be okay," David assured her. He stroked Lizzie's hair. "Take care of our little rug rat, and take a picture of him every day for the photo album. That way, I won't feel like I missed so much once I get back."

Lizzie walked behind the couch to hide her tears from David, embracing him from behind and kissing his cheeks as she whispered in his ear, "I love you with all my heart and soul, David Cohen. You're the most loving, compassionate, wise, intelligent, funny, giving man I've ever known. I don't deserve you."

He kissed her hands on his chest. "Well, I guess we're a perfect match, because that's how I'd describe you too. And I love you heart and soul too. You know that."

When David felt Lizzie's tears on his cheek, he whispered back, "Please don't be sad. It makes *me* sad."

"Okay, okay. Enough sadness. Now that Jonathan's out of earshot, give me as many details as you can so I can try to track exactly where you'll be and what you'll be doing."

"It all stems from when the Rwandese Patriotic Front started a civil war with the Hutu extremists, in 1990, I think. The RPF was made up mostly of Tutsi refugees whose families had fled to Uganda following previous Hutu violence against the Tutsi."

"The Hutu and the Tutsi are really like the Montagues and the Capulets."

"And then some. Both are certainly fueled by hatred and settle things through violence. Relief organizations are putting together an emergency action plan for implementation for when the local hospitals can't handle all the influx of the wounded that the intelligence indicates will be coming in. The situation in Kigali isn't good and it's primed for violence. Nobody knows what's going to happen exactly, but they know it's ready to erupt."

"Sounds like another Somalia."

"Yesterday, the PSPP assisted another agency in opening an admissions center for the wounded in Kigali. Since the hospital has limited capacity, we'll set up tents to screen the patients. We were specifically asked to come in response to a fax from the Head of Mission in Rwanda in preparation for the anticipated violence. We'll have to be ready to handle a large number of wounded, and of course they're desperate for surgeons."

"Wait. I thought you'd be at the camps. Not Kigali."

"No, Kigali."

Lizzie hands began to shake. "So you're stepping smack-dab into the arena right when the lions come out for feeding? I can't stand to hear this."

"We won't be alone. We'll be assisting other organizations in preparing the Kigali hospital complex. They put a huge water tank in and are setting up tents at the entrance to make a triage center. Unfortunately, the whole peace process is failing badly. We've been told the wounded will mostly be civilian."

"Oh God ..."

"You know Liz, there comes a point in most life travels, usually in the autumn of our journey, when we challenge the status quo with an inner wisdom and knowledge that there's a deeper meaning to life."

"Enough!" Feeling physically sick from David's words, Lizzie grabbed their coffee cups and headed to the kitchen. "No more. I can't hear any more. Let's just go to bed. Make love to me and hold me all night. I know why you're going, I just don't want you to go."

David complied, silently following his wife upstairs, where they slept all night with their arms and legs intertwined.

Only Lizzie had barely slept a wink when the alarm went off. She tiptoed down to the kitchen, careful not to wake Jonathan, and poured David a travel mug of coffee. By the time he followed her down the stairs, hair still wet from the shower, a car was waiting out front to take him to the airport.

At the front door, Lizzie stared at David—no, she looked *through* David, as though she'd traveled in a time machine to the first time she'd seen his kind, smiling face.

They hugged and kissed, not saying much, both trying to hold back tears and put on a brave front for the other.

"No good-byes," he said at last. "I love you, my darling. With all my heart."

"I love you too. Be safe."

As the car drove away, Lizzie collapsed on the floor in tears.

CHAPTER 43
APRIL 1994

L IZZIE WASN'T THINKING about getting Jonathan ready for school. She wasn't thinking about what to wear to work. Her thoughts were constantly on David. She needed to hear from him—she needed to hear his voice. Instead, she received information from former co-workers at the PSPP, a journalist friend who sent reports, and assorted news faxes from overseas contacts who'd promised to keep her informed. She read an incoming fax:

```
It is, yet again, a bad time in the history of
mankind, and a perfect storm is brewing. The end
result is likely to be a country ripped apart by
mass killings. It has all led up to this. For
over forty years, tensions have been rising in
Rwanda, like a dormant volcano starting to brew,
waiting to erupt.
```

This is the last thing I need to hear right now, she thought, searching for a fingernail to bite but finding no more available. She was acutely aware that the situation in Rwanda was escalating like a pressure cooker. But seeing these updates in print always shook her to her core.

By the third of the month, Lizzie had heard all sorts of rumors suggesting that something disastrous was going to happen. On April 6, the impetus triggering the violence actually occurred, when an aircraft carrying the Rwandan president and the Burundian president was hit by a missile over the Kigali airport. *Oh, God, I wish I would hear from him.*

Shortly after the incident, Lizzie received another fax from a co-worker. As much as she dreaded reading it, she was too hungry for news to resist devouring it as it came over line by line:

```
... and leaders of political opposition groups were
killed, followed by the systematic massacre of
the Tutsi. Any Hutus who sided with the Tutsi
were also designated to die. Soldiers and militia
began to use Rwandans' national identity cards
to determine ethnicity and kill the Tutsi—the
genocidal killings had begun. Hutu were ordered
to kill, plunder, rape, and massacre the Tutsi
community.

The forces organized the Hutu civilians to arm
themselves in any way they could. Since bullets
were expensive, most Tutsis were killed by hand
weapons, such as machetes or knives. Some of the
victims were given the choice of paying for a
bullet so they'd have a faster death. Many were
tortured before being killed. Women were brutally
beaten and raped.

On April 8, the PSPP sent a surgical team along
with medical and surgical supplies into Kigali to
help the victims of the fighting that had exploded
over the past two days while ...
```

Finally, *finally,* David reached Lizzie by phone. At last, she heard his voice, although the connection was choppy at best. He told her that he'd arrived in the city prior to the plane crash and that the other PSPP expatriate staff stationed in Kigali were essentially confined to their homes because of the fighting. Some remained in the capital to serve the wounded, hoping to be backed up by the surgical teams on standby as soon as their transfer was possible. As soon as it could be arranged, the nonessential staff was to be evacuated.

"This is crazy," she told David. "Get the hell out of there and come home!"

"I'm working on that right now," he said. "Liz, I love you."

But then another report came in, causing Lizzie to break down in tears. She felt helpless and scared reading the horrifying words:

```
The country is engulfed in terror. No one is
safe from the barbarity. It seems the world
had gone insane. Moving around the city has
become nearly impossible, with roadblocks and
barriers everywhere. The country is hemorrhaging
brutality.
```

Lizzie didn't know what to do. So she just sat on the couch crying and drinking coffee.

Matthew stopped by on his way home from work. "Hey, kiddo, how are you holding up?" He gave her a big one-armed hug. "Have you heard any more news?"

"I'm not holding up, and I've heard nothing more than what I already told Sophie this afternoon. But it sounds like it's turned into hell over there, more every minute. I can't read, I can't concentrate, I can't sleep. I've never been so afraid. Why doesn't he get out of there *now*? I know they're evacuating the staff soon, but it can't be soon enough for me. I just want him home, Matthew."

Her hands shook as she spoke; it seemed she was always shaking lately. Her nerves were constantly on edge, and she didn't feel like herself. She thought it was odd that she'd never felt this way—this scared, this frantic—when she'd been on dangerous assignments herself, but being the one left behind this time, being the one at home waiting and not knowing what was going on, was torture.

"You and Jonathan are going to have dinner with us. You shouldn't be alone now," Matthew said. "Since Jonathan's already with Sophie at our place, come with me. I'll drive you over and bring you back home later. It would do you good to talk to Sophie while I toss a ball around with Jonathan or something."

"Yeah, okay, thanks, that sounds good. But I want to take a shower first. I'll meet you over there in less than an hour, okay?"

And it did do Lizzie good to be with friends that evening, to find solace in freely expressing her sorrow and receiving their sympathy in return. But after she was back home, having tucked Jonathan in for the night, she found herself back downstairs on the couch, staring into the darkness, rehashing every word of their last conversation.

David had told her she wouldn't believe the horrors he was witnessing—he was glad she wasn't there to experience them with him. The beautiful country had turned into an ugly, giant graveyard—a land filled with senseless violence, the mark of mankind gone terribly wrong. Twisted decomposing bodies. Amputated limbs. Decapitated heads. Pieces of human bodies thrown down hills, floating in the water. Smoke from burning villages.

Carnage.

Fear.

Hatred.

He'd described it as though some evil force were blowing through the country, infecting human brains with something dark, vengeful, and evil. Tens of thousands of people, pushed to extremes by intense emotions, had made their choices. And the rest of the world was standing by with shaded eyes, refusing to watch the slaughter of men, women, children, and the elderly. The systematic killing continued for days on end, exterminating people as though they were pesky bugs.

Lizzie couldn't believe her husband, her David, was stuck in the middle of all that. She couldn't believe that all the good work he felt compelled to do had led him to this incredibly bad situation. Feeling exhausted from worry and utterly useless to do anything to help, she finally closed her eyes and drifted off into a restless, dreamless sleep.

*

The next day, Lizzie received news that David's surgical team was scheduled to remain in Kigali for two more days to surgically treat the latest round of gruesome injuries—machete and gunshot wounds, beatings and blows to the head and body, amputations. All too rapidly, the hospital had reached maximum capacity, so tents had been erected on the grounds. Although the roads were virtually impassable, each day, at risk of execution, personnel scoured the city to find the injured and deliver them to the field hospital. They just couldn't leave them out there, dying in the dirt.

In an effort to help, one of Lizzie's friends from the PSPP kept forwarding her the string of memos coming in, apparently without reading all of them herself first. Lizzie sat at the kitchen table with her cup of coffee going through them all … until she came to the one that would change her life forever:

On Friday, April 15, a team of PSPP surgeons went with a larger group of rescue workers to search for injured in a nearby district of Kigali. Radio messages reported that the area stunk from thick smoke and that the team was met by strong resistance from the militia at each barrier they went through. When leaving the district, the militia thoroughly checked all vehicles in the convoy for Tutsi escapees.

At one checkpoint, twelve men stood under a banana tree manning the roadblock. Next to them, along the side of the road, was a pile of bodies, one tossed on top of another. The men were armed with clubs and machetes, one had a machine gun over his arm and several grenades in his belt.

As the third truck prepared to pass through the barricade, the men surrounded it and started rocking the vehicle. One of them bashed in a glass window with his club and then attempted to drag out a dark-skinned female worker, demanding to see her papers.

As the woman was being pulled by her arms by several militia through the jagged glass, kicking and screaming, the surgeon sitting next to her, identified as Dr. David Cohen of California, USA, held on to her legs, trying to pull her back in and shouting to the men that she was Hutu.

The man with the machine gun shouted something, then turned the gun on Dr. Cohen—one of the "lucky ones" to be killed by an expensive bullet. All fell quiet.

The men succeeded in pulling the woman out of the vehicle, dragged her to the underbrush, and then proceeded to brutalize her with …

There it was. In black and white. The words Lizzie dreaded more than any others she could imagine.

David had been shot. He'd been killed. He was dead.

Dead!

Gone forever.

She gasped, doubled over at the waist, knocking her coffee cup off the table, smashing it to pieces on the floor. She herself fell to the ground in what felt like slow motion. Everything, in fact, looked like it was moving in slow motion. Until she didn't see anything at all.

Lizzie didn't know how much time passed before they came to the house to officially inform her of the news. Mechanically, automatically, she opened the door, accepted the envelope of papers held out to her, offered them coffee. After they left, she moved lethargically, nothing seemed real. She forced herself to climb the stairs, put on clothes, call Sophie to pick up Jonathan. Lizzie fought against sinking into the mire, minute by minute, hour by hour. She had a child who needed her. Already, there was no anger or rage—in their place, apathy slid in, a protective shield against the sickening truth. *Thank God I have Jonathan. If it weren't for him …*

*

David's body was shipped home. Lizzie allowed Matthew and Sophie to take over all the arrangements for the graveside funeral, including making the reservations to fly out David's parents, who were rendered impotent from their grief.

Lizzie herself was numb, barely functioning except to attend to Jonathan's basic needs. She couldn't even produce tears. She felt empty and emotionless, as though her spirit had disappeared and she was left with only a vacant shell inside. The modern calendar is separated by B.C. and A.D.—Lizzie now divided her life into W.D. and A.D., "with David" and "after David." The line between the two was distinct. She thought about nothing other than David, playing the sound of his voice over and over in her head like a melancholy record.

On the day of the funeral, Lizzie stood by the coffin, stiff-backed, stoic, palms clasped tightly together to stop the shaking. She felt like the only thing holding her up was Jonathan's presence beside her. She knew she had to be strong for him. There was no other choice. He grabbed for one of her hands and gripped it so tightly, her knuckles turned white. She felt him draw the little strength she had left into him, as though her arm were a conduit of energy he needed to survive.

Jonathan teetered, and Lizzie bent to pick him up. She was afraid she'd be too weak to lift him, but she simply had to hold him close to her. She didn't know what else she could do to help him. Against her chest, he lightly closed his eyes, his eyelids quivering each time he blew out a long, sustained breath.

Lizzie was relieved that Matthew had agreed to speak on behalf of the immediate family. As he began his eulogy, Jonathan nuzzled into her neck and she clung to him, listening but not really hearing.

"David, our beloved David, was tragically taken from us, and we profoundly mourn his loss. He was a husband, a father, a son, a friend, a doctor, a healer, and a humanitarian. He was one of the few who stayed behind in Rwanda during the most difficult of times as others fled. He tried to save those so desperate for assistance. That's simply who David was.

"David was an honorable, kind, and admirable man. Many doctors work in less than desirable conditions, but only a small number work in the most dispiriting of situations, like conflict zones, refugee camps, and disaster sites. David and his wife, Lizzie, worked extensively to help their fellow man wherever they were needed most.

"All we can extract from the brutality of this situation are lessons—lessons to improve our world so that David's death will not be in vain. David talked a lot about life choices. He said we all need to be aware that each moment in life is a choice. We have to determine how we, as individuals, envision the world and see ourselves fitting into it and, ultimately, what actions we'll take. Life is always about choices. David weighed out his options and made his own choices. As he said to me before leaving on this mission, 'I have no choice but to follow my convictions.'

"I look up to him as a role model. What kind of role model should each of us strive to be? One that allows future generations to turn their backs on the rest of the world? As David often said, we all need to increase our consciousness and motivate our fellow human beings to band together. We're all one. We're all interconnected.

"Without much rhetoric, David was a man who lived in the present moment and put his convictions into action. He leaves behind a most admirable legacy.

"I've lost a dear friend—a man I respected and held in the highest esteem. Although he was passionate in his humanitarian efforts, his greatest passion was his love for his wife, Lizzie, his son, Jonathan, and his mother and father. I grieve for the loss we're all experiencing today. For all of you who knew David, you know he loved quotes. So I'll end with one of his favorites, attributed to Albert Einstein from *The World As I See It:* 'How strange is the lot of us mortals! Each of us is here for a brief sojourn; for what purpose he knows not, though he sometimes thinks he senses it. But without deeper reflection one knows from daily life that one exists for other people—first of all for those upon whose smiles and well-being our own happiness is wholly dependent, and then for the many, unknown to us, to whose destinies we are bound by the ties of sympathy.'

"David, we gather here today as one, sending you the same light and love you brought to each of us. We won't forget what you taught us and how you served mankind. Rest in peace."

Weeks later, Lizzie read in the paper:

> In the end, over 800,000 people, some say up to a million, were murdered and brutally slaughtered in the Rwandan genocide. It will go down in history as the time when Rwanda's Hutu majority turned against the Tutsis with hundreds of thousands massacred—the Rwanda genocide of 1994.

But to Lizzie, it was the time when her beloved died, when her husband was brutally taken away from her. And life thereafter would never, ever be the same.

Chapter 44
The Astral Plane

Malach: David Cohen has returned home to us, as planned. Let the healing and the learning begin for those left behind.

Pneuma: Let me know what to do to help.

Malach: Actually, you already started some time back when you sent an inspiration I requested of you. How about trying another one now, Pneuma, to help Jonathan?

Pneuma: Send him some love? Do you have something specific in mind?

Malach: I do. Some unconditional love. Give Lizzie the inspiration to encounter a dog that's going to have puppies—puppies that will be ready to leave their mother in time for Jonathan's next birthday. It's time to send in Betty Rose.

Pneuma: It may take a bit of work. Lizzie is closed off from us right now and may not allow herself to receive this message. But I'll give it my best shot.

CHAPTER 45
JULY 8, 1994

ONTHS HAD PASSED since they'd lost David. Jonathan thought about him every day. To Jonathan, the death of his father simply seemed like the wrong plot twist in a story. It all could have turned out so differently, he felt, if his father hadn't gone away. He didn't understand why his father's story had to play out the way it did. He was consumed with an internally directed anger at David's decision to leave. He couldn't comprehend why he and his mom weren't enough to make him stay home. *Why did he stay with those people instead of coming home to me and Mommy? Did he love those people more?* When lying in bed, amid the softness of his blankets and his sheets, in a place somewhere between sleep and wakefulness, in his mind's eye, David would come to him. The sensation of David's physical presence filled Jonathan's darkened bedroom as he remembered how his father lifted him onto his shoulders. He felt so secure and safe, placing his trust in his daddy, feeling his strong arms holding his legs and hearing his playful, lighthearted laughter. *Daddy, I miss you so much.*

That was how Jonathan related to his father—like his life was a story, one that had come to a tragic end. Sometimes even when he wasn't in that twilight zone of sleep, out in the real world, Jonathan sensed his dad near him. A waft of his cologne would linger in the air, finding home in Jonathan's nostrils, or he'd feel the sensation of David's strong hand on the top of his head, tousling his hair, or he'd sense him being near when the light in his bedroom would flicker precisely three times.

Just as his father used to tell him countless bedtime stories, Jonathan divulged his own stories to his dad as he lay in bed under the covers, ready to fall asleep. "I've a whopper of a story to tell you tonight, Dad," he'd say. Sometimes he'd confess his fears. "Daddy, are you there? I can feel you. Daddy, I'm afraid. I'm afraid of things in this world. I worry about monsters and boogeymen and sharks … What if Mommy dies, too, and I'm all by myself?" It felt good to share these things with his dad, and even though he never received an answer, he knew David could hear him. He just knew it.

Shortly after David died, Jonathan snuck into Lizzie and David's bedroom and snatched David's pillow, replacing it with his own, finding the comfort and tranquility he craved when he snuggled with it every night. One day, he caught Lizzie stripping his bed to wash the sheets, and she pulled the pillowcase off David's pillow and put it in the pile with the sheets. Jonathan walked into the room at that moment and screamed bloody murder. "Don't. Don't take Daddy's pillowcase. No, don't! It smells like him." He grabbed the pillowcase and pulled it tight to his chest, as if he were trying to squeeze himself out of existence, then crumpled to the ground on the floor and cried, "I want you back, Daddy. I want you back now!"

In the past, David was always the one to take Jonathan to his taekwondo lessons, and after class, they would go out for a hot-fudge sundae together—a special father-son ritual that Jonathan looked forward to every week. After David died, Jonathan would sit at taekwondo class and watch the other kids with their dads, which left him feeling different—lonely and empty. "Mommy, I'm not going to taekwondo anymore," he said. He couldn't tell her how he felt about David because he hated seeing her eyes go hollow and the corners of her mouth droop, her shoulders caving in like she was an old lady.

He couldn't save his dad, and he couldn't save his mother, either. Sometimes he'd see a few flickers of light in her eyes—the old Mommy he used to know, the real her, but those moments were few and far between. Sometimes he felt like he was the parent and Lizzie the child, reminding her she needed to eat or go to bed. It was a monumental burden for one so young. His dad had always been his lighthouse, guiding his way when there was fog. Now he felt like he was navigating on his own.

To Lizzie, life was a swirling, dark abyss. The house was far too quiet with David gone. She missed the sound of his razor buzzing in the morning. His once-annoying snoring now seemed sweet, like an old love song. Her despair grew like a weed inside her heart. When cleaning out one of his dresser drawers, she found his handwritten bucket list. When she read, *Walking down the aisle with Liz at Jonathan's wedding,* she broke. She protected her grief as though it were her secret lover.

Although she avoided mirrors, she knew she didn't look well. She felt herself walking like she wore lead weights, with a vacant and nebulous expression. The few times she did see her reflection, she saw a hollow and distant look in her eyes, as though she were physically there but living in another time, somewhere in the past. She kept thinking about how she'd just assumed she and David would grow old together like the two gnarled oaks in their backyard. She'd thought wrong. She couldn't muster up any joy or cheer, barely tolerating the day-to-day routine of getting by. She allowed silence to settle in the house like dust in the desert after a windstorm.

One day she'd been stripping the linens off Jonathan's bed, feeling lower than low, literally forcing herself to attend to household chores. When Jonathan walked into the room, he'd screamed, "Don't take Daddy's pillowcase! It smells like him." Lizzie had no idea that he'd swapped his pillow with David's, and she was ill equipped to soothe him. What could she say? She'd had no words. So she let him clutch the pillowcase for dear life, knelt on the floor next to him, and held him from behind as he sobbed. She didn't know what else to do. She just didn't know what to do. Then he refused to go to taekwondo, but he wouldn't say why. He simply wouldn't go. Sometimes she'd let him sleep in the bed with her, but she didn't want either of them to become dependent on that. Even in her severe depression, she knew that was a step that could descend down a slippery slope. She worried she would never be a good mother again. *Why can't I snap out of this for my little boy?*

Sophie's focus following David's death was providing shelter from the storm for her friend. She wanted to do all she could to comfort her, but having lost her own husband tragically and unexpectedly, she knew Lizzie would have to find her own path out of the dark in her own time. She also understood some of Jonathan's fears and pain, having lost her own father as a child, then her mother as an adult, and as much as she wanted to soothe his soul and mend his broken heart, she knew she didn't have the power to do that, either. Her inability to give Lizzie and her godson what they both wanted most left her feeling helpless and useless.

On Lizzie's worst days, Sophie would stay over in the guesthouse. She'd bring them dinner, she'd take Jonathan to the park, she'd help him with his letters and numbers over the summer break. *What else can I do to support them? How can I make them smile?*

Knowing that Jonathan's birthday was coming up and that Lizzie wouldn't have the energy to plan anything, she settled on a party. She'd throw him a very special party. Adults couldn't always rise up out of their grief when in deep mourning, but kids were more resilient, she knew from her years in the social services, and she hoped that Jonathan would rise to the occasion. He needed a celebration, and she was determined to give him one. She didn't know what else she could do.

CHAPTER 46

AUGUST 6, 1994

A FEW WEEKS BEFORE Jonathan's birthday, the idea came
to Sophie late one night: It would be a Mad Scientist party!
Jonathan had always been infatuated with Albert Einstein,
as had his father, so the theme would give her lots to work with even
as it served as a sentimental homage to David, on this, Jonathan's first
birthday without him. Matthew was all for the idea of hosting the party
at their place so that Lizzie wouldn't have to be inconvenienced with the
preparations at all. In fact, he loved the idea of a houseful of fun-loving,
boisterous little kids who would hopefully lift Jonathan's spirits.

She'd started in on the planning and the shopping and the cake
design the very next morning. By now, mostly everything was done, so
Sophie felt quite relaxed and content as she sashayed into the kitchen
the morning of the party to find Matthew sitting at the island, eating a
blueberry muffin.

She planted a kiss on his cheek. "You have to come out and see how
I set up the table. Everything looks so cute!"

"Sit down and rest a minute. Tell me all about it while I finish my
muffin, and let me know what I can do to help."

Matthew peeled the liner off a second muffin and started buttering
it as Sophie reached down into one of the shopping bags on the kitchen
floor and removed several items to show him. "Look at these cool white

lab coats and safety glasses I got for all the kids to wear! And check out this Albert Einstein wig for Jonathan!" She held up a balding latex headpiece with white, fluffy hair around the sides and back. "I made a lot of the things, but I bought some too. I just want him to love this party!"

"How could he not?" Matthew said between bites with a smile.

"Oh! And I ordered these petri dishes. Let me show you what I did with them." Sophie walked over to the refrigerator and pulled out a tray. "What do you think? I filled the petri dishes with clear gelatin, then I added colored sprinkles to look like colonizing bacteria. Aren't they so creepy-cool?"

Matthew's smiled widened. "Yeah, I saw those when I got the butter. Very creepy-cool. Sophie, everything is so clever. The kids are going to love this. How many are definitely coming?"

"Well, Lizzie sent out the invites, and she got eight positive RSVPs, a few more maybes. There're separate tables outside for the treats, for food, and for scientific experiments."

Matthew put his arm around Sophie's waist as they walked out to the backyard together to inspect the setup.

"And what are these?" he asked her, pointing to a line of paper bags atop a table, each with a name tag on it.

"They're the party favors to take home. Look inside."

He gingerly peeked into one of the bags, careful not to disturb the arrangement of the favors too much. "A magnifying glass, a test tube filled with candy, lab goggles … Really great job, Sophie, really cute. And what's my role? What can I do? Want me to go buy some dry ice to put in the beakers and the punch bowl? That would look awesome, wouldn't it?"

"Great idea. While you do that, I want to stop over at Lizzie's—bring some breakfast and Jonathan's gift." They kissed good-bye. "See you back here before party time!"

Jonathan woke as the sun poured through his bedroom window. His first thought was that it was his sixth birthday. A warm breeze blew in through the half-open window, rustling the curtains with faded sailboats on them. For some reason, he didn't feel excited, not even at the crepe paper decorations and balloons his mother must have hung in his room while he was sleeping. He plodded down the steps in his Ninja Turtle pajamas, slapping his bare feet on each step, yawning as he went.

"Mom, where are you?"

"In the kitchen, drinking coffee. Happy birthday, sweetie," Lizzie said as he came through the doorway. "Want anything special for your birthday breakfast?"

Jonathan plopped himself down at the kitchen table, his hair sticking up at various angles and his eyes still half closed. "Just a bowl of cereal, Mom."

"No chocolate chip pancakes? I'm in a pancake-making mood!"

"Nah, cereal is fine. Thanks for decorating my room."

"You're welcome, sweetie. I just wanted you to start your special day off with something special. Hey, would you like to open some presents now? Your big one is for later."

"I'll open them all later."

"You'll love them—are you sure?"

"Yep."

Lizzie looked at Jonathan's sad eyes with her own, trying again to bring some sparkle to them: "Are you excited about your party today?" No answer. "Be sure to thank Sophie and Matthew, okay? Sophie's worked so hard on this party to make it special for you."

"I will. I'm still kind of sleepy. I'm going to go watch cartoons."

"Okay, I'll bring you a bowl of cereal," Lizzie said to his back as he shuffled into the family room.

A few minutes later, the front doorbell rang with Sophie's distinctive ring. She stood outside with a knot in her belly, a bag of gifts in one hand and a white bakery bag in the other. How she missed the days when Jonathan would squeal with delight at the sound of her approach, scampering to the door to greet her. The knot remained in place when it was Lizzie, not Jonathan, who opened the door.

Lizzie gave Sophie a big hug. "You're such a gem to do this for him."

"It's my pleasure. You know I love doing this stuff." Sophie handed Lizzie the bakery bag. "I brought us some apple fritters and fresh coffee."

"Oh, great. I was going to make pancakes, but he isn't interested," Lizzie said with a nod toward the family room, signaling Sophie where Jonathan was.

Sophie headed into the family room to find Jonathan sitting on the floor, leaning against the leather couch, eating cereal while watching TV.

"Happy birthday, Bunkies!" she said brightly. "Come give me a hug."

He did as he was asked, hugging her warmly. "Thanks, Toffee."

"I need to give you six spankings. And a pinch to grow an inch. You know today is one of the best days of my life 'cause it's the day you were born." After she playfully spanked and pinched him, she asked, "Want an apple fritter?"

"Sure."

After she delivered one to him on a plate with a napkin, she said, "Let me have some coffee with your mom first, and then I'm giving you your presents. Wait until you see all the decorations and treats for your party. I think you'll love everything, and we're going to have a lot of fun!"

"We will, Toffee," Jonathan agreed, then he quietly turned back to the TV and munched on his fritter.

"He doesn't seem too excited," Sophie said to Lizzie as she walked into the kitchen, glancing back at Jonathan over her shoulder.

"I know. That's what worries me. Nothing seems to excite him. He seems more in the dumps than ever. I see moments when the old Jonathan emerges, but then he goes back inside himself again."

"Kind of like you, huh?"

"Hmm … I guess so."

"I got him a cassette recorder from Matthew and me. You know how he loves to create stories, and he told me he wants to record them. So I thought it would be a pretty cool gift that would interest him. He's extremely creative."

"I like that idea. But I gotta tell you, some of the stories he tells are pretty dark and upsetting. I can relate to that. I feel the same way. One day your life is going along great, and the next, the rug is suddenly pulled out from under you. But I'm preaching to the choir, aren't I? You know very well how that goes."

"I do. And I know what a long process it can be to heal."

"Heal," Lizzie repeated sullenly. "What does that even mean? For me, just trying to get by and function and not seem too sad for Jonathan, I guess."

"Oh, honey," Sophie said with a sigh. "Let me know what I can do to help."

"There's nothing anyone can do. You know that."

"I'm sitting in your heart, feeling your pain, my friend. But today, what we need to do is concentrate on Jonathan's healing ... help him create a happy story. So you go collect yourself and I'll be right back. I want to give him his presents before the party."

But when Sophie returned to the family room, Jonathan was no longer there. Climbing the steps to his bedroom, she stopped to look at the family portraits lining the wall above the rail. David and Lizzie at their wedding ... David on his back on the floor, holding Jonathan up in the air like an airplane, with his arms straight out ... the family portrait of the three of them when Jonathan was four. That world was now in the past.

As she suspected, Jonathan was in his bedroom with the door closed. She knocked. "Can I come in, honey?"

"Sure." He was sitting on his bed, staring at his feet.

"Time to open your presents!"

She handed him a box wrapped in purple-and-white-striped paper. There was a time, not too long ago, when the sight of wrapped presents made him act like he was on amphetamines, jumping up and down and tearing the paper off with gusto. This time, he slowly unwrapped the gift like a person on antidepressants.

"Wow, Toffee, a whole bunch of storybooks. Thanks so much. These are the ones I wanted." He leaned over and hugged her.

"I know how you love stories. And now—ta-da!—something to help you create your own." She handed him a second box.

He was a bit more animated this time, tearing off the wrapping paper.

"Whoa! A tape recorder." He eagerly turned the box this way and that. "Thanks, Toffee. This is a great present—you remembered that I want to make my own recordings."

"I got you a bunch of tapes, too," Sophie said, smiling widely now and handing him a smaller bag filled with cassettes.

"I have a story I want to record right now. Can I do that?"

"Of course, do you want me to help you read the directions—figure out how to use it?"

"No, I want to try myself. I think it'll be easy. You can go back downstairs now."

Sophie was a little hurt at how abruptly he was dismissing her, but she didn't let her disappointment show. "You have to get dressed for your party soon."

"Okay," he answered, not looking up from the box. But on her way out the door, he called, "Wait. I have a question."

She turned back and looked at him. "Shoot. What is it?"

"Remember when I was a little kid and we went to the cemetery to help free Neil? And you told me about the line between the date he was born and when he died on his gravestone—that the line was the story of his life?"

She was a little stunned that he remembered that conversation so vividly. "Yes, I remember. What about it?"

"Well, because Daddy and Neil didn't wait until they were old to die, does that mean the line between their numbers is shorter than other people's?"

She hesitated, trying to think of the best way to respond. "No, it doesn't. All the lines are the same length."

"Oh, okay, thanks. See you later." Then he went about setting up his tape recorder.

Sophie rejoined Lizzie in the kitchen. Lizzie poured her a hot cup of coffee, and they sat at the table.

"Well, the presents aroused a bit of excitement in him, so that's good. I'm hoping this will be a good day."

"Glad he liked them."

"Matthew is helping me put the finishing touches on the party. It's going to be so cute. He's going to show the boys how to make slime, and then they can all take it home with them."

"Slime?"

"Don't you remember ever making that?"

"Nope."

"The secret recipe is clear Elmer's glue, water, glow-in-the-dark paint, neon-green food coloring, and borax. It makes the best goop. They'll each make their own batch in a zip-top bag. The parents may hate me, but the kids will love it. I'm really excited."

"I can tell. You're so good at these kinds of things."

Sophie was eager to share all the details with Lizzie. "There's also pizza, punch, games, and a cupcake station—I baked and frosted a bunch of cupcakes, and the kids can decorate them any way they want. ... And I of course designed Jonathan his annual signature birthday cake, but that's just for us, for after the party."

"It sounds wonderful, Soph. You and Matthew have done so much for this. Very cute." Although she was smiling, tears started rolling down Lizzie's face. "Thank you for doing this for him. But *I* should be doing it—I know that. I don't know what's the matter with me—that I can't pull it together." She bent over, hands covering her face, and wept with deep, heaving sobs.

Lizzie's pain was palpable. Sophie could almost feel the loneliness and despair seeping out of her body through her tears. She looked broken— like a little bird curled up with broken wings—and Sophie didn't know the words to soothe her. She stood behind her friend, stroking her hair and gathering it into a ponytail, embracing her with pure empathy.

"Go ahead and cry. Let it out. Let yourself feel it. It'll be okay, Lizzie. You'll be okay. We'll get through this together. I promise. I promise it will get easier."

She continued stroking Lizzie's hair until the sobbing slowed. Then Sophie pulled Lizzie to her feet, hugged her, handed her a box of tissues, and told her to go wash up before Jonathan saw her.

"I'm going to take him back to the house with me while you get dressed. He can help us finish up and be there early to greet his guests. In the meantime, you pull yourself together, take a hot shower, and come over when you're ready. Good? And, Lizzie, wear something other than sweats, okay? You remember how tired you got of seeing me in my pajamas for months?"

The corners of Lizzie's mouth angled upward a little at the memory. "Okay."

"You'll feel okay again one day. You really will. You'll get through this," Sophie repeated. "It *will* get better."

Then Sophie shouted up the stairs. "You ready, Jonathan? Time to head over to the Mad Scientist's laboratory!"

CHAPTER 47

AUGUST 6, 1994

ALTHOUGH SHE WASN'T in the mood, Lizzie got ready for the birthday party. Sitting at her dressing table, she picked up the small pearl earrings—an anniversary gift from David—and put them on, her face averted from the mirror to avoid seeing her reflection. She didn't want to see it; she didn't need to. All of her parts had been fastened together by David's love, and now all those shattered pieces shifted and rolled around inside her like a kaleidoscope. During their years of marriage, he'd been there to fill in her gaps, fortify her deficits. Now there were all these empty spaces and places around and through her, and she wasn't adapting well to all of the things that had changed so fast. Looking at her watch, she abruptly stood and straightened her dress, slipped on her sandals, vowing to herself that she'd rally for her little boy.

By the time she got to the party, all of the children had already arrived and the festivities were well under way. When Sophie saw her coming up the walk, she breathed a sigh of relief, not realizing until just then that she hadn't been positive Lizzie would show. Although she'd just seen her a few hours ago, she greeted her with a tender hug and led her to the kitchen, where they could see the kids running around the backyard through the sliding glass doors. Lizzie smiled at the sight of their white lab coats and safety glasses as they ran from Matthew, who was chasing them around with some gross-looking "lab cultures" dangling from a stick and laughing as much as the kids were. Jonathan had *loved* the Albert Einstein hairpiece, and when he'd put it on, it's as though the disguise had freed him to be a kid again. It was so wonderful to see him laughing and playing and having a good time—Lizzie and Sophie even caught him glancing at the gift table a few times with an animated look on his face.

After lunch and a few more games, it was time to make the slime, which definitely turned out to be the pièce de résistance of the party. Matthew donned his own lab jacket and goggles to demonstrate how to make the neon-green concoction, giving instructions in his best German accent. Sophie had thought the kids would want to take home the slime as souvenirs, but when it was all done, they instead decided to throw it at Matthew, the best part of the "experiment" for them. As Sophie watched him being pelted by one messy blob at a time and clearly enjoying the whole interaction, she couldn't help but acknowledge how great he was with kids, how much of a kid at heart he was himself.

Judging by the level of fun everyone was having—including Lizzie, who set up shop at one of the tables with the kids, mixing mystery medicines and potions from water and food coloring in the collection of beakers Sophie had provided—the party was a smashing success. Everything was going even better than Sophie had hoped … until dessert. As the kids were decorating their cupcakes with jelly beans, sprinkles, and licorice pieces, Josh, the tallest kid in the group with the blondest hair, said to Jonathan, "This is a cool party. One of the best I've ever been to. And your dad is awesome."

Jonathan's joy immediately fell flat, like a balloon deflating, leaving a shriveled and flaccid form. He tore off his Albert Einstein wig and threw it to the ground. His face turned beet red, he knitted his brow, and he clenched his jaw. Then he glared at Josh with piercing eyes and erupted. *"He's not my dad!"* he screamed, pointing at Matthew. "He's. Not. My. Dad. My dad is dead. My dad is DEAD!"

All the kids stopped what they were doing and stared at him as he stomped his foot with every word he yelled out. Jonathan burst into tears and ran into the house, leaving everyone in stunned silence.

"Oh my God, no," Lizzie whispered under her breath.

"You go after him," Sophie hold her, "and we'll wrap up the party."

Sophie and Matthew quickly assured the kids that everything would be okay, that everything was fine. "Why don't you finish up your cupcakes and enjoy them before your parents pick you up?" And sure enough, by the time parents started stringing in a few minutes later, all the kids were laughing and joyous again, frosting lining their lips. Each happily left the party with favor bag in hand, oohing and aahing over the contents inside.

"Cool party, Dr. Hobbs," one boy said over his shoulder, waving his hand.

"Thanks for having me. Say good-bye to Jonathan for me," a little girl said.

When it was Josh's turn to leave, he approached Matthew with his head hung low. "I'm sorry I ruined the party."

"You did no such thing, young man," Matthew replied. "Don't you worry about it. You didn't know, and that's okay. Jonathan's really sad about losing his dad, but this day was really fun for him, and you helped make it that way. Everyone had a good time, right? So don't give it any more thought." He gave Josh a pat on the back.

Josh's chin lifted and he breathed deeply, as though Matthew had lifted a heavy weight off his shoulders. "Okay, thanks."

Sophie and Matthew cleaned everything up while Lizzie was in their bedroom with Jonathan. When they finally emerged later, Sophie's heart melted at the sight of Jonathan's red, swollen eyes and tearstained cheeks. He looked exhausted, downtrodden, spent. She remembered all too well the distraught, rhythmic beat of a broken heart: *I'm angry. I'm sad. I'm angry.* It was hard enough to recover from the loss of a spouse. How was such a little boy supposed to cope with the enormity of his pain and suffering? All she wanted to do was make him feel better. *Now.*

"Hey, buddy," she said, going over to him and pulling him to her. "You're okay, sweetie. You're okay now," she soothed, stroking his matted hair from his forehead. "You know what might make you feel better? I have one more surprise. Want to see it?"

"Sure," he said, shoulders slouched, head still bowed.

"It's your special cake for this year," Sophie said as she brought the cake out from the fridge. "An Albert Einstein cake. And it's your favorite—carrot cake."

"Wow, Toffee, that really looks like him. I like how you used cotton candy for his hair."

"Well, you didn't have a cupcake, so why don't we light the candles on this right now and you can blow them out."

"Okay. But I'm not going to make a wish, because I know it won't come true."

Matthew put a comforting arm around Lizzie when she audibly gasped at his remark, but then he broke into singing "Happy Birthday" to break the silence and lighten the mood.

And it worked. Everyone enjoyed their cake, and after Matthew stuffed the last bite of his slice in his mouth, he jumped up from his chair and rubbed his hands together. "Guess what? It's time for your present from your mom ... because it's been here all day and it literally can't wait a moment longer," Matthew said, sounding genuinely excited. "You ready for something truly special? Your new best friend?" he asked Jonathan, who was now all wide-eyed and open-eared. "Close your eyes and hold out your arms," he said, then he disappeared into the back bedroom for a minute.

When Jonathan opened his eyes, his arms were filled with a warm, wriggling Rottweiler puppy. He jumped for joy and squealed with delight. Lizzie's eyes filled with tears.

"*There* you are," Jonathan whispered to his new pup, cradling and rocking her with the hugest grin covering his face. "I knew you'd come."

Lizzie couldn't have been more relieved. "What are you going to name her?" she asked.

"Betty Rose," he answered without hesitation.

"Betty Rose? That's a pretty odd name for a puppy. Why Betty?"

"Because I already know her. I just don't know her in *this* body." Jonathan buried his head into her fur and kissed her neck. "Hi, Betty. It's so good to see you again."

Sophie and Matthew exchanged a knowing look while Lizzie just stood there. It had been a while since Jonathan had said something like that—since before David's death, if she stopped to think about it—but she knew her son well enough by now not to question him or doubt his beliefs. She'd learned to just listen to him, feeling much more open to the possibilities.

Later that evening, with Betty Rose sleeping soundly in her cage in Jonathan's room, Lizzie tucked him in for bed. "Happy birthday, my big six-year-old boy. I hope you had a good birthday."

"I did, Mommy. But I'm sorry I messed up my party."

"Honey, you didn't mess up anything. You got a little emotional, that's all. And you have reason to be. We all have meltdowns now and then. It was a great party, and all your guests had a wonderful time. Now get some sleep and have good dreams tonight. Let that dream catcher catch anything bad."

"Night, Mommy. I love you."

"Love you more," she said, kissing his forehead.

When she'd left the room, leaving his door open just a crack, Jonathan pulled the covers up to his chin and snuggled David's pillow. Catching a whiff of his father's familiar cologne, he asked aloud, "Daddy, are you here? … You were supposed to be at my party today. I wanted my daddy at my birthday." Soft tears rolled down his cheeks, tears of love this time. "Did you see my new puppy? I think you did—I think you sent her to me. I love her. But I miss you, Daddy. I always miss you."

He crawled out of bed, quietly opened Betty's cage, and pulled her into bed with him. "Thank you for coming, Betty Rose. I really need you."

Cuddling his pup, the warmth of her tiny body pressed up against his aching heart, he slept.

CHAPTER 48

MARCH 1996

LIZZIE WATCHED JONATHAN as he stood at the sink in the bathroom—having grown so much just since he'd started second grade in the fall, he no longer needed a stool to reach the faucet. As he brushed his teeth, his mouth frothed like a rabid dog.

"How do you produce that much foam?" she asked him, shaking her head but laughing.

He turned toward her, white bubbles sliding down his chin. "I brush hard."

"Gross. Don't talk, just listen. I'm glad you agreed to go back to taekwondo. Your teacher said he's missed you. I have to drive up to San Clemente to go to a meeting for a fund-raiser—one of your dad's favorite charities—but I'll be back to pick you up by five. Tyler's mom is going to drop you off at class after school. Meet me out front when you're done, okay?"

Jonathan nodded, spitting a wad of foam into the sink.

Lizzie headed toward her bedroom to get dressed, thinking about ways to help him with his anger issues—more unpredictable now that he was older, with sudden outbursts of rage or displays of acting out hitting him at random times, with random triggers. She hoped that getting him back into taekwondo would do more good than counseling had. When they'd tried therapy over the last year, Jonathan would just sit there silently without interacting with the counselor, so she figured there was no point continuing on with it if he wasn't yet willing or able to open up. But maybe the physical release of martial arts—combined with its mental and spiritual aspects—would provide a safe way for Jonathan to express his anger under controlled conditions and help him learn some self-control and discipline.

It was late afternoon now, and Lizzie's meeting had gone well—the planning committee had chosen a theme and a venue. In the hopes of avoiding rush hour, she had snuck out a bit early to give herself a few extra minutes to get back home in time. She hated driving in traffic.

At least we're moving for now. Hopefully, there won't be any accidents.

With the cars flowing smoothly, it was a good time to think. Her mind wandered to other things she hated besides traffic, like the quarterly parent-teacher conferences she had come to dread. It seemed as though there was always something negative Jonathan's teachers had to say.

Just last week, she'd met with Miss Potter. She'd thought about cancelling, making up some excuse, but had decided she better not. So she'd slinked into the classroom with apprehension and anxiety, wondering what issues his teacher would bring up this time.

"Good evening, Dr. Cohen. Have a seat over there, please, and thanks for coming in tonight."

Miss Potter appeared to be in her late twenties and didn't look anything like the teachers Lizzie had had when she went to elementary school. Miss Potter was tall, about five foot ten, wearing an impeccably styled lavender suit and high heels, her blonde hair, long and loose, framing her tanned, oval-shaped face. She wore different rings on each of her well-manicured fingers, excluding her thumbs, the polish perfectly matching her pale pink lipstick.

Lizzie had sat in an uncomfortable child-sized chair opposite Miss Potter, who sat behind her perfectly organized desk. Lizzie hid her unpolished fingernails from view.

"So how's Jonathan doing at home?" Miss Potter asked.

Lizzie twirled a strand of hair. "Not much change since the last time we talked, I'm afraid. My biggest concern is his internalized anger, which bubbles up and bursts out at inopportune times."

"How's the therapy going?"

Lizzie shook her head and let out a heaving sigh. "It's not. He'd sit in the doctor's office and refuse to talk, so we've put that on hold for now … I'll try revisiting it in a few months. That was the doctor's recommendation. Evidently, talk therapy isn't for everyone."

"That's too bad. It'll be two years this spring since his father died, correct? I was hoping he might have moved a bit more forward by this time."

Wrong thing to say! Lizzie yelled inside her head, visibly stiffening at the teacher's comment. Through gritted teeth, she replied, "I didn't know there was a deadline on how long a child has to grieve for his dead parent." She shifted in her chair and leaned forward. "And for the record, I don't meet that deadline, either."

Miss Potter also leaned forward and interlaced her fingers together. "I didn't mean any offense by that at all, Dr. Cohen. I'm just trying to figure out how to help him. I thought he might have adjusted a bit more by now, and I'm worried because his emotional state is interfering with his learning. He's unfocused and distractible. He's a bright boy, but he doesn't put effort into things. I find it hard to motivate him. He does have a great imagination, and he's a creative child who does well telling stories. Maybe we can use that in some fashion to develop more motivation. Has medication been discussed?"

Lizzie knew she had her own anger issues, because she wanted to punch this woman in the face. *How dare she ask me that!*

"Thanks so much for your opinion, based on your *vast* experience," she'd said, "but no, I'm not considering drugging him."

Lizzie's emotions could still flip on a dime. A moment before, she'd been filled with indignation; the next moment, she was gripped by a wave of nausea and a sensation of oxygen being sucked from her lungs. On the verge of crying, she'd opened her purse and reached in for a packet of tissues.

"I signed him up for taekwondo classes again. He started when he was three and quit when his dad died. I'm hoping it will help him channel his anger. Depression is often a sign of unexpressed anger, and I don't want that to happen, either, so I'm searching for ways for him to vent his feelings more appropriately. As I mentioned, talking about them doesn't seem to be the best method for him."

"That sounds like a good approach to try," Miss Potter had said. "I'm so sorry. I really am, Dr. Cohen. I know you're both going through so much. Let me know if there's anything I can do to help."

What would help is not provoking me with stupid comments, Lizzie had thought as she'd gathered her things to leave.

Feeling a bit sleepy from driving now, she decided to take the next exit and get a cup of coffee. As she waited in a long line at the coffee shop, she continued to think about Jonathan.

It was hard for her to find fault with his actions when she was doing the same thing—experiencing fits of anger followed by periods of apathy. The apathy scared her more, because she worried about the days when she just didn't care about anything. At times, she felt like she'd simply flatlined, unable to muster up energy to do anything. Working at the hospital was a good distraction, and she was able to release some of her self-pity when she was concentrating on sick kids, grateful that Jonathan was at least healthy, if not exactly happy right now.

Jonathan was also able to find release for some of his emotions through his stories—by creating them and dictating them. The tape recorder Sophie had gotten him for his birthday a few years back had proved a godsend. Lizzie had taken to transcribing his writings for him on paper, then illustrating them with pen-and-ink drawings. The creative outlet was good for both of them. She resented all the people who said their grieving time should be over. She didn't think it was right for anyone to put them on a timeline. What was normal where grieving was concerned?

The minute Lizzie reentered the freeway, she regretted stopping for coffee. Traffic had slowed to a crawl, and she started panicking at the thought of disappointing Jonathan, failing to show up on time for him after his very first class when he'd only agreed to return to taekwondo to please her.

Ten minutes later, when she'd only passed one more exit, the stress started to mount. She had her pager from the hospital on her, but that only received incoming messages, it couldn't transmit anything out. *Do I get off again and find a phone? Or just keep going and hope this opens up sometime soon?*

Lizzie heard sirens in the distance. That could be good news or bad. If this wasn't gridlock but only a fender bender, they could start moving again quickly once the authorities cleared the way. On the other hand, if something serious had happened, she could be stuck here a very long time. She looked at her watch and decided she'd likely make it on time if she could get through whatever was blocking the way. She turned on the radio, bit her nails, and inched forward, bit by bit.

Jonathan sat on a bench in the taekwondo studio, dressed in his dobok with his bare feet swinging back and forth, watching the other kids finish the class before his. *I wish I didn't have to be here,* he thought. *I just want to be home.*

Sah Bum Nim Rogly, his instructor, approached the bench and nodded. "How are you doing these days, Jonathan? It's been quite a while since I've seen you."

"I'm doing okay, sir."

"I know this has been a rough time for you. I'm sorry about that. My own father died when I was about your age—did you know that? I promise you it will get better over time. Hang in there."

"Yes, sir."

"Have you been studying and getting good grades?"

Jonathan looked down sheepishly and picked at his belt. "Not really, sir. My grades aren't that good."

"And what are you going to do about that?"

"I don't know, sir."

"I want you to think about it, and let me know what you come up with next week. It's important to keep your focus in school just like you have to do when you're sparring. I want you to feel empowered and confident. Don't worry, we'll work on these things together. As you work toward your blue belt, practice your spin kicks. Work on turning your hips. We'll practice, but today you will spar."

"I'm sparring today? Already?" Jonathan squealed. He knew it—he knew this would happen! He didn't want to spar. Just the thought of it made him upset.

Sah Bum Nim didn't respond to Jonathan's alarm. "Yes. We're going to pick up right where you left off. Just stay focused. Remember: mind focus, eye focus, and body focus. Have faith in yourself."

"Yes, sir," Jonathan mumbled.

It was already 4:40, and Lizzie had gotten only as far as Oceanside. She wasn't going to make it by five o'clock. Trying as best she could to move rightward toward the next exit ramp, drivers wouldn't seem to let her change lanes. She beeped, waved, and honked, but everyone seemed as frustrated in their cars as she was in hers. Finally, she made her way off the freeway and quickly found a gas station with an outdoor pay phone. She didn't have the number for the studio on her—she'd have to call Sophie.

"Soph, thank goodness you're home. You gotta help me. I can't get to Jonathan in time to pick him up from his taekwondo class. I'm stuck in the traffic from hell. I don't want to worry him—you know how he gets. Any chance you can get over there as quickly as possible and get him for me? Pretty please?"

"Of course, of course. No problem at all. I'm glad you thought to call me. I'll leave right now. So don't drive crazy trying to get here. I've got this—I've got him. I'm on my way."

Jonathan liked doing forms and practicing his kicks, but he didn't like sparring. He halfheartedly lined up with the rest of his class, bowed, stretched, and began the series of calisthenics. After warming up, followed by the day's lesson, he reluctantly put on his protective gear, hearing Lizzie's voice in his head, reminding him to use his mouth and groin guards.

Sah Bum Nim matched him with an older boy wearing a blue belt. Jonathan walked on the mat and bowed. His opponent was older and taller and the first to make a move. Jonathan got one kick in, and then his opponent made a fast roundhouse kick directly to the side of his helmet. He went down immediately after the kick and didn't get up.

Sah Bum Nim kneeled down to assess the situation. "You okay?" he asked.

Jonathan didn't say anything but got up slowly with downcast eyes, refusing to look at anyone. *I wish Mom were here,* he thought.

"Jonathan, do you feel dizzy? Look at me."

He sat up. "No, I don't. I'm okay," he said.

"You hurt anywhere?"

"No, sir."

"Please sit down over on the mat there. You're done for the day. I want to talk to your mother as soon as she gets here."

Jonathan sat and sat, counting the seconds until the end of class. He just wanted to leave, to never come back here again. The minute his group was excused for the day, he raced outside, away from the noise, into the fresh air. But he didn't see his mother's car, so he sat on the steps.

By a quarter past five, Jonathan was getting very edgy. The next class was starting at 5:30, and people were piling in past him. Where was his mom? Feeling deflated, angry, and alone, he felt one of his meltdowns coming on. He tried to fight it, not wanting to humiliate himself more than he already had today. When everyone was inside and he was alone again on the curb, he released the tears that had been bubbling up. He didn't want anyone to see him crying like a baby.

Where's Mom? Where is she? Why isn't she here? He stayed on the steps, clasping his hands and nervously tapping his feet. *What's happened to her? ... Oh my God, she got in a crash on the way here. Oh my God, Mom is dead! Now she's dead too!*

Jonathan's meltdown escalated rapidly, until he completely lost control. One of the fathers inside the studio, close to the door and watching the warm-ups, heard sobbing and came out to see what was wrong. He found Jonathan curled up in the fetal position at the side of the stairs, crying and muttering that his mom had died. The man sat Jonathan up and tried to decipher what was going on, but Jonathan wouldn't talk to him.

Before Sophie left home, she'd tried to call the dojo, but no one had picked up. When she finally arrived outside the building, she didn't even bother to park—she saw Jonathan on the ground next to a strange man and left the car running at the curb, racing to him.

Seeing Sophie made matters worse for Jonathan, not better. "Where's my mom?" he screeched. "She's the one who's supposed to pick me up! She died, didn't she? She's dead, isn't she?"

Sophie held him tightly in her arms, stroking his hair and talking in soothing tones. "No, no, no, honey, she's okay. She's fine. She just got stuck in traffic and couldn't get here fast enough. I would have been here sooner, but I got stuck in rush hour myself. She's fine, sweetie. She's absolutely fine."

"Why didn't she call the front desk? Why didn't they tell me?"

"She was on the freeway, Jonathan. It was hard for her to get to a phone. She's so sorry. Don't you worry any more. You're okay and she's okay—everything is going to be okay."

But Jonathan wasn't calming down like he usually did after one of his outbursts, which was making Sophie nervous. And once he said that his head hurt from getting kicked, she said, "That's it. I'm taking you to get looked at."

She turned to the man who'd been trying to help Jonathan. "Can you watch him for one more minute while I run inside to make a quick call?" Without waiting for an answer, she hurried into the dojo lobby and grabbed the phone at the front desk. She left a message on Lizzie's machine at home, telling her she was taking Jonathan to the urgent care clinic closest to their house. "Don't worry, it's nothing serious, I don't think," Sophie said into the receiver, "I just want to get him checked out after a little mishap at taekwondo. Meet us there, okay?"

When Sophie came back outside, Jonathan was still shaking and crying inconsolably. She thanked the man profusely for his help, then slowly walked Jonathan to her car, more worried about him than she'd ever been.

*

Lizzie herself was in an escalated state when she got home to find, not her son and her best friend preparing dinner in the kitchen, but an alarming phone message severely lacking in details. *What could have happened? Could he have sprained an ankle, broken his wrist? On his first day back?* She raced back out to her car and over to the care center, not breathing freely until she arrived and saw Jonathan safe and sound on a waiting room chair.

When he saw her, he ran to her and cried, "Don't ever do that again, Mom. I thought you were dead. I thought you'd died." He wrapped his arms tightly around her waist and cried into her belly.

Instantly, guilt flowed over Lizzie like a rushing river. Everything hit her all at once. Guilt that she wasn't at class with him, that she'd made him take the class in the first place. Guilt that she'd been busy with something for herself when he'd clearly needed her the most. Guilt that she couldn't bring David back. Guilt that she couldn't be both mother and father to her son. Guilt that she couldn't put her life back together if only for the sake of her child. In utter desperation, she wanted to heal it all, to make all the pain go away, but she felt impotent to do anything other than exist in this endless, bottomless pit of guilt that kept her up late at night and ate away at her soul.

As the doctor examined Jonathan, Sophie filled Lizzie in on what had happened. It wasn't really the kick that had worried her—he'd been wearing his headpiece, after all—it's how frantic he had been when she'd gotten to him, perhaps having a panic attack, Sophie gently suggested. Lizzie just looked down at her purse in her lap, slowing shaking her head back and forth and listening to Sophie's words.

Once the doctor cleared Jonathan, assuring Lizzie that he could find nothing wrong with him, no signs of concussion, he told her to nevertheless watch for signs like headache, dizziness, and vomiting over the next few days. She wanted to snap at everyone in the room, telling them that she was a pediatrician and knew just what to do better than anyone, but in her current frame of mind, she doubted even her professional skills at the moment. She didn't trust anything about herself these days—she simply felt on overload.

Mentally exhausted, she got Jonathan home and resting on the couch, then met Sophie in the kitchen, where she was putting on water for tea. Matthew was on his way over with takeout for everyone, so the two sat down across from each other with their mugs, neither talking. Lizzie didn't know what to say, what to do. And Sophie didn't need words to know what Lizzie was telling her with her silence.

At last their reverie was broken by Matthew's knock on the back door. "How is he?" he asked, setting multiple bags of fast food on the counter.

Lizzie shook her head. "Matthew, I don't know what to do. I don't know how to help him. He's like a little lost soul. Any advice?"

Matthew sat with them at the table and was quiet for a few minutes. "Lizzie, I say this with the deepest love and respect for you. The deepest sympathy as well. But I think it's time you lead by example. Mourning, grieving, and crying are vital to the healing process. However, I think it's time to make a concerted effort to rebuild a full life for yourself, not this half life you've been living, for Jonathan's benefit, for his welfare. He has too much on his plate to feel responsible for you as well as for himself. He's floundering in fear, and you need to show him the way out. It's time to show him how to move forward. My advice? Don't be a victim anymore. Be emotionally present for him."

Lizzie forced out a deep sigh. "You're right," she said. "This is my wake-up call. I need to pull it together. And I need to do it now."

"Don't tell him how to be, Lizzie. Show him."

Lizzie heard his message, without an ounce of defensiveness, with only gratitude. It was time for her to wake up. Time to make a change. Maybe she didn't have the motivation to do it for herself, but she could do it for Jonathan.

That night, Lizzie let Jonathan sleep in her bed. She made a sandwich out of their family—Lizzie on one side, Jonathan in the middle, and Betty Rose stretched out along the other side of him. It was good to feel safe.

No, it was necessary to feel safe.

CHAPTER 49
THE ASTRAL PLANE

Malach: What are you working on, Ruach?

Ruach: An inspiration for a fishing trip for Jonathan Cohen and Matthew Hobbs.

Malach: Thinking maybe it's time for the two of them to bond alone?

Ruach: Yes. He's going on nine years old now—his father's been gone for three years in human time. I think he's ready now to receive Matthew's intended role in his life.

Malach: Give it a go.

CHAPTER 50

SPRING/SUMMER 1997

MATTHEW WAS STANDING in line at a sporting goods store with swim fins in hand, a gift for Sophie's brother's son, Danny. He was going on a class trip over the Easter holiday and needed the fins before the weekend. As the cashier checked out the customers in front of Matthew, a colorful brochure on the counter caught his eye. He got a prickly feeling on the crown of his head—a sign that he was receiving an intuitive message—so he picked up the brochure and reviewed it with great interest. *Hmm, a fishing expedition. This looks great.*

When it was Matthew's turn to check out, the cashier said to him, "If you're interested in that trip, you should call soon—it fills up fast for the summer. But I've been there—really good place, worth the wait," he said.

"Thanks," Matthew said. "I appreciate the tip. This might be just what I've been looking for."

Back home, he hurried into the kitchen, eager to share his idea with Sophie. She was in the middle of tossing a salad for dinner and stretched up to him as he kissed her cheek. "Hey, were you able to find the fins for Danny?"

"I was. Mission accomplished. Do you want me to mail them out tomorrow?"

"No, thanks, I will. I have to go to the post office for stamps anyway."

"Take a look at this and tell me what you think." He held the brochure out to her, and she wiped her hands on a dishtowel to take it.

As she started reading it, she smiled and nodded.

Looking for a tranquil and peaceful vacation? Look no further than Shanti Lake Lodge, located in the Chippewa National Forest on Sand Lake in Itasca County, Minnesota, approximately an hour north of Grand Rapids. This fun family resort has oodles of activities for everyone, making it a perfect location for reunions and retreats, all-guy or all-gal fishing trips, stress-busting getaways, and family vacations.

Calling all anglers—this fishing mecca is a slice of heaven. Imagine your boat gliding out of the slip before dawn, then spending the day catching walleye, yellow perch, crappies, and northern pike. We've got the boats, the motors, the bait, and the tackle. You just bring your pole!

The lodge hosts 15 cozy cabins that sleep from 1 to 10 guests. Each clean, comfortable cabin comes complete with cable TV, air-conditioning, fireplace, fresh clean linens and towels, fully equipped kitchens, fire pits, and BBQ grill.

Gather at our lodge to meet other fellow vacationers for our Sunday buffet breakfast. We're also known for our flavor-of the-day homemade frozen custard during the summer. And you have to come to our s'mores fest. There's something for everyone.

"So," Matthew said, "are you thinking what I'm thinking?

Sophie nodded enthusiastically. "Yes. For his birthday, right? Go for it."

Matthew called the number right away and was on the phone quite a while as Sophie finished preparing dinner. When they sat down to eat, he told her, "Well, we're in luck. Usually, they're filled up by now for the summer, but the guy told me that someone cancelled today—they have precisely one cabin open on the dates I wanted to book."

Sophie squeezed Matthew's hand. "See? It's meant to be."

Lizzie stood in her kitchen, testing out the new knife skills she'd learned in her latest cooking class. In the past year, she'd tried her hand at several new pursuits—computer classes, a painting workshop, even a weekend meditation seminar—but when she'd noticed that their local kitchen supply store offered a series of culinary classes for the whole family, she thought it would be a great way to spend some quality time with Jonathan, just the two of them concentrated on healing and nurturing each other. Sometimes he came with her, some classes didn't interest him so much, but they both were benefiting greatly by her new goal to feed them fresh, whole foods cooked at home. No more uninspired takeout dinners in front of the TV. No more cold pizza for breakfast. It was as though the change in their lives had started in the kitchen—in committing to nourish the two of them from the inside out—and all the other growth and adjustment had stemmed from there.

She hummed as she masterfully chopped up cubes of cold chicken, pecans, celery, and grapes, surprised that she was actually enjoying making lunch. There was a smoother rhythm to their lives lately, and it had started to bring her peace. Her part-time schedule at the hospital was still working well for her, still allowing her to be at home with Jonathan most days, and when she was working or involved in a charity event, he and Sophie still spent ample time together, baking her cakes and taking long hikes and working on his homework. Third grade had gone so much better than second—in fact, with her and Sophie tutoring Jonathan, his teacher had said he was all caught up by the end of the school year—that Lizzie was letting him take the whole summer off to just enjoy himself and relax and hang out with his friends.

He sauntered into the kitchen now, wearing khaki shorts, a T-shirt, and flip-flops. "What's for lunch? I'm starving."

"Chicken salad stuffed avocados. And guess what I made, from scratch? Homemade sweet potato chips."

He grabbed a few and stuffed them in his mouth. "Mom, I'm loving those cooking classes. These are so good. Crispy and sweet."

Jonathan set the plates on the table and poured them both freshly squeezed lemonade. He'd become a more helpful child, often anticipating what needed to be done without asking or being told. Lizzie couldn't put into words how relieved she was that his emotional outbursts were now much fewer and farther between; actually, she could hardly believe how much he'd improved—had just seemed more content and more "normal"—since she'd also allowed herself to let go of some of the pain, to stop looking backward so much, to start looking toward the future with as much optimism as she could muster. The two of them set goals now to keep them facing forward, like Jonathan's recent promotion to blue belt status in taekwondo.

They sat at the table enjoying their meal together. Secretly, Jonathan snuck a few chips to Betty.

Lizzie waited to speak until her mouth wasn't full. "So it's time to start talking about your birthday. If we're going to plan a party, we'd better start planning now. Boy, your birthdays roll around fast, don't they? Nine already!"

"I don't want a party this year."

As Jonathan reached for more chips from the bowl, Lizzie playfully slapped his hand away. "Hey, save some for me," she said with a laugh. "Why not? Why don't you want a party?" she asked him more seriously.

"Just don't. No reason."

"Well then, what *would* you like to do for your special day? Because just last night—"

He interrupted with, "I want to go fishing. Like I used to do with Dad when I was little."

Lizzie's fork froze in the air for a moment, her mouth open. "Oh my God, if this isn't a coincidence! That's *exactly* what I was going to say! Matthew called me just last night after you went to bed. He reminded me that his birthday is the day after yours, and he said he'd like to celebrate it by going on a fishing trip. He's got a reservation on some lake, but Sophie isn't the rugged type. He wondered if you'd like to go with him."

"Yeah," Jonathan answered nonchalantly. "I'll go with him. That would be cool." He kept popping potato chips into his mouth, not saying anything more.

"You don't want to know the details?" Lizzie prodded. "Like when and where?"

"Okay, where?"

"A lodge in Minnesota, so you'd fly there the actual week of your birthday. It's a fishing resort in the Chippewa National Forest on Sand Lake."

"Like I said, sounds cool."

"All right, then, that's settled! Let's call Matthew later and let him know you're in." As Lizzie started clearing the dishes, an unhappy thought crossed her mind. "It means you won't be with me on your birthday, though … for the very first time."

Jonathan laughed. "You'll live, Mom." She scrunched up her face and stuck her tongue out at him. "We can do something together to celebrate when I get back. I'll go call Matthew."

CHAPTER 51

AUGUST 5/6, 1997

MATTHEW, A DETAILED kind of guy, had made a to-do list and had checked off each item he accomplished as the trip neared: confirming reservations at the fishing lodge, booking plane tickets, securing fishing licenses, reserving a rental car, and purchasing gear. He'd even made up menus for all their meals and a shopping list of the necessary groceries for once they got there. He loved to fish, and he was genuinely looking forward to spending time with Jonathan. On departure day, he was up at the crack of dawn, packed and ready to go, waiting for Sophie to finish her coffee before they picked Jonathan up for the airport. Intuitively, he just knew it was going to be a great adventure for the two of them.

Lizzie, however, had mixed feelings about the trip—not just being separated from Jonathan on his birthday now that they were both back on track, but just having her little boy fly halfway across the country without her. But all her reservations were put to rest when she saw how excited he was, like a kid on his first trip to Disneyland. He, too, had been up since 6:00 a.m., dressed, packed, and constantly looking out the window for Matthew and Sophie to arrive. Finally, they drove up and honked the horn.

"Get in, guys," Sophie said. Lizzie had decided she wanted to take the drive with them, and Sophie said she'd be happy for the company on the ride back.

Jonathan tossed his bags into the trunk of the car, and he and Lizzie climbed into the backseat.

On the way there, Jonathan teased his mother. "Mom, you better not cry. You already look like you might. It's only for a few days, and besides, you and Sophie can have some girl time together."

Sophie still flinched a little whenever Jonathan used her given name—something he'd just started doing in the past year—but she knew it had to happen sometime. So instead of wallowing in self-pity over the loss, she was training herself to just be grateful for all the years she had as his "Toffee."

"We'll miss you guys on your birthdays," she said now, "but we know you'll have a wonderful time."

"And, Jonathan," Lizzie added, "don't forget to change your underwear, don't even step outside without putting on sunscreen, and always wear your life jacket when you're in the boat."

"Mom! You're embarrassing me!"

"That's my job."

When Sophie pulled up to the terminal, Lizzie jumped out of the car too to give Jonathan a hug and a kiss. Since that last hug and kiss with David, good-byes to loved ones had become almost unbearable, and it took all of her discipline now to fight her emotions, to push down her fears. *They serve no purpose,* she reminded herself. *Things happen in life that you can't control, and I refuse to hold Jonathan back from living his fullest life possible.* Still, in parting, she whispered in his ear, "Just be safe. Please, be safe."

"Happy birthday," she and Sophie both yelled out the window as the guys grabbed their bags and hustled inside.

They flew out of Lindbergh Field to the Grand Rapids–Itasca County Airport. When they landed, they collected their bags and gear and retrieved their rental car, giddy as teenagers on the way to prom. They had been on the road for only fifteen minutes when Jonathan declared he was hungry.

They stopped at Pedro's Homemade Tacos and feasted on whitefish tacos amid a friendly crowd of locals, tourists, regulars, bikers, and older couples. Next on Matthew's list was procuring food, beverages, and ice at a grocery store, where Jonathan went a little crazy putting snack foods into the cart.

It was after 4:00 p.m. by the time they arrived at the lodge, checking into cabin number nine. It was a comfortable two-bedroom cabin with double beds, ceiling fans, a full kitchen, an outdoor grill, and a fireplace—not that they thought they would use it in August. Matthew was pleased with the accommodations: quiet, peaceful, and overlooking the lake. They took a hike around the area to get the lay of the land, ate ham and cheese sandwiches for dinner, and turned in early. Well, Jonathan turned in shortly after dinner; Matthew, not wanting to look like a fool in front of Jonathan, stayed up to set up the fishing lines for the next morning. Sitting outside on the porch by the light of a lantern, with only the chirping insects to break the silence, he was perfectly content. Almost. *I only wish David were here with us.*

After a restful night's sleep, Jonathan woke to the sound of the cabin phone ringing. He wasn't surprised—he knew his mother would call first thing on his birthday—but he *was* surprised at how early she was up, given the time difference between them. "Gosh, Mom, did you even go to sleep?" he asked her playfully.

Matthew came out into the common room and waved good morning, then headed to the kitchen to make coffee. He listened to Jonathan's end of the conversation with a smile on his face, pleased that Lizzie had taken this big step in allowing Jonathan to go away without her and even more pleased to hear how happy Jonathan sounded—as fresh and bubbly as a popped bottle of champagne.

"Mom, this place is awesome!" Jonathan gushed. "The flight was really cool. No one was in the third seat, so we had tons of room, and I got the window seat. Then we rented a convertible and drove here with the top down. This cabin is great. We've got tons of food, and Matthew even bought me a birthday cake with candles. We're going to fish for walleye today."

Matthew started frying up sausage, hash browns, and eggs as he continued listening to their phone conversation. He poured Jonathan a glass of orange juice and walked it over to him as he was saying, "Okay, yeah, I'll open the presents you got me when we get home. Thanks, Mom. Wish me luck on the water. ... Love you. Don't miss me too much."

Then he hung up the phone and joined Matthew at the table. As they settled into their hearty breakfast, Jonathan virtually inhaled all the food on his plate, eager to get their fishing expedition started.

Matthew refilled his coffee cup and sat back down at the table. "Hey, sport, I'm glad you're enjoying bouncing off the walls, but I've gotta get more coffee in me before we go. Speaking of which, be sure to go to the bathroom right before we leave. We've got a short fishing seminar to go to, then we can lug stuff to the boat."

"Do we have to do the seminar?"

"If we want to know what we're doing, yes," Matthew said with a laugh.

So they took the requisite training course, learning important tips about boat safety, fishing rules in the area, and the local geography. Afterward, Jonathan took several trips down the dock with the fishing equipment while Matthew paid for the boat and motor he'd reserved. They met up at the bait shop and bought live bait, more ice, and gas.

"Let's see," Matthew said. "Do we have everything? Life jackets?"

"Check."

"Sunscreen and sunglasses?"

"Check."

"Hat with visor?"

"Check."

"Cooler, ice, water bottles, and lunch?"

"Check."

"Insect repellant and first aid kit?"

"Check."

"Okay, we've got all the gear, right? Poles, tackle?"

"Yes, yes, and yes!" Jonathan yelled. "Let's go fishing!"

They happily walked out on the dock and located their Lund Rebel boat, equipped with a 40-horsepower motor. It was a pleasant day, and the weather report had predicted a high of about 80 degrees. The sky was a bit overcast, and the lake was calm.

"I promised your mom that you'd keep your life jacket on at all times and that you'd wear plenty of sunscreen. So put this on." Matthew tossed Jonathan a tube of zinc oxide.

"Can I drive the boat?"

"Sorry, but the rule is, you have to be eighteen. Don't worry—you'll be busy enough with the fishing. I haven't fished for walleye before, so this will be a new experience for me too. Who knew there was so much to learn about fishing?"

"My dad knew a lot about it."

"He sure did, and hopefully, we will too after this adventure."

Matthew studied the hot-spot map, started the boat, and took off on Sand Lake. "We'll keep the night crawlers fresh and lively in this worm box in our cooler," he yelled to Jonathan. "And I dropped some ice on it to keep the worms spunky. Walleye feed a couple of feet from the bottom, so we'll take the boat along the edge of the lake where the weeds are visible from the surface. The guy said to stay near the edge of an underwater weed bed because the walleye stay in the weeds 'cause there's food and cover in there."

Matthew slowed the boat way down. "Here we are—I think it's about ten to twelve feet of water here, right in the weed bed. Ready to catch some fish?"

"I hope we do. This is really cool."

"Well, let's up our chances by doing what that guy told us this morning—the Lindy Rig technique for catching walleye. Remember? We're supposed to match the size of the hook with the bait. So, okay … ," Matthew thought out loud. "We have worms and number eight bait hooks. We'll put the night crawler on like he showed us … watch me do it first. This takes a bit of practice, and I don't want you jamming the hook into your fingers. Okay?"

"Yep."

Jonathan slid next to Matthew to watch, and Matthew demonstrated threading the worm on the hook.

"Doing it this way will keep the worm from spinning when we reel it in. Also, remember when you get a bite to give the fish a moment to eat the worm and actually get the hook in its mouth."

Jonathan picked out his night crawler and worked it on the hook. He seemed a bit frustrated, but he eventually accomplished the task without stabbing himself. "Okay. Got it."

"We can troll or cast, but let's try casting. Like this." As Matthew demonstrated the technique, he felt a pang in his stomach, again wishing David were with them.

They both practiced a few times, with Jonathan often collapsing into fits of laughter. It was easy, relaxed, and nonstressful between them.

"Leave the spool open and your finger on the line, and when the fish takes the bait, you might feel a tug. Then feed him some line. Now let's flip them out there, and then you can put the rod in the holder."

"Now what?" Jonathan asked.

"Now we wait."

"Now *you* wait. I eat."

"Jonathan, how does your mom afford to feed you?" He laughed. "What do you feel like? Do you want your sandwich already? Or just something to snack on? Fruit, corn chips, M&M's?"

"Chips and a banana for now."

Matthew reached into the cooler and retrieved the requested items. "Having fun?"

"Yeah. Being outside like this makes my brain be quiet."

"I know what you mean. It's called 'peace of mind.' Nature can do that for you. It's like meditating. Your thoughts are still, so you don't feel anxious and you can hear your inner voice."

"Yeah, sometimes I think too much and I can't focus. Can I ask you a question?"

"Anything. Shoot."

"Are you going to marry my godmother?"

Matthew wondered what had provoked that question.

"Not sure. We've talked about it, but Sophie isn't sure she wants to marry again. We love each other whether we do or not. I'm leaving that up to her. You know we've both been married before."

"I know. Her husband, Neil, killed himself."

"Yeah. My wife, Susan, died too—she had cancer—and that was a difficult time for me to get through. Dealing with the death of someone we love is one of the hardest things we have to do."

"Why do people have to die? It really sucks."

"There's one thing that's for sure—everyone dies."

"Well, it sucks."

"It's hard for the people who are left behind, but I don't think it sucks for the person who's died. Sometimes we don't get to keep relationships and sometimes the relationships we have don't work out the way we wish, but we experience them for a reason."

"Sophie and I helped Neil set his soul free. She said that he went into the light to go home and that she'll see him again."

"You'll see the soul of your dad again when you've finished what you need to do too. You don't remember this, Jonathan, but one of the things your spirit came to Earth to accomplish was to let Sophie know that the spirit inside the person's body never dies. We're here for a period of time to learn and complete our missions and spiritual growth, and then we return to the spiritual dimension."

"I came to let her know that?" As Jonathan raised his eyebrows, the sun poured in his eyes and he tipped his baseball cap farther down to provide some shade. He scrunched up his nose, dotted with little brown freckles.

"You did. And it was a very important thing to help her heal in this life. You showed her that the day you were born. Because she was your mom in another life, she was unbearably sad when you died, like you are now about your dad. The problem was she spent the rest of that life being miserable and didn't complete her own life plan because you weren't there. She didn't realize your spirit still existed and she'd be with you again. Do you remember any of that?"

"When I was an American Indian, right? I don't really remember it, but Sophie told me about it. She said it wasn't sad for me when I died, but it was very sad for her."

"And when you came to be born on Earth this time, it healed a part of her soul because she now knows that when people die, their body goes away, but the spirit, who they are inside, is still alive and is always alive. Just like with your dad. The people left behind aren't meant to be sad and miserable forever. They need to grieve, but then they should go on and fulfill their own missions."

"I don't think people should have to die until they're really, really old," Jonathan said. "I guess I wasn't old when I was an Indian, and Neil wasn't old, and my dad wasn't, either."

Matthew nodded in understanding. "People go when they have completed their missions and life plans."

"What was my dad's plan?"

"I'm not sure, kiddo. There're lots of possibilities. But as an example, he could have mastered something he needed to learn pretty quickly … or he might have made a soul contract with your mom and you and other people to help them learn something about death and dying in this lifetime, the same way you taught Sophie. Also, I think your dad was here to demonstrate and teach others about being a humanitarian. He had a courageous, good heart, and he stood firmly behind what he believed in. He didn't just talk about it. He took action. He got in there and did what he believed was right for people. He was kind and benevolent to all human beings and spent his life helping people in need."

"Grandpa Cohen said he was a real hero."

"I agree with that. Many people turn their backs on others and only get involved in something if it negatively impacts them. Your dad stood up for all people. He was an example for all of us. He talked about the goal of someday seeing the coming together of all human beings. Maybe someday he'll return to Earth to see that."

Matthew saw the tears welling in Jonathan's eyes. *It's good for him to feel the emotion and release it. Hopefully, this will help heal the pain.*

"That's really important, isn't it?" Jonathan said very quietly.

"Indeed, it's very important."

"What am *I* supposed to do while I'm here?"

"That's something you'll need to figure out. Each person makes a plan when they're a spirit before they're born. They figure out the things they need to learn to help evolve the soul, help others with their missions, and what they want to accomplish." Matthew paused for just a moment before adding, "I can work on that with you if you want—we can try to figure it out together. Sometimes it has to do with something you feel passionate about, something that energizes you. Like, I'm betting your mission has something to do with your writing—the stories you write. I think you have messages to share with the world."

Matthew smiled when he saw that his comment sent Jonathan deep in thought.

Gentle gusts of wind had caused the boat to drift sideways by then, so Matthew took the opportunity of the lull in their conversation to motor to a better location. He knew they weren't done talking, and he was prepared for Jonathan's next question right when he cut the motor.

"So after I die, I'm going to come back again?"

"Not every soul reincarnates, but I believe you will again—only in a different time and place and as a different person with a different life. You won't be Jonathan Cohen on the outside because your spirit will get a different body and personality." He paused again, allowing time for this to sink in. "Remember when your mom took you to see the play *Peter Pan*? Obviously, those people weren't really Wendy, Peter, Captain Hook, and the Lost Boys, were they? They were actors who played a role, and they lived in a certain place and dressed in a certain way. They took off the costumes and went home when the play was over. Those actors may then choose to be in another play, set in a different place, with a different story, wearing different costumes, and playing a different role. That's a simplified version of what life is really like. We do the same thing. Our spirit picks a time and place to be born, as well as the lessons and goals to work on. Then it plays out that role, dies, and returns to the spirit world to absorb lessons learned and to decide on the next experience when ready."

The whole time Matthew was talking, Jonathan listened intently, nodding at times, looking up or down to consider some point, seeming to understand. They continued chatting for the next few hours—sometimes seriously, sometimes more lightheartedly. As Matthew had hoped, fishing with Jonathan got him to open up—side by side, as men do, instead of face-to-face, as women do. As the sun climbed in the sky, Matthew found Jonathan confiding in him about school, his friends, all the changes at home over the past year. He talked a little more about his father and quite a bit about Betty Rose. And all the while, the fishing created an easiness between them, an activity they could concentrate on as the talk flowed as naturally as the cast lines. As in Matthew's practice, he found that a little silence and patience work the best. And the outing so far was the best Matthew could have hoped for.

Finally, early in the afternoon, Jonathan jumped up from his seat, rocking the boat a bit.

"Matthew! Matthew! I felt a tug—I think I have something playing with my line. What do I do next?"

"Wow, looks like you *do* have something! Okay, walleye are slow biters, so give him a chance to swallow the bait, then set the hook, giving the rod a firm pull. He'll probably put up a steady battle, pulling to the bottom, so hang in there."

As directed, Jonathan stood and pulled upward with the pole.

Matthew moved closer to the side of the boat, ready to help when needed, coaching Jonathan the whole way. "Reel it in slowly … slowly. That's a feisty one! Keep cranking a bit. Once I can, I'll get him with the net."

When the fish was close enough to the boat, Matthew scooped the net underneath it and caught it up clean. The fish thrashed violently, intent on escaping, but to no avail.

"Buddy, you got the first walleye! And what a beaut!"

Jonathan burst out laughing. "So we can eat this one?"

"Yep, but we have to store it properly immediately if we plan to eat it. Fish goes bad really quickly."

Matthew jabbed the walleye with the iki spike and added it to the chilly bin filled with some water and lots of ice.

"You beat me in getting the first fish—great beginner's luck." He slapped Jonathan on the back. "Atta boy!"

Matthew chuckled as he watched Jonathan act like someone with an IV of caffeine in his vein, doing a victory dance in the boat, beaming, and chanting in a singsong voice, "It's my birthday luck. I got it 'cause it's my birthday luck."

If Matthew felt this experience with Jonathan was going well before, he was thrilled with how it was going now.

I love this kid, he thought. *I really love him.*

As the afternoon wore on, they continued to laugh, eat, joke around, make up silly riddles, and catch fish. They had enough for dinner, so they agreed to release anything else they snagged. Matthew caught a walleye that was too small, and they both caught and released a small perch, which made Jonathan happy.

When the sun began to sink into the lake, Matthew realized all the other boats were gone. He turned theirs around and headed back toward the lodge. "If we go back to shore now, we'll have time for a quick spin in the kayaks before dinner."

"Let's do it!" Jonathan enthusiastically agreed.

Matthew pulled the boat into the slip as smoothly as he could, and then they both started collecting as much gear as they could carry, storing it in the dockside storage room for the next day.

"We don't want to wait too long to clean the fish, but this is perfect kayaking time. Let's make the most of it while we can, then I'll show you how to prep our catch. Deal?"

"Deal."

Less than an hour later, after another fun-filled activity, Matthew and Jonathan headed to the fish-cleaning room. As they walked, Jonathan thought about what a great birthday he was having; in fact, he didn't think he could feel happier. Once they got to the room—with its three sinks, multiple cutting boards, and lots of countertop space—Matthew hoisted the cooler atop one of the counters, and Jonathan peeked into the chilly bin to look at the walleye he caught. It was long and slender with a bronze metallic tone to it, olive shading, and what looked little puddles of black ink poured over it. Its belly was white.

"It's too cool-looking to eat. I'm kind of sorry for the fish," he told Matthew. As he stared at it, he started feeling sick to his stomach.

Head down and intent on the task at hand, Matthew didn't notice. "Jonathan, take the fish out of the cooler, but leave it in the chilly bin. Then wash off a cutting board, would you?"

Jonathan followed Matthew's directions, but he kept looking inside the chilly bin at the fish. He wasn't sure why he was so sad at the thought of eating him—and he did think of the fish as a "him." Maybe this male fish was a father, and all his fish children would be sad and miss their dad. The thought caused a knot in his stomach.

"Hold the fish up and let me take your picture," Matthew said cheerfully.

Again, Jonathan did as he was told, thinking that the fish, which had once flopped around so vigorously, was now utterly lifeless in his hands.

Matthew opened a soft pouch containing his fillet knife. "You can put it on the cutting board now."

Jonathan pulled up a stool to watch. "Matthew, do fish have souls? What happened to the life inside him now that just his body is left?"

"I believe every creation has a spirit. And everything has an energy vibration."

"I think I should thank him for being food for me."

Matthew stopped sharpening his knife and glanced up. "That's very compassionate, Jonathan. That would be a great thing to do. Do you know that the Inuit people have a belief that *anua,* or souls, exist in all people and animals? They honor all the animals by recognizing them as spiritually aware. Some of the hunting tribes would ask permission of the spirit of the animal before they killed it for food. I like the idea of thanking the spirit of the fish for giving us food."

Matthew took his knife to the fish, beginning the cleaning and filleting process.

"You run the knife along the backbone to the tail, like this. Then you do it on the other side, like this."

Jonathan leaned in closer as Matthew worked, but he said, "I think I'll let you be the one to cut up the fish." And now and then, he turned away to avoid watching. "Can I ask you another question—about what we were talking about before, I mean?"

Without missing a beat between skinning the fillets, washing them, and packing them on ice, Matthew replied, "Ask me any question you want, anytime you want. I'll always do my best to answer, and if I don't have an answer, I'll try to help you find one."

"So, okay ... if I lived lives before, why did I forget them? And why did I remember my life as an American Indian when I was a little kid, but I don't remember it anymore?"

"Those are good questions," Matthew said. "We know and remember everything when we're pure energy spirits in the other dimension. When we're born on Earth, though, we power down our energy so we can be physical in a three-dimensional world. When you incarnate, come to Earth to be born, you go behind the 'veil,' as it's often called. It's just a phrase meaning we forget who we are and where we come from. If we remembered everything, focusing on the new life we're starting would be hard. Some people remember for a few years, actually, and as they get involved in their new lives and start to learn the things society teaches them, they forget."

"Like what happened to me."

"Yes. I think you started to forget when you were around five or six. If we remembered everything, our brains would be on overload with all the things that happened in all the different lifetimes and keeping all the people straight and what roles they served. It could be overwhelming."

"It's hard enough to remember everything from one life, huh?"

"I agree. And we know this is going to happen before we're born. We know we're going to forget. But more and more people are remembering and awakening. Everyone can wake up his or her consciousness more. We can meditate and listen to our spirit guides. They have messages for us when we learn to listen. Sometimes the messages come in an unexpected way. When we're in our bodies, our soul communicates with us, and we need to listen to that too. It communicates with us by our feelings. When you're experiencing loving, kind, and joyful emotions, it means you're on the right track with your spirit self. If you're feeling lonely, angry, upset, or sad, you're off track. It's a good way to measure."

Jonathan grinned. "I'm on track today."

"You sure are. Now let's take these fillets back to the cabin and get that grill going!"

After a wonderful dinner of the freshest fish Matthew and Jonathan had ever tasted, they sat back at the wooden table, sated and happy. Matthew felt so relaxed. *This is exactly the kind of day I wanted.*

He got up suddenly and went to the fridge, quickly returning with Jonathan's birthday cake, candles lit and flickering in the slight breeze coming through the screened door. "Quick, make a wish, buddy."

Jonathan closed his eyes for a moment and then blew out the flames. Matthew cut slices of the cake and served them up with chocolate ice cream.

"What a fantastic day," Matthew said after his last spoonful. "Know what I want to do now?"

"No, what?"

"Sit outside and listen to the loons. That will be our joint happy birthday song."

"Is a loon a duck?"

"No, it's a cool aquatic bird. The one I saw yesterday had black-and-white checkerboard feathers on his back and a white necklace around his neck. And loons have kind of spooky, red eyes."

Curiosity piqued, Jonathan followed Matthew outside, and they took seats around the glowing red embers in the fire pit. Jonathan soaked in all the beauty around him and enjoyed the peace. He felt quiet inside, and he liked the feeling. The lake was as smooth as glass, and the silhouette the trees reflected on the water looked silvery and shimmery in the moonlight.

Matthew put his finger to his lips. "Shhh. Listen. If you're very quiet, you can hear it—the moon."

As Jonathan tried to hear what the moon sounded like, one of the loons let out an eerie wailing sound. Seconds later, another responded,

Ooooooooooo-Ooooooo. Jonathan's mind flashed to a distant memory of an American Indian flute, yet he was entirely in the present at the same time. It had been a perfect day.

"Hey, Matthew?"

"Yeah?"

"Thanks. Thanks for everything. I really mean it."

"You're really welcome, bud. Happy birthday."

"You too."

CHAPTER 52
THE ASTRAL PLANE

Ruach: As they say on Earth, there's good news and there's bad news. The good news is, the fishing trip was a big success and Jonathan had a great time. The bad news is, he's now clearly stated that he doesn't remember. Looks like he's behind the veil. I know you promised him otherwise, Malach, but would it be so bad if he lived out his life without remembering the spiritual plane?

Malach: I made a contract with him, Ruach. I'm going to work on formalizing the details for plan B. I'll start preparing for it now, but the plan is extensive, and since we're dealing with earthly time, it could take a while.

CHAPTER 53

ASTRAL PLANE

Malach: Since we don't live in a dimension with time, it often is not in our awareness. But many Earth years have passed since we last spoke of plan B, Ruach, and Jonathan is now fifteen. It's time to enact the plan, once we work out a couple more things.

Ruach: Let me know what you want me to do.

Malach: We've got two things to deal with. Please give Sophie an inspiration to go to the cemetery to put flowers on the graves of David and Neil. I have a bigger task to handle. I need to keep Jonathan from going to the Spring Fling dance at his high school.

Ruach: I'll go do my part right now.

CHAPTER 54

APRIL 24, 2004

I T WAS THE kind of Saturday where just breathing seemed exhilarating. It was spring—a time of new beginnings. A sunny day and a transparent blue sky created the perfect conditions for a road trip.

Sophie drank her second cup of morning coffee, pleased that she didn't have any cakes to make that day. She'd woken up with a sudden urge to take a drive to the cemetery. She hadn't been there for a long time and had the inclination to take flowers to Neil's and David's gravesites and spruce them up with a bit of spring-cleaning. But she wanted some company, so Sophie picked up her phone and called Jonathan, not actually expecting him to answer.

"Hi, Sophie," he said.

"Hey, Jonathan. Nice day, good weather, and it's springtime! Can you change any plans you have for today? Are you up for a drive with me?"

"Where to?"

"The cemetery. I'm going to drive out there and take some flowers to Neil and your dad in celebration of the season. Want to come?"

"When?"

"Now."

"I have such good and bad memories of that place. I remember when we went to free Neil—it's weird how clear that memory is to me. But I hated burying my dad there." He paused for a moment, apparently deciding whether or not to go. "Sure, I'll come. I'd like to talk to my dad, and maybe in such a peaceful place like that, I'll hear him talking to me too."

"Ask your mom if she wants to go."

"She can't. She's working. Can I bring Betty?"

"Sure, but bring her sling so she can ride in the backseat and also her car harness with the tether. Okay, so it'll be the three of us, buddy. I'll pick you up in a half hour in Mark's car."

"Cool. I'll be waiting outside."

Sophie pulled up to the house in a silver Saab convertible with the top down. "Going my way?" she called out to Jonathan, revving the engine for his pleasure.

"Awesome wheels. How'd you get your hands on it?"

"You know Mark goes on assignment for a few months at a time. Well, he asked us to drive his car now and then, so I thought this was a perfect opportunity to take it for a spin."

"I can't wait till I have my license."

"Won't be long now."

Jonathan placed the sling in the back of the car and adjusted the tether on Betty's harness. Then he hopped in the passenger seat and buckled his seat belt.

As they took off, Sophie glanced at the boy she loved so much—not a boy anymore, actually, but a young adult now, with his long, loose brunette waves blowing in the wind of the open car. Once he'd started high school, getting him to open up to her had become more of a challenge, but she was hoping the long drive would give them a chance to have a heart-to-heart.

"You're looking good," she said to him, "your usual handsome self. How are things going for you these days? We haven't really talked for weeks."

"I'm fine. Okay enough. Just kind of tired."

He didn't sound all that fine to Sophie. "I want to know the real story, honey—what's going on with you underneath all the small talk. It's me ... talk to me."

She didn't get a response at first—just the sounds of the highway all around them.

"I don't know," he finally said hesitantly. "Sometimes I don't feel like everyone else. So many of the kids at school seem to have their lives all mapped out. But I sure don't."

"Really? At fifteen years old? That sounds so unreal to me."

"Yeah. Like, they know what grade point average they need to get into the colleges of their choice, what they want to major in, what clubs they'll join, even where they want to work after graduation. They have it all planned out. I mean, how do they know what they want to do already? I don't even know what I want to do tomorrow. I don't feel like I'm like anyone I know."

"First, I'm sure not *everyone* knows what they want their lives to be like—maybe a few kids, or their parents, *think* they know, but it doesn't mean it'll happen. Second, from my experience, being like everyone else is way overrated. Good grief, you're only a sophomore. All of the answers will come to you when the time is right."

Jonathan shrugged and shook his head. "I just feel like I'm floundering and not measuring up to others."

"What happened to make you feel you aren't measuring up?"

He bit a fingernail. "Nothing, I guess."

"Jonathan, this I can guarantee: There'll be times when you'll feel insignificant, and there'll be times you have low self-esteem or feel like you're not enough. But this is a lesson for you to learn: You're enough. Exactly the way you are, you're *so* enough. You need to work on allowing."

"Allowing what?"

"Allowing things to flow as they need to. Just melting into the now and letting yourself feel what's going on in the moment. Things will fall into place, but not if you're on the wrong path. You miss out on what's going on *now* if you always sit in your future planning it out."

"Yeah, maybe."

"You love quotes. Do you know this one from Woody Allen? 'If you want to make God laugh, tell him about your plans.' I've found that plans don't usually work out as intended anyway. Life always seems to have some surprises in store for us that redirect our path. You'll come into what you're meant to do in good time."

"Matthew told me he thought my purpose might have something to do with my writing. I've never forgotten that."

"That's for you to discover, but I think that very well could be. It's always been a passion of yours and something you're good at."

"It doesn't seem like something important, though, like what my dad did. He was a doctor who healed people and was a real hero."

"Everyone has their own path to follow, sweetie. That was his. You have yours. They aren't meant to be the same. And although we each may have a main life mission, we actually have a number of goals to achieve in a lifetime. One of the things I'm here learning about is forgiveness, like with Neil. You know, some people spend a lifetime striving to be a clone of everyone else. So many people think that's what's important—to follow the same path, think the same things. I say break the mold and celebrate your uniqueness. High school is a time when everyone wants to be the same—I do get that. But one of your gifts is that you're a bit of a nonconformist. I love that about you."

"Maybe ..."

"Remember, differences are scary because they're unfamiliar."

"But if I decide to become a writer—to write movie scripts or books—what would I write about that's important?"

"You don't have to decide that now—that's the beauty of it. Just keep practicing your craft and keep that career option in your back pocket, and see how it opens up for you."

Jonathan was quiet, appearing to let the information sink in.

Sensing it was time to change the subject, Sophie lightened the mood. "You hungry? I could use some lunch."

"You know me, I can always eat. You keep driving, and I'll be on the lookout for a good place to stop."

They drove in silence for several minutes, with Sophie happy to give him his space, something she'd learned to do long ago. As with any teenager, too much talking about a particular topic at one time could shut him down. *Little bits at a time,* she reminded herself. *Let him control the pace.*

"Swing a U-turn, Soph. We just passed a diner. Sign said chicken pot pies. I could use some comfort food."

"I haven't had a chicken pot pie for years. I think the last one I had was when we came out to the cemetery for Neil."

The tires squealed loudly as Sophie took a 180-degree turn.

Jonathan chuckled. "Way to drive."

After she'd pulled into the lot and parked, she told Jonathan to take Betty over near the stand of trees. "While she does her business, I'll put the top up so she'll be comfortable in the car while we're eating."

A few minutes later, they walked into the diner together—and were immediately transported to the 1950s. There were red booths and white Formica tables, black-and-white floor tiles and tableside jukeboxes, ketchup-stained menus and torn plastic seats. Their waitress, about sixty years old, with wrinkles like tire treads and a silver-blue beehive hairdo, took a pencil out from behind her ear and wrote down their order. They each decided on chicken pot pie with coleslaw and a roll.

As they waited for their food, Jonathan drummed his fingers on the tabletop, absently playing along to a song in his head.

Sophie knew something was bothering him—she could feel it. Something was on his mind, and he was holding back.

"You seem a bit distracted, like something's wrong," she said casually. "Still thinking about what we were talking about before? Something else? Spill."

"Why do you think something's wrong?"

"Because I know you, and I feel it in my bones."

His cheeks reddened at her comment, and he turned the upper half of his body away from her. "It's embarrassing."

"You don't ever need to feel embarrassed around me. I'm always on your side, and I don't judge you. I'm here to offer whatever assistance and support I can."

She looked directly at his perfectly symmetrical features while he kept his eyes averted, his shoulders sagged.

"It's … it's about a girl, I guess."

She grinned. "Ah, a topic I know something about!"

"You're not like these girls." He shook his head. "I've had a thing for this girl, Lisa, for a long time."

"Oh, I think I know which one she is—the tall girl with the long blonde hair who came to the house the last time I was there?"

He rolled his eyes at her. "Sophie, they're *all* tall blonde girls at my school."

"Yep, that's true. Go on."

She tried to keep her vision locked on the plate of food that had just been delivered in front of her. She knew he was more likely to talk without direct eye contact.

Jonathan rhythmically hit his closed fist into the open palm of his other hand and pursed his lips. He took a bite of his roll, then said, "I asked her to the Spring Fling dance, and she said yes. I was really happy about that. Kind of a high, you know? I told the guys I was going with her, and I even got new clothes and everything. … Anyway, she tells me yesterday—and the dance is *tonight*—that she isn't going to go with me after all, because Brad Stager asked her, and she'd rather go with him."

Sophie took a long, controlled breath. She wanted to break that bitch's skinny neck. How dare she do something like that? And why? Why say yes, then hurt his feelings? And the day before the dance, no less. So rude! But she stifled her anger for Jonathan's sake. She didn't want to make him feel worse than he already did by having a dramatic reaction. Besides, the goose bumps on her arms were telling her that there was a reason it had happened—she trusted that.

Jonathan glanced up just then at the smiling waitress, who'd brought him an extra roll.

When she was gone, Sophie finally asked, "So how did you handle it?"

Clearly uncomfortable discussing it, but seeming to want Sophie's input, Jonathan winced a little as he answered her, his voice cracking as he spoke. "I asked her why, and she said she thought Brad had a better shot at becoming someone important in life than I did."

He turned away in his seat again, looking off to the side, his fork frozen in his hand.

It all made sense to Sophie now—why Jonathan was talking earlier about feeling like he wasn't measuring up. As upset as she was for him, she was relieved when he returned his attention to his plate and slowly started eating his pot pie as he confided in her.

"Okay, so I'm not Brad Stager, future governor of California or anything. But I want to be successful—I want to make my mom proud and myself proud too—I just don't know how I'm supposed to make that happen starting now, if I should even be worrying about that now."

As Jonathan talked, Sophie could tell the reason Lisa had given him for bailing on their date had struck a deep chord in him. She pictured him standing on a bridge somewhere between poor self-esteem and inadequacy. The view from the bridge was foggy—his horizon cloudy in front of him. There seemed to be an internal struggle going on between his present and his future.

"Some of my friends' parents push them—really hard. You should see how they're constantly measuring the progress they're making or not making. At least Mom never does that. I mean, I know I don't want to follow in their paths by setting my sights on Harvard or Stanford, but when I tell people what I want to do, they say, 'Come on, get real—how many people make it as famous writers or screenwriters?' "

Sophie aggressively buttered her roll, empathizing with his pain and worried that he was feeling so much pressure. The kids she'd known who hadn't been able to keep up with their parents' expectations suffered with their self-esteem. She knew the pressure wasn't coming from Lizzie, so where *was* it coming from? Probably a self-imposed paralysis caused by comparing himself with his friends and listening to them instead of to his inner voice—not fully affording himself the freedom to explore what *he* wanted to do and instead placing himself in a box of what other people thought he should do.

"Anyway," Jonathan continued, "guess Lisa thinks my goal is a pipe dream too."

Bloody hell, Sophie thought. She wanted to give that Lisa a piece of her mind! Instead, she told Jonathan, "But you only asked her to a dance, honey, you didn't propose marriage. I had no idea kids were thinking like this these days."

"It sucks."

"It sure does. Life is filled with things that make us feel like crap, but rejection is right at the top of the list. The key is to not let someone else determine your self-worth. Never let another person define you. We all seem to get tested in this area. Try not to fall into that trap. You'll meet many people who aren't going to be right for you. In your teen years, there's a big gap between who you are intended to be and your self-perception. You'll build your own self-esteem, but when you do, don't base it on other people's misconceptions. If you allow them, people will place their limitations on you. Oh, they may try to talk you out of your dreams, but remember this—you don't need their approval. I've never met a teenager who I think has the capacity to fully assess someone's character or predict their future. I can guarantee you that little Miss Lisa doesn't have a magic crystal ball that can predict her own future, much less yours or Brad Stager's."

"Yeah, like I said, it sucks. … But enough on that. Let's bolt."

Sophie signaled the waitress for the check, and as she brought it over, she pointedly smiled at Jonathan again.

He returned the smile. "Can I get a couple of pieces of bacon to go—for my dog?" he asked her. "Thanks for lunch, Sophie. I'm gonna go see Betty."

As Sophie paid the bill and waited by the cash register for the bacon, she gazed at him walking toward the car through the restaurant window, which cast golden highlights on his strikingly angular face—like his father's. He had a way of appearing as though he were always posed for a photograph. The best word she could think of to describe him was "beautiful." His soft eyes—sometimes green, sometimes golden brown—had seen grief, but they were soulful, and she heard a symphony when she looked into them. But then, she was also a fan of his chiseled nose, his slightly long eyebrows, his thick head of hair—no longer a towhead. She noticed that people stared at him when he entered a room, not only because of his handsome good looks, but a natural charm and charisma that sucked people in. Just looking at him made her heart melt. *You've loved that kid since the day he was born. What else is new?* She snapped herself out of her reverie and headed out the door. *That Lisa is an idiot.*

The rest of the drive was even more lovely than before as they rode deeper into the mountains and the fresh country air grew warmer. Sophie pulled into the same parking lot they'd used close to a dozen years ago when they'd come for Neil—only this time, things looked different in the spring than they had in the fall. The grass was greener, and there was a bounty of yellow daffodils blooming.

Jonathan let Betty out of the car and clipped on her leash, then let her lead him down the path. Sophie had to rush from behind to keep up with them. They came to David's gravestone first. "You talk to your dad while I go put these flowers on Neil's gravesite," she said a little breathlessly. "Here, put this bunch on his stone." She thrust a bouquet at him.

But he didn't take them. "No, bring those to Neil too. I brought something else for Dad."

"Oh, okay. You just take your time, then, and I'll be back in a few minutes."

"We'll be right here."

Once Sophie was gone, Jonathan commanded Betty to sit. It wasn't hard—at her age, getting her to recline on soft cool grass was no problem.

The minute he looked at his father's stone, all the grief rushed back through his veins—all the memories of the worst day of his life. His eyes brimmed with tears, and his breathing became labored and heavy, as if he were under water, unable to catch his breath. Every time he thought the nightmare was over, something happened to remind him that he'd never wake from it, it would never end—that relentless ache of knowing his father was no longer present in this world. His father's death still seemed so unbearably wrong to him. He thought he'd watch his dad grow into an old man, he thought he'd be a grandpa to his own children. He felt so cheated.

Kneeling down, Jonathan's voice quavered as he spoke. "I miss you, Dad. I know I can always talk to you, but I wish I could hear you talk back. I need to ask you questions and get some answers. I know you're around—I need your advice. I can't tell anyone this, but I've even thought of ending this sad life of mine and coming to join you. I don't fit in, don't know where I'm heading, and I'm sad all the time. I wish you would tell me what to do.

"I have this feeling I'm here for some special reason, but I don't know what it is. It's hard to live up to you, Dad. You're a hero, and everyone talks about you being a humanitarian. Maybe I should be a doctor like you were and be like you, but I'm not. I hope that's okay. So many of my friends are planning to follow in their fathers' footsteps—same schools, same profession—but I think I have a different path. I don't know ... I guess I just want to know if that's okay. I could really use a sign from you."

Jonathan closed his eyes and waited silently for ten minutes, but he didn't hear anything. With an overwhelming sense of disappointment weighing on his chest, he let out a deep sigh. "I didn't think so," he mumbled.

Before getting up, he reached out to brush off some debris in front of the gravestone and caught a glimpse of a shiny object. He picked it up and noticed it was a silver coin. *That's weird,* he thought, shoving it in his front pocket. Then he pulled the special stone he'd brought for his dad out of the same pocket and placed it on the gravestone.

When Sophie returned a minute later, Jonathan's posture said it all: downcast eyes, slumped shoulders, a crumpled face. He looked like a deflated beach ball, and her heart sank at the sight of him. Even Betty looked sad next to him, resting her head on her front paws.

"So did you talk to him?" she asked quietly.

"I always talk to him, but he doesn't talk back. I feel like he's around me, but I never hear him. I don't know why I expected this time to be any different." He kicked a rock into a tree.

"I have a hint for you that I think will help," Sophie offered, desperate to ease his anguish. "You need to look for different ways of communicating with him. Most people don't hear from spirits directly, but they can get messages to you. The answers to your questions will come in different ways—sometimes through inspirations, sometimes through signs. Messages appear to me in all sorts of ways when I'm open to receiving them. They may come to me in a book I'm reading or in a movie or TV show I'm watching. Once, a book fell right in front of me in a bookstore, and it was the book containing my answer."

"For real?"

"For real. ... Or you might feel reactions in your body, like chills going down your spine or a sensation of needles and pins. Be observant, quiet your mind, and watch for things that seem to be coincidences—because there are no coincidences."

She placed her hand on his shoulder. "Dreams are a means of communication too. Keep a pad of paper and a pen on your nightstand, and as soon as you wake up, jot down your dreams so you don't forget them. Ask your dad your questions right before you fall asleep. You can always meet up with him in your dreams. You need to quiet the mind clutter interfering with your reception. That's why meditation is good. When you're quiet, hear the messages and wisdom within that silence."

"That can work?"

"Absolutely. I kid you not."

Although Jonathan's disappointment was still evident—he thought for sure he'd hear from his dad today—he revived just enough to remember something else he wanted to do. He pulled a folded piece of rice paper and three crayons from his back packet.

"I want to do a rubbing of my dad's story before we leave, Sophie."

He placed the paper over his dad's stone and started vigorously coloring the epitaph there, the date of birth in blue, the date of death in green, and the dash—that powerful, meaningful part that represented his dad's story—in bright red. Staring at the finished product, he was inspired.

Hmmm, he thought. *Maybe I need to tell my dad's story since he couldn't tell it himself.*

The ride back home was much quieter than the ride out. But finally, Sophie couldn't take it anymore—she'd so hoped that this trip would be uplifting for Jonathan, not disheartening. She opened her mouth to speak, but Jonathan cut her off.

"Sophie, don't say anything too mushy, it'll make me cry, and I definitely don't want to cry right now."

"Okay, nothing mushy. I only want to tell you my feelings about your talent. Your gift is your creativity—it has been all your life. When you said stories aren't important, that's so not true. Stories have stood the test of time. They've always have been around and always will be. We *are* our stories. They're the best means of communicating information from one human to another. You can direct whatever messages you wish to relay into novels, movie scripts, whatever you like. Stories comfort, inspire, motivate, educate, record, entertain, and connect us as human beings."

"Just doesn't seem as important as Dad's work."

"Don't compare the two and rate them by importance. They're *both* important. Stories are the best way for people to learn in a powerful way. A story can take a message and drive it right into a person's brain and heart. The emotions and the feelings you create with your words are absorbed into others. We love stories because they make us feel. People involve themselves in stories every day. You tell your mom what happened at school. That's a story. We watch TV and movies and go to plays. All stories. We read books and listen to songs and look at photos like the ones Mark takes—all telling us their stories. Life is a story."

He nodded. "Sure, I guess everything creative that has meaning tells a story."

"Yes! When people dance, when I paint, when your mom draws, my tapestry—we're all conveying a story we want people to *get*. When you hear a story, you leave the confines of your own life for a moment as you're transported into a world of imagination. A story has the power to connect us to the meaning underlying our life experiences."

"Okay, okay, I hear you. You should have been an attorney. You make a great case. I get your message."

After that, the atmosphere in the car loosened up, and Jonathan's spirits seemed to rise in kind. They were making good time.

"You want a piece of gum, Sophie?" Jonathan asked her, searching his pants pockets for his pack. His hand grazed the coin and he pulled it out. Fingering it, he said, "I found this silver coin next to my dad's gravestone."

"Oh, yeah? What is it, a quarter someone dropped?"

"I don't know, let's see." He examined it, realizing it was a foreign coin. "It's silver with some writing on it: Republique Francaise ... 50 Francs ... 1978."

"Oh my God!" Sophie gasped so dramatically, Jonathan didn't know what was going on. She immediately pulled over to the side of the road, gripping the steering wheel so tight, her knuckles went white. Then she lowered her head and pressed three fingers to her brow before slowly looking up at Jonathan, her eyes misty.

"What's wrong? Are you okay?" he asked, a little panicked.

"Jonathan, your dad *did* speak to you today! In his own way. He did, he did. You have your sign. Oh my God, you have your sign!"

"What? I don't understand."

"Oh my God ... okay ... you were so young, not even four years old, and your mom and dad went to France for a seminar. You were really interested in coins when you were little, and your dad brought back a souvenir for you: a silver, 1978, 50-francs piece. Finding coins is often a way spirit gives a message of support and guidance. It's your father speaking to you!"

Chills traveled down Jonathan's spine as he gave Sophie a look of pure joy. His dad had answered his question—he was free to walk his own path.

Thank you, Dad. He closed his eyes and tilted his head upward to the open sky. *Thank you.*

Sophie was overcome with emotion too, and they both rode the rest of the way home tingling with electricity. They spoke in fits and starts, beaming the whole time. When Sophie dropped off Jonathan and Betty, she asked, "How much do I love you?"

"More than I'll ever know," he answered automatically. "Sophie, I ..."

"Yes, sweetie?"

"I love you too."

Her day—her world!—was complete.

She blew him a kiss. "Call you later."

The next morning, Jonathan woke still bubbling with excitement over his dad's message. As he pulled on some clothes, made his bed, and then walked around the upstairs hall brushing his teeth, he could hear his mother on the phone with Sophie in the kitchen, but he couldn't make out much of what she was saying. It was like she was trying to whisper, but she was too animated to pull it off. He caught snatches of "dance," "afterward," "Spring Fling."

Curiosity piqued, he made his way into the kitchen and sat at the table while Lizzie said her good-byes and hung up. When she turned to him, she was visibly shaken and her eyes were wet.

"What's happened, Mom? Sounds like something at the dance?"

Lizzie collapsed into the chair across from him and covered her face with her hands. "Jonathan, I have some terrible, terrible news. Give me your hand."

At the word "terrible," he waited for the hammer to hit. It had been like that since his dad.

"Your friend Lisa," Lizzie started, "I know how fond you are of her. ... Well, Lisa drove to the dance last night with her date, Brad. Unfortunately, Lisa was drinking at the dance or after the dance, I'm not sure which. Either way, in spite of drinking too much, she still decided to drive Brad and herself home. No one stopped her." Lizzie paused to take a sip of her cold coffee. "She caused a serious car accident, honey, a head-on collision. She's in intensive care with a severe head injury, and—I'm so sorry to tell you this—but Brad died in the crash last night." She got up to come around the table and hugged Jonathan. "I'm so emotionally torn," she sputtered out, crying. "I feel devastated that that young man is dead ... but I'm beyond grateful it wasn't you in that car with her."

The hammer hit Jonathan as though he were a block of ice, shattering into shards upon impact. He had a sudden urge to bolt. He grabbed Betty's leash, and together they ran out the front door, leaving it wide open. They ran fast and furious, until Jonathan eventually stopped to lean against a tree to catch his breath. Thoughts were jumbled in his head, some mirroring his mother's.

That could have been me. Oh my God, that was supposed to have been me. Is someone protecting me? Is that you, Dad? Are you looking out for me? ... God, poor Lisa. Poor Brad. Now he'll never have that future. Maybe Sophie was right about concentrating on the now. ... Oh my God, this can't be happening.

Jonathan bowed his head in profound sadness.

Sensing his distress, Betty licked his face as if to say, *I'm so glad it wasn't you.*

CHAPTER 55

JULY 19, 2004

I T HAD BEEN three months since Lisa and Brad's accident, and a black cloud still hung in the air; the impact on Jonathan and his friends had been profound. He'd signed up to take a Spanish class during summer school to give himself an advantage in the fall, but he was having trouble focusing on his studies. After another unsatisfying day at school, Jonathan was just happy to be home and blew in through the front door like a storm gust, intent on releasing his frustrations on a run with Betty. Normally, she anticipated his arrival and was waiting at the door with her eager tail wagging. But when she wasn't there to greet him, he wondered if she was out in the backyard. He walked into the kitchen.

"Mom, are you home?" he yelled.

No answer. Circling the house, he saw her in the living room. Betty Rose. Motionless on the floor. Lifeless. Blood discharged from her nose. She was still, like the walleye he caught on his fishing trip with Matthew. He felt like he was going to vomit and bent over clutching his stomach. He squeezed his eyes shut to erase the image in front of him, trying to breathe through the nausea enveloping him. Grabbing at his mouth, he tried to muffle the sounds escaping it, but they came out anyway. His heart was beating violently, and every muscle in his body was tense.

No! No, not now. Not yet. No, Betty, no. I'm not ready for you to go yet.

He fell to his knees next to her—there was no rise and fall of her rib cage. Instinct kicked in. He held her mouth closed, cupped his hand around her snout, and blew two breaths into her nose. Good, it seemed like the air went in. He racked his brain trying to remember how many breaths. One breath for every three seconds? He checked again for a heartbeat. Nothing. She was already on her right side, so he located the spot on her chest where her left elbow touched her rib cage and began his compressions. His first-aid training was coming back to him. Three compressions every two seconds. After fifteen quick compressions, two breaths.

From the kitchen, the sound of the back door opening. Then the rustle of paper grocery bags being set on the counter. "Jonathan, I'm home! Can you come help me bring in the groceries?"

When she heard no voice in reply but instead odd sounds coming from the living room, she headed there thinking, *What now?*

What she saw there stopped her in her tracks and broke her heart at the same time. The desperation coursing through her son's face and body was palpable. She quickly knelt next to him as he tried to save the life of his best friend.

"How long have you been going?" she asked, taking over the CPR.

"Maybe ten minutes," he said.

For Jonathan's sake, she continued a bit longer, but she could tell Betty was gone. Lizzie suspected she'd been dead about an hour.

"I'm sorry, honey," she said, shaking her head and petting the dog. "She's left us."

"No, Mom, no! You're a doctor! You have to do something!"

He pulled Betty to him, embracing her lifeless body. Gut-wrenching sobs finally erupted from somewhere deep within his soul, and Lizzie began to cry with him.

Why now? she wondered, even as she realized the futility of her question. There was never a good time, a better time for death.

Mother and son sat in the living room sobbing, swimming in the pain of loss that felt so familiar to both of them.

*

Jonathan was devastated. While Lizzie made the necessary calls and waited downstairs for Betty's body to be picked up, Jonathan threw himself on his bed, weeping so violently into his pillow, as though his desperate wailing could somehow resurrect her.

He finally ran out of tears, and his exhaustion led to sleep. When he woke hours later, Lizzie was curled behind him on the bed—spooning him the way she had so many nights after David died.

With his eyes almost swollen shut and his red nose coated in dried mucus, he told her, "Mom, we're going to have a memorial service for Betty. We have to."

"And so we will," she readily agreed.

By the next day, the vet had called with the likely cause of the sudden death: a tumor of the spleen—something rottweilers, in particular, are at risk for. There wasn't anything they could have done, nothing they'd failed to notice.

After Betty was cremated, Jonathan was given a beautiful cedar box containing her ashes. On top of the box, at Lizzie's request, the pet funeral home had engraved her paw print, her name, and her life span: 1994–2004. As had become a bittersweet ritual for him by now, Jonathan placed a piece of rice paper over the engraving and colored over the dash to preserve Betty's life story—it was a story of unconditional love, loyalty, and devotion. He placed it in his top drawer alongside Neil's and his dad's rubbings.

Later in the week, Sophie and Matthew joined Lizzie and Jonathan for a ceremony to commemorate their beloved Betty. Jonathan dug a hole in the backyard—in a shady spot where Betty loved to nap—placed the cedar box in it, and covered it with dirt. Then they each set a stone atop the mound as they eulogized her.

When it was Jonathan's turn to speak, his voice was clearly laced in pain. "Betty Rose, there's no greater gift I could have been given than you, with your cartoon-like face, wagging tail, and soulful eyes. You came to me when I needed you the most. It was a dark time, and you brought me the light I needed and gave me the unconditional love only you could give. You've been a loyal and faithful friend to me: the best friend I've ever had. And I'll never forget you. I wish you could be alive and here with me until I die. But I know you'll come back to me again.

"We're meant to be together. I love you, Betty. I'll miss you more than you'll know. I'll miss you waking me in the morning with your leash in your mouth, ready for a run. I'll miss how your whole body shakes and wiggles with joy when I come home. I'll miss how you snore loudly and wake me during the night. My sweet girl. I hope you're with my dad right now. Please come and hang around with me sometime. Give me a sign you're with me, like your dog tags jingling. I don't know how I can go running without you at my side. I love you, Betty."

Though he thought he was out of tears, they came streaming down again. He turned and walked away.

For the rest of the summer, Jonathan took Betty Rose's passing hard. Lizzie tried to comfort him by filling a collage picture frame with photos of the two of them together and hanging it in his bedroom.

But every night, clutching her dog tags, he'd place his pillow over his face to muffle his cries. He felt lost again, completely adrift.

How am I supposed to deal without her? I just want to be numb, he thought. *I want to stop feeling all of this pain. My existence on this Earth is pointless. Every night as I lie here trying to fall asleep, that's what I think. My existence is pointless.*

Betty, why did you have to go?

CHAPTER 56
THE ASTRAL PLANE

Malach: I had to interfere with Jonathan going to that school dance. It wasn't his time to exit. However, he wants to know his purpose on Earth and is feeling lost and disconnected. Clear signs that he's completely behind the veil.

Ruach: I'm sorry plan A didn't work, Malach.

Malach: He's now been on the physical plane for sixteen years, and things are finally in place and ready to go for me to honor my commitment. It took years to confirm if my plan worked or not, but now Jonathan is acting and behaving in ways that indicate he doesn't remember where he came from or the missions he's intent on accomplishing.

Ruach: I agree. The original plan didn't work. He sure planned a heavy load of loss this incarnation, didn't he? I guess it's nothing more than he can bear, but it seems like a lot right now. So what are you thinking?

Malach: I made him a promise, and I intend to keep my word. It's time to resort to plan B.

Ruach: How can I help?

Malach: You know Dylan Connors? Jonathan's friend? Nudge his uncle to give him a Christmas gift of vacation time at his condo in Park City.

Ruach: Consider it done.

Malach: And, Ruach, don't forget to give Sophie the inspiration we talked about. It's extremely important.

Ruach: I won't forget. I'll do it now.

Malach: As we go into plan B, I will need you and Pneuma to assist, as we've discussed. We'll see everything that is happening and know what they are feeling, of course. I'll explain during the actual event. Nothing better go wrong this time.

Ruach: It better not.

PART III

CHAPTER 57
DECEMBER 27, 2004

S CRUBBING THE CAST-IRON frying pan, coated with burned batter from the remains of the blueberry pancakes Sophie had made for Matthew that morning, required muscular effort. The dish scrubber she'd found at the state fair didn't work as promised. She was concentrating intensely when the ringing phone startled her, and she yanked off her soapy dish gloves to answer it.

"Hello?"

"Sophie, it's Jonathan."

"Hi, sweetie. How are you?" She immediately relaxed. Just hearing his voice was like taking a warm bubble bath.

"Good. Hey, what are you doing tomorrow? I thought I'd stop by. I also have a favor to ask. My friend Dylan and the rest of the powder hounds and I are going snowboarding over winter break. Would you take care of Einstein while I'm gone? Pretty please? I could drop him off before we leave. Mom's going to drive us and go skiing herself. You should come and keep her company. Matthew could watch Einstein."

Sophie was very fond of Jonathan's new golden retriever puppy, Einstein, but he was a bundle of energy, and she wasn't sure she could keep up with him while wearing a cast that had been on since an unfortunate ice-skating fall she took shortly before Christmas.

"I broke my ankle, remember? I won't be skiing this year. I'll be staying home, hobbling around or renting movies."

"Oh, yeah, I forgot. Sorry to hear that. Are you doing okay?"

"Yeah, but the cast is annoying. So how long will you be gone and where are you going?"

"Four days. And we're going to Utah."

"Who are the 'powder hounds'?"

"My group of friends. We're craving some powder. There'll be four of us and Mom."

"Sure, I'll take care of your pup. When are you leaving?"

"Early Wednesday morning. So I thought I'd come by with Einstein sometime tomorrow afternoon—say, three o'clock?"

"Is that Jonathan time or real time? And don't forget his dog food and treats—some chewy toys, too."

"Very funny. I'll do my best to be on time."

"See you. Love you."

"Love you too."

After Sophie hung up, she poured herself another cup of coffee and sat down at the kitchen counter. As much as she knew Jonathan needed a getaway before school started back up—having fun with his friends and doing something he loved to do—and as relieved as she was that Lizzie would be the one to drive them and chaperone them, something about the whole trip nagged at her. She trusted her intuition—all her life, the messages she received from that source had provided her with her inner guidance; and now, her gut reaction to Jonathan's news had created an ominous cloud hanging over her head.

So she threw on some clothes, grabbed her purse, and hobbled to her car, grateful that she still had use of her right foot to drive. Following her instincts, she headed to a nearby sporting goods store, where she found a young male salesclerk who was an avid snowboarder himself. She confided what she was worried about and asked for his advice.

"I hear your concerns, and they aren't unfounded," he said. "As much of a rush as it is, snowboarding *can* be dangerous."

He walked her over to a shelf, then held up a simple-looking device with a tube—sort of like a snorkel with straps. "I recommend you get your godson this: the AvaLung. It's an easy-to-use, helpful tool for those 'just in case' situations. A customer last month told me it saved his friend's life. Get this! He was buried in six feet of snow for twenty-five minutes, and he survived because of this."

Sophie was all ears and asked him to tell her more.

"Well, the AvaLung is a cool device because if the worst happens and if you use one of these babies the right way, you have a way better chance of making it 'cause it helps you breathe while you're buried under snow."

"Can you show me how it works?"

"Sure." He started gesturing with his hands. "When the snow covers you and you have airspace around your face, the warmth of your breath begins to ice up that space. It's called an 'ice mask,' and it can quickly suffocate you.

"But this little gizmo lets you breathe in air but doesn't form an ice mask near your mouth. Too much CO_2 is what asphyxiates you. So on this device, the intake for the air is here." He pointed to a spot on the device. "And the exhaust is in a different place. There've been reports of some people buried in the snow for forty-five minutes with this.

"But tell your godson two things. They're really important, so don't forget. One, he has to have the mouthpiece in his mouth *before* an avalanche gets under way, so he needs to be wearing it. Not wearing it? It won't save him. Second, it needs to be on the outside of his clothing. Very important."

Sophie pressed the open palm of her hand against her throat and exhaled slowly. "I'm actually getting more worried about this trip, not less. Wrap it up, I'll take it."

The salesclerk rung up her purchase. "I'm saving up for a snowboarding trip myself, to Canada. It's a dream of mine to go to Whistler. Tell him I hope he has a great time."

"Will do and thanks." Sophie left with the package, feeling only slightly relieved about the concerns plaguing her.

The next afternoon, Jonathan was late, as usual. He finally rushed into Sophie's house close to 4:00 p.m.

"Wow," said Sophie as she bent down to pat Einstein's head. "He gets bigger every time I see him. It's crazy how fast they grow."

"Well, he's fully housebroken now, so no worries about that."

"Good to know. But I think I'll keep my favorite shoes out of his way."

Jonathan ruffled the hair on Einstein's head. "Leather is a gourmet treat for you, isn't it, boy?"

"Unfortunately," Sophie said with a laugh, "I found that out the hard way. Can you stay for dinner? Please?"

"I'm really sorry, but I can't. I've still got to get a few things and pack up before we go, and as you can tell, I'm running late." Jonathan kissed her cheek. "Make it up to you when I pick him up, though?"

He strolled toward the kitchen, two bags in hand. As he set them on the island and started unloading them, he said, "Here are the cans of food. Give him a scoop of dry and half a can of the moist stuff twice a day. One omega-3 bone and a treat at bedtime. Easy, right?" He reached out to give Sophie a hug. "Thanks a lot. Love you." Then he started heading back to the front door.

"Whoa, wait up a minute, mister. I have something for you before you leave."

She grabbed the white paper sack off the dining room table.

"Can I get it when I pick him up?" Jonathan asked, still heading toward the door.

"No, it's for your trip. For your safety. Please, Jonathan, hear me out." The gravity of her voice made Jonathan stop and face her. "I have an intuition, and I want you to take it seriously." She pulled the device from the sack. "This is an AvaLung mouthpiece—a filtration system that could save your life if you're ever in an avalanche. It pulls in the air directly from the snowpack, so you can breathe if you get trapped, God forbid."

"I know what it is, but I don't need that thing."

Sophie didn't like the smug grin on his face.

"I know how to be safe to avoid an avalanche. I took a class," Jonathan said more respectfully. "And to give you peace of mind, we hired a guide to go with us when we go into the backcountry."

"Going to the backcountry is *exactly* what I'm worried about," Sophie replied firmly. She couldn't get the knot out of her stomach. "Jonathan, *please* practice putting this on before you snowboard and promise me you'll actually wear it." She proceeded to relay to him the two critical points the salesclerk had emphasized.

When Jonathan still didn't respond, Sophie thrust the bag at him and held it there until he took it. "Jonathan, do you hear that I'm actually begging you? I'm very worried—I just have a … a feeling. Look, I know I can't talk you out of going, but do this for me. Please. I don't ask much of you, but I'm asking this."

"Sophie, you worry too much. You really do. William James said, 'If you believe that feeling bad or worrying long enough will change a past or future event, then you're residing on another planet with a different reality system.'"

She scowled at him and sighed heavily. "I don't think my worrying will change an event, but I think this could."

"Okay, okay," he finally said, caving in at her exasperation.

She smiled and pressed the bag tighter against his chest. "Thank you. Don't blow me off, okay, kiddo? Promise me you'll wear this whenever you're in the backcountry. It means everything to me."

"I promise."

He kissed her on the cheek one more time, gave Einstein a few more good-bye pats, then bolted out the door, calling over his shoulder, "We'll have dinner together when I get back."

"That would be great," she called back. Then, unable to resist, "How much do I love you?"

He waved from the car. "More than I'll ever know."

Sophie closed the door behind her and walked Einstein into the kitchen to get him one of her homemade peanut butter and bacon dog treats. Bending down to pick up the puppy, she looked him square in the eyes. " I still don't feel good about this, Einstein. Not good at all."

The next morning, Lizzie woke up thinking, *This is going to be fun.* But the trip didn't exactly start out as planned. The intent was to leave at

5:30 a.m., but everyone wasn't at the house and ready to go until 7:00. It was going to be a very long day of driving—with 750 miles to travel—so she headed out on the I-15 North toward I-215 North, with four rambunctious, continually hungry teens in tow. Before long, her Toyota Land Cruiser smelled like unwashed towels and the backseat was littered with the kind of mess that only teenage boys can generate: candy bar wrappers tossed on the floor from Dylan, crushed soda cans from Tyler, and empty bags of chips from Nate. Jonathan rode up front with Lizzie.

"Mom, relax and slow down," he said. "You don't have to go so fast. If you get a ticket, you'll only delay us. Besides, you're setting a bad example to a certain person in this car who recently got his driver's license."

The rest of the boys burst out laughing.

"This is just how I drive, darling. Jonathan, grab one of those garbage bags at your feet and toss it in the backseat so you boys don't turn my brand-new car into a pigsty."

"Can we stop at the next fast-food joint we see for some burgers? Then I'll drive and give you a break."

"Yes, but good grief, how are you guys hungry? You're like dogs—all you do is eat and pee. It's mind-boggling. But it's a good idea to let you take a turn at the wheel before it's dark. I want to be the one who's doing the high-elevation, nighttime driving. I'm more experienced."

"Yeah, but I'm younger with better reflexes," Jonathan countered.

With every foot of elevation the car climbed, with every degree the temperature went down, the boys became more impatient and excited. A berm of snow was left on the right side of the road by passing plows, piling it up much higher than the actual snow level. The scenery looked like a painting of itself, with crusted pine trees and snow-capped mountains in the distance.

They arrived in Park City late that evening, with its low-moisture snow and backcountry access. Lizzie felt the energy of everyone's anticipation.

It pays to know someone who knows someone, she thought. Dylan's uncle had given him a Christmas gift of free lodging at his condo: three bedrooms, three bathrooms, a gourmet kitchen, two fireplaces (one gas, one wood burning), hot tub, one-car garage, two TVs, and boot heaters. It was going to be a luxurious couple of days.

After the long ride, everyone was anxious to get out of the car and stretch their legs. Long, jagged icicles hung from the roof of the A-framed condo, and Dylan couldn't resist picking one off and starting a sword fight with Jonathan. Lizzie envied their youthful energy, but she did find it amusing that she was the one who drove most of the way and didn't feel one bit tired, and they were the ones heading for bed. She was still wired, and after unpacking the car, she planned to indulge in a glass of wine. Fresh snow, wine, and a vacation with the boys … what more could she want?

"Mom, we're getting up early in the morning. Our guide is going to meet us at the front office. Are you going to hit the slopes tomorrow or take a few brush-up lessons first?"

"Yep, I'm hitting the slopes. Just little old me doing that old-fashioned thing called skiing."

"You should try snowboarding. You'd be good at it. You'd like it."

"Going to stick with what I know. What time are you guys getting up? I'm planning to make you a hearty breakfast before you go."

"Up at seven. Meeting the guide at eight," Jonathan said.

In jest, Lizzie swatted him with a rolled-up magazine. "What? I thought you said early! The day is half over by then. Love you, baby. Sleep well."

Lizzie kissed Jonathan's cheek and tousled his hair. "Go get a good night's sleep. I want you guys to be well rested and alert for tomorrow."

"You too, Mama Bear. Thanks for doing all this for us. You're the best."

Once Jonathan was gone, Lizzie blew air out between her lips in a deep sigh of contentment. This was the happiest she'd seen him in a long time. The worst of last year's prom accident and Betty Rose's passing seemed to be over, but she never stopped worrying about him ever since David's death. She still wished he had more motivation and that he'd get his grades up in school, but she was hoping this trip with his friends and all the fresh air and nature around them would start the year off on the right foot. All she wanted for her child—day after day and year after year—was for more and more life to creep into him.

After a restful night's sleep, Lizzie woke early and, staring out the window of the condo, she noticed the snow falling softly like feathers. They'd all slept well and woke to a picture-perfect day. It had snowed during the night, leaving several inches of new powder, and the clouds looked as though big, puffy marshmallows were tossed into a mixing bowl and whisked around into long strands of white fluff. The smell of coffee, frying potatoes, and omelets drifted into the bedrooms, waking the ever-hungry boys.

"Mom, I'm impressed. I told the guys we'd be eating fast food this week," Jonathan said. He laughed and snapped her with a dishtowel.

"Stop it, that hurt," she said. She loved seeing him so playful. "But it's not a big deal—anyone can put on some coffee, cook up some frozen hash browns, and scramble up some eggs. And Sophie made two dozen cherry-nut muffins for us. So dig in."

Jonathan continued his lighthearted ribbing and joking with the boys.

"This is great, Dr. C. I'm starving," Nate said. "I guess you carted all this food along. Thanks." He shoveled potatoes into his mouth.

"Dude, chew or you'll choke," Tyler teased him.

When Jonathan finished his breakfast, he started looking around the room for something. "I can't find my gloves. Mom, did you bring my gloves?" Even as he was speaking, he was looking out the window, marveling at all the fresh powder. *Should be a great day,* he thought.

"No, you're old enough to pack your own stuff. That was your responsibility," Lizzie answered.

"Hold on," Dylan said, going into his bedroom and rummaging through his suitcase. He reemerged a moment later. "Here," he said, shoving a pair of gloves at Jonathan. "I have an extra pair. Bright red, but they work."

"I'll look like a clown. But thanks, I'll use 'em. Mom, we'll do a few warm-up runs and then head for the backcountry."

"Please, can't you stay within the boundaries?"

"Mom, you arranged a guide for us specifically for that reason! We took a safety class. And Sophie got me an AvaLung. We'll be okay. It's you I'm worried about. I wish Sophie had come with you to keep you company."

Lizzie scowled, standing with her hands on her hips. "Sophie got you a what?"

"An AvaLung—it's an emergency breathing device if you get caught in an avalanche. You know how she is, a chronic worrywart," he said, chuckling a little. "But I promised her I'd use it because she had a bad vibe or something, so she ran out to get it for me."

Lizzie raised her eyebrows. "That's not funny. Knowing she's concerned makes me uncomfortable."

"I shouldn't have told you—you always act like she's psychic or something. It's all good, Mom. No worries."

Lizzie shook off her anxiety, not wanting to ruin the day worrying about things she had no control over. "Give me a hug. Each of you. I love you to pieces. You boys look out for each other out there and have fun! We'll meet back here for dinner."

"See you for dinner, Mom. You have fun too."

Jonathan was the last in line out the door, behind his friends, and as they headed toward the meeting point, he double-checked that the AvaLung was in his pack. He'd read the directions last night in bed and figured it couldn't hurt to bring it along. *I'm sure I won't need this,* he reasoned, *but I did promise Sophie. And a promise is a promise.*

The boys met their guide at 8:00 a.m. sharp. His name was Will Norris, a mellow guy who looked to be in his mid-fifties and who wore his surfer-dude look well. His parched skin was like leather, damaged from hours under the sun, and his curly blonde hair was tied back at the nape of his neck. Jonathan instantly took a liking to him.

Nate leaned over and whispered, "I bet this guy cost your mom a chunk of change."

"Yeah. But Will's going to chase the best conditions for us. That's what we hired him for. My mom's willing to cough up the money for his expertise."

Jonathan shook Will's hand. "I'm Jonathan. Really nice to meet you, man. I'm looking forward to this. This is Nate, Dylan, and Tyler. Been working here long?"

"Yep, I've been guiding and instructing for over twenty-five years and have skied from Alaska to the Alps."

"Impressive. Ever been in an avalanche?" Jonathan asked.

"Had a close call two winters ago. I was lucky enough to avoid one in Jackson Hole by a hairsbreadth. I was on one side of the bowl, and the avalanche happened on the other. But I'm well trained and have participated in a few rescues."

"You were lucky, dude—lucky," Nate said.

"Okay, guys," Will instructed, "after a mandatory safety talk and demonstration, we'll warm up a bit, then head out to the backcountry, where you guys will experience some of the best runs you've ever had. We'll issue you an avalanche beacon, shovel, and probe pole and instruct you in their use."

So far so good, Jonathan thought. There was something familiar about Will. Maybe they could stay in touch after this vacation.

Following the requisite training, the boys took a few warm-up runs as planned, then stood in line to take the chairlift to the top of the mountain to gain altitude. Once on top, they hiked out a distance to get to untracked powder.

"This is going to be epic!" Tyler enthused. "Guess I didn't realize how snow starved I've been."

"Glad we could do this," Jonathan agreed, having a Zen-like moment of pure contentment with his buddies.

They all gathered at the crown, which was about fifteen feet at its thickest on a southwest-facing slope with a thirty-eight-degree steepness. When Will saw Jonathan fumbling with the AvaLung, he helped him strap it on. The boys got antsy waiting for him.

"Jonny, dude, hurry up, will you?" Tyler yelled. He started swaying his hips and knees, his boots already snapped into their bindings. "The virgin snow is so inviting!"

"Sorry," Jonathan said quietly to Will. "I promised my godmother I'd wear this thing and ..."

"No apology necessary," Will assured him. "It's a smart move. You're good to go now."

Jonathan inserted the mouthpiece and bit down on it. "Let's start shreddin', guys," he said. "I'm set."

"You want to go first since your uncle's the one who's letting us use his awesome condo?" Nate asked Dylan.

"Sure, I'm going to drop," Dylan replied. "This way, powder hounds!"

Dylan pushed off and began his run, carving in and out with tight turns as he crossed the bowl. Nate went next, then Tyler.

As Jonathan dropped, a surge of exhilaration took over his body, topped by the ultimate of all adrenaline rushes. But he had only made four turns before fractures formed in front of his eyes—the earth beneath him literally started cracking. *What the heck?* In an instant, all that powdery fresh snow became the enemy and the intense excitement he'd just felt was replaced by a sickening sensation.

This can't be happening. This can't be happening. No, this can't possibly be!

Something sounding like a huge collapse—followed by cracks propagating upward and outward—released the whole bowl.

Will was still at the crown, trying to keep an eye on each boy, when he saw what was happening. He immediately yelled the dreaded warning: "Avalanche!"

He hoped he was as well trained as he thought. He'd heard of an avalanche being referred to as "breath of the white dragon," and this white dragon had some powerful breath. He figured it was the result of new snow on top of large grain facets, knowing it's the flat, icy flakes that are the real problem because they can't hold on to the layers above and below.

Will saw each boy get swallowed up by the white dragon as it picked them off one by one and swept them downhill under a giant cascade of snow. His training kicked in, and he knew he had to act fast.

*

Jonathan was shocked when he noticed a three- to four-foot fracture appear, followed by an instant change in the snowpack. When he pushed down, the whole slope released beneath him.

He tried to head straight downhill in hopes of building up some speed, so he could then veer off to the side of the moving slab. He knew if an avalanche was bearing down, he needed to get away from its track.

But there was no time!

The impact was so jolting, it shoved him from behind, and he plummeted into space. It was as though he were tumbling around inside a giant cement mixer that turned into a class five white-water rafting ride over a waterfall, traveling faster than fifty miles per hour.

He was at the mercy of the avalanche, flung about and tousled under the power of the snow waves that flew over rocks and crashed through the trees, snapping off their limbs like they were toothpicks.

When he felt it slow down, Jonathan knew it meant he was getting close to its runout zone, where it would all stop. He tried to roll to his back with his feet going downhill to do the backstroke, but there wasn't time to get into place. One of his gloves had been stripped off, but he was grateful he had inserted the mouth device before taking off. He took a big breath to expand his lungs.

The cement mixer spewed him out along with its viscous ice-cement that immediately turned into hard concrete encasing him in an ice tomb. Unable to move even his fingers, buried alive in cold snow-concrete, he panicked.

He knew there weren't many options for him: one, to be rescued by one of his friends who'd made it; or two, to die here alone and melt out with the snow in April.

So this is it. This is how it's ending for me. Terror and sadness washed over him. Sadness for his mom, who had already suffered so much from the loss of his dad. Sadness for Sophie, for his friends, for Einstein, but most of all for himself. Sadness for all the life he wouldn't live.

He was well aware that many avalanche deaths result from suffocation—if you don't go off a cliff or slam into a rock or tree first. Fortunately, his AvaLung remained properly positioned. He breathed in and out of the mouthpiece held in his teeth. As he exhaled, the carbon dioxide–saturated breath exited through the bottom end of the apparatus, around his side, and behind his back. He could still breathe in small shallow gasps with the mouthpiece. His left hand was immobilized alongside his head, but at least he was in an upright position.

The panic intensified, until it overtook him. Adrenaline coursed through his body, but he couldn't move.

Mom, Mom, save me. Please!

In an avalanche, he knew every second counts. In safety class, he'd learned that after the first seven to eight minutes of being buried, brain damage can occur. At the fifteen-minute mark, around 30 percent of victims are already dead. At thirty minutes, about 90 percent are dead. Jonathan counted backward from sixty to one in his head. How many minutes had already gone by? How many minutes of life did he have left?

It was a short life, he thought, *and I wasted a lot of it. If I die, I don't want to take my best friends with me. This will kill my mother—and Sophie too. I wanted to live a life with no regrets, and here I am, full of regrets.*

He thought about his father's death. *Dad, Dad can you hear me? Dad, please help me. Get me out of this and I'll turn things around. I don't want my final moments to be in an ice coffin. Maybe Will or one of the guys will save me? Dad, I don't want to die. Dad, please help me. Please.*

Was it too late for him? Would he never get to live with the knowledge that each moment of life was a precious gift?

From the large mountain-facing window in the lodge, Lizzie saw the snow barreling down the mountain. She'd been sitting in front of the fireplace sipping a hot toddy when sweat broke out on her forehead and she had an image of Jonathan in trouble.

She knew at once.

She knew.

A mother knows.

Her baby, her boy, was in that avalanche.

Before the horror of it all could even set in, she released an anguished scream and started running for help. Everyone in the lodge stared at her as she passed.

Why did I let them do this? Oh my God, why? I'm the one who hired the guide to take them outside the boundary. Oh my God, this is all my fault. This is all on me!

On the mountain, Will communicated with the Ski Patrol and learned that they, along with Search and Rescue, had already been alerted and were responding immediately. The medical helicopter was on its way. Two rescue dogs, stationed at Ski Patrol headquarters, were riding to the site on the laps of two patrollers on a snowmobile. Will knew one avalanche dog could cover an extensive amount of ground more meticulously than a line of people with probing poles, covering over two acres in thirty minutes.

He breathed a sigh of relief when he saw one of the boys trudging toward him. It was Nate. He must have been only partially buried and dug himself out! Thank God, he didn't appear to have any injuries.

Once he safely delivered Nate to the patrollers, Will switched his beacon to receive mode and began his own search on foot, waiting for the blessed sound of a responding signal. Almost immediately, he got something. He oriented to the most powerful radio signal—about forty feet away—and followed it. He reoriented at the five-foot mark, drawing his transmitter across the ground, listening to where it was stronger and where it was weaker. At the point where the signal was most intense, he scratched a box in the snow with his finger, then probed with his pole in concentric circles until he located where to dig with his shovel.

He found one of the boys! Dylan wasn't buried too deeply, and Will easily pulled him to the surface. He was alive and appeared to be shaken, but otherwise okay. *Two down, two to go,* Will thought, as only a small wave of relief crested inside him. He knew he couldn't live with himself if any of the boys died on his watch.

Jonathan was still upright, but buried deep. Being unable to move was almost unbearable—it was as though he were wearing a body cast. Trying to gauge how much time he had left before he died, he kept counting the minutes backward slowly in his head, over and over again. He thought he'd counted eight already. He knew time was running out. His head throbbed and his heart ached. A combination of anguish and love washed over him.

I'm sorry, everyone. I'm so sorry, Mom. I love you all. Three ... two ... one. Nine minutes.

Will's heart raced when he saw the helicopter land on a clearing not far away. The rescue team arrived on its heels, and then everything played out like a well-rehearsed script. Energetic avalanche rescue dogs carried out maneuvers called zee's as they criss-crossed the field of the slide area, trained to pick up the strong scent of still-conscious humans percolating through the snow.

Within minutes, one of the dogs caught a scent and started barking, then vigorously digging with his front paws.

Two patrollers took over with their shovels, dug four feet down, and carefully extracted a hand ... then an arm ... then a whole torso. It was Tyler. Good news: He'd been found in a supine position, aided by an air pocket. Although he was conscious, he appeared to have facial lacerations and other injuries. Once he was safely removed from the snow, the medical team stepped in.

That left only Jonathan.

Under the snow, the minutes continued to tick away. To stave off his increasing claustrophobia, Jonathan told himself to breathe slowly. *Just keep breathing through the mouthpiece, slowly. ... Just keep counting the minutes, second by second.* He'd learned in class that brain damage actually starts well before death, but as long as he could think and count, he knew his mind was intact.

But he was worried. Extremely worried. The head and the neck are especially vulnerable to the enormous impact of an avalanche, and his head was in serious pain.

Jonathan's air channel remained open, but within moments, he started to lose track of his counting. Then he heard a distinct sound: Betty Rose's dog tags jingling.

This is it. I'm slipping away. This is the day I die. I love you, Mom. I'm so sorry to die on you.

At ground level, Lizzie had been frantic this whole time, but she was told in no uncertain terms to wait at the bottom of the mountain and let the teams do their work. She'd be informed the minute they knew anything.

One second she was standing there, pacing like a caged animal, and the next, a chill ran up her spine and out through her ears, and it was as though she could hear Jonathan's thoughts beaming directly into them.

Don't you dare, she replied. *Don't you dare leave me. You stick this out. Stay with me. Do you hear me? Do you hear me?*

She telepathically beamed her thoughts right back at him, commanding him to live. She was totally unaware of the protective arm of one of the ski patrol staff around her, holding her up from collapsing.

The rescue mission was completely buzzing now—an orderly, methodical mix of transceivers and beeping signals as men and women, wearing the familiar red jackets with the white cross, probed the snow with poles—and Will continued to assist in the search. He was grateful that everyone knew their job so well and carried it out so precisely, but he also knew the unanswered questions on everyone's mind: Three alive. But would the fourth survive? Would the fourth even be *found*?

Tick tock.

Time was moving too quickly for Will, with each passing second posing imminent danger. Finally, finally, he heard a dog handler yell out, "Hershey's got something!" The chocolate Lab, a level A certified avalanche dog, had picked up a scent and was aggressively wagging her tail.

Yes! In fifteen minutes, she'd done what it would have taken a probe line several hours to accomplish.

As the rescue workers shoveled, Will stood ready for the extraction. The first thing he saw was Jonathan's red glove. Shovelful by shovelful, the team dug him out, taking extreme measures to protect his head. When they reached his face, they checked his airways and then proceeded to dig out his shoulders and the rest of his body, carefully extracting him from his ice tomb.

It wasn't what Will wanted to see—Jonathan was no longer conscious. But he didn't want to panic, either. The helicopter crew was waiting and quickly whisked him to the nearest medical center. Will stood on the mountain watching the chopper fly away, with only one thought left in his mind: Would he live or would he die?

From the daily newspaper:

> PARK CITY, UTAH (Friday, December 31, 2004) – An avalanche swept four male snowboarders down a southwestern slope of the backcountry yesterday. Summit County Sheriff Ogden Meyers said the four teenagers and their adult guide survived, with two of the boys (both aged 16) remaining in critical condition at Cranston Medical Center. Names of the victims, as minors, are being withheld until all family members have been contacted.
>
> One of the boys was able to dig himself out of the debris on his own and make it to safety. The second boy, who sustained no injuries, was located and recovered by the guide, Will Norris. Rescue dogs led to the discovery of the two remaining boys, both of whom were buried beneath the snow. Both have serious injuries, but only one of them—the one submerged under the snow the longest—remains unconscious.
>
> Two observers reported that they saw massive amounts of snow roaring down the side of the mountain as the visible snowboarders tried to escape, but they quickly lost sight of the boys.
>
> Utah Avalanche Center forecaster Marvin Currler learned, in talking with the guide and two of the boys, that they were all experienced boarders who were prepared for their backcountry trip and were equipped with appropriate rescue gear.

Local authorities had issued only a category one warning for the area at the time of the snowslide. Thursday's slide was 380 yards wide, two to six feet deep, and could have ended tragically. Although the four identified snowboarders were unexpectedly caught by the cascading mass of snow within minutes, all survived and no other persons have been reported missing or injured by the avalanche.

CHAPTER 58

JONATHAN
JANUARY 2005

S OMETHING BIZARRE HAPPENED to me. One minute
I was buried in my snow tomb, and the next I was hearing an
odd sound like a couple of loud clicks. Then I felt myself moving
through the top of my head—a kind of whooshing—like an intense
roller-coaster ride. I was floating above, looking down at my body,
observing my rescue. Hershey, the chocolate-brown Labrador rescue dog,
was vigorously digging with her front paws to find me, followed by two
ski patrollers who took up the rest of the digging with shovels. I could
hear their conversation.

"Hershey found him!" one said.

"Think he's under about two meters," another said.

"That's his red glove," the other said.

"Looks like his head is up, so ease up a bit."

From my counting, I estimated I was buried about twenty-three
minutes before I lost consciousness. Lots of people were gathered around
giving their opinions. From my vantage point, I could see that Nate,
Dylan, and Will were okay, but I didn't see Tyler. As they dug me out,
the first thing they saw was my head with the AvaLung still attached to

me. I couldn't have been unconscious for more than a couple of minutes. The guys carefully pulled me out and loaded my body into the helicopter.

It was so weird not to feel the sensation of a body. Very light. Very freeing. I could transport myself with just a thought, kind of like watching different scenes on TV.

I switched to a scene watching my mom break down emotionally. She was on a phone in some lobby somewhere, sobbing and begging Sophie to get to Utah immediately. She was really frantic.

Then switch. In the next scene, I was on a table in a hospital room with physicians and nurses working on me. My body didn't look too banged up or physically harmed in any way.

My mom stood in the corridor outside the room, watching through the window, super distraught. I wasn't in any pain at all and felt light and at peace. I heard people saying things like "head injury," "unconscious," and "coma." I knew enough about comas to know they can last days, weeks, or years.

The doctor was saying something to my mom about achieving medical stability, medical management, and prevention of medical crisis. No way to predict how long I'd be in the coma. I felt so sorry for her. She was not consolable.

After a few hours, Sophie and Matthew arrived. Right after getting my mom's call, they'd dropped Einstein off with a friend and headed to the airport. Sophie tried to comfort my mom, but she was unable to, as she couldn't be pacified herself. It was good that Matthew was there for the two of them.

I was acutely aware of everything—I could even tell what people were thinking. Although I felt no pain for myself, hearing and feeling the anguish of all the people around me, especially my mom, was almost unbearable.

Observing my body, I simply looked like I was sleeping, but the tubes, wires, and pieces of medical equipment attached to it were freaking them out.

There was a tugging sensation and some pressure. Then I heard that unusual sound again—those clicks—followed by the roller-coaster whoosh again. After the clicking sounds, I sped through a narrow wall of darkness, emerging into an area of bright and beautiful light.

Holy crap! I knew the beings there. Everyone was familiar. I even knew their names: Malach, Ruach, Pneuma, my dad.

My dad!

They appeared as transparent, vibrating light to me, but I *knew* them and communicated with them through thought.

I had such profound awareness, and I remembered everything about this place from before. They were all transmitting an overwhelming sense of love—it was mesmerizing. The whole place was love. I could even carry on a conversation with them telepathically.

Malach: Hey, Nephesh, good to see you, man.

Jonathan: Malach, wow, does this mean I, I mean Jonathan, died?

Malach: No, Nephesh. This is plan B. I had to resort to plan B. The original plan to keep you remembering this dimension didn't work because of birth complications. So the only way I could rectify the problem was to implement our backup plan. I had to find a way to bring you back here so we could remind you of where you're from and you could retain the memories of this dimension when you return to Earth. You've gotten a bit off your intended track, my friend, and that's okay, but I know you were emphatic about remembering and completing your various missions, and I couldn't let you down. Once you leave here, you won't be under the influence of the amnesia of the veil anymore.

Jonathan: So plan A didn't work, huh? Birth complications …

Malach: You want to see a summary of your life so far?

Jonathan: Not really, Malach. I'm kind of flunking life in the human dimension.

Malach: You know there's no flunking. You're evolving. You're learning. Just as you're meant to. There's not a soul here to judge you. You know that's not what this is about at all. And now you're here to remember what you set out to do.

Jonathan: Okay. Let me see it.

It was like a movie fast-forwarding on a large screen—everything that had happened to me during the past sixteen years, only I could actually feel how each of my actions had impacted others. I could sense how others felt. I could see what I did well and how I might have done better. I saw that many of the group souls I incarnated with were working on dealing with the loss of a loved one in one shape or form. It was our opportunity to grow through the experiences and to learn that, although we'd briefly be separated, we'd always be together again. Loss is not a permanent state.

Jonathan: I really want to stay here. I forgot the beauty and the sense of freedom and the love.

Malach: Maybe not the best option. I don't think you're ready to come back yet and stay, but it's totally up to you. This is plan B. This is your reminder, your wake-up call. Come home or continue on with your life. It's your choice.

Strong feelings of extreme familiarity and comfort washed over me. I thought and thought hard, and as enticing as it was to stay, I knew I couldn't leave my mom—the whole course of her life would completely change if I died. And Sophie. I realized that this would be a repeat of the life she had when she was my mother. This would alter her life as well.

Malach: We'll be here when the time comes for you to come back.

Jonathan: It would be devastating to my mom and Sophie if I return and stay in a coma forever. In fact, it would ruin their lives even more than if I die.

Malach: You won't remain in a coma. We created this scenario to reach you. You'll be fully whole again.

Pneuma: My burning question for you is, how's the pizza?

Jonathan: That's funny. Worth the trip, my friend. It's good stuff.

Ruach: Good to see you, Nephesh. Your father, David, is here. But we know him as Anua.

Jonathan: Dad! Oh, Dad, it's great to be able to talk to you. I've been trying hard to communicate with you. I miss you so much.

Anua: I do send you messages. You know that now because of the coin you found, right? When you go back now, you'll be able to receive my messages more easily. I'm sorry to have left you, but your soul wanted to learn to deal with loss, and my death was part of our contract in our role together. I want you to know that I love you so much, and I'm incredibly proud of you. Don't let my departure lead you off your path. You have much to accomplish. Know I'm with you and feel my love for you. Always.

Jonathan: I remember now. I love you and miss you so much.

Anua: Remember to listen to your inner voice. You won't go wrong. You need to go back and complete your missions, as well as being a support for your mother, Sophie, and all the new people coming into your life who are counting on you. I'm always with you. Don't lose sight of that. I'm currently not incarnated, but my love is there with you always. Give my love, my deepest love, to your mother and tell her I'm always with her. Remind her of her own missions, please.

Jonathan: Okay, I will, Dad. I'm going back. I love all of you very much. Thank you for being there for me.

Anua: We love you too. Now go complete your missions. I'm here for you.

Jonathan: And Betty Rose! You're here too. Thank you so much for helping me through a rough time. I love you, Betty.

Being in the realm of the Source, well, there are no earthly words for it. It was peace, harmony, and love. The veil was lifted. The awakening happened, and I remembered my missions. I knew I had a life purpose, missions to accomplish, and spiritual evolution I wanted to achieve for my own soul growth. And I wanted to be with my mom.

So I made my decision.

Oh, but how good it was to see my dad, Malach, Ruach, Pneuma, Betty, and all the others! But I knew I'd see them again when it was time. Life on Earth seems long, but it's a mere blip on the screen, looking at it from that dimension.

Now I know that I want to share the stories of what I know about this realm and the marvelous, exciting things I've learned. I want to help people move beyond their suffering and recognize their own life purpose and missions. Each person has their own contribution—some big, some small, but all valuable and worthwhile. Life and all its experiences ... it's a gift to appreciate, and life is real and authentic when it unfolds in the present moment.

The human dimension is all about the experiences, and nothing is meant to be pleasurable or uplifting all of the time. We can only truly appreciate what we have through the contrasts we experience in the physical world: good/evil, joy/sadness, hope/despair, love/fear.

I know all of that now. I remember all of it.

The click and the whirl again. Suddenly, I was gone from that dimension. I woke up in a hospital room. In spite of the attempts to make it seem homey, it still had a medicinal smell.

My mom was sitting next to me, holding my hand and reading to me, and Sophie was exercising my legs.

It was awesome to be back with them again. There was this "instant knowing" that came over me, and I knew—despite his injuries—that Tyler would heal and be okay and that the other guys on the trip with me would be fine, but I also had the awareness that life as I knew it was forever changed.

I remembered the things I needed to do. I realized that all the events in life have significance, even those we consider insignificant—each one directing us toward finding greater harmony, balance, grace, and an expanded awareness.

After that panoramic view of my sixteen years on Earth, I realized, like Sophie told me, that each life is an awe-inspiring tapestry of endless threads of experience woven into intricate patterns. Many of the threads running through it are just the plain stuff of everyday living, but there are also dark ones scattered throughout, representing when times are difficult, and there are shimmering, golden, jewel-toned threads, reflecting times of joy—all these intertwined threads making up the totality of a life. No threads of experience should be judged as good or bad—they just are … it's the gestalt of all the threads in combination that creates each soul's own unique, personal story.

I woke up feeling so much wiser. The secrets of the universe are there for anyone open to receiving them.

CHAPTER 59

JANUARY 2016

AFTER HIS EPIC journey to the nonphysical realm, Jonathan understood that, relatively speaking, even for those who live to a ripe old age, one's life on Earth is startlingly short in contrast to the immortality of the soul. As humanity evolves in consciousness to a higher vibration, it appears as though time is actually speeding up. At least, that's how it seemed to Jonathan.

Time moved quickly after the turning point of the avalanche experience, which changed his attitude toward and approach to life. He knew his purpose. His life's work was to creatively share his stories, to impart his knowledge of the nonphysical world with those on Earth.

Following his "out-of-body experience," as many refer to it (but known as "plan B" to others), Jonathan's life carried on per his original plan.

As the years wore on, what he'd first realized in that hospital bed sunk in deeper and deeper, until he had a profound understanding of the life cycle as an opportunity to choose experiences from a great big pot filled with all the complementary forces in the universe, all interconnected—like a casserole of contrasts. And that casserole plays the role of teacher, serving up lessons. He no longer viewed life as light or dark, positive or negative; rather, with the dark comes the light, and life just *is*.

*

After graduating high school, Jonathan moved to Australia to attend Bond University's School of Film and Television. There, he was able to refine his craft and establish his artistic voice on paper, opening up a part of himself that he desperately wanted to share with the world as his contribution, his talent. He wrote, acted in, and produced his first movie, and during the filming, he fell in love with one of the producers, Aria Russo. The two married, and of course Sophie made the most astonishing cake for the wedding.

The home Jonathan and Aria made together in Los Angeles was an ideal blend of their personalities—quiet and secluded for his writing, yet also perfect for entertaining. There was a spacious sunken living room with an old-fashioned stone fireplace and a formal dining room with French doors that opened to a lovely, grassy yard for old Einstein and their new pup, Cadbury. Cadbury's mother was Hershey, the chocolate Lab that had located Jonathan in the avalanche debris.

One pleasant California evening in this home, Jonathan fervently typed at his computer, set up in a nook in the kitchen area. About ten books were haphazardly piled on the table next to him, along with five empty paper coffee cup—remnants of his late-night writing habit, no cream, no sugar.

He took several deep breaths, closed his eyes, and savored the moment—prolonged it, even. Pushing himself back from the computer, he threw his head back and bit his lower lip as he expelled a slow breath, actually feeling the weight of his task lifting from his shoulders. The sigh of relief was followed by a gleeful smile. He was elated but welled up with emotion at the same time. *I did it,* he thought. *I finished.* A sensation of satisfaction flowed through him from the base of his spine to the top of his head, as though an inner emptiness had finally been filled. A warm glow expanded throughout his body as his spirit friends in another realm sent him a congratulatory light, signaling their support of his completion of one of his missions.

He swiveled on his rolling chair and watched the woman standing at the stove, stirring a bubbling pot of chili. He loved this woman so—in her late twenties, with her olive skin, lightly tanned, and her ink-colored, shoulder-length hair pulled into a high ponytail. He'd relinquished all those tall, blonde girls long ago.

He paused before calling her over, just to drink her in and watch her longer. There was something about the way she crossed the room with the effortless grace of a lithe ballet dancer, in spite of her nine-month baby bump, that captivated him. When he looked into the depth of her gray eyes, he believed she held the secrets of the universe in her soul, but those eyes always looked as though they were ready to laugh as well, sparkling with little flickers of light. From his knowledge of the other realm, he knew what authentic love was, and he'd recognized that feeling immediately when he'd first connected with Aria.

With genuine satisfaction in his voice, he announced, "Aria, I'm finished. My book is done. Come look."

He wanted her to see the written words: *The End.*

Baby-heavy, she moved slowly to his side, chili spoon in hand, and put one arm around his neck as she kissed his cheek. "Jonny, I'm so thrilled for you! This is a big day for you. Your book … it's finished! How does it feel?"

"It's hard to describe. But I guess I'd say it's an all-encompassing sense of contentment and fulfillment. I feel really good. Really good. It's funny, but I'm going to miss my characters. They've been a part of my life for a long time now. It's like saying good-bye to people I care about."

He jumped up, vigorously rubbed his hands together, and gave her the biggest bear hug he could considering her protruding belly. They both laughed like little kids.

"I can't wait to sit down and read the whole thing through, beginning to end," she told him.

He reached into the refrigerator for the bottle of champagne he'd been keeping chilled for this occasion, along with a bottle of sparkling cider for Aria. "I'm excited to show it to Sophie especially. My mom has been reading the drafts all along, but I've kept the whole thing a surprise from Sophie—she knows I've been writing a book, but not what it's about."

"I'd love to kick my feet up for a while as the chili cooks, so let's go into the living room and you can start reading it to me from page one."

Glasses and bottles in hand, they made their way down the steps and settled in their favorite chairs in front of the cozy fire burning in the fireplace—black leather recliner for him, padded rocking chair for her.

"Cheers, my love," she said. "To the joy of accomplishment. Now, Jonny, please begin. I love it when you read to me."

She closed her eyes, ready to listen.

He opened his laptop and began:

PART I

CHAPTER 1

August 21, 1987

The framed photo of her husband, Neil, fell from the wall as Sophie Beaumont plodded down the steps, in her pajamas, still wiping the sleep from her eyes. Bits of shattered glass covered the wooden floor near the bottom step. She stopped in her tracks, wondering if it was an earthquake; after all, their house sat on the Rose Canyon fault. No, nothing was shaking. Seeing no reason for the strange occurrence, she continued down the steps, carefully avoiding the pieces of glass, surprised the noise hadn't seemed to wake her sleeping husband. She ...

Jonathan glanced up at Aria to see her reclining with her eyes closed, but she was wincing and steadily rubbing her belly in clockwise circles. Their "read aloud" time was sacred to both of them, but he grew concerned when she let out a long, low groan, then pushed down on the armrests of her chair as she struggled to stand.

"Honey, I think the book is going to have to wait a bit. It's time, Jonny. I think my water just broke—my dress is damp. The baby is coming!" She was up now and waddling quickly toward their bedroom. "We've still got time, but call the doctor and your mom, and get my bag, please, while I put on some shoes. I don't want to get caught in traffic."

Jonathan frantically jumped from his chair and did as he was instructed, making the calls and loading Aria into the car, then speeding down the highway—in the style of all expectant fathers—toward the hospital. Just moments after they arrived and Aria was wheeled to the maternity ward to prep for labor, Lizzie, Sophie, Matthew, Mark, and Aria's parents paraded in one by one, congregating in the waiting room in anticipation together.

They didn't have long to wait. The birth was short and, thankfully, without complications—all went well for both mother and daughter.

Jonathan's daughter, Samantha.

Jonathan had been in the delivery room with Aria, watching the wonder of the birth unfold. Their eyes locked—no words needed to be spoken between them. They were resonating together, riding the same wave in time, sharing an inner knowing and understanding.

When the nurse placed his baby girl in his arms, Jonathan grasped the magic of a soul connecting with physical life.

It was so right—this little being he knew instantly and intimately the moment he gazed at her face. She looked back at him, newborn eyes fluttering, as though they were saying, *I picked you as my father because of our mutual love for each other. It's going to be grand! Of course there are going to be bumpy moments, dips and crescendos, but oh what a ride we'll have together!*

Samantha. Jonathan cradled her closely as she suckled his finger. His cheeks glistened with salty tears; his joy, indescribable. He saw the familiarity in her eyes and responded to them: *There you are. Safe and sound. Let the journey begin.*

I knew you'd come … I knew you'd come.

EPILOGUE

J ONATHAN'S FAMILY AND friends were profoundly impacted by his near-death experience as well, and through the knowledge they gained from it, they were all able to move forward in their lives with more confidence and a greater sense of peace and understanding. His visit to the other realm had reminded them all that life in the physical world is fleeting, yes, but it also has purpose.

Matthew continued his life's work of providing spiritual guidance to those in need. He enjoyed teaching and taught seminars all over the world. He wrote two more books and became a regular contributor to *Empowering You* magazine.

Intertwined as she was with Jonathan's "plan B," Lizzie experienced a fuller awakening to the spirit world and was eventually able to accept David's death with grace and with the understanding that it was part of their mutual plan for soul growth. She learned it was necessary to grieve but to not remain stuck like a needle in a groove of an old record; she realized she needed to move forward to accomplish her own life missions and lessons. Life is meant to be lived in the now, she realized, each moment a treasure. And although there are no guarantees of more to come—no promises of time to make up for lost moments—her vocation as a physician infused her with true fulfillment and allowed her to provide service and healing to others. In gratitude to the clerk at the sporting goods store who suggested the AvaLung for Jonathan's adventure in Park City, Lizzie bought him a trip for two to Whistler; and in appreciation to the rescue team that saved her son, she made a large donation to the WBR International Dog School's Avalanche Rescue K-9 program. Once able to open her heart again to romance, she found a joyful, rewarding, and loving relationship with Matthew's brother, Mark Hobbs.

Sophie was grateful for the gift she'd been given of her journey to wholeness—from a person lacking in self-worth to her evolution into a confident, self-reliant woman who found peace in her life. Learning to forgive was a powerful tool for her, and during her metamorphosis, she developed fortitude and an unshakable faith that grounded her during the subsequent ups and downs of her life. She mastered the art of celebration with her successful cake and cupcake shop and enjoyed making people happy with her creations. She and Matthew married, in a small ceremony, with Jonathan and Lizzie at her side, giving her away. She also made donations to the homeless and worked at a soup kitchen monthly, as she'd promised the universe at the time of Jonathan's birth.

As for the team of spirit guides loving and watching out for this group of people on Earth, they continued supporting, guiding, nudging, and providing them with inspirations.

Upon the incarnation of the newest soul in this family, the guides met to discuss the event:

Malach: Everything is on track, and we rejoice for our friends and the new life they've brought to Earth. As for us, there's a new challenge to take on—guiding this new soul as we've planned.

Ruach: We're ready for the challenge.

Pneuma: Malach and Ruach, if you think I'm ready, I want to be one of Samantha's main guides. I've learned a great deal, sat in on her life planning meetings, and I feel I have the understanding and perspective to take this on.

Malach: You've done well, Pneuma. Share with us. What's one of the more enlightening things you've learned?

Pneuma: So many things come to mind, but I can sum it up in one phrase.

Malach: What is it?

Pneuma: It isn't about the happily ever after . . . it's about the story.

Message received.

ACKNOWLEDGEMENTS

To me, gratitude is the heart's way of saying thank you. And for those people who supported and helped me give birth to my novel, words cannot express how grateful I am.

To my beta readers, David Linnell, Betty Martin, Marjorie Knauer, and Janet Rosenthal, thank you for the time and energy you put into reading my story and giving me such inspirational feedback. Your encouragement, your opinions, your input were vital to the process.

To those in my spiritual group who shared your very interesting life stories and uniquely fascinating experiences, and to those in my various writing groups who provided me with critiques and guidance on my long journey, heartfelt thanks.

To Janet Rosenthal—a primary member of my tribe, the one who's put countless Band-Aids on my soul wounds, my best friend and comrade in life—thank you for consoling me when the worst things in the world have happened to me and for rejoicing and celebrating in my triumphs. You have been my rock throughout my life. What writer doesn't need a sounding board? Thank you for sitting for hours with me on Skype discussing characters and motivations; for crying together over the death of a favorite character; for your totally honest critiques that forced me to think and clarify my thoughts; for laughing with me when my characters would do something amusing; and for giving your valuable input on draft after draft after draft. Sometimes in life what we need the most is someone who believes in us and supports our dreams. It empowers us during the times—and they always come—when we think we should surrender. For your ongoing support in my life, my deepest gratitude.

To my copy editor Cindy Nixon of Bookmarker Editorial Services: I'm profoundly happy I came across such an incredibly talented professional as you. Your entry into my life was simply meant to be. I thought you were an editor, but you're really an alchemist who can transmute lead into gold. Your attention to detail thoroughly amazes me, and you've displayed the most astonishing skills. You brilliantly buff, polish, and make things shiny. Thank you for making my manuscript more accurate, cleaner, and tighter.

To Marjorie Knauer, my mom: thank you for buying me the book *Sal Fisher at Girl Scout Camp,* which first showed me I wanted to be a writer.

Thanks to those of you who read this book and find something meaningful to take away from it—that's my hope and dream: that the messages within speak to you.

To everyone out there in the vast universe who has mirrored to me, taught me, and given me fodder for my characters—and you know who you are—my endless gratitude.

AUTHOR'S NOTE

This book uses the term *American Indian* (and, less frequently, *Native American*) to refer to peoples indigenous to North America.

Wikipedia, on the topic of the Native American name controversy, states: "As of 1995, according to the US Census Bureau, 50% of people who identified as indigenous preferred the term American Indian, 37% preferred Native American, and the remainder preferred other terms or had no preference" (at: https://en.wikipedia.org/wiki/Native_American_name_controversy#cite_ref-17, citing Clyde Tucker, Brian Kojetin, and Roderick Harrison, "A Statistical Analysis of the CPS Supplement on Race and Ethnic Origin," Census.gov, Bureau of Labor Statistics, Bureau of the Census, May 1995, retrieved December 13, 2013).

According to infoplease (http://www.infoplease.com/spot/aihmterms.html): "Now almost every style and usage guide describes these terms as synonyms that can be used interchangeably. In recent decades, other terms have also come into use, including *Amerindian, indigenous people,* and *Native,* expanding the vocabulary for referring to indigenous people of the United States rather than circumscribing it."

It was very important to the author to be sensitive to this issue, and based on the above research, it seemed more than acceptable to use the term *American Indian* in the book to match the name of the actual American Indian Culture Days festival—a wonderful annual event in Balboa Park, San Diego, that the characters in the story attend in 1992. (This note applies to the use of *pow-wow* as well, also to match the treatment used in the festival's promotional material.)

About the Author

BEVERLY KNAUER LIVES in sunny San Diego, California. She's the retired Chief of Rehabilitation Services for the County of San Diego. She received her bachelor's degree from the University of Wisconsin–Madison and her master's degree from San Diego State University. She has always loved exploring esoteric wisdom and chose to become a writer to communicate transformative life experiences in the form of visionary fiction. *The Line Between* is her debut work. Currently, she's busy working on her second novel, *The Soul's Hope*. She can be contacted at: beverlyknauerauthor@gmail.com or at authorbeverlyknauer.com.